ADVENTURES
OF A
YOUNG MAN

ADVENTURES OF A YOUNG MAN

A Novel

JOHN DOS PASSOS

Copyright © 1938, 1939 by John Dos Passos

Cover design by Kat JK Lee

ISBN: 978-1-5040-1551-6

Distributed in 2015 by Open Road Distribution
345 Hudson Street
New York, NY 10014
www.openroadmedia.com

ADVENTURES
OF A
YOUNG MAN

I. THE PARENTAL BENT

1

THE BIRD COCKED HIS HEAD as he hopped out into the sun from between the flowers behind the hoops round the flowerbed. He kept his feet side by side when he hopped. When he cocked his head his eye was looking right in the little boy's eye. He pecked hard into the damp dirt between his feet. When he hopped again a pink worm was wiggling in his beak. The little boy yelled to Old Soul to look he'd taught a worm. Old Soul raised his cane into the sky and sighted along it at the bird as he flew and made a popping noise with his lips. "Bagged him, Glenn," he said, and the middle of his eyes were bright and black like the bird's eyes, in his white face that ended in drooping white whiskers that hid his chin and most of his necktie. "Now he's dead," yelled the little boy.

Old Soul said the bird was dead as a door nail and that made the little boy laugh. Then he said that when he'd been a little boy, bigger than Glenn but still a little boy, he had been reputed a good shot with a rifle, he could shoot a railbird's head off at a hundred paces and not ruffle the feathers, but he'd seen too much shooting along the Potomac and in the Wilderness and besieged in Petersburg and now he wouldn't shoot a living thing. "Shoot him," said the little boy, pointing at the gentleman on the horse who was taking off his hat while his horse stood on his hind legs. Old Soul said he wouldn't shoot him, he was General Andrew Jackson of Tennessee, whatever might have been said against him he had been a great heart and a Christian Gentleman.

The lady in the big white hat with flowers on it coming towards them down the path was Mother. The little boy ran to meet her yelling, "Oh, Muddy, Old Thoul thot a bird." Mother's skirts swished as she stooped and hugged him and he could smell the sachetpowder smell of her clothes. She said Old Soul wouldn't hurt a fly.

He pulled her by the hand to where Old Soul was slowly getting up off the bench, taking off his black hat with a sweep like the Christian Gentleman on the horse. From under his hat skimpy white silk hairs shone in the sun round a pink bald head. Mother kissed Old Soul at the corner of his whiskers and asked Papa darling had the little imp been good. Old Soul said a regular little preacher. Then Old Soul took his hat off again and said Granny would be worrying if he were late, Granny would think he was out skylarking, and Glenn and Mother watched Old Soul, limping a little and leaning on his cane, walk off slowly down the gravel path between the hoops that kept you off the sunshiny grass where the birds hopped looking for worms. Straight as a ramrod at eightytwo and a Christian Gentleman, was what Mother said Old Soul was, and that that was what little Glenn must always be. They started off the other way towards home, Glenn holding tight to Mother's hand that was warm inside its white glove.

2

Glenn and Dad were taking a walk downtown; he had a stitch in his side from trying to keep up with Dad's long steps after all the stuffing and mashed potatoes and gravy of Mother's Sunday dinner. Glenn's high black shoes pinched his toes and a frayed place on the stiff Eton collar sawed at his neck. The blue serge suit he'd been bought for sundayschool and was beginning to grow out of bound him under the arms. It was Sunday afternoon and he hated it. He was afraid Dad would say something about his black eye. Dad hadn't said anything about it yet. Dad stopped short at the corner to look at a headline on a newspaper on a rack outside of the drugstore. Now he was going to say something. The paper was yesterday's and was all gritty and curled at the edges from being out all day in the dusty fall sun. Glenn gulped a breath. The stitch in his side eased up.

"Puffing, eh?" was what Dad said, looking down with his head on one side the way he had.

Dad took his spectacles out of his case he carried in the inside pocket of his coat, and put them on to see the headline better. Then he said for Glenn to tell him about the fight. Glenn felt his face go all hot; he couldn't say anything but just swallowed a lump.

Dad's glasses were so thick that the way the light struck them it looked like he didn't have any eyes behind the glasses. He was saying slowly that Mother had said Glenn had gotten into a fight sticking up for a smaller boy, and that it was a Christian Gentleman's duty to protect the weak, but it was just as well not to do it in school hours when it was against the rules. Glenn gasped that some big guys who were big bullies had jumped him in recess. Dad went on, pronouncing every letter of each word in the careful poised way he had, like he was speaking to an audience in a hall, to say that guy was an English word for scarecrow and he didn't want his boy picking up slang and fighting and bad manners in school, and he went on telling about Guy Fawkes and the Gunpowder Plot and blowing up the Houses of Parliament in England in the reign of King James and the dreadful tortures they had in the olden days, and how they used to burn people at the stake.

Ed Welsh and Joe Herman had had Piggy Green tied up against a post in the basement and had him almost scared to death telling him they were going to burn him at the stake when Glenn had come out of the toilet and said it was a shame. Ed had come towards him on his toes shadowboxing with his fists and asked what did he want to make of it, and Glenn had said all he'd said was that it was a shame, and Ed had socked him right in the eye so that he saw stars like in the funnies, and Joe had tripped him up from behind, and he'd bumped his head on the floor, and that minute the bell had rung and Ed and Joe had beat it and there was Mr. Hines standing over him, and Piggy, the dirty little snitch, had said it was Glenn had tied him up, and Glenn had been sent still blubbering up to the principal and he'd been kept in every day for a week and had to copy *A bully is the most despicable of men* five hundred times. But he couldn't explain all that to Dad; all he could say was, "Yes, Dad," "No, Dad," while Dad went on lecturing him.

3

The kids were all fooling round the pond when Jack Simmonds said let's play Washington at Valley Forge. Freddy said it was a slick idea, he always did back up anything Jack said, and Jack said he'd be George Washington and Freddy could be Monseer Lafayette and the rest of them could be the army. When Freddy yelled out that the Kid had to play Benedict Arnold it made Glenn feel all chilly inside. They didn't need to call him the Kid even if he was the youngest of the bunch. He said he didn't want to play Benedict Arnold.

Jack was already George Washington and he had a lath for a sword and Skinny Ames was making him a wig out of a piece of gunnysack. Freddy was saying hadn't they better start with the Declaration of Independence, but Jack said to hell with that, they were at Valley Forge and it was snowing something awful.

Freddy said that would cost Jack a penny because he'd said the first guy that cussed or talked dirty would have to pay a fine. Jack said it didn't count because it was in the part. Freddy said sure George Washington swore awful but he didn't tell lies or say shit. Jack said that would cost Monseer Lafayette a nickel. Freddy said he hadn't said it, he'd just said that George Washington didn't say it. George Washington said all right but the next guy that cussed or talked dirty got a kick in the pants.

Then he said to Benedict Arnold to start his treason and bowed low to Freddy and said in his best elocution voice that it was snowing something awful and that the troops had their feet bound in bloody rags and that the redcoats were all around them and that they were encamped in the valley by the forge and that he hoped there weren't any traitors around because he and Monseer Lafayette were going into their tents to get a few winks of sleep.

Glenn said there weren't any traitors around because he wasn't going to play Benedict Arnold, he wanted to be the Green Mountain Boys and attack the redcoats from the rear; and George Washington jumped up from where he was lying in the grass under the willow tree and said Glenn would damn well play Benedict Arnold or get his block knocked off, and Freddy made a fist under his nose and said sure the Kid was cut out to play Benedict Arnold because his old man was against preparedness and that was the same as a traitor, that was what Freddy had heard his Uncle Will say, he didn't care if that damn Spotswood was a preacher he was against preparedness and that was the same thing as being a traitor to the flag.

Glenn stood facing them with his fists clenched blinking without being able to say anything, until Skinny came towards them across the grass frowning and said well he guessed Freddy was fined that time. Freddy said it was Uncle Will talking but Jack said it didn't work unless he said quotation mark, and just for that Freddy would have to play Cornwallis when they got around to the Surrender of Yorktown.

Freddy said that first they'd ought to try Benedict Arnold for treason and then they'd hang him to a sour apple tree. George Washington said that would be great and made a big speech to the army saying that there was treason in the camp and some caitiff had sold the country to the redcoats and to go, men, and hang the traitor to yon sour apple tree. Glenn felt he was going to cry. He turned and bolted off through the bushes, blubbering as he ran, with all the bunch yelling quitter after him.

There was a little footpath round the edge of the pond that wound between yellowtwigged willows that already had tiny green leaves on them because it was spring. The hoots of the bunch got fainter as Glenn ran, they weren't coming after him. He sat down on a rock at the edge of a little cove. Tadpoles wiggled out of sight when he reached for them. He folded an old piece of theme he had in his pocket into a toy boat. Hoptoads were trilling along the edges of the pond. A little chilly breeze started just as the sun came out and took the boat out of reach into the blue center of the pond.

It was Skinny Ames who had a longer reach than Glenn who fished it back with a stick. Skinny had come up behind him, talking tough out of the side of his mouth, and saying to hell wid 'em he was trough wid dat bunch, let's Glenn and him be outlaws and act like they damn please. Glenn said if he was a traitor he might as well be a traitor. Skinny said solemnly shake, traitor, meet outlaw, and said he'd damn well like to see Jack or any other son of a bitch call either of them a traitor. They'd be outlaws the both of them.

They roamed round the pond, getting their feet wet in the swampy places where the skunkcabbages were thrusting up their fat slushy green leaves, catching tadpoles in an old tin can, watching the hop-toads sitting on each other's backs all round the edges of the water. Glenn asked what the hoptoads were doing. Skinny threw back his head and laughed, shaking his thin sides the way he did and said couldn't he see?

Glenn got cold all over. Skinny said go ahead say it, it wouldn't burn him. Glenn said it and blushed red. Then Skinny caught a couple and showed him how the little one on top with the dark markings was the male and the big fat one was the female and how she was laying her eggs in a long jelly ribbon little by little. The eggs wouldn't hatch out without the male sitting on top and squirting out his jelly on them. Even in Skinny's wet hand the top one went on trilling, puffing out his white neck like a little balloon. Wouldn't they give you warts, Glenn stammered. Skinny screwed up his nose and said he bet Glenn believed in Santa Claus, naw, things didn't hurt you if you weren't ascared of 'em.

They were walking up the brook to a place in the birchwood where Skinny was going to build a treehouse and he was saying he'd let Glenn help and they'd have a slick time trapping muskrats and catching bull-frogs and be outlaws, when they heard the supperbell tinkling distant and silvery through the still afternoon. The sun was setting all yellow and bright behind the birches.

They began to run. Skinny was ahead. About halfway up to the Home House he turned around and said breathless, "Snap it up, boy, stretch 'em."

Dr. Cope was just saying the blessing. They had to stand in the

8

door holding their mouths shut so as not to pant right out. They were in luck because there were two sixthformers late too and they slipped into their places right after them. Glenn looked to see if Mr. Atkins at the end of the table pulled out his book but he didn't; he was talking and laughing about something with the mathematics teacher at the next table. Glenn's heart was pounding so he could hardly eat.

It was reading night, and after supper in the livingroom, Dr. Cope read about Richard Coeur de Lion in his booming voice that faded off now and then and made the words sound so far away and long ago. It ended about how after Richard Coeur de Lion had died in the Holy Land his faithful retainers were bringing back his heart to England and fell into an ambuscade and threw his heart into the center of the fray. When Dr. Cope stopped reading everybody was so quiet you could hear the bids washing dishes in the kitchen and Glenn was all chilly down his back thinking that Skinny's name was Richard too, and that if he'd been his faithful retainer bringing his heart back from the Crusades he never would have thrown it away like that. But Dr. Cope went on booming about the Crusades, and how, when boys went out from these walls and entered the various callings and professions of the great world, he hoped they too would always be crusaders for what was right and just without fear or favor; and he told the story about a town out west where he'd once taught, where there had been an accident to the sewer, and due to some labor disturbance or other there had been nobody to mend that sewer, so that the town was in danger of an epidemic and the boys from the school had volunteered to go down and mend that sewer.

Some boy giggled. Dr. Cope glared round the room and said severely that he'd rather go down into a sewer than into the mind of the boy who giggled. Filing in to study hall Glenn caught himself blushing thinking it was an outlaw he said he'd be with Skinny not a knight. Maybe they could be outlaw knights. Through the open window next his desk as he worked over his French he could smell the skunkcabbagy smell of spring and from way off down at the pond came the trilling of the hoptoads laying their eggs in a long jelly ribbon round the edges of the water.

4

Glenn had just finished packing his trunk to leave that school because Dad had written he didn't have enough money to keep him there now that he'd lost his position at Columbia on account of this war business, and when he'd come out on the landing with his overcoat on and his hockeystick under his arm, and his skates in his hand that he hadn't been able to get into the trunk, he'd found Skinny there waiting for him. There wasn't anybody else there and Skinny said he'd sneaked out of study hall to say Goodby and Jesus Christ he was sorry Glenn was going. Then he suddenly ran over to Glenn and kissed him on the cheek and Glenn didn't know what to say and all he could say was he was scared. "So am I," said Skinny, and that was the last time Glenn ever saw Skinny Ames.

5

There was the time Uncle Mat and Aunt Harriet came to Thanksgiving Dinner. The sizzly smell of the turkey and the spices in the stuffing filled the kitchen every time Mother opened the oven door to baste. Glenn had helped lay the table in the cramped diningroom of the little apartment and had filled the two china swans with red white and blue candies and, carefully, with only one or two smudges, had printed out the names on the placecards.

Dad had been around the house all morning getting into Mother's way in the kitchen and frowning as he sat bent almost double reading, with his green eyeshade on, at his desk in the corner of the livingroom. A letter had come from Tyler overseas that morning that had upset Dad a good deal. The letter had said that Tyler wasn't coming home with his outfit but that he had just gotten under the line with his commission at Saumur before the armistice and was going to be sent to Coblenz in the Army of Occupation. Glenn was too excited about Thanksgiving and everybody coming to dinner to pay much attention. He and Mother were attending to everything and Dad was just mooning around, now and then pulling at his sandy mustache with that worried look and taking down first one big book and then another from the top of his desk and setting them down on chairs and forgetting to put them back.

Mother, in her pink apron with her hair in curlers, was leaning over the oven of the gasstove basting the turkey. Glenn was standing beside her with his mouth watering as he watched the little splashes of juice sizzle as they trickled off the kitchen spoon onto the brown tight skin of the turkey. Mother was out of breath. He said couldn't he do that because she'd promised him and Dad she wouldn't do too much. She said never mind, darling, for him to run around the corner to get the icecream at Etienne's. It was all ordered but she was afraid they wouldn't bring it in time, and twentyfive cents' worth of salted almonds, and to be sure to wear his muffler because it was a terribly raw day.

Glenn ran down the three flights of steps two at a time and almost fell on his neck in the lower hall. Outside, in the broad streets, behind the trees rusty with fall, the waving flags and the bunting showed up bright and candystriped under the gray blustery sky. Down at the end of the street there must have been a parade or something because a marching band was playing "Over There."

In the French candy store on the avenue it was warm and smelt of chocolate and baking cake. The fat lady behind the counter gave Glenn the icecream and the salted nuts in a little fancy pink carton tied with ribbons at the top and, first thing he knew, he'd bought a plaster turkey with little tiny gumdrops in it for seventyfive cents out of his own money. That sort of thing helped to garnish the table, the fat lady agreed in her wheedling French accent. When he got home he ran up the three steep flights of the back stairs and broke breathless into the apartment through the back kitchen door.

Dad was in his shirtsleeves mashing the potatoes and saying, Ada, he couldn't help feeling bad about the thought of our boy in a uniform strutting around lording it over those miserable defeated Germans. "I'm afraid he'll never be good for anything again." Mother was whispering she could only feel thankful that he was safe.

Yes, indeed, Dad intoned in a loud false voice that made nothing seem fun any more to Glenn, it was a real Thanksgiving day for the Spotswood family all right, wasn't it, my boy; and then he said for him to help his mother beat the potatoes, because he had to change his clothes; the family would soon be coming and it would never do for them to find him like this; they had a poor enough opinion of him as it was. And Glenn set to beating the mashed potatoes with all his might with a big fork while Mother poured in a little milk from a cup. Then she put the mashed potatoes on the stove in a double boiler to keep hot.

My, they looked good, he said, he was so hungry he could eat an elephant, and Mother told him to run along now and brush his hair and wash his hands, because they'd soon be there, and to tell his father to come and open the oysters.

He'd hardly gotten into his bedroom when the bell rang and he ran to the door, and there they were, Uncle Mat and Aunt Harriet and Lorna. Aunt Harriet and Lorna smelt of perfume and furs and Uncle Mat smelt of bayrum like a barbershop. They had so many coats and mufflers and furs to hang up that Glenn was still in the coatcloset when Cousin Jane and Miss Jenks arrived in tweedy outofdoorslooking wraps, and everybody was crying out, my dear, what a wonderful Thanksgiving it was, and the news about Tyler, imagine his coming back an officer and going to the Army of Occupation and maybe he'd have a career in the regular army, and when Mother came out of the kitchen in her new silky-ruffly dress and with her hair all curls there was such squealing and kissing and, my dear, you look like a schoolgirl, and to think that Tyler's a second lieutenant at twenty; and out of it came Uncle Mat's voice grumbling that Tyler had ought to have gotten his commission before he went over like the other college boys did; but Miss Jenks screeched that Herbert hadn't wanted him to, he'd wanted him to rise from the ranks, it was so much more democratic, and she thought it was splendid.

Mother said for Glenn to go help Dad bring in the oysters and Uncle Mat followed into the kitchen where Dad was standing by the sink. Dad had a couple of plates of oysters ready but he'd jabbed himself with the oysterknife and was standing there looking down with that slow puzzled look he had at a little drop of dark blood swelling up in the palm of his hand.

Uncle Mat roared that it was too bad, Herbert, and that he'd ought to use a leather mit, and grabbed the oysterknife out of Dad's hand and started to open the oysters at a great rate while Dad and Glenn carried the plates into the diningroom where the table had every leaf in it and they'd hung paper festoons round the electriclightfixture that Mother always said was so ugly. Glenn went around straightening the old linen tablecloth with its stiff creases and Mother's best silver spoons and forks that had belonged to Grandmama Carroll. Uncle Mat caught him at it and slapped him on the back so hard it hurt and said he was darned if they hadn't turned little Glenn into a regular parlormaid, and Glenn felt his face getting red, and went out in the back hall and stood looking out the window at the garbage cans and the spilt ashes in the back yard, where there was still an oak all golden with fall and a scraggly privet bush with green leaves on it. Somebody had stuck a faded paper American flag at the top of the privet bush.

When Glenn got back they were all at their places and Dad was standing still with his eyes drooping, waiting to say grace. As soon as they'd sat down Aunt Harriet said, now dear Ada mustn't do another thing, she was afraid she'd overdone. Mother shook her head, but she did look pale instead of looking flushed like she had in the kitchen. Her voice sounded tired when she said she'd so looked forward to having everybody at her house this Thanksgiving so that they could be happy with her because she was so happy, and tears began to run down her cheeks.

Well, now the Huns would get what was coming to them, Uncle Mat said. He was lifting an oyster dripping with cocktail sauce into his fat mouth. He smacked his lips and said he for one hoped they'd hang the Kaiser and burn Berlin to the ground, teach 'em a lesson, that was all they understood.

Two wrongs didn't make a right; Dad was speaking his carefully pronounced words from the end of the table, when Lorna began to kick up a row because she'd found an oyster-crab in her oyster. Uncle Mat roared that she must eat it and Glenn said he thought they were cute and Lorna screeched that they were horrid, and Dad said nothing that was Nature was horrid, they were just cute little pink crabs that lived in the oysters. Lorna dared Glenn and doubledared him to eat it and poked it across the table at him on her spoon. The tiny crab crawled a little on his tongue but he crunched it up and swallowed it. Then Lorna kicked him in the shins under the table and said now she thought he was horrid.

Uncle Mat got red in the face laughing and spilt cocktail sauce on his chin gulping down his oysters, so that he looked like he'd cut himself shaving. He said he didn't think the younger generation appreciated oysters, so he distributed Lorna's oysters among the grownups and Glenn lost some of his too, though he liked them fine. When Uncle Mat had eaten his last oyster he pushed back his chair a little and Aunt Harriet made him wipe the cocktail sauce off his chin and he declared that nothing in the world could beat a Potomac oyster. But now that we'd won the war the Huns would have to pay for it, he said looking straight at Dad. Mother and Cousin Jane were fluttering around taking away the plates.

Dad got that cornered look on his face. He took off his glasses and rubbed his gray bulging eyes and leaned forward across his plate before he spoke. He hoped that those really responsible for the war would be made to pay for it, instead of the poor people of Germany who were its first victims, he said, his voice trembling a little; he had confidence that the President . . . Cousin Jane came to the door and said in her businesslike way that Herbert must come help them with the turkey, they were afraid they'd drop it, it was so heavy, and wasn't little Glenn coming to act as headwaiter, so that his poor mother could sit down and entertain her guests a little.

When Glenn was through passing the vegetables with a napkin on his arm like a real waiter, he sat down and began to eat. Oh, she hoped the turkey wasn't dry, Mother kept saying as she watched Dad shakily carving. Everybody was eating the turkey and saying how good the stuffing was and please pass the cranberry sauce or the piccalilli, and it wasn't until the second helpings had gone around that Uncle Mat started to argue with Dad some more. Of course, Uncle Mat said, he was for backing the President but he thought the leniency shown to conscientious objectors and disloyal elements in this country was a scandal. Dad flared up and said did he call twenty years in jail lenient when the Constitution . . . Uncle Mat interrupted that that kind of talk was disloyal at a time like this when our boys were giving their lives to defend the very principles . . . "After all, Brother Matthew, Tyler's our son," Mother said with a shy smile, "and we ought to know about sacrifice." Then she told little Glenn to clear the table and bring in the icecream. She said for Lorna to help him but Lorna didn't move.

When Glenn brought out the icecream it slithered back and forth on the platter. Cousin Jane, who was following with a silver sauceboat of chocolate sauce, cried, "Whoops, my boy," in her jolly way that made him feel good again. But Uncle Mat was still talking about how pacifism was giving aid and comfort to the enemy and at a time like this. . . . Dad looked very pale and stern and was spacing his words slowly and saying that he realized that a great deal of dogma was out of date and rather obscured the gospels than clarified them but that he could find no justification for a Christian to take part in war and that he thought the application of Christianity to war was not only spiritual but practical.

Uncle Mat pushed back his chair and got very red and said he hadn't come to listen to a sermon but in his opinion all pacifists were yellow. "Mat, now you promised me you wouldn't," Aunt Harriet was whining in a singsong voice. Cousin Jane added in her snappy cheerful tone that this was Thanksgiving dinner and that arguing at meals gave people indigestion.

"Herbert, don't argue with him please," Mother whispered down the table, and made Glenn get Uncle Mat's plate and gave him another helping of icecream. It made Glenn feel awful to see how her hand was trembling when she poured out the bitter fudge sauce. "I should think his own sons would be ashamed," Uncle Mat muttered as he helped himself to another piece of fruit cake.

Lorna started giggling. Aunt Harriet kept hissing hush across the table. Uncle Mat went on rumbling in his throat that it was a surprise to him Herbert hadn't been arrested before this for his disloyal utterances and us with him for listening to 'em.

Dad had gotten to his feet, leaving his icecream untouched on his plate. "After all, Matthew, you are my guest and Ada's." He walked over to the window and stood there looking out with his thin hands clasped behind his back.

"Mercy," broke out Miss Jenks, who hadn't said much during dinner because her new set of false teeth bothered her, but had sat there, with her little pursedup mouth munching fast like a rabbit's, in the middle of her bright little lined pink and white face. "You wouldn't think the war was over, would you?"

Then Aunt Harriet suggested that Glenn take his little cousin Lorna for a walk around the zoo. Lorna pushed her face out in a big pout and said she hated the old zoo but everybody thought it was a lovely idea and Uncle Mat gave them a half dollar to buy peanuts for the elephant with and they were bundled up and shooed out of the house into the chilly twilight of the streets.

"Aw, it'll be closed anyway by the time we get there," Glenn drawled out of the corner of his mouth, trying to talk tough. Lorna put her hand on his arm and said, "Let's us go downtown and go to the movies. My Uncle Herbert's a big sissy, isn't he?" That made Glenn sore and he wouldn't speak to her all the time they were in the movie.

6

It was beginning to get dark. They'd been a long time without saying anything in the chilly stuffy little apartment, Dad sitting with his head bowed over his desk and Tyler walking up and down with his tunic open and the belt of his uniform dangling, smoking cigarette after cigarette and scowling out the window, Glenn on the davenport trying to read a book of Howard Pyle's he'd read when he was a little kid. The steampipes began to clank. That was Charley the janitor stoking up the furnace like he always did at six o'clock. Glenn got to his feet.

"Suppose I scramble up some eggs," he said. His voice broke. "We'll have to eat."

"You can't cook," said Tyler sourly.

"You tell him, Dad."

"You can do anything you put your mind to, never forget that, boys," said Dad without turning around from his desk. Something about the way he said it set Glenn's teeth on edge. It was a relief to get away from the others and to start doing something. He closed the kitchen door behind him and turned on the light.

When Glenn found himself alone in the small kitchen he couldn't keep the tears out of his eyes, it looked so much like it used to times he'd helped Mother get meals or had washed the dishes for her. There was the pink scalloped paper she'd cut out for the shelves of the china cupboard, the row of old porcelain jars she used to tell him Grandmama Carroll had painted the flowers on, her apron with lace round it still hanging behind the door. The tears didn't run down his face, so he wasn't exactly crying, but his eyes swam. He lit the gas and filled the teakettle with water and got out knives and forks and plates. He found some eggs and a tomato and a few strips of bacon in the icebox and got a yellow mixing bowl down from the upper shelf of the cupboard. The kettle had begun to purr. He lit another gasburner.

The sweet smell of the gas brought back to his mind the sweet smell of the lilies that morning, the sorry closeness of black clothes that came from Aunt Harriet and all the cousins who had come to the funeral, and Charley Nice's, Dad's college friend's, newly pressed black suit that smelt of the cleaner's. Glenn could still see Charley Nice's round face pale and pursed above his parson's collar, the undertaker's long yellow teeth bared in a kind of doleful grin, the closed-up careful faces of the undertaker's two helpers who looked too young and healthy for it. He could still see Mother's wax face, motionless under glass, that looked like her but didn't really look like her, and the dirty nails and big redknuckled hands of the young helper who had taken off his black gloves to screw down the top of the coffin with a shiny new patent screwdriver with a red handle, and hear the creak of their shoes and the way their breath hissed through their teeth when they carried the coffin through the door and down the narrow stairs. He had felt better when he and Tyler had had to help. The metal handle had pinched his fingers and the corner of the coffin had gouged into his shoulder as the five of them had wrestled with the heavy oblong bulk lurching down the narrow stairs.

Glenn sliced the tomato and while it was frying in a little butter went through the livingroom to lay the table in the diningroom. Dad and Tyler were sitting in the dark without saying anything. It made Glenn sore the way they sat there. He lit the light in the diningroom. He wanted to say something but his throat was too stiff and he couldn't think what to say. As he went back into the kitchen he yelled back over his shoulder in a voice he hadn't meant to be so raucous, "I put on some hot water, would you like some tea?" "Allright, son, anything'll do," came Dad's tired voice back.

"Haven't you got any coffee?" grumbled Tyler. Glenn didn't answer, but went ahead and made the tea. He had some toast on and stirred up the scrambled eggs with the tomatoes and fried up some bacon in a separate pan. Then he buttered the toast and brought everything in on a tray, calling, "All right, gents, come and get it," in as cheerful a tone as he could.

The three of them sat down at the table and began to eat. Dad poured out the tea. "This is very thoughtful of you, Glenn," Dad said. "I guess the kid was hungry," said Tyler, smiling. The color had come back into Tyler's brown face. He was looking at Glenn with friendly brown eyes under his straight black brows. "Hey, I'm not a kid any more," said Glenn.

"I guess not, Mister's in long pants now."

Dad couldn't eat anything but he drank a couple of cups of tea. Then, while the boys ate, he began to talk in his slow even lecturer's voice about how happy their two lives had been when she was perfectly well, before the Caesarean she had in Cleveland when Glenn was born. Of course that probably hadn't been the cause of the cancer, but she'd never been so well after it, that was a certainty. He remembered so well the night he took her to the hospital. He'd been giving a talk about citizenship at the Y.M.C.A., and he'd walked home out the boulevard feeling frisky as a colt in pasture because, although the boys had been restless at first, he had managed to get their attention and to hold it; that was in the days when everybody was in earnest about reform, and thought the democracy would be saved if we could only get honest men in office, T.R. and the progressives. Well, he still thought he'd been right. But that night was the first time he'd really felt he could convince others by talking to them man to man. He'd walked home feeling like a million dollars in spite of the heat. They lived a couple of miles out in three rooms they rented from a Methodist minister's widow.

"Sure, I remember waking up scared to death and how Mrs. Appleton dressed me to go to school and did everything wrong," said Tyler.

"How can you remember?" Glenn asked.

"I was nearly six, wasn't I, Dad?"

"You were nearly seven, Tyler," Dad said.

Glenn was sitting on his hands and rocking back and forth uneasily on his chair. Why did they have to talk about it, he kept asking himself. He could see that Dad felt better now that he was talking about it. He'd even started to eat a piece of toast. Glenn and Tyler had eaten up everything else. Dad was saying that those years in Cleveland had been the most hopeful time in his life, he'd felt full of faith in himself and the great new age that was opening for America and he'd been able to make great audiences feel that way too. Then had come the appointment to Columbia University. Dad's voice got hoarse, he took a gulp of the milky tea that was already cold in the cup before him, and wiped his sandy mustache first on one side then the other with his crumpled napkin.

Glenn felt his mouth hardening with dislike as he looked across the table at his father's pale lumpy face with its scraggly mustache trimmed a little uneven and the thin nose with the enlarged pores down the sides and the red marks the glasses left on either side of the bridge and a few blond hairs on the flattened end of it, and the big gray eyes bulging out of red rims. He's only thinking of himself, Glenn was thinking. Dad picked up the teacup again and drank the rest of his tea, choked a little and said, "You know I've always tried to impress it on you boys that no matter how overcrowded the professions are, there's always room at the top."

The teacup was one of a set Glenn had won playing the Japanese ball game at Atlantic City the time Mother took him there for a week after he'd had the measles. They were Japanese eggshell china and each had a picture of Fujiyama, the sacred mountain. They were so thin they'd all gotten broken but that one. Glenn felt he was going to bawl out loud like a kid.

He got up from the table and went to the bathroom. He slammed the door after him and locked it and sat down on the edge of the tub and began to cry. On the wall opposite was a picture of the Bay of Naples at night, with Vesuvius in eruption in the distance. The lights in the houses and the sails of the fishingboats and the lava running down the side of the volcano were inlaid with mother of pearl. Mother had bought it in Italy the summer Grandmama Carroll had taken her and Aunt Harriet abroad when they were girls. Glenn found himself making believe that he was sailing that fishingboat across that midnight bay under that mother of pearl moon. There had been sleet in the wind that lashed across the raw new monuments of the cemetery as they all stood in a straggle round the open grave. Charley Nice's nose was red and running and he kept having to dab it with his handkerchief as he read the service. What Glenn had hated most had been his Uncle Mat's pompous official look in his black overcoat with its black velvet collar and the way his pink neck made a bulge above the white silk muffler as he stood with his arm around poor slim Aunt Harriet who almost broke down. Some glistening clods of red clay had rolled out from under the flowers and hemlock boughs that covered the mound of earth behind the grave. It had made Glenn sick the way the relatives stepped around them and gave each other little warning nudges. They didn't care about anything but themselves, he'd kept thinking. When it was over Glenn had wanted to stay after everybody else was gone to help the men shovel the red clay into the grave, he'd feel better if he could only do something, he kept telling himself, but Tyler had grabbed his arm with a strong grip that ground the muscle against the bone and pulled him along after the others. "Let me go. I'll come," he'd whispered through clenched teeth and yanked his arm away.

As he sat on the edge of the bathtub wiping his face with a wet washrag Glenn happened to look down at his black shoes. They still had a little of the red mud of the cemetery on them. That was all over now.

Glenn wiped his face and went back to the diningroom. Dad was talking to Tyler in his natural voice, carefully pronouncing his words as if he were in the classroom. "You boys have got to know sometime and might as well know now that our financial situation is going to be definitely straitened. . . . Sit down, Glenn, you are old enough to understand these things. . . . With your mother's death her annuity ceases and the capital reverts to the other branch of the family. You might as well know that your grandmother did not consider me exactly a suitable match for her daughter for reasons that we won't go into now; that was the arrangement she made. If I had been able to keep my situation at Columbia everything would have been all right. On that score I don't think I owe any apologies to anybody. A man's first duty is to his belief in what's right and what's wrong. I believed that our entering the war was an act of criminal folly and I still believe it."

"Don't I know it?" said Tyler without any expression on his glum tanned face. He blushed red. "Oh, hell, I don't give a damn one way or the other."

Dad didn't say anything about Tyler's cussing. All Glenn could think of was could he finish his year at school and start taking the college board exams. Dad said that had already been arranged for and Glenn just caught himself shouting Hurray. They all got red and sat looking at each other without saying anything.

Tyler pushed back his chair and got to his feet. "I guess that puts it up to me to go out and scratch," he said, and started buttoning up his tunic. He drew a deep breath. "Dad, I'm goin' out for a walk and kinder try and pull myself together." "Can I come, Tyler?" Glenn jumped up too.

"That's bully," said Dad. "You boys go out and take a walk. . . . I'll clean up the dishes. It'll give me something to do." Dad got to his feet and awkwardly put a thin hand on each of their shoulders. "You've got your future ahead of you. Try to forget these terrible . . ." Something seemed to choke him. He slumped down in his chair again and sat rubbing his fingers up and down his face.

Tyler was already off down the stairs. Glenn grabbed his hat and coat and ran after him. Breathless, he caught up with Tyler's long stride at the street door. "Mind if I come, Tyler? . . . Where are you going?"

"Damned if I know. I don't suppose you know any place you can get a drink in this man's town?"

"Gosh, Tyler, I didn't know you drank," panted Glenn.

Tyler didn't answer. They walked fast a long time without saying anything. It was a raw hazy night. The bare trees dripped and the wheels of automobiles made a hissing noise over the wet asphalt. At a crowded street they stopped at the curb to let some cars go by. "I guess you'd just as soon not have me along," said Glenn. "Aw, have it your own way, Glenn."

After they'd walked a few more blocks Tyler stopped suddenly in his tracks and said, "Hell, my feet are wet and I'm all in. I think there's a buddy of mine staying at a hotel down the line. Maybe we'll go over and see him." At the corner he went into a drugstore to phone. "Wait a sec. . . . Want a soda?" Glenn shook his head. When Tyler came out of the booth he was grinning. "Sure, he's there. He's got a bottle of rye." Glenn scruffed with his feet on the tiled floor of the drugstore. The glare in there made his eyes smart after the dark streets. "I guess I better go along home," he said hoarsely. "No, come along and meet him. He's a great feller. We won't eat you."

As they walked through the lobby of the hotel Glenn felt that all the bigfaced men with their hats on lolling in the deep chairs and smoking cigars and spitting into the big brass spittoons were staring at him. The colored man in a sloppy uniform in the elevator seemed to be eyeing him funnily. The hall smelt of stale cigarsmoke and old green carpet. Tyler knocked at a door. "Entray," roared a voice. Tyler fumbled with the doorknob. "Come in, God damn it," roared the voice again. "Hey, Duke, the door's locked," shouted Tyler through the transom. "My mistake," came the voice. The door was opened by a big redfaced man in his undershirt, who grabbed Tyler by his shoulders and hauled him into the room. "Come in, Toby, you old c—r . . . Jesus Christ, it does me good to see you."

"Well, Duke, you old son of a bitch, what do you think of the nation's capital?"

"Aw, shit. . . . Ever hear of the Washington Run Around? Well, that's what the returned sogerboy's getting. . . . But by God, Toby, I'm goin' to stick till I get results."

"Thataboy, Duke. The first fifty years'll be the hardest."

Glenn was standing against the wall twisting his hat around in his hand. Duke's big rolling eye caught his. "Is this the kid brother?" He strode up to Glenn and wrenched at his hand with a meaty red fist. "Howdy, Bud?"

"Excuse me," said Tyler. "Glenn, I want you to meet Captain Jerry Evans. We were buddies in training camp and on the other side."

"Glad to meet you, sir," said Glenn.

"An' we're goin' to stick together on this side until all these goddam embusquays who've been polishing their asses on swivel chairs get it into their heads that us doughboys fought a war for 'em. Ain't that so, Toby?"

"You tell 'em, Duke, and I'll mark time."

"What we need's a drink," said Duke, letting himself drop into the armchair. "Say, Toby, you'll find a bottle of whiskey and some glasses in the bathroom, mix us up a couple, will you? Does the kid drink?" Tyler shook his head. "Hand me that telephone, Bud. You'll drink a bottle of gingerale, won't you?" Glenn nodded.

Tyler came out of the bathroom with two ambercolored glasses. Glenn caught a sweet strong whiff of the whiskey. "Hell," Duke was saying. "The war's over. We might as well have some ice. . . . You call down and tell 'em to send up some ice with the gingerale, Bud. . . . Well, Toby, here's to the clappedup ladies of Paree."

Glenn caught himself blushing. The bellboy came with the gingerale. Glenn sat on a stiff chair in a corner of the hotel room watching them drink and listening and drinking the fizzy gingerale in big gulps. It kept going down the wrong way and he kept choking. He felt he was making an ass of himself. When he'd finished it he got to his feet and stammered that he guessed he'd better go home, Dad might be wanting something.

"All right, Glenn," said Tyler, getting to his feet. He'd taken off his tunic and opened his shirt and his eyes had a bright moist look.

"Good night, Captain Evans," said Glenn. "Thank you for the gingerale."

"Okay, Bud, always glad to meet a brother of Toby's," said Duke with a wave of a big flipper from out of the armchair. Tyler walked with Glenn to the door and put an arm round his shoulder. As he brought his face near Glenn's Glenn could smell the grainy smell of whiskey on his breath. His lips brushed Glenn's ear. "Say, Glenn," he whispered. "Don't tell Dad I went out to get fried. . . . I just had to get things off my mind, see? You run along home. . . . I won't be late."

Glenn pulled away from him. "Of course not, Tyler, what do you think I am?"

Their laughter came roaring out over the transom as he stood in the hall waiting for the elevator. He felt lonely and scared walking home through the dripping dullylighted streets. The entry with its bells and mailboxes and the creaking stairs of the walkup Mother and Dad had lived in these years looked dingier than ever. As he climbed the two flights he found he was dead tired.

There wasn't a sound in the apartment. The only light came from the door of Mother's and Dad's room. Glenn looked in. Dad was stretched out on the bed with his clothes on fast asleep. Glenn tiptoed in and threw the comforter over him and then switched the light off and closed the door as softly as he could. With all the lights on in the livingroom he stood there a while listening to his own breathing. The steampipes were hissing softly and a sound of a dripping tap came from the kitchen. He tiptoed in there and turned on the light. Dad had stacked the dishes but he hadn't washed them. That was just like him.

Glenn washed the dishes and dried them and put them away in their places the way Mother used to. Then he went into his little room, where the books and the muskrat skins and the skunk he'd stuffed himself when he'd taken the correspondence course in taxidermy, and the crossed American flags over Tyler's picture in his private's uniform taken when he'd first enlisted in the National Guard, and the Columbia University banner and the shed antlers Glenn had picked up in the woods near Cumberland that summer, all looked like they belonged to somebody else. That was all over now.

He got out of his clothes and into his pyjamas and turned out the light. Before he got into bed he started to kneel down to say his prayers, but what was the use now; he'd only done it to please Mother. The raw air made him shiver when he opened the window. He got into his cot and lay there for a long time with his teeth clenched to keep them from chattering.

7

The train pulled out, taking its shadow with it and leaving the platform sunny and empty. On the street side of the station an elderly man in overalls was helping two girls in middy blouses into a Ford. The other cars had already left and were grinding down the dusty road towards the town. Hurrying round the end of the station Glenn bumped into the stationagent, a short man in a blue shirt too big for him, held up at the sleeves with rubber bands, who stared out of dull redrimmed eyes when Glenn asked breathlessly if there'd been anybody down from Camp Winnesquam to meet the train, and drawled: "So the folks are gettin' you off their hands for the summer, eh?" Glenn pulled his shoulders back and said stiffly, "I am a counsellor at the camp."

The agent took his cap off and scratched his head in a leisurely way and unexpectedly burst out laughing. "No offense, son." His voice warmed up a little. "They've got a sort of little truck with an Indian head painted on it. It was around town this morning. You better wait till they come for you unless you want a twenty-mile hike. Doc Talcott's probably layin' down the law some place around. You'll hear him talkin' before he comes in sight."

"Thank you very much," said Glenn and hurried back into the waitingroom for fear somebody might have copped the big old yellow suitcase Dad had loaned him. The suitcase was there all right, looking more battered than ever with its torn labels and its worn corners, forlorn in a beam of dusty sunlight that came in through an unwashed window. Glenn sat down beside it on the bench. He felt hot and sticky from the long traintrip but it was hard to sit still and wait.

He jumped to his feet and began to walk back and forth jingling the change he had in his pants pocket. Then he dropped a cent in the slotmachine and got a pair of chiclets in a little yellow box. He had another penny so he thought he might as well weigh himself. The black needle jumped up to no, then went back to 107 and up again by jerks to 108½. For five feet six, sixteen and a half years old, he was underweight according to the table. He fell into a kind of daze looking at half his face in the narrow strip of mirror that edged the dial of the scales. He hated how he looked. His nose had a knobby pasty look. His reddish hair had a silly-looking wave in it. One gray eye looked back at him dolefully. Mother used to say they were hazel like hers instead of blue like Dad's. Mustn't stoop. He pulled his shoulders back and straightened his striped necktie.

There was a step behind him. "Your name Spotswood?" asked a deep pleasantsounding voice.

Glenn turned red as a beet. The scales gave a clank as he stepped off them. He was looking into the eyes, brown under straight black brows like Tyler's, of a tall skinny young man with big knees and big elbows and a big adamsapple, who was dressed in khaki shorts and a kind of boyscout blouse. He looked a couple of years older than Glenn. Glenn nodded, grinning. "I was just seeing how much I weighed." He couldn't help letting out a silly giggle.

"My name's Paul Graves. . . . Glad to meet you."

"Gosh, I was scared there wasn't anybody coming." Glenn's voice broke at the end of the sentence instead of being deep and steady like Paul Graves' was. "Dr. Talcott's over at the garage with the flivver. He said to come over and fetch you. Got any more bags?" Paul Graves picked the suitcase up. "No, I'll carry it," stammered Glenn. Paul Graves was already striding off with it.

"Gosh, thanks. . . . Say, you're a southerner, aren't you?" said Glenn, running after him.

"Tarheel."

Glenn didn't know what that meant so he just nodded and grinned. They were walking down a street of gray frame buildings with empty-looking stores in them. The sunlight had a slaty look on the rough asphalt of the street.

"Lordy . . . What you got in this here grip, rocks?" Paul Graves had set the suitcase down. Glenn made a grab for it, talking fast, "I know it's heavy. Books . . . I'm studying for the collegeboard exams."

"Ever met the Doc?" asked Paul Graves, drawling out of the corner of his mouth. Glenn shook his head.

"Well, you'll meet him soon enough."

They turned a corner past a drugstore. In a thicket of scarred birchtrees past which the road led out of town towards some low green hills Glenn could see the red spindle-shape of a gasoline pump and the glint of sun on some cars grouped round a garage. Behind the other cars there was a yellow stationwagon with an Indian head on it and the back of a man in a blue shirt leaning over the front axle. Beside the mechanic stood a tall man in a khaki shooting jacket and knickerbockers with a patch of bald head that caught the sun in the midst of a mop of fine gray hair. As they drew nearer they could hear a voice addressed to the mechanic's back and two or three scrawnyfaced countrymen who stood chewing tobacco and rubbing their shoulders against the wall of the garage to keep out of the chilly northwest wind that came off a little pond in back.

"The outdoors," came the voice. "The outdoors is our great heritage." Paul and Glenn set down the suitcase in front of the dented radiator of an old Ford and stood behind the broad khaki butt of Dr. Talcott's breeches waiting for him to turn around. He was saying, why David, he'd give his right hand if he were so situated that he could spend his whole life up there among the New Hampshire lakes and streams. "Wouldn't be so bad if 'twarn't so slack winters," came the cracked voice of the mechanic from under the mudguard.

Paul cleared his throat and Dr. Talcott turned around. Glenn found himself looking at a pair of thick spectacles set on a hooked nose sunburned to crimson in the middle of a red face puffing into jowls towards the neck. The broad mouth spread into a smile that deepened the lines that curved from the wide nostrils to the corners of the mouth. "Ah, here's the neophyte. . . . Welcome to Winnesquam. . . . I'm glad to see you, young Spotswood. Your father and I were great cronies, we were a couple of cubs together. . . . Days of lofty thinking, nights of midnight oil. . . . I imagine he has spoken of me often. . . . What's your first name, son?"

Glenn swallowed and said hoarsely, "Glenn." "Of course, Glenn, I remember. . . . You and Paul are already friends, I gather. I am sure you will come to think of him as highly as we do. . . . Meet my friend David Perkins and these gentlemen . . . ."

Glenn held out his hand. The mechanic stood up with a groan as he unbent his back. Two small bright blue eyes were set close together in a smudged puttycolored face. He rubbed his hand off on the seat of his overalls. "Mit's kinder greasy," he said and gave Glenn two black bony fingers which he shook. "There's no hand I'd rather shake," said Dr. Talcott in his resonant voice, "than a hand soiled with honest work. At Winnesquam we honor honest work out of doors above everything, above wealth and the false pride of birth and position. Let us give David a hand with the wheel since we don't want to keep them waiting for supper at Winnesquam. . . . David and I exchange homespun philosophies, don't we, David?"

David had a cotterpin in his mouth so he didn't answer. Paul rolled the wheel over from where it was leaning against the wall and David put it back on the axle. Then they all watched him while he finished the job.

It was chilly sitting in the back of the stationwagon as they bowled along the stony country roads. The northwest wind ruffled the birchleaves and combed back the fine silver needles of the pines. Reaches of the lakes where the wind had full force were lashed into a brownish purple and ridged with tiny whitecaps. Finally they turned into a grassy lane between thickets of sumach and drove up to a group of low buildings on a little knoll fronting a piece of lake ruffled to purpleblack from the wind, and Glenn piled out stiff and numb from among the packages.

After they had unloaded and stowed away all the stuff, Paul picked up Glenn's suitcase and said he'd show him where he could bunk that night. After this they'd each have to take a big U. S. Army tent with the small fry, they'd start coming tomorrow, though camp didn't officially open until the fifth. "I'll bet my bottom dollar their folks are glad to get rid of some of the little darlings. . . . Here, take a towel. Supper bell'll ring in a minute. Old lady looks crosseyed at us if we're late." They washed up in a showerroom where there was a large sign in fancy lettering over the spotted lookingglasses above the washbowls: LEND A HAND.

They were still washing when they heard the clang of a handbell from the direction of the kitchen. Paul hustled Glenn around to the front of the big glassedin porch of the main building. Dr. Talcott was standing with his feet wide apart, swaying a little from side to side, staring out over the lake and tapping with his finger on the broad plateglass window in front of him. He remarked sourly that late was better than never and took Glenn by the arm and pushed him in the direction of the big fieldstone fireplace where some birchlogs were blazing, saying that now he must meet our little circle of dear friends.

"Mother, this is the new counsellor, my dear old friend Herbert Spotswood's younger son; Madam Talcott." Glenn found himself first shaking the cold tremulous hand of an old lady with fixed bright eyes and yellowish white hair that teetered in artificiallooking waves under a hairnet strong enough to catch birds, then the brisk hand of a dumpling-shaped redfaced lady with a cosy smile who wore her gray hair pulled back from her forehead under a similar hairnet, "My wife . . . Mrs. Talcott," and last the limp hand of a younger woman who was shaped just like her mother but was paler and less smiling and had her hair pulled back under a net too. "Our only daughter, Mrs. Elgin. . . . Blaise, I suppose," went on Dr. Talcott, dragging the name out sarcastically, "is late as usual."

The daughter answered in a timid browbeaten voice that he'd be right in, he was just putting sunburn lotion on his neck. Blaise Elgin turned out to be a plump young man with a cleft chin in a red turtleneck sweater who strolled in with his hands in his pockets saying in an apologetic Harvard drawl that he'd been delayed by tennis and tea at the Eriksons', they'd asked him to stay to tea and he'd hardly known how to refuse, and he couldn't very well swallow his tea and run, could he? At Winnesquam, Dr. Talcott was intoning, punctuality and a respect for those who did the hard work of the day were considered of more importance than social amenities.

Meanwhile they had been taking their places at a large oblong oak table set without a cloth in the dark back part of the room. Glenn was politely hauling out the chair for Mrs. Elgin when Paul pulled at his sleeve. They were all standing behind their chairs with their eyes on the blue willow plates, in a hush broken only by the sound of the cook pounding something that came from the kitchen, while Dr. Talcott's bushy head nodded a little above his chest. "Oh, Lord," he broke out, "amid these beautiful lakes and woodlands in the heart of nature which is thy tabernacle may we be thankful to thy great fatherhood for this simple repast, may it strengthen us in thy service and in the service of our fellowman." "Amen," said Madam Talcott in a sharp everyday tone, and they all sat down to watery tomato soup a little cold from standing in the plates.

When they got up from the table, Dr. Talcott gave his arm to Madam Talcott, who walked with a stick, and they marched stiffly out through the screendoors onto the pineneedle terrace. Mrs. Talcott and Mrs. Elgin followed them and the rest straggled after. Behind them they could hear the scrawny farmer's wife who did the cooking clattering the dishes as she cleared the table.

For a while everybody looked out through the birch trunks at the lake full of dazzle from the sun already low in the west. Nobody spoke until the old lady said she was chilly and that she was going in. "Mother, you won't miss the sunset," Dr. Talcott called after her. "Edgar, you know I never miss the sunset," the old lady called back tartly as she went into the house.

At Winnesquam, his voice resounded, they walked up every evening to the old pasture hill to see the lake in the sunset, and when the boys were here he read to them after supper. Just at sunset it was the custom for Paul to play tattoo on the bugle as the flag was lowered. Then followed a short prayer. Then after a few moments of silent communion the chosen boy ignited the campfire and they sang. Lights were out at nine o'clock sharp. "If you have never experienced it, Glenn, the dreamless sleep of openair life will be a revelation to you."

After that the doctor sent the boys down to look over the canoes. They set to work lifting the canoes off their racks in the cobwebby boathouse and laying them out in a row out on the float. Paul shook his head as he looked at their ragged bottoms and said that if that old canuck could fix them he was a better man than he was, Gunga Din.

By the time they had the last of the two big war canoes dragged out, the sun was setting and Dr. Talcott's voice came ringing down the hillside after them. They ran up the hill to where the doctor and the three women were standing and looking solemnly out over slaty-silver reaches of lake, dotted with wooded islands, that ran long shining fingers into the hunchedup purple of the hills under the sunset. "Paul, you forgot your bugle," Dr. Talcott said sharply. "I declare I did," mumbled Paul, frowning. "You know how important I consider these ceremonies." Dr. Talcott's voice had a rasp in it. Then his face drooped back into the attitude of rapture. "Majestic," he said in a deep voice as he stared out over the lake at the orange sheen under the clouds into which the red sun had melted. "Majestic," said Madam Talcott, still panting a little from the climb up the hill and leaning heavily on her granddaughter's arm.

Mrs. Talcott sighed audibly.

"We make it a point, Glenn," said Dr. Talcott, letting out his voice as if Glenn were a congregation, "not to miss Nature's crowning of the day."

Glenn said, gosh, this was a beautiful place, still quite carried away with it all, after he and Paul had gone down through the dusk to their tent. Paul was bent over fussing with an acetylene lamp. A stench of carbide filled the tent. Finally he got it lit, muttering that Glenn would find out it was hell's own nuisance keeping the kids from setting themselves on fire with lamps.

Glenn undressed and put on his pyjamas and then put his bare feet back into his shoes to walk up to the washroom to clean his teeth. The wind had dropped and the night was absolutely still. There was no moon. The Milky Way made a glowing smudge across the sky. The braken along the path were wet from dew. Glenn had to roll up the pants of his pyjamas to keep them from getting soaked. In the washroom a few mosquitoes whined round the unshaded bulb. On his way back Glenn stopped in his tracks to watch, through a gap in the trees, the stars shakily reflected in the lake. As he watched a long "Whoo" came across the water and sent a little shiver down his spine. Behind him the tent glowed cosy orange. "Say, Paul," he called.

"Yeah?" Paul stuck his head out, blinking. When he opened the flap the light turned the shapes of braken and the leaves of the birches into a series of bright green cutouts against the black. "Say, Paul, come out and tell me if this is a screech owl." Paul stepped out with nothing on but a jockstrap, lifting his long bare legs high on account of the wet grass. "Ouch," he said, "the dew's cold."

"Say, won't you catch your death of cold?"

"Need to toughen up a little," Paul whispered with a shiver in his voice.

"There he goes again . . . shush."

The who, whoo, whooo, came loud across the lake. "That's a barred owl . . . swamp owl some people call 'em. . . . I heard him last night." Paul's teeth were chattering.

"I kinder thought you'd know," said Glenn.

They were both shivering now. They went back into the tent and Paul hopped into his blankets.

"Ever stuffed any birds? I took a course in taxidermy once," said Glenn, pulling the blanket up to his chin.

Paul let out one of his heehaw laughs. "I bet you learned a lot."

"Let's try and get some specimens this summer."

"Okay, I been tryin' to identify species. Out of about two hundred and eighty-three different birds you're like to see in the state of New Hampshire I checked about fifty last summer."

"I'll tell you what, let's each keep a list and we'll see who identifies the most."

"You wait till you see how hard it is to identify these damn kids."

A hand with a wristwatch pulled open the tentflap. Blaise Elgin stuck in his round towcolored head. "You men turned in? I thought I might stir up some interest in a game of rummy."

"We got to be up at the crack of day to help Toussaint with those canoes."

Blaise pulled his big body, made bigger by several sweaters with H's on them, into the tent and sat down glumly on the campstool beside the cardtable where the lamp was. "Got a fag, Mr. . . . . er?"

"Spotswood don't smoke, either. . . . You're out of luck, professor."

"I forgot to get any when I was in the metropolis. Dr. Talcott says it's all right for me to smoke if I do it out of sight of the boys. We mustn't put ideas in their heads. . . . Anyway, Lucile and I are going down to Ipswich for the Fourth."

"Well, goodnight, Blaise," said Paul firmly. "Put the light out for us, won't you, and tie back both flaps."

"All right. Sweet dreams. Bless you, my children."

They could hear Blaise humming, "The crimson in triumph flashing . . ." to himself as he walked back up towards the house. The sweet cold air from outside that smelt of birchbark and pineneedles cleared out the rank carbide stench from the lamp.

They were quiet. Glenn was seeing red blotches where the lamp had been. As his eyes got used to the blackness he began to make out, through the open end of the tent, the shapes of trees against the starry sky. The whoo whoo of the owl came across the lake again. Glenn was feeling warm and cosy in his blankets. "Say, Paul," he asked suddenly. "Do you believe in God?"

Paul gave a low laugh. "That's a nice question to ask a feller who's just droppin' off to sleep. . . . Well, my grandfather was the hellroarinest Baptist minister in five counties. . . . Had any biology?"

"No, but I'm going to when I get to college."

"Well, the protoplasm's immortal, isn't it? Maybe you need the idea of God in science like the square root of minus one in math. But we don't know enough to answer one way or the other yet, see?"

"What's the square root of minus one?"

"It's somethin' mighty funny."

"Things like that owl and the Milky Way make me think of things like that."

"I'm goin' to sleep, let's cut the philosophy."

"Goodnight, Paul."

"Goodnight."

Glenn was so excited by meeting Paul and sleeping in a tent and the talking and everything that he couldn't get to sleep. For a long time he lay flat on his back listening to the drip of the dew off the tent while all the day's happenings went round and round in his head. He kept his ears strained, hoping to hear the owl again. But the owl was quiet.

8

It was hard paddling on account of the brisk northwest wind that blew down the lake and gave everything a bleak flinty look. Already Fats was laying down on the job at the bow. "A little more elbowgrease there, Franklin," Glenn kept saying coaxingly. Glenn was tired. He and Paul had worked like beavers for three days getting the tents ready and patching the canoes and checking and rechecking the list of groceries and the first aid kits, and last night nobody had slept for excitement. Still he felt good. His was the lead canoe and he pushed on the paddle until his arms cracked with the effort of keeping the bow into the wind. Now and then Fats caught a crab and drenched him with water. Glenn had an idea that the little rat was doing it on purpose, but he had to remember each time that he was a counsellor at Winnesquam and to say in a sugary voice, "Have a heart there, Franklin. . . . You don't want to swamp the boat, do you?"

After about an hour's tough paddling they got into the lee of the west shore of the lake. Glenn was winded and had scraped one knuckle raw against the side of the canoe. "Take it easy now, Franklin. I can take her now through the quiet water," he sang out. Fats had been taking it easy for some time.

The sun was warm now that they were out of the wind. The canoe slipped evenly across the gray water where the wind ran in little flaws. White shivering birches stood along the bank and a smell of birchbark and sweetfern and mushrooms and wild strawberries came through on each gust of warm wind from the woods. In the marshy places blue pickerelweed and glistening white arrowhead grew out into the water. A kingfisher flashed by with his long bill stretched out ahead of him.

"There goes a kingfisher, Franklin."

"A what?" Fats said, almost tipping the canoe over as he turned to stare at Glenn with beady eyes out of a round freckled face. "Kingfisher. That's a bird that fishes." "Oh," said Fats. "Hey there, keep your weight steady."

Glenn let the canoe swing around a few feet from the shore and looked back at the other canoes following, two green and two red, paddles flashing and spray sparkling off their curved bows. The canoe that Paul paddled had the flag of the camp with the Indian head on it stuck up on the thwart amidships.

The canoes looked fine, and the slateblue lake and the green hills and the big white July clouds sailing overhead.

"Let's go ashore," Fats started whining. "No, we're going right along." "But I gotto, honest, I gotto." "Can't you do it over the bow, that's the way the guides do it." "But it's number two." "All right, hurry up . . . we don't want to get left."

By the time they got started again the others were tiny specks way out on the lake and Glenn had almost to pull his arms out of their sockets catching up. Crossing over to the island Fats caught a crab that was a beaut and let go his paddle so that Glenn had to circle around and shipped a wave that almost swamped them. That scared Fats so that he started to blubber arid paddled for dear life for the rest of the trip. By the time they slid into the little island cove where the rest of the canoes were drawn up on the sickleshaped beach Fats was merry as a cricket again. "Lookit, Mr. Graves," he yelled as they landed. "Mr. Spotswood nearly swamped us."

"Come ahead, everybody, and get busy." Paul was shouting orders. "Wiggleswood, you're on the kindlin' detail."

While they were eating their supper of bacon and eggs and fried potatoes they began to hear the whir of an outboard motor down the lake. Paul made the kids pick up all the stuff that they'd left laying around and straighten out their blankets inside of the waterproof covers. The outboard came pop-pop-popping louder until the big green sponson canoe stuck its nose round the point where the tall pines were and they saw Dr. Talcott waving his khaki hat as Blaise cut off the motor, letting the canoe slide silently across the cove. "Take it slowly, Blaise," the Doctor was enunciating over his shoulder. The canoe shot up the sandy beach with a jolt that nearly threw them both on their faces. Some of the kids laughed. Glenn wanted to laugh too but he kept his face straight like Paul's was, except for a kind of gulping chortle that he hid under a cough.

"Well, boys, how do you like your coral isle?" said Dr. Talcott after a furious glare over his shoulder at Blaise who was stumbling sheepishly out of the canoe with his chin pulled down in his Harvard sweater. "A real treasure island where the treasures are peace and solitude," the Doctor's voice resounded.

"Have a cup of cocoa with us, sir," asked Paul. Dr. Talcott took a deep breath. "I don't mind if I do. This wind is sharp and invigorating. . . . Makes the blood tingle, eh? Has everybody been behaving?"

The boys nodded and smiled. "All full of health and sunshine, eh?" Fats had to come out with, "We nearly got drowned crossing over to the island." "Who?" The mean rasp came back into Dr. Talcott's voice. "Mr. Spotswood and I."

"That wasn't anythin," spoke up Paul. "They shipped a wave because little Franklin dropped his paddle."

Before they pushed off, Blaise brought out a package of cocoanut cookies Mrs. Larkin had made as a treat for the campers and some letters for Paul and Glenn. "Goodnight and God bless you." The Doctor let his voice out so that the pines resounded. It was drowned by the starting of the outboard motor. After they'd had the sunset exercises and the kids, sleepy from the long day, had turned in, Paul and Glenn threw some dry chips of pine wood on the fire to make a blaze and sprawled beside it on a blanket to read their letters.

Glenn's was from Dad in Madison, Wisconsin.

Dearest boy,

The employment bureau justified its name for once and enabled me to procure a temporary instructorship in philosophy at the summer school here. It's with the greatest difficulty that I take up the strings of my life again. Fortunately you boys are a couple of fine manly fellows and already standing on your own feet in the world. Since your dear mother's passing, I have not I confess been able to shake off a haunting sense of futility. I know it is wrong and I pray continually for help and guidance so that I may take up the tasks of life with my old enthusiasm. The cup is bitter and I must drink it to the dregs.

A very nice letter from Edgar Talcott, who says you are doing very nicely at the camp, was a consolation to me. His influence and the whole atmosphere of the place will I am sure, be congenial to you. You will meet the sons of many men prominent in various walks of life. I am glad that your companion is the kind of boy we would want him to be. You are now reaching an age when the proper friendships and associations mean a great deal. I know I can trust you to pick clean ambitious and intelligent companions. I wish I could say the same of Tyler who seems a stranger to us since his return from the war. However your Uncle Matthew has offered him a position in his law office that will allow him to study for the bar evenings. I hope Tyler has the application necessary to take full advantage of this great opportunity.

As for your taking the rest of the college board examinations and trying to enter Columbia in September, I hardly think I would advise it. What worries me is how you are going to work your way through. I wonder if some middlewestern school wouldn't be easier. Anyway there will still be time to talk about that when we see each other in September. If I manage to secure anything like the position I hope this winter, I shall be able to help you with at least some of your expenses. It's with the greatest shame and humiliation that I have to admit that I shall be unable to do more . . . .

Glenn tucked the letter into his back pocket and stared in the fire with his eyes unaccountably wet.

"Bad news?" asked Paul.

"It's all been bad news since Mother died. . . . I guess I won't be able to go to Columbia."

"Sure you will."

They went around with a flashlight to see if the kids were covered up all right. Then they banked up the fire and turned in, each in the entrance to one of the big tents. Paul wouldn't sleep on a cot but spread his bedroll on pineneedles on the ground, so Glenn did too. Before he went to sleep Glenn rolled over on his elbow and whispered, "Say, Paul?"

"Yare?"

"Say, Paul, why does the Doctor keep that little Fats?"

Paul let out a low whistle.

"All these New England schools and camps like to have a few Back Bay kids, kinder like decoy ducks."

"But the Doctor's always talking about how birth and wealth don't mean a thing."

"He's from Boston, ain't he? . . . *The city of beans and of cod, Where the Lowells speak only to Cabots, And the Cabots speak only to God.*"

Glenn let out a hoot. "Hey, let's pipe down," whispered Paul. "It's about time we got some sleep."

The next morning was gray and cold. The wind was in the east.

They had a hard time keeping the kids busy and cheerful, as it was too cold for swimming. That was the day Paul invented the new game. He'd been reading up about the Russian Revolution and he divided up the kids into Reds and Whites instead of cops and robbers. At first none of them wanted to be reds because they all said that reds were terrible people. Paul explained that the reds were just workers and peasants; but nobody wanted to be a worker or a peasant either until. Paul said that just meant embattled farmers and regular guys, like the Spirit of '76, and that, besides, they were winning all the battles. That made Fats want to be a red too, but everybody said he'd have to be General Scratchitch, leader of the white forces. His voice got whiny and he said he wouldn't play, until Paul told him the white general would have to shoot all his prisoners. "Oh, boy," Fats said, and led the attack on Moscow, that was a big rockpile in the center of the island. It was against the rules to throw anything or hit anybody, but they were all armed with quarterstaves and anybody who was touched was a prisoner. The whites shot theirs and they had to lie down and keep out of the game, but the reds made propaganda speeches at theirs and turned them into more reds. They named it the Red Army game and the reds were winning and everybody was having the time of their lives when somebody's hand slipped and General Scratchitch got a crack over the noddle with a quarterstave, and went off crying, saying he was going to tell Dr. Talcott.

After they had cooked up dinner and fixed a tarpaulin over the table to keep the mean drizzle that had come up off the kids while they ate it, somebody asked where was General Scratchitch. Paul slipped his poncho over his head and ran out. There was Fats just pushing off in a canoe. Paul yelled to him to come back, but Fats said he was going back to camp to tell Dr. Talcott they were just a bunch of dirty reds.

Paul jumped into a canoe to go after him. Glenn went out in another one to head him off. When Fats hit the choppy water in the full wind he seemed to lose his nerve and tried to turn back. First thing they knew the canoe had upset and Fats was in the drink. He seemed to be having trouble swimming so Paul pulled his shoes off and slid overboard after him. When Glenn caught up to them the kid's face was white and water was pouring out of his mouth, but Paul had a firm hold on him and was towing him into shore at a great rate, so Glenn went out to collect the drifting canoes and the paddles.

It took him a long time in that wind and he was drenched to the skin by the time he got in. He found the kids all giving Fats first aid. He'd come to after he'd thrown up a little water he'd swallowed from fright, but Paul said they'd give him first aid anyway to make sure. It would be good practice. They gave him first aid until he howled for mercy.

Next day was fine and everybody was sunny, but when time came for sunset exercises Fats was gone again and so was a canoe. Nobody had seen him go. Paul put Herm Detweiler in charge of the camp and he and Glenn went off grimly like Hiawatha into the sunset to look for the little brat. First they paddled clear round the island, then they made for the nearest shore.

Paul was paddling in the stern. They were both in good training by this time and their paddling was easy and smooth. The lake was slick liquid copper under a flaming yellow sky, green and purple in the ripples. Glenn was worried, but he couldn't help enjoying the long paddle across the still lake. Once a pair of birds rose heavily off the water ahead of them, each leaving a little purple streak. "Say, Paul, are those woodducks?"

"Shelldrakes . . . mergansers more "likely. . . . If he had tipped over and drowned we'd see the canoe floatin.'"

"I bet he went across to Hicks' store to get a chocolate bar . . . he's a fool for chocolate bars."

"We'll go there first. I'd like to whale the livin' daylights out of him."

There were several farmers and a couple of canucks loafing around outside the store. No, none of them had seen a fat boy in a boyscout suit. Inside, an old man was just lighting the big lamp in the center of the store. It was stuffy in there, and smelt of coaloil and old crackerboxes and mice. The old man was deaf and told them a long story about a boy who had drowned in that end of the lake last year and how they had dragged three days before they found the body and how the fish had eaten the face off it, but he hadn't seen a fat boy in a boyscout suit.

They left the store ready to cry from worry. It was dark; they had

JOHN DOS PASSOS

a hard time finding their way through the woods to the place where
they'd left the canoe. The mosquitoes ate the hides off them. "Well,
we're up shit creek without any paddle," said Paul.

In camp the kids were all sitting around snivelling. No sign of Fats.
Paul was swell. "He probably got lost down the lake somewhere and
decided some of those camps had better grub than we have. We'll find
him in the morning," he said cheerily, and made everybody turn in.

Glenn was awakened by Paul tugging at his blanket when there
was only a single streak of pale yellow light in the east behind the big
pines on the point. "Didn't seem to spoil your sleep. . . . Gosh, I worried all night. We'll go over and phone at Mr. Erikson's. I ought to have
phoned last night."

Glenn was so stiff from all the paddling that it was hard rolling
out of the warm blankets. Paul had some cocoa hot on the fire that
he'd built up. They each swallowed a tin cupful and were off. The sky
was brightening to violet as they cut across the broad center of the
lake. There was nobody stirring at the Eriksons' big gray bungalow. A
polished mahogany speed boat was tied up at the float. Glenn sat in
the canoe holding it away from the float while Paul went in the house.

"The Eriksons bawled hell out of me for wakin' 'em up," Paul said,
grinning, when he came back. "We're to work up the lakeshore from
here and they'll cover the lower end with the outboard. . . . Gosh, the
Doc was wild . . . he's always crabby in the mornin' anyway and Fats
is the apple of his eye. He hoped if he could make a man out of Fats
he could get a raft of rich social register kids to Winnesquam. A fat
chance."

"Say, Paul," said Glenn huffily. "I think Dr. Talcott's all right."

As they paddled along the lakeshore all the little downy clouds
overhead got first rosy and then golden and then the sun popped
up with a burst of warmth from behind the hills across the lake. Just
before sunrise they saw two woodducks feeding on the glassy black
surface of a little cove. The new sunlight lit up all their colors as they
flew off across the cattails.

"Aw gee, I wish you and me were off for a long canoe trip, just the
two of us."

"Let's you and me paddle down the Mackenzie River to the Arctic

40

Circle . . . I've always wanted to do that," said Paul. "It's a promise." Paul leaned forward from his seat in the stern and stretched out his hand. Glenn crawled back and solemnly shook it. "And after that we'll try the Yenesei," he shouted.

It was noon and the hot sun was beating down on their shoulders when, as they spun round a rocky point, they caught sight of the Indian head on the end of a green canoe pulled up in a bunch of sweet-flag. A flock of redwing blackbirds flew up as they landed.

"Now," said Paul, stretching, after they'd pulled the canoe out of the water and turned it over in the shade, "let's see what kinder trackers we are." A paddle was floating among the flags. They fished it out and pulled up the canoe into a place where it could be seen from the lake. There were the kid's tracks all right in the marshy sod, but they disappeared as soon as the bank got rocky again. "He was lookin' for a store to buy candy . . . we mustn't forget that," said Paul.

They followed along the shore until it got too steep for them, then they found themselves on a path through an old clearing all overgrown with alder and giant fireweed. At the end of the clearing they came out on a rutted road that led them through a patch of scraggly corn, just beginning to tassel, to an old red farmhouse. While they were opening the gate they heard the voices of kids yelling, and there, behind a red swaybacked barn, was Fats playing prisoner's base with the farmer's kids.

Paul was so mad he wouldn't speak to him. "Hello," said Fats cheerily. "I been with the workers and peasants." He went on that he'd gotten lost trying to find Hicks' store and that he'd had to spend the night at the farm. A toothless woman with her hair screwed off her head came to the farmhouse door, so Paul and Glenn had to smile and thank the lady.

As they marched off down the road, Fats turned and yelled over his shoulder, "I'll bring you the twentytwo when my people come." Then he winked at Glenn. "I promised 'em a twentytwo rifle. They didn't know I had my fingers crossed."

"Dr. Talcott's all over the lake lookin' for you," said Paul. "If it was up to me I'd send you home." "You just wait," said Fats, "until I tell Dr. Talcott you are all reds. Gee," Fats went on as he settled happily

41

amidships in the canoe and waited to be paddled back to camp, "those workers and peasants sleep three in a bed and something bit me, and the only make of car they know's a flivver. . . . I made those workers and peasants sit up."

When they got back to the island dead tired and perishing with hunger the first thing they saw was Dr. Talcott's broad felt hat bobbing in and out of the tents. His voice rang across the water that he'd been kept waiting all day, that they must come ashore immediately.

Late that evening after the kids had gone to bed Glenn and Paul sat talking a while beside the fire before they went to sleep. "What did I tell you," said Paul, yawning. "I was the one that caught hell . . . and Fats told the Doc all about the Red Army game. . . . The Doc said to can it. . . . Say, suppose you and me go off and make some real dough instead of this charity work?"

"But what could we do, Paul?"

"Wouldn't hurt us to go to work, would it?"

Anyway Fats was off their hands for the rest of the campingtrip, because Dr. Talcott took him back to Winnesquam on probation. When they got back at the end of the week the kids all said they'd had the time of their lives and none of them could do too much for Glenn and Paul, but Dr. Talcott and Mrs. Talcott and Madam Talcott and Mrs. Elgin were all distinctly cool and kept their noses in the air.

Then one morning Fats woke up complaining of a sore throat. It was Paul he showed his throat to right after breakfast. Paul looked in and felt his pulse and hurried him right up to the main house to see Dr. Talcott. He told Glenn about what had happened while they were patching a canoe that one of the kids had ripped open on a snag.

"That kid's got something contagious. . . . He caught something at that damn farmhouse. . . . You oughta seen Mrs. Talcott's face when she took his temperature. . . . I told the Doc he oughta call up Dr. Rivers right away. He puffed out his chest like he does and boomed that Nature was a great healer." They both started to laugh. "Glenn, get me that shellac on the shelf just inside the door of the boathouse."

When Glenn got back with the shellac, Blaise was standing beside Paul in his rubber cap and wet bathingsuit shaking his head gloomily. Paul gave that dry heehaw laugh he had. "Say, Glenn, Blaise has got a sore throat too, can you beat it?" Blaise was shivering. "I have the rottenest luck. . . . If it's not one thing it's another. . . . Well, cheerio, I got to get through my swimming lesson."

"For a big husky guy he gets sick more'n anybody I ever saw."

"Hell," said Paul in a low voice. "If I had that family on my neck all the time I'd get sick too."

"Why, I think they are very nice people."

Paul kept his face stiff the way he did when he was sore about something.

The next day it rained. Fats was kept in bed in the upstairs room they used for an infirmary, and when they saw Dr. Rivers' car drive up all the kids sat around on their cots looking blue. Somebody had scared them by starting the story that Fats had typhoid fever and that they'd all get it.

Around eleven o'clock, which was the time on rainy days when the boys were usually let in to play games in the livingroom, Blaise came down from the house to get Paul and Glenn saying Dr. Talcott wanted to speak to them. He had on a heavy sweater under his raincoat. "How's the boy, Blaise?" "Terrible . . . I've caught something, sure as fate." Paul poked Glenn with his elbow but he kept his face straight.

They pulled ponchos over their heads and ran up through the downpour to the house. The family was sitting round the fieldstone fireplace. Madam Talcott was knitting and gave a disapproving click now and then with her steel needles. Mrs. Talcott and Mrs. Elgin were rolling yarn into balls. Their faces both had the same gloomy frightened flustered look. Dr. Talcott was striding back and forth with his gray hair standing out around his head where he'd been running his fingers through it. "It means our season at Winnesquam is ruined. It will be impossible for us to meet our indebtedness. . . . The loss of the summer's profit means ruin, the end of Winnesquam," he was intoning in a singsong voice. He stopped dead in his tracks when he caught sight of Glenn and Paul and pointed a shaking finger at them. "This is the result of your carelessness, young men . . . still I shall not be hasty . . . I shall not allow myself to be hasty." Paul's face got red and his jaw set with a click. Glenn just stood there wondering where to put his hands.

Dr. Talcott said that young Wiggleswood had scarlet fever or scarlatina, the doctor could not determine which for a few days yet, and that he would have to be dispatched immediately to a hospital and his parents notified and that of course if he had been under the proper supervision when he had been entrusted to the care of the counsellors who Dr. Talcott had taken into his family like his own sons trusting to their lively gratitude and sense of responsibility, this never would have happened. They had betrayed Winnesquam.

Staring at the ground at Dr. Talcott's feet Paul said that he thought the responsibility was mutual. His face was red and he was frowning.

Mrs. Talcott jumped to her feet saying she wasn't going to sit by and hear such insolence to Dr. Talcott. She had thrown down her yarn so hard that the ball rolled out of her lap and the daughter had to run out across the floor after it like a kitten.

Madam Talcott stopped her knitting long enough to glare across the room and echo "Insolence" in a quivering voice.

"Well, sir," Paul went on firmly, "I'm terribly sorry the kid got away but I do feel it was not entirely my fault and it certainly was not Glenn's fault because I was in charge of the camping party."

Glenn found himself piping up, "But it was Paul that found him. . . . Honestly, that kid is so spoiled you can't do anything with him."

"You were both careless," snapped Mrs. Talcott, "but Paul Graves' conduct is indefensible."

"Indefensible," echoed Madam Talcott with a click of knitting needles.

Dr. Talcott said he would never allow himself to be carried away by righteous indignation, and that he hoped Paul was sensible of the trouble and loss he had brought on Winnesquam where he had been so affectionately received, and what was this about this silly game he had started the boys playing, surely it had been most unwise.

Paul said he thought it was good for kids to know what was happening in the world, and made a little bow and walked out of the room. Glenn was going to follow when Dr. Talcott said in a choked voice to wait a minute, he wanted to talk to him alone.

The phone rang. Mrs. Elgin ran to answer. It was long distance. Dr. Talcott strode over and snatched the receiver out of her hand. As he listened his expression changed. When he spoke his voice was all sweetness, "Yes, Colonel Wiggleswood, it's most unfortunate, we hope it's only a light case of scarlatina. . . . That's what we can't understand on our beautiful lake . . . in our lifegiving air. The only possible explanation is that due to the carelessness of one of the counsellors in whom perhaps I had misplaced confidence . . . I can assure you that the young man is receiving his walking papers and that no such negligence shall ever be tolerated at Winnesquam."

"Well, it serves him right," whispered Mrs. Talcott as she and her daughter started winding the yarn on their fingers again. "He always seemed a surly sort of boy."

"You know they say in the South, mother," said Mrs. Elgin, "that no amount of education can change a poor white. . . . I'm afraid Paul Graves' people were a little ordinary." They picked up the yarn and started to wind it again.

"Ordinary," said Madam Talcott through the click of her knitting needles.

Dr. Talcott put down the phone and went back to striding back and forth in front of the big window. "Well, Colonel Wiggleswood will meet us in Laconia at the hospital this afternoon. He insists that the boy be taken there in an ambulance. If there's one more case we close up Winnesquam and send the boys home. It will be a severe financial blow."

"Severe," said Madam Talcott.

Mrs. Talcott was making signalling gestures with her head at the Doctor as her hands were tied up with the yarn. Suddenly he remembered Glenn who was scruffing his feet on the Navajo rug.

"Glenn, this is a very unfortunate situation."

"Yes, sir," Glenn found himself saying in a pleading tone, "but it's not fair to blame Paul."

The Doctor stared at him for a moment and then blew up: it was a conspiracy to ruin Winnesquam, the last thing he would have expected was that the son of an old friend and classmate should be conspiring against him with the enemy within the gates. Hadn't he been greeted with every kindness and consideration? Mrs. Talcott and the daughter dropped their yarn again and jumped to their feet. All talking at once they gradually backed Glenn towards the door. "But I don't think it's fair," he kept stammering. "I shall not tolerate such impertinence," thundered the Doctor. "Impertinence," said Madam Talcott.

"If you fire Paul you'd better fire me too," Glenn said, almost crying, and stepped out the door, missing the top step in his excitement and turning his ankle as he fell out into the rain.

Paul beckoned to him from the door of the washroom as he limped past. Glenn ducked in out of the downpour. "Well?" Paul looked in Glenn's face with his straight black brows drawn together. Glenn said he'd told them it wasn't fair.

"Wasn't any skin off your ass."

"But it wasn't fair. It was his fault for letting Fats go on the trip."

"You'd oughta kept your mouth shut."

9

It was quiet in the little whitepainted softdrink parlor down the road from the Lakeview. Paul and Glenn sat side by side at the oilcloth counter with their feet twisted round the wire legs of the stools, reading letters from home and making their chocolate milkshakes and hardboiledegg sandwiches last as long as they could. Big latesummer moths bumped against the windowscreen. An occasional sigh came from the fat girl with glasses who was slumped down behind the counter reading a pulp.

Glenn didn't read all his letter; he just peeped at scraps of it:

Your first failure to make good in the world of men has been, I must frankly confess, a severe blow to me. . . . The added aggravation of discourtesy and ingratitude to an old friend from whose association I had many hopes for you cuts deep. . . . Edgar Talcott's reasonable and fairminded letter a bombshell. . . . Naturally after what has happened you will be unable to accept any remuneration for the time you were there, though the whole sum agreed upon was most generously offered. I am confident that no

son of mine will accept one cent of it under the circumstances. . . .
It is with the gloomiest forebodings that I read of your present
activities and associations . . . beg you to remember the ideals
your dear mother tried to inculcate in you. Her memory, I pray
God, may be a protection from the coarsening and cheapening
effect of the temptations and brutalities of life that will from now
on surround you and from which your home and schooling have
shielded you thus far . . . .

Glenn rammed his letter into the back pocket of his trousers and
asked in a stiff kind of voice what Paul's old man had said. All Paul's
old man had said was that Paul had been born noaccount and would
probably be noaccount for the rest of his life like the rest of the Graves
family. Paul seemed pretty cheerful about it. Glenn's eyes were stinging. He sucked up some of his chocolate milk and then blew bubbles
in it. Neither of them said anything. Glenn went on blowing bubbles
in his chocolate milk.

"I'll tell the world," Paul broke out suddenly. "Keepin' that bus in
shape and carryin' the guests' baggage to and fro from the station is less
work and better pay than wetnursin' those darn kids at Winnesquam."

"Young man," mouthed Glenn, puffing out his cheeks, "you have
betrayed the cathedral of the woods."

Paul let out his heehaw laugh that always made Glenn feel good.
Glenn went on to say that gosh, he hoped he could save up some
dough. The one thing he didn't like was taking tips from the guests.
Paul said that in a couple of weeks maybe he could get Glenn on the
truck. He'd oughta learn to drive a truck anyways. Driving a truck was
a useful thing in this life. Old Otto was going to have to go to the hospital because he'd ruptured himself.

"My, the other boys talk dirty, lots of 'em are collegeboys too."

"I like ole Otto. He's got a wife and five children. Ole Otto don't
worry about things like that. I guess bellhops are jus' naturally trashy."

"All they seem to think about is dirty stories and peeping in keyholes."

Paul nudged him and Glenn remembered that the fat girl with
glasses could hear what they were saying. He felt the blush starting on
his neck at the edge of the sweatshirt and creeping up his cheeks. He

gulped down the rest of the milkshake and leaned back on his stool looking up at the dustymillers skidding round the single electriclight bulb that hung between the flyspecked pink paper festoons over their heads.

"Shall we shove, Paul?" Glenn slid off his stool. "I've got to review some Plane if I can keep my eyes open. . . . There's a darn nice pantryman who's an Armenian and reads all the time. He slips me a cup of coffee outa the kitchen sometimes so's I can keep awake. . . . He's the only one who doesn't spend all his time shooting craps and talking smut."

"Never mind, boy," Paul said in his deep comforting voice. "Just give me a week to work on Mr. Haines and you and me'll be on the bus together. Outside work for mine every time. . . . Well, goodnight, constant reader." When they got outside he laughed. "My soul an' body if we didn't get a smile out of little vinegarpuss."

"I guess she's afraid guys'll get fresh."

"A hot chance with those glasses."

"And that face."

"It's not the face it's the figgur."

They were hooting with laughter as they hopskipped along the black road taking pokes at each other with their flat hands. Beyond the pines along the road the full moon was high over the lake, so bright that the broad sheen over the milky water flashed here and there with pink and green light in the ripples. Crickets cheeped in the bushes and katydids kept up a shrill sawing in the pines overhead.

"Gosh, what a night," said Paul, suddenly serious. Glenn fell into step with him. "Say," he said, clearing a husk out of his throat. "Doesn't it make you want to go places?"

"Gosh, I always want to go places."

"Say, Paul, let's start next summer and make up for lost time."

"Where'll we go?"

"We'll have to beat our way someplace. Collegeboys get jobs on those Grace Line boats to South America."

"We won't have enough jack for the outfits we'd need to try the Mackenzie River. We'll have to make some money before we can do that."

"We might try working as harvest hands out in the Northwest."

"Do you think you could take it, Glenn?"

Glenn nodded excitedly. "Gosh, I wish it was next summer right now. Gee, we got jobs easy this time."

"A feller can get plenty jobs, Glenn. The problem is to find a job that pays money."

They walked on a while without saying anything. Their steps crunched in time on the sand that had been sprinkled over the newly asphalted road. They began to see ahead the tiers of lights of the hotel twinkling along the lakeshore. Glenn began to feel the sinking in his stomach he always felt coming back from an evening off. The lights of a car came suddenly around the bend in front of them. The headlights bore down on them dazzling. Glenn gave a yank at Paul's arm and pulled him into the tall grass at the side of the road. The car whizzed past. They felt its wind in their faces. Paul let out a whistle through his clenched teeth. "Golly, that was close."

They had hardly gotten the dazzle of the headlights out of their eyes when they found there was a man walking along the road beside them, going in the same direction, dragging one foot as he walked. As Glenn got abreast of him he caught a whiff of sweat dried into rank unwashed clothes. Glenn was speeding up his step to pass on ahead when a heavy hand caught his arm. "What's your hurry, Johnny?" came a low hoarse voice. "Say, cough up a nickel like a good kid. I ain't eaten in three days." All Glenn could see in the moonlight was a cap pulled down on a thick broken nose.

Paul squared off in front of them. "What's the trouble?"

"Ain't goin' to be no trouble if you slip me some chink. I can knock the goddam block off either one of you punks if it's trouble you want." The man's voice rattled in his chest. Glenn tried to yank his arm loose but the man's grip tightened until the muscle ground against the bone. "Now come across."

"We haven't got any money," said Paul, raising his fists. "Why don't you go get some honest work?"

"So you know all the answers, eh?" The man brought his fist up with a sudden jab at Glenn's chin. Glenn threw himself sideways just in time, pulling his arm loose as he fell and leaving the sleeve of his sweatshirt in the man's hand. Paul hauled him to his feet and they ran off down the road. The man didn't try to follow but stood teetering in his tracks, yelling a string of curses at them in a crazy bawling voice.

"The son of a bitch is nuts," said Paul when he began to catch his breath. "Never seen anybody like that around here. Must be some crazy tramp. They come through from Canada sometimes."

"I'd liked to have talked to him," panted Glenn.

"You can't talk to a guy when he's nuts."

"If he was hungry we ought to have given him something, Paul. I've a great mind to go back."

Paul laughed his heehaw laugh and grabbed Glenn by the shoulders and started pushing him down the path between two long hedges that led into the service entrance of the hotel.

After Paul had hit the hay Glenn sat in his undershirt under the dim electric bulb, in the pineboarded passage outside the room where the others were asleep, trying to keep his eyes open long enough to get the square of the hypotenuse equals the sum of the squares into his head. He could still feel the soreness on his arm where the crazy tramp had gripped it and smell the stink of bad teeth and hungry sweat and unwashed clothes that had come from him. He still tingled inside with the cold scare that had gone through him as the big fist had whizzed past his ear. Every time he tried to put his mind on one of the figures in the plane geometry book he'd have to be able to draw on that examination paper, the three of them snarling at each other at the side of the road beside the lake in the moonlight swam in front of the page.

Finally he fell asleep and dropped the book. He woke up with a scared start and got to his feet stretching and yawning. He opened the bedroom door softly. The room was full of deep breaths. Somebody was snoring. Glenn tiptoed in past the other cots with the dormer full of moonlight bright and dazzling in front of him. When he sat down on his creaky cot and bent over to unlace his shoes he felt his arm sore where the tramp had grabbed it, and remembered the unwashed reek of his body. He sat there with one shoe off and one shoe on, trying drowsily to shake off the scared chill he still felt up and down his spine. Temptations and brutalities, was what Dad had said in his letter.

II. SCHOOLING AND YOUTHFUL ERRORS

I

THE LAST SEMESTER OF FRESHMAN YEAR Glenn roomed with George Dilling in an old redshingled rooming house with broad shaky porches, scornfully known to the dwellers in Fraternity Row as Mrs. Kraus's Ark, that had the reputation of being the home of freaks and misfits. Glenn and George had decided that frats were undemocratic and would not pledge themselves to the only sophomore society that was willing to rush them, though they knew everybody would say it was sour grapes because they hadn't made any of the Big Three. They lettered out a sign saying LET THE HEATHEN RAVE that they tacked up over the brickedup fireplace. George used to look up at it from time to time as he sat under the bare dangling electriclight bulb evenings, reading Henry George's Progress and Poverty, with his hair that was black and stringy as an Indian's pushed back under a green eyeshade. George was older and stockier than Glenn. He was the sixth son of a Methodist Episcopal bishop from whom he'd inherited a singsong voice and a pulpit manner of reading aloud that soon converted Glenn to Single Tax too.

They were both working their way through, waiting on table and washing dishes at the Faculty Club. When they finished work they'd go back to the Ark and wrangle with the other freaks about unearned increment instead of preparing their courses. They even founded a Single Tax Association with a typewritten constitution and bylaws, of which George was duly elected president and Glenn secretary and treasurer. Their great disappointment was that they never could get anybody who'd made his letter or who was prominent in campus activities to come to meetings.

As the days got longer and warmer, George and Glenn mowed lawns and weeded flowergardens for a little extra cash, and found it harder and harder to take notes in classrooms that smelt of last winter's dust, where the voices of the profs tended to blur more and more with the buzz of flies caught between the raised windows. They couldn't help listening instead to the yells of kids playing baseball on faraway backlots and the occasional tiny crack of a bat hitting a ball and the plop of a fast ball caught in an oiled mitt. Evenings it took more and more black coffee and wet towels to keep them awake to review the year's work for the final exams, and Glenn had half the time a creepy feeling that he was going to flunk out. The only thing that kept them going was the plan they were cooking up to beat their way up into the northwest that summer to study conditions among the migratory workers in the harvest fields.

They didn't wait around for Commencement or the prom, because neither one of them had a dress suit and for that matter they didn't know any girls well enough to ask. They were in such a hurry to get out of town that they blew themselves the trip to Detroit on the boat.

When, finally, late one steaming afternoon, they stood against the rail, with a paper suitcase on the tin deck between them; and felt the screech of the whistle in their ears and the steamboat trembling under their feet as the paddlewheels started, and began to see the oredocks and the rusty whalebacks and the great viaduct shuttling with cars and the rows of black chimneys of the dirty old river backing away and fading into the reddish mist, and felt the wind of the paleblue lake chill their sweaty shirts, George gave Glenn a thump in the ribs and yelled out in a voice that made all the other passengers turn around, "We're a lucky couple of sons of guns, shucks!"; that was as near cussing as George ever came.

They put their suitcase in the men's cabin and walked round and round the deck as the sun began to set and the city faded into its long smudge of smoke, and, for the first time in weeks, got back to their old argument about the Scriptures. George was hot for the idea that you could prove single tax by the laws of Moses, but Glenn argued that it didn't matter, all you needed to prove anything by was your own sense of right and wrong. Glenn had along the Oxford Book of English Verse and claimed to be a pantheist. That gave George cold chills because he was full of his father's old time religion, although he was intending to study law himself. When it got dark and chilly George began to get very blue and to tell Glenn that if his faith was undermined it was associating with a pantheist that had done it.

In the morning they piled out feeling stuffy and rumpled from having slept in their clothes, in time to see the great oblong masses and the ranks of chimneys of a new automobile plant stalk shining through the morning mist. They had them each a fifteen-cent breakfast at a lunchwagon near the wharf. There they picked up a little Finn, who was eating his breakfast too, who said he'd give them a hitch on the truck loaded with spare parts he was driving down to a dealer in South Chicago. They paid for his breakfast on the strength of it and he sure had eaten plenty.

It was after midnight when they got into South Chicago that was a terrible dump. They couldn't get out of it quick enough. The flops all looked so lousy they couldn't think of anything to do but buy themselves traintickets into Chi. They fell asleep in the station and missed the last train, so they had to go on sitting there dozing on the hard bench until the tickettaker woke them up and put them on the milktrain in the morning. On the plush seats of the daycoach they fell asleep again like logs and stayed there until a colored man who was cleaning the car routed them out. The car was in the yards.

They had to go stumbling back between the tracks into the station, their heads buzzing and their eyes smarting with sleepiness. Glenn wanted to go some place to get cleaned up, but George said Chicago was a city of gangsters and bootleggers, and if they didn't want to get stuck up and their money taken away from them, the thing to do was to make a beeline for the North Shore. He had an idea that if they could get to Evanston they'd find college men with cars who'd give them a hitch. But, gee, Glenn kept saying, if they were out to study conditions, oughtn't they to start where conditions were worst?

Still it was hot and the streets were crowded with cars and trucks, and the pavements, once they stepped out of the station, were jammed with toughlooking people in a hurry who kept bumping into them and shoving them out of the way as they argued, and neither of them had ever been on the loose in a big city before; so they piled into the first El station they found and took a northbound train. George said they'd go as far as a five-cent fare would take them and that would get them through the worst of it. But, George, Glenn kept arguing, the worst of it was what they'd oughta see.

When they got off the El they were hungry again, because all they had for breakfast had been a cup of coffee in the station. They went into a whitefront and before they knew what they were doing they had eaten up ninetyfive cents' worth of grub. That reduced their capital to eleven dollars and thirty cents.

Taking turns carrying the suitcase they hoofed it for miles along the North Shore Drive. All the cars were going too fast. The afternoon was hot and airless, with big cloudheads building up over the lake and an occasional rumble of thunder. Drops the size of quarters were spattering the pavement when a battered Dodge touring car driven by a fat Italian finally stopped for them at the curb. "You boys goin' to Evanston? All aboard," he said, grinning.

The rain was over and the pavements were beginning to steam dry in the sun again when he stopped to let them off at the corner of the campus. As they were thanking him he handed them out some cards reading *Tony, Delicatessen and Specialties*. "Summer school too hot," he said. "Boys sometimes want nice glass of beer, gin, whiskey, wine, anything, all cut rates."

George handed him back the cards, frowning, saying that they didn't drink and besides they didn't believe in breaking the law. As they roamed around, keeping an eye out for a car that looked as if it might be headed for Milwaukee, they argued about whether it was their moral duty as good citizens to call a cop whenever they discovered that the law was being violated.

They pulled into Milwaukee next evening, sitting on the kegs of a nearbeer truck feeling absolutely pooped. They had spent the night under some pinetrees at the side of the road and it had rained on them. At the farmhouses where they'd asked to chop wood for a meal, none of the people would let them in, and one old farmer had sicked his dog on them, and they'd been so disgusted that, when a big Swede at a filling station had offered to run them into town for fifty cents a head, they'd climbed aboard without caring whether the beer they smelt in the empty kegs was legal or illegal. The Swede gave them the address of a rooming house he said was clean and cheap, and they went around there and shaved before going to the postoffice to see if they had any mail.

A telegram for George had been waiting two days at General Delivery that said his father was sick with double pneumonia and his mother wanted him home. It gave Glenn a cold chill down his spine; that would leave him on his own all right.

Next morning Glenn saw George off at the station. After the train had gone he sat for some time on a bench in the waitingroom staring at the scruffed toes of his unshined shoes. He felt trembly and vacant inside. He had a worn blue suit, some workclothes and the Oxford Book of English Verse in the battered suitcase and the copy of Progress and Poverty, that George had given him as a parting gift, under his arm. He had four dollars and seventy-five cents in his pocket. He was scared to death.

You're on your own and that's what you wanted, he kept telling himself. He had to do something right away, so he put the book in his suitcase and checked it, bought himself a paper and sat up on one of the thronelike chairs of the shoeshine parlor. While the colored boy shined them up, he went through the paper looking for Help Wanted ads. Having his shoes shined made him feel better; he'd read some place that if you were going to look for a job the first thing to do was to get your shoes shined.

The trouble was that there weren't any Help Wanted ads, all he found were the addresses of a couple of employment agencies, so he decided he'd go around to the Y.M.C.A. The secretary was a gray sharp-faced little man who heard Glenn's story looking him up and down all the time out of suspicious redrimmed eyes. Then he pursed up his lips as if he'd just tasted something sour and asked him if he'd ever heard of unemployment. Glenn said he had but he believed that a man who was willing to work could always get some kind of a job. "That's what you think," said the Y.M.C.A. secretary peevishly. He said he'd put his name down on the waiting list, but that of course local members received consideration before people from out of town. Then he tried to sell him a ticket for a singfest their glee club was giving next week. Glenn shook his head and walked out and went around to take a look at the employment agencies.

There he found that it would be three weeks before they'd be hiring harvest hands. One guy in dirty overalls told him that if he had any dough the thing to do was to go to Minneapolis, always plenty jobs in the Twin Cities, but another guy gave him the horse laugh and said hell, he hadn't noticed any and he'd just come from there last Friday. The ratfaced fink who sat chewing on a cigarbutt behind the counter said he couldn't even talk about a job unless he had a two-dollar deposit, so Glenn took a walk around the block to think it over.

In the end he found a lunchroom with a roughly scrawled sign, *Dishwasher wanted*, leaning against the rubberplant in the corner of the window. The boss was a dumpy tallowfaced man with a blue chin, some kind of a foreigner but Glenn didn't know what; he asked Glenn did he know how to run a dishwashing machine. Glenn nodded. Then he said did he understand all breakages were deducted. Glenn said okay and he was hired and found himself up to his armpits in grease for ten hours a day for the rest of the time he stayed in Milwaukee.

The two weeks he spent there were the hardest he ever remembered. It was like washing dishes at the Faculty Club only a hundred per cent worse, and when payday came around the breakage amounted to about half his pay. The cuts in his hands wouldn't heal; no matter how hard he scrubbed himself with soap and water when he got back to the rooming house he couldn't get the smell of stale grease out of his nose. His back ached all the time. The nights were hot. Dead tired as he was when he got home he'd sit halfasleep on the stoop for an hour waiting for his little room at the top of the house to cool off before he went up to roll around sleepless on his lumpy mattress.

One night he fell to talking with a lanky longjawed older man who was sitting out there too, with his wet shirt open, waiting till it was cool enough to go to bed; he said he was from North Dakota and that his name was Ben Noe, Benjamin Franklin Noe. They each passed a couple of remarks about the hot weather; then Ben Noe leaned forward with a little chuckling noise in his throat and asked Glenn, well, collegeboy, how did he like the life of a working stiff. Glenn said he didn't call pearldiving work, it was a pain in the neck. Here he'd worked like the dickens to save up to go to college and what did he do when he got there, wash dishes; and now he'd set out to get a job in the open as a harvest hand, and where had he ended up, washing dishes.

Ben Noe leaned back against the step behind him and laughed. When Glenn asked how did he know he was a collegeboy, he just laughed some more and said that you must never tell your landlady anything you didn't want the whole street to know. Then he moved up beside Glenn and tapped him on the knee with his knobbed forefinger and said all right, kid, he guessed he'd been around enough to know when a kid was on the level, he guessed Glenn had better string along with him if it was work in the harvest fields he wanted. If a stiff tried this game without somebody who was wise the finks would take the hide right off'n him, they'd had his hide often enough so he'd oughta know. He said he was going to run a threshing machine for old Spike Parker up on the river that season and if Glenn wanted to come along he'd take him if he'd promise to do one thing.

Glenn said he guessed he'd better know what it was. Ben Noe cleared his throat and stammered a little and said it was like this, he'd never had no more eddication than a gopher, but he guessed Glenn was pretty well up on grammar and punctuation and spelling and that kind of hokum. Glenn drew himself up and said he just missed getting an A in Freshman English. Ben Noe leaned over mysteriously and talked right into Glenn's ear and said he did some correspondence, see, for a paper, see, a workingman's paper in Chicago, and he'd like to have Glenn straighten out the grammar for him, but that the whole business was on the q.t. and he'd never run with anybody who didn't know when to keep his mouth shut, no more talking to landladies, see?

"You mean it's a socialist paper?"

Ben Noe shook his head. "Naw, politicians never helped the workin' class none."

Glenn said sure he knew how to keep his mouth shut and besides he was a Single Taxer. Before they went to bed he made Ben Noe take his copy of Progress and Poverty. Ben said he couldn't read such small print without his glasses and he'd lost 'em in the jungle down by the lakeshore where he'd been taking the night air for his health when he'd been down on his uppers a while back. Glenn made him take it along anyway saying he wanted a real workingman's opinion of it.

Next evening Glenn had the pleasure of telling the boss at the Arctic Lunch that he was resigning Saturday. When he left that night he saw the same old sign, only a little more flyspecked, *Dishwasher wanted*, leaning against the dusty rubberplant in the corner of the window.

Glenn felt wonderful when he woke up with a start to find that Ben had stuck his head in the door, one Sunday morning before day, and was whispering hoarsely what was the matter, was he waiting for the landlady to bring up his breakfast to him in bed. The arclights were still shining and the streets were blue with dawn as they walked across the city towards the Chicago and Northwestern freightyards. Ben said he knew a nice slow freight that would take them out to the river in no time. Glenn said, gee, he hoped they wouldn't get arrested. Ben said a stiff never needed to get arrested unless he wanted to get arrested, like in a free-speech fight or somepin, and besides he happened to know that this was the time the yard dicks were all out laying pipe.

They went into an allnight coffeestand near the depot and Glenn, who was leaving Milwaukee with just about the same amount of jack he'd hit the town with, set up to coffee and doughnuts. The coffeestand smelt sour. There were two grimylooking drunks wrangling soggily at the end of the counter. Glenn was half through his coffee when one of them lurched to the door and vomited out over the pavement. It turned Glenn's stomach and he couldn't finish his breakfast.

It was a relief to be out in the sweet pale morning air again. Gosh, Ben, he said, he didn't see how a man could get so low as to make a beast of himself with liquor. Ben had a funny look on his face. His thick lower lip quivered and he stammered a little as he said that sure the kid was right, especially a rebel oughtn't to tank up, but, kerist, a stiff sometimes got so goddam disgusted.

Glenn was relieved they didn't have to ride the rods. They sat down in an empty gondola and watched the sun come up and cast a brassy gleam over the freightyards while the rails rang with shunted cars and the yardengine tooted pleasantly in the distance. Once the freight pulled out they didn't even have to keep out of sight. "The times ain't so bad yet, kid, that a red card won't get you by," Ben yelled in his ear. Glenn didn't ask him what he meant. Anyway the train was making too much racket to talk.

Spike Parker's house was a tall old brown house with blank windows, sitting up on a new brick foundation in the middle of a cowpasture. It was near sunset, and Glenn's arm was about pulled out of its socket lugging his suitcase all the way across country from the watertank, by the time they turned in from a lane full of sweetclover, through the gate that led to the house. "There he is, I'll have to bawl him out for not sending James to meet us with the limousine," said Ben and pointed to a tall, stooped figure with a lot of white hair standing in blue overalls out in the middle of the yard between the big old red barn and the house. Behind him was a new silo and some sheds built of unpainted new pineboards that tailed off into leantos and chickenwire runs in the appleorchard out back.

Glenn had to stop to close the gate and to fiddle with the latch that was busted and wouldn't stay closed, so he just caught up on the trot as Ben was pointing to him with a jerk of the thumb over his shoulder. "That's my helper, Spike, he's a good worker even if he is a college boy." Spike looked Glenn up and down with a cold blue eye and said in his cracked voice that if he didn't suit they could always throw him out.

"What's your name, son?"

"His folks named him Glenn but I call him Sandy. I can't have a guy around me named Glenn."

"All right, Sandy. I can't pay you mor'na dollar a day as helper until I find out if you're any good. You kin ketch up on the missus's grub. . . . It's plain but there's plenty of it. Ben, you know where you sleep. . . . Does he smoke?"

"No, sir, he don't smoke or drink. He's a good clean boy."

"About all they learn in these here colleges is smoking cigarettes to my way of thinking. . . . If you got any matches you'd better hand 'em over. I don't allow no matches in my barn."

Glenn flushed as he handed over a box of matches he'd been carrying in case they needed to camp out. Then he followed Ben across the barnyard. Rhode Island Reds scattered underfoot as they went in the barn door. In a rich smell of sweetgrass hay they climbed a small dark stairway into the harness-room that smelt of sweated leather and stale mule. There they found a row of old cornshuck mattresses under a small square window. Ben picked himself out the best one with a knowing look and unrolled his blanket and took out soap and a towel and a comb and his shaving things. Glenn tried to figure out the next best and laid his suitcase on it. Ben stretched himself and took a bite off his plug of tobacco and said well, Sandy, what did he think of the Harvest Hotel?

Glenn said what was worrying him was that he'd been expecting to make two dollars and a half. Ben said he'd talk to old Spike, old Spike was on the level and that as soon as he found the kid could do a day's work he'd pay him for a day's work. Glenn said, hadn't Ben just been telling him the working class and the employer class didn't have any interests in common, and that a working stiff should never trust his master. Ben made a funny face and said that was in the preamble all right but Spike was an exception. A sort of schoolbell started ringing from the house before Glenn had time to think up an answer. "That's supper. Don't worry, kid, old Spike's a slavedriver like all the employing class but he won't gyp us."

The kitchen was clean and dingy. Mrs. Parker was a quiet dingy-looking unsmiling round woman. She and her two gawky daughters hovered around the stove and the sink while the men ate, as if they were fussed by strangers being there. At the table, besides old Spike, was young Spike, a redfaced young fellow about twenty who showed a mouthful of white teeth when he smiled, but didn't say a word, and a tiredlooking old hired man named Sydnor who took care of the cows, and, at the end, the youngest of the family, a spoiled noisy little boy they all called Buster. Glenn and Ben were hungry and ate up a big plate of cold fried eggs with slices of fat smoked shoulder and some doughy biscuits, washed down with several cups of hot weak coffee.

They hadn't swallowed the last mouthful before Spike was after them to start taking the machinery out of the shed so that they could be ready to do the oiling and repairwork in the morning. First they had to pull out an old buggy and a rusty cornhusker and a lot of dustcovered eggcrates. In the dusk Glenn couldn't tell which piece of ungodlyshaped machinery fitted in with which. Finally, old Spike brought a lantern. He kept them at it until they were ready to drop in their tracks.

He wouldn't let them take the lantern up in the harness-room so they had to undress in the dark. Although the night was warm a patch of mist from the river bottom now and then filtered chilly through the moonlit window. Glenn didn't have a blanket so Ben said, okay, they'd bunk together and give his fleas a college eddication. Ben was asleep right away, but Glenn lay awake a long time feeling stiff and sore and strange on the rustling shucks, next to Ben's angular figure that smelt of dry sweat and pipes and chewing tobacco, listening to the barnyard noises, the occasional sleepy cluck of a hen, the champing from the cowshed, the stamp of a horse from the stable below, or the sudden crowing of a rooster that the moon had waked up.

It seemed to Glenn that he'd hardly dropped off to sleep when the kitchen bell was ringing right inside his head. He jumped up not knowing where he was. It was pitch black. He could hear Ben cursing under his breath as he fumbled for his shoes. They half fell down the steep boxed stairs and pumped water for each other at the horsetrough. The water was so cold it stung when it ran down behind the ears. In the east the sky was just getting silvery.

Mrs. Parker was moving quietly around the kitchen in the orange glow of the lamp. Old Spike was sitting in a rocker beside the table reading the Bible through steelrimmed spectacles perched on the end of his nose. A light roaring came from the draft of the stove. The kitchen was full of the smell of applesauce simmering in an iron kettle. Early as it was, they hadn't gotten up early enough to find the biscuits or the fried eggs hot. The coffee seemed to be last night's brew with hot water added. They still had their mouths full of buttered biscuit when old Spike got to his feet, carefully put away his Bible and his glasses on the mantelpiece, and routed them out.

All that day they scraped rust off the rickety old steam engine, cleaned parts with emorypaper and oiled and greased and spliced busted pieces together with haywire. Meanwhile the whir of the reaper and binder, now near now far, came to them across the fields.

At dinner there were four more hands at the long oilclothcovered kitchen table and Mrs. Parker and the girls were grim and redfaced from their work at the stove. That afternoon they set up the rig in the pasture back of the barn and the next morning, as soon as the sun had dried out the wheat, they started threshing.

Glenn's job was stoking the engine. He worked in a blaze of heat from the split birchlogs he had to keep feeding in every minute and from the blistering sun overhead. His head spun from the wheezing rattle of the thresher and the yells of the men feeding in the shucks and carrying away the full sacks of grain from the end of the chute. His shoulders were sunburned and the sharp chaff itched under his armpits and under his drenched undershirt. He sweated till his pants were sticking to his knees. Ben had to yell at him at the top of his voice to make himself heard above the din. The only letup was when the belt slipped or broke and the whole contraption stopped, and Glenn was able to straighten up and stretch his back for a minute, and to stand there, in the sudden sunny silence, looking at the green flicker of locust trees along the fence against the bright blue sky, and white pigeons strutting along the ledge of the high upper window of the barn, hearing Ben's low cursing as he fiddled with the belt, and the sound of the wagons clanking over the dry earth of the wheatfields, and the men yelling at the mules, and old Spike's cracked voice rasping, "What's the trouble now?" as he strode round the end of the barn. Then Ben would yell for Sandy to go get a new lacing or for Sandy to bring the oil can and they'd be off again.

When Ben let them have the whistle at twelve o'clock the hands all made a beeline for the kitchen. By the time Glenn had washed the chaff off his face and his stinging neck, and had put on his dry blue denim shirt, there wasn't enough left to eat on the table to feed a chicken. At supper he ate first and washed afterwards. But it made him feel good, as good as when he'd found out he'd passed freshman year in the first ten, when he heard old Spike telling Ben, who was smoking his pipe after supper outside the kitchen door, that he could tell that helper of his his fingers were all thumbs but he reckoned he could have his two dollars. All he asked of a man was that he didn't die on his feet.

That night Spike Parker slept six of them in the harness room, but Glenn was so dead to the world he couldn't stay awake to hear what the other hands were saying as they settled themselves grumbling and kidding on their mattresses. It took four more days of feverish stoking, and broiling sun and driving chaff, to finish up Spike Parker's wheat-crop; then they moved lock-stock-and-barrel over to the Crowell farm about a mile down the road. It wasn't till Glenn woke up one morning and found that there wasn't any work and that it was Sunday that he had a chance to think things over.

He was sleeping on the hay in a big loft with swallows in it. Ben and the other hands had gone to breakfast. Glenn turned over and stretched. He was sore all over but he felt hard and sunburned and tired and happy. He and Ben ought to be running a combine instead of that miserable little teakettle. But he was a harvest hand all right. In a week he'd have made twelve bucks clear. Well, it was an experience. This would be a trip he could write to Paul about all right. He began making up a letter to Paul in his head, but sleep began buzzing through his blood and he fell back in a warm doze again.

When he woke up the loft was stifling hot. Flies were bumbling round his nose. He found a bucket of clean water at the barn door and washed and shaved in a splinter of mirror propped up on a harness-rack. Outside the dim barn the sunlight fell dazzling like a blow on the back of the neck.

When Glenn slid in the kitchen door the hands laughed and kid-ded him, everybody said they'd thought he'd be laying there sawing wood right on through to Monday morning. They were finishing up their pie. The table looked like a tornado had struck it. Mrs. Crowell, who was still bustling around the kitchen, brought him over a big heaped tin plate of spareribs and cabbage she had kept hot on the back of the stove, and hovered over him while he ate it after the others had stamped out belching and picking their teeth.

She was a tall woman with yellow teeth and a cheerful gaunt manner. She'd heard that he was working his way through school and
wanted to hear all the details of how he did it. Her boys were not old
enough yet, only ten and twelve, but she sure did want them to get a
good schooling. Glenn felt quite a guy as he sat there at the end of the
oilcloth table, eating his third piece of pie and giving Mrs. Crowell the
lowdown on a college education.

When he'd finished he went out to join the other hands who were
perched in a row in clean undershirts smoking and sweating along
an old log in the shade of the woodshed. The afternoon was hot and
airless. They all started to kid him about being such a big sleeper. Ray,
who was a foulmouthed guy from Iowa with a thin pointed face and
prominent ratteeth, who never said a sentence without slipping in a
dirty word, started them off by asking in a false serious voice what
the kid had been doing to himself last night that he slept so hard, he'd
never come to no good if he couldn't leave himself alone till payday.
They all roared. Ray piped up again that he'd seen him in the cowbarn
with it in his hand. Brownfaced Karl said, talking through the spear of
grass he had between his teeth, he'd bet a dollar he'd been out after the
sheep out in the fiveacrelot, that was why he'd slept so hard.

Glenn blushed crimson and began to get sore. "Lay off me, will
you," he muttered. He was the one who was alayin' on it, said Ray, out
of the corner of his nastily curled lips, he bet he could change hands
without losing a stroke.

Glenn was on his feet and hauling off to swing on him when Ben
grabbed his belt and hauled him back on the log and said to hold his
horses, Ray was just bullshitting, he didn't mean nothing and who did
Sandy think he was anyway, the Virgin Mary. That was about the size
of it, roared Ray, the kid was a virgin.

Ben turned the laugh on Ray by saying he'd a damn sight rather
be a virgin than one of your damn scissorbills with more balls than
brains, what did a working stiff get out of that stuff anyway except
a doctor's bill. If the working class would lay off the nookie and the
booze and spend their dough organizing for just one year you'd see a
hell of a lot of difference in this country. They'd start to do something
about shaking off the parasites and bloodsuckers. This way what did a

stiff do as soon as he got twentyfive bucks in his jeans? He went down to some damn honkytonk and let the broads and the bootleggers take it away from him and spent the next three months slaving to pay the doctor to cure him up. Ray laughed and spat between his eyeteeth and said Ben was speaking for himself, so he'd gotten burned when they went the rounds down at the junction last fall, had he, well, it was tough luck, old horse.

Ben grunted and said a stiff got so damn disgusted trying to get a little sense into the heads of you slaves it was a wonder he ever sobered up at all. Anyway it was better'n getting married and breeding up a lot of kids that didn't have no chance in the world.

That made big Ole sore and he spoke up and said a man had to have a vooman, what a man ought to do was to get him a nice hardworking vooman, and a little farm, and raise a lot of nice kids to help with the vork and mind his own business. And spend your life on your knees to the storekeeper for a little credit and run yourself ragged to fatten up the crooks who ran the wheatpit and the commission merchant and the smalltown banker, shouted Ben. Karl laughed and said none of your bohunks ud ever earn enough to fatten up a turkey buzzard.

Ben shook his head gloomily. Warn't no laughing matter, he'd seen more'n one good fellowworker fatten up the buzzards. Karl said well, so long as a guy was young and quick on his feet he could keep moving on after the good wages. Ray got up and kicked the toe of his boot against the log: "You tell us where, boy. But you wobblies ain't so smart, all you did was git beat up and land in Atlanta penitentiary for war slackers while the wise guys was makin' eight dollars a day in the munition plants."

Ben got up and spat out his quid of tobacco and said he didn't notice as how Ray had held on to any of it, or he wouldn't be hiring himself out for two dollars to John Farmer, at least the fellowworkers who went to jail had the satisfaction of knowing they'd put up a fight for their own class.

Ray asked him why he wasn't in jail himself if he was such a hell-roarin' red. Ben said he'd been in jail plenty but this time the D. of J. hadn't caught up with him. "A hardworkin' man who minds his own business can make out good in dis coontry," said big Ole.

"In the pig's a.h." said Ben. "A workin' stiff is lucky to end in a decent poorhouse when he gets old." Then he yelled to Glenn to come along, he was disgusted with these scissorbills and was going to wash out his underclothes in the creek. Big Ole had the last word: "You get you a good nice hardworkin' vooman and she'll do your washin' for yous."

Glenn had just about toughened up to the work by the time old Spike was through with his threshing and ready to put his rig back in the barn and go home to pull his cornfodder. He stayed on for a day after the other hands had been paid off to help Ben oil and clean up the engine and the thresher. The hands went off talking about the Red River country, and Ben said him and the kid would hotfoot after the rest of 'em, and they'd work up into Manitoba. Him and the kid was going to lay them by a stake that summer.

After Glenn and Ben had shaken hands all around with the Parker family they walked off down the lane to the watertank to hop a freight to the junction. Ben had his blanket roll on his shoulder and Glenn was still toting his suitcase. Ben had about fifty bucks in his jeans and Glenn had a little less than forty.

There had been thundershowers in the night, followed by a northwest wind that had lashed a fine sparkle into the air. All the way Ben talked big about how they were going to save two hundred dollars apiece that summer and that would be enough to get them up to Alaska. There was easy money to be made digging gold up to Nome. He knew guys who had made a pile in three years. What Ben wanted to do was to make him a little pile and buy him some kind of little gasoline station out on the Coast somewhere, just something he could live on, and then he'd set up a little paper to tell the truth to the working class, how about it, Sandy?

The freight whistled way down around the bend and slowed to a stop at the watertank. The couplings clashed all down the long train as the engineer put on the brakes hard. As cocky as two passengers getting on a daycoach, Glenn and Ben tried the boxcar doors until they found one unlocked, then they swung in and pulled the door to after them.

Glenn was still blinking from the darkness of the boxcar when a hoarse voice came out of the corner, well, he'd be goddamned if that warn't old Ben Noe, Benjamin Franklin Noe. "Is that you, Teebone? Well, it never fails. Meet my sidekick, Teebone." Glenn found his hand squeezed in a big hard grip. "Old Teebone and me pulled out the fruit-pickers together and we was cellmates in Fresno jail." Ben slapped his knees, laughing. "He's the orneriest pokerplayer you ever saw." They were all laughing.

The train was rumbling so loud they couldn't yell over the racket of the trucks. All that Glenn could make out was that Teebone was bound north and west for the harvest with the rest of them.

As the freight slowed for the junction the three of them piled out in a hurry and slid down the side of the embankment to keep out of sight of the yard dick who Teebone said was a tough hombre. Glenn fell on his face and slid halfway down the cinderbank on his knees with his suitcase on top of him. When he got to his feet he found he'd torn one leg of his khaki pants and taken the skin off his knee.

Ben and Teebone laughed, and Ben said he guessed they didn't teach him hoppin' freights at that cowcollege of his. Now that they were out in the day again Glenn could see that Teebone was a big red-haired husk in a ragged sweater with a red freckled face and a neck creased and wrinkled like elephant hide. He and Ben walked off talk-ing about old times. Glenn followed after them limping, down a road past a lumberyard, towards a collection of shacks with high board fronts along a rutted dusty street. "First thing, let's eat," Ben was say-ing. "There used to be a widow woman down the line that put up a darn good two bit meal." Teebone said that was just two bits more than he had in his jeans. Ben said to forget it, him and the kid was in the money. "Look out for this feller, Sandy, he'll take your money away if he gets to rollin' the ivories." Glenn said he thought gambling was a big mistake. "You said it, brother," said Teebone.

Glenn went into the general store and bought himself a new pair of khaki pants. He changed a ten-dollar bill to pay for the pants. The thought that he'd started from scratch and made forty dollars at real work made him feel great.

He met up with the others at Mrs. Adamic's Railroad Boarding-house. They were already hunched over the table shovelling in the grub. After they'd eaten they all felt good and wandered around the junction in the late afternoon chewing toothpicks. Teebone had begun to talk about how this would be the time for a couple of drinks and a little crapgame, just a little friendly game and one or two drinks, no more.

There was quite a bunch of men standing out on the piece of concrete pavement in front of the poolparlor. Teebone and Ben elbowed their way through, kind of nosing around, and Glenn tagged after them. A little guy in dirty sneakers with his hair growing very low on his narrow forehead was leaning against the jamb of a door at the end of the poolroom that led out back. Teebone whispered something to him and he let them slip past him and then slouched back so as to fill up the door again. In a corner of a concrete yard, that had a couple of big pairs of wagonwheels standing in the middle of it, sunburned men in dusty clothes were sitting on their heels in a circle round a big pile of bills. All their eyes were on the bones that clicked gently as they rolled.

"Well, ain't that a coincidence?" said Teebone in a silky voice and borrowed a dollar off Ben to get in the game. After a minute Ben got in the game himself. Glenn felt silly looking on leaning against the clapboard wall. A tall man in blue overalls with gray towhair standing up straight on his head had a bottle that he was passing around. When the bottle was empty Ben beckoned to the little guy with the sneakers and slipped a dollar in his hand.

Glenn took Ben by the arm and whispered that maybe they'd better make themselves scarce, wasn't there a westbound train out that night? Ben put on a serious poker face and said for Sandy to watch himself, them boes was tough company. By that time the little guy in the sneakers was back with a pint of whitishlooking stuff. Ben said, have a swig, it was regular tigerpiss. Glenn shook his head; then Ben said, why didn't Sandy go and get 'em a flop at Mrs. Adamic's, him and Teebone had a little business here might take 'em all evening.

As Glenn brushed past the little guy in the door, he looked out at him and said, hello, buddy, how about some gash, he could get him dated up swell. Glenn shook his head and walked out through the poolroom, where the lights were just going on over the tables.

Glenn walked over to the boardinghouse and got them a ground floor room that just held three cots with their heads against a small screened window. The room was stifling and smelt of bedbug powder, but it was cheap. Then he went to the rickety bathroom lit by a blue gasflame and shaved and washed up. After that he took a turn around to the poolroom to see how the crapgame was getting on. The corner of the yard was lit by an acetylene lantern that shone in the men's eyes and gave their taut faces a white skeleton glare. Teebone was talking to the dice as he rolled them. There was a big crowd around looking on and several men were pretty drunk.

Glenn couldn't catch Ben's eye, so he went back to the boarding-house and lay down on the cot without getting undressed so that the bedbugs would have less of a chance at him. He'd just gone to sleep when there was Ben fumbling around between the cots holding up a match. Ben's face was all sweaty, and his eyes were bright and wet, and his heavy lower lip sagged on his chin. Sandy, old cock, he said, and a reek of liquor came out of him, him and Teebone was agoin' to make a killin', them boes was gettin' cold feet an' Teebone was in a run of luck, all they needed was a little more jack, now it was up to Sandy to come across with his wad, they'd split the winnin's three ways, see?

Glenn sat up in bed. "But shucks, Ben, suppose they clean you." "Them bindlestiffs ain't got it in 'em. Didn't I tell you Teebone was the greatest crapshooter north of the Mason and Dixon line?" Glenn said if they'd take his advice they'd come back here and go to bed before they got sick off rotgut liquor.

The match went out. Ben lit another that he held up between two shaky black fingers and stuck his face into Glenn's. Glenn could feel his drunk eyes boring into him. Kid, he said, if a stiff was a sidekick of his, it was share and share alike in spite of hell and high water, and he didn't expect any little snotnosed punk from a jerkwater cowcollege to hold out his roll on him just because he was a stuckup college student from the Y.M.C.A.

"Well, if you feel that way about it," said Glenn, and handed him a ten-dollar bill; and he went off mumbling that there was near four hundred dollars in the kitty, and Teebone was going to make the killing of his life. After he'd gone Glenn took the precaution of putting his three remaining fives in the lining of his boot. Then he lay down again. He felt bad about Ben's going off the deep end like that, and every now and then he got a bite around the wrist or ankle that must have been a bedbug, but he was so sleepy he dropped off just the same.

A shrill giggling woke him. The gaslight was lit. There was a rank smell of perfume in the room. Ben and Teebone were standing over him wrestling with a couple of girls. They were all reeling drunk. "Hey, for crying out loud," Glenn said, jumping up. "Shush," said Teebone, "if they wake up they'll run us out of this joint." Ben said to pipe down, Sandy, old boy, he could lay a little pipe himself when they were through. Ben's girl broke out in a giggle and Ben put his hand over her mouth to shut her up. Teebone already had his down on the cot.

Glenn felt his knees trembling. He walked out of the room and went and sat on the empty boardinghouse porch. There was a gnawed sliver of the tailend of a moon behind the cottonwood trees, and the shrill screech of dryflies went through his head. In a minute Ben came lurching after him in his bare feet and whispered in his ear that he got to come across with four dollars, them hookers was fightin' like hell-cats and wouldn't do nothing till they they got their money.

Glenn dragged all his loose change out of his trousers pocket and said after this he was through. Ben said, good old Sandy, all he wanted was make a man of him, better come in and have some human companionship. Glenn sat there in a cold sweat a long time listening to the squeals and giggles and scuffling noises that came from the room. Then Mrs. Adamic and her husband woke up and he could hear them knocking on the door and raising cain in the hall, saying they'd have to get out of there, all of them, this was a respectable boardinghouse. The hookers scuttled out past Glenn in a hurry with Ben and Teebone hotfoot after them. Ben was so drunk he didn't notice him. He was barefoot and carrying his shoes in one hand and his blanketroll in the other.

Then Glenn went in and tried to explain that it wasn't his fault to two squat angry figures with blankets round their shoulders, sputtering at him in bad English, but all they'd say was git and git quick, so Glenn closed up his suitcase and laced up his boots and went out. There was already a streak of day behind the lumberyard in the east. As he walked towards the freight depot he heard the whistle of a locomotive way off.

2

Glenn got back to college in high spirits the day after Labor Day with thirtyfive dollars in his pocket and a good tan and a fine set of calluses on his hands; but he couldn't find anybody he knew. The gypsymoth had eaten all the leaves off the trees on the campus and everything had a dusty abandoned look. At the Ark he found, covered with dust on the settee in the hall, a long letter full of Single Tax and the laws of Moses from George, saying he wouldn't be back north because his dad had died and he was going to have to stay home to take care of his mother and had been taken on as office boy in a lawoffice where he hoped to study for the bar nights. Beside it was a scrawl on a postalcard from Paul Graves saying he'd married the sweetest girl in the world and that they were going to have a baby.

It gave Glenn a funny lonely feeling reading that Paul was married. He didn't have time to think about it; what he had to do just then was line up a job for the winter. There was nobody in yet at the college employment office. So, just on chance, he went around to see Edmund Carmichael Gulick, a sociology prof he'd had several friendly arguments with last spring about the importance of Henry George. Glenn had a hunch he might be able to suggest something that paid better than waiting on table.

He felt lonesome and blue as he stood shuffling his feet in the brick entryway of the Gulicks' apartment after ringing the bell over their mailbox. He was just turning away to leave when the buzzer answered and a voice down the speaking tube said to come on up, third floor right.

Mrs. Gulick met him at the door with a feather duster in her hand. She wore a stained and rumpled artists' smock of bright pink material. Her bobbed hair cut in a straight bang across her forehead flopped over her black eyes that had a peevish teasing look about them. The rouge on her lips had smeared and there was a smudge of dust on her small turnedup nose.

Glenn stammered that he guessed she didn't remember him, he was Glenn Spotswood. She started chattering, as if he were her oldest friend in the world, that Mike had been offered an instructorship at Columbia so they were moving to New York, and of course the twins' nurse had taken the opportunity to get sick and they were almost crazy with packing. Maybe Glenn could help them pack.

He said sure, he hadn't a thing in the world to do, and he followed her into the tornup livingroom where they found Edmund Carmichael Gulick standing in the middle of a packingcase holding a teetering pile of books to his chest. He was a tall skinny whitefaced man with high cheekbones and thin sandy hair plastered carefully across a high narrow forehead. There was a good deal of classroom manner about his way of talking. He didn't seem to remember Glenn either but seemed delighted when he offered to help them pack.

Edmund Carmichael Gulick had a way of looking up in the air and sticking out his adamsapple when he asked a question, and then going on talking without paying any attention to the answer. While they packed he asked Glenn several times what he'd been doing that summer. When he finally caught on to the fact that he'd been working in the harvest fields he straightened up and looked right at him and said by golly, he was just the man he wanted to talk to because he was writing his Ph.D. thesis on migratory labor. "But goodness, Mike," Mrs. Gulick almost shrieked, "he's been trying to tell you for the last half hour he was a migratory worker."

It ended by Glenn's doing all the packing while the Gulicks stood over him and asked him questions about the Northwest. By the time he'd nailed up the last case of books for them it was midnight. Nobody had had any supper so they all went downtown in the Gulicks' car, which Mrs. Gulick drove, to a Chinese restaurant. There they sat for hours over chow mein and tea while Glenn told about life as a harvest hand. He felt he was making a hit with the pair of them and before he knew it he was talking his head off.

When they got up to go home because the chink was closing he said his dad had taught at Columbia years ago and he sure wanted to transfer his credits there but the question was how he could swing it. Gulick asked was that Herbert Spotswood? Glenn nodded, pressing his lips together. "He's one of my heroes," cried Mrs. Gulick.

"I should venture to say there had been a definite change of opinion in academic circles in regard to the Spotswood case," said Gulick solemnly. "It was very much too bad."

As they were driving home through empty streets Mrs. Gulick suddenly said she had an idea; why couldn't Glenn drive their car to New York for them. It would be cheaper than shipping it, and Mike couldn't drive on account of his eyesight. Glenn said he'd like nothing better, but that wouldn't help him to find a paying job for the winter that wouldn't take too much time from his college work. They, said for Glenn to sleep on the proposition and they'd see what they could dope out. By the time the Gulicks said goodnight to Glenn at Mrs. Kraus's Ark they were all calling each other by their first names. Glenn went to sleep in Mrs. Kraus's hall bedroom all aglow with the thought that Marice Gulick was the swellest girl he had ever met in his life.

It was eleven o'clock when Glenn woke up. He jumped into his clothes and hurried around to the Gulicks'. They were sitting over their breakfast coffee in their bathrobes not knowing what to do next. The twins were all over the place.

Glenn went on packing and nailing down boxes as best he could and phoned the transfer company for them and ended by helping Marice pack her dresses. They both kept saying Glenn had saved their lives, and that he must come to New York with them. They explained that Marice had inherited an old brownstone house on Morningside Heights. Glenn would live there with them and take care of the furnace and do the chores for his board and lodging. That would just leave his clothes and tuition to be handled. Mike said he was sure he could get a scholarship. Marice said she would recommend him for a packer anywhere.

So he went home to his room that afternoon, after the Gulicks had set him up to a good lunch in a downtown restaurant, to write to Dad to see if he couldn't let him have a little money that winter on account of the wonderful opportunity that had come up, and to George and Paul blowing about how he was going to take his sophomore year at Columbia, no more freshwater colleges for him.

Glenn arrived in New York late on a rainy afternoon with the car so jammed with cartons and paperboxes that the state cops had stopped him for a bootlegger in Easton, Pennsylvania. After a long push through sludging traffic and wet streets he found the Gulicks' old brownstone house and ran up the steps to ring the bell.

It was Marice herself who opened the door, looking very neat in a new pearlgray tailored suit. Oh, Glenn, she said, she was glad he'd come, maybe he could tell her what to do about this house, wasn't it awful, she thought she'd move everything out and paint it bright red like the A. & P. Without knowing what to say Glenn followed her around the long dark rooms cluttered with bulky furniture draped under dustcloths, here and there moving a table or peeping into a closet full of hooded articles that smelt of mothballs, and up into the attic that was full of broken chairs and dusty cutglass, where they found themselves gazing solemnly at a row of old chamberpots with roses painted on them and burst out laughing.

Glenn was anxious to be useful, but they couldn't seem to decide where to begin. They went back down to the big front bedroom and he helped her drag some overstuffed sofas around. She was wearing two silver bracelets that jangled when she moved and she left a little trail of perfume behind her. When the backs of their hands brushed each other as they moved the dressing table, Glenn felt himself blushing red. It made him feel awkward being alone with Marice in the close warm air of the old house where she'd lived when she was a little girl.

The front doorbell rang. Glenn ran down the stairs two at a time. It was a relief to have to answer the doorbell. Standing outside bareheaded in the rain was Mike; he had lost his latchkey.

When Marice heard Mike had lost his latchkey she cried out, what again, and made an awful fuss. She said you had to, read the Psychopathology of Everyday Life to see what that meant. Mike was quite peeved and said he wished he'd never started her reading Freud. She said tartly she'd read Freud before Mike had ever heard of him. Glenn didn't know what on earth they were talking about.

That night, after supper, that Glenn had been sent out to buy at the delicatessen around the corner, and that the three of them had eaten cosily at the huge mahogany table, under the chandelier draped in cheesecloth, in the diningroom, while Marice and Mike went on wrangling about whether Mike's losing his latchkey really meant that he'd ceased to care, Marice said that a couple of friends were coming in for a little housewarming.

When the bell rang Glenn tried to slip off to bed, but Marice caught him by the arm saying he mustn't be inhibited and dragged him down to the foot of the stairs again, and he found himself being introduced as a migratory worker to a redfaced young man with a small black mustache, who came in staggering under two gallon jugs badly wrapped in newspaper, and to a man and his wife who were both very blond and had a look of eyestrain under their glasses, and were research workers. Then a couple of graduate students came in and a gaudylooking girlfriend of Marice's who was studying at dramatic school.

They were all crazy to hear about Glenn's experiences, they said; Marice had told them so much about him. He must tell them about conditions among the migratory workers. But by the time Glenn had gotten around to thinking up something to say, everybody had started talking at the top of their voices again. It was all about Freud. Glenn couldn't get a word in edgewise.

Mike filled Marice's father's cutglass carafes with the dago red. They all sat around the big table arguing, and Glenn sat back and listened, feeling he was in the big city for fair. Marice's friend, Eileen Paradise, who wanted to go on the stage, had been to a psychoanalyst that very day because her inhibitions were interfering with her acting, she was afraid she had an Oedipus complex; she declared she knew Marice would get one, bringing her husband back to her father's house like that. Mike got a little huffy and said well, if a healthy pair of twins wasn't the sign of a successful transference he didn't know what was. Then somebody asked Glenn to tell about the sexlife of migratory workers and he blushed red and stammered that it was pretty bad and everybody laughed.

Eggy Harriman, who was a cub reporter and a great wisecracker, said sex was sex the whole world over and the only trouble was you couldn't get enough of it. That shocked everybody and Eileen Paradise shook her finger at him and said, what about the libido. Eggy said he didn't bring his out in public and Marice said, "Eggy, none of your barroom manners," and hurriedly changed the subject.

While Mike was filling up the glasses again Glenn made his get-away and went up to bed; his head was swimming, he was so sleepy after the long day's drive through the rain.

There was so much painting and scraping to be done around the Gulicks' house, as they'd decided to redecorate it themselves, that Glenn didn't get him any other job. What with his college work and a little basketball and tending the furnace and carting out the ashes and the garbage can and occasionally driving the car for Marice, he didn't have a spare moment all winter.

The Gulicks treated him like a member of the family. He got to be very fond of them. He was getting a little too fond of Marice and had dreams about her at night and it made him uncomfortable to be alone with her, but he told himself that nobody in the world would ever know; Mike Gulick was his friend and that was enough.

Eggy Harriman was around the house a great deal, especially at noon when Mike was always in his office at the university. He'd come around to have a cup of coffee with Marice, who was anything but an early riser, before going downtown to work. On his day off he'd call up, if he wasn't too plastered, to take her to a matinée. He got to be ratpoison to Glenn, who never could think of a comeback to any of his wisecracks until afterwards when it was too late. Glenn would find himself sitting at a lecture stewing about it, telling himself that Eggy was a waster and a bum and a bad friend of Mike's and that he ought to punch his face in. Then one day, when Glenn came home at an unusual time in the afternoon on account of a course being called off because the instructor had the flu, he heard a man's voice, that certainly wasn't Mike's, coming from the Gulicks' bedroom as he passed their door on his way up to his own room on the third floor. His heart started pounding so he could hardly breathe.

He tried to settle down to reading Marx's Capital at his table, but the print on the page kept melting into white blotches. In spite of him his ears kept straining for voices from downstairs. He even tiptoed over to the stairs and listened. He couldn't hear a sound.

He went back into his room and threw himself face down on the bed. As if it were somebody else, he noticed coldly that he was sobbing and whispering into his pillow, oh, Marice, Marice. Then he sat on the edge of the bed making up a story in which he followed Eggy out of the house and mashed his head in with the coalshovel and then went and gave himself up to the police, and Mike and Marice lived happily ever afterwards, and nobody knew but Marice that he'd sacrificed his life to save her marriage. He told himself not to be a damn fool, that it was all imagination and went and washed his face. It was time to stoke the furnace anyway so he put on his workclothes and went downstairs.

The light was out in the Gulicks' room and the door was open, but as he went on down to the ground floor, his knees shaky and his hands cold, he heard Eggy's whinnying laugh and Marice's warm voice and the clink of ice from a cocktail shaker. "That you, Glenn?" Marice called as he passed the parlor door. "Come on in."

He stood in the doorway and looked in. Marice looked prettier than he'd ever seen her in the warm light of the floorlamp. She was sitting on the horsehair sofa with a tray with glasses and the shaker and a plate of shrimps in mayonnaise in front of her. Eggy was in his shirtsleeves. He got up from where he'd been sitting on the sofa beside her when he saw Glenn, and started walking up and down, in front of the gaslogs in the black marble fireplace, with his hands in his pockets, scruffing at the bear rug with his feet.

"Hadn't you better have a cocktail, Glenn?" Marice said in a laughing kidding voice. "It's an awfully gloomy afternoon . . . Eggy's dreadfully gloomy. He just called up the office and said he was sick in bed. It feels like Sunday."

Glenn shook his head. "I don't like the taste of it," he said, and stood rolling on the balls of his feet in the doorway. "Mike come home yet?" Marice shook her head, laughing easily and happily. "He's gone to tea with a lot of professors."

"Better try one," said Eggy. "It's the best Martini I ever made and the driest."

Glenn shook his head. Marice laughed again. "He's got a complex about drinking. He's a very inhibited young man."

"Jeez, I thought the migrants were the toughest eggs in the world. I suppose the harvest hands all go down on payday and have a good big glass of milk," said Eggy. Glenn blushed and was just ready to walk over and sock the little smartaleck in the jaw, when Marice said in a serious deep voice, no, that Glenn was quite right; and would he mind taking a look at the twins after he was through with the furnace as it was Agnes's night out. She was coming up to give them their suppers in a minute. Glenn couldn't help pulling the door sharply to after him as he turned to go.

He took some of it out shaking down the furnace so hard he just about dumped the fire. By the time he'd gotten the fire going again and had carted out the ashes into the areaway under the steps and had messed with the hotwaterheater that was out of order, he was telling himself it wasn't any business of his, he was just a hired hand. When he went back up to his room he was still so upset he couldn't trust himself to talk to Marice and Mike at supper, so he dressed and went out for a walk.

A foggy warm winter evening was blurring the lights and softening the last caked remnants of snow in the gutter into slush. Glenn walked and walked. His feet got wet and he was too hot in his raincoat. He walked down Broadway through the suppertime crowds, stopping now and then to read headlines on newspapers or the menus announced in frames of white enamel letters in the windows of lunchrooms. He stopped under the jiggling electric lights at the entrance to a moving picture theatre, and halfdecided to go in, but found he didn't have a cent in his pocket.

He felt awful. Mike and Marice had meant a whole lot to him since he'd been east. Now everything was over. By the time he'd gotten to the spinning roar of traffic round the monument, that jutted up dark in the red glare of Columbus Circle, he'd decided he ought to tell Mike that Eggy was breaking up his home. He ought to talk to Marice and tell her it was wrong. He ought to go to see Eggy and push his face in.

His legs were beginning to get tired and his feet were wet. He began to feel he was catching cold. He turned uptown again through the park, where the lights from the streets and the tall buildings cast a glow over patches of pockmarked snow and gleaming wet paths between black trees. Suddenly he felt dead tired and plunked down a bench with his feet stuck out in front of him.

He closed his eyes for a second: girls' faces, eyes, lips, cheeks, girls' legs on billboards, the buttocks jiggling up and down under her raincoat as she walked of a girl he'd followed for a block down Broadway, all unreeled in flaring lights and shadows in the blackness in front of his eyes.

He felt somebody sit down on the bench beside him. A Bostonian-sounding voice was saying did he like foggy nights like that. Glenn straightened himself up and muttered that they were all right if you had some place to go. He glanced at the man who had sat down on the bench beside him; something about the wet look in the eyes too close together that looked at him from under a pulleddown hatbrim made Glenn turn his face away.

The man was saying that foggy nights made a fellow feel lonely. Glenn said it was tough when you thought of all the people who had no place to go.

The man said it oughtn't to be like that, we ought to have beauty and companionship in our lives, and not wear all these ugly clothes. He said he had a friend who had a studio where a fellow could get warm and dry his feet, and see interesting photographs, beautiful photographs of the nude that showed everything, and that sometimes if he met up with a nice friendly fellow who knew how to keep his mouth shut he'd take him over there. The man's voice was getting husky. His hand in a black glove trembled as he poked a cigarette at Glenn. Glenn said that he didn't smoke and got up and walked on.

When he got home his nose was itching and he felt he was catching cold. He went in the basement entry so as not to meet anybody. Banking the furnace he spilt a shovelful of coal on the floor and slammed the furnace door to in a sudden rage and went up to bed. He could hear people laughing in the front room and Mike's highpitched voice laying down the law about something. He locked the door of his room, took off his clothes and got shivering into bed.

He was dead tired but he couldn't sleep. He kept remembering the perfume Marice wore, the smell of her hair, the soft small look of her breasts under the boyish blouses she wore, and half wished he'd gone to see the photographs with the man in the park. The Bostonian-sounding voice went on and on in his head after he fell asleep and feverish dreams of streets and naked bodies and Marice kept blooming and fading in a glare like the foggy lights downtown. He woke up wet and sticky and had to change his pyjamas.

Next morning Mike met him on the stairs as he was going out to classes and took one look at him and said he looked like he had the flu and he'd better let him take his temperature. They found he had a fever of a hundred and one. Marice came out from taking her bath, smelling of heliotrope bath salts and wearing a blue negligee, and they both talked to him like Dutch uncles and put him to bed on a diet of aspirin and bicarbonate.

It made him feel like a kid again the three days he stayed in bed; Marice brought up his meals herself, and he read Hugh Walpole's Fortitude and a lot of Marx; and Boris Spingarn, a Brooklyn boy who was studying chemistry he'd met at a socialist rally, came to see him every afternoon to argue about whether the capitalist system was on the way out or just groggy from the last war.

The last afternoon he stayed in bed Marice came up to talk to him, bringing up a pot of tea and some toast with marmalade on it and a cup for each of them. She said she loved having somebody sick in the house on a snowy afternoon, it made things so cosy. She said she didn't love Mike half so well since he'd taken up handball and didn't have all those colds he used to have, she guessed it was the maternal instinct. That's what Dr. Blumenthal said, he said she was the earth mother or Demeter type.

They both got to laughing at that, but Marice said they'd have to be serious because it was especially about Dr. Blumenthal she'd come to talk to Glenn. He'd noticed him at the party the other night, when he'd helped Mike bring in the punchbowl and glasses, and said he looked like a very inhibited young man. Dr. Blumenthal was one of the four leading psychoanalysts outside of Vienna, and he was taking cases at very low rates now, because he wanted to observe complexes in various social stratifications, and complained all the cases he got were either very rich or very crazy. Dr. Blumenthal had said Glenn looked like a very typical adolescent narcist, and Marice said she thought he ought to consult him before his neurosis got any worse.

She'd been several times and he'd already done her a great deal of good. She'd been so unhappy since the twins were born, she'd been at her wit's end because Mike didn't seem to satisfy her any more. The first year they'd been married it had been so wonderful, they'd been like two beautiful young animals, but now Mike didn't seem pagan any more, he was so preoccupied with his work and everything. Dr. Blumenthal had said it was because she was an earth mother and advised her to have another baby instead of acting like a perfect bitch and that was just what she was going to do.

But she thought Glenn ought to see Dr. Blumenthal right away before he got to be an introvert, she thought herself he had a little Oedipus complex that made him all tied up inside so that he couldn't fall in love; that's how young men got to be homosexuals. Dr. Blumenthal could help him effect a transference.

Glenn turned red and stammered that he didn't see what use it would be unless he could find some way of making some more dough, after all it was an economic problem too. Marice said now Glenn mustn't be crass, that was just the kind of rationalization Eggy Harriman would make, he mustn't get to be a smartaleck, that was all just a mechanism. Then she gathered up the teathings and went downstairs leaving Glenn feeling like he'd been run over by a steamroller.

The next time Glenn met Boris Spingarn at a meeting of the Social Problems Club he said there was something he wanted to talk to him about and would he come out for a walk after the meeting. They walked up the Drive towards Grant's Tomb with a lashing northwest wind in their faces in the bright icy night, and when Glenn said he'd been advised to consult a psychoanalyst, Boris asked who by. "Well, she's somebody I think a lot of," Glenn muttered sheepishly. Boris laughed like he'd split and said if any woman advised him to do anything like that he'd lay her good and proper. Glenn said but suppose she was the wife of a friend. Boris said they lived in a world in decay and it was no use having bourgeois prejudices and that besides the wives of friends were a whole lot more practical than trying to pick up floosies on Ninth Avenue.

He said Glenn ought to feel himself a member of the revolutionary workingclass and to stop associating with bourgeois liberals whose ideas were the main support of decaying capitalism. All this talk about sex was bourgeois liberalism and made him sick. What a working man needed was plenty of bed exercise and to shut up about it, and revolutionary marxists ought to live like working men.

Glenn said haltingly he didn't think he was a marxist, though he was all for the working man getting an honest return for what he produced, but he guessed he'd have to pull out from the Gulicks' house and get him a job. He'd go around to the employment office and see what they could do for him. "That's the stuff, no compromise with the bourgeoisie," said Boris. By that time their ears were so cold they turned across to Broadway and went into a fifteen cent movingpicture house to get warm. "You're right, Boris," said Glenn, after they had sat through the newsreel of the battleship being launched and were looking at sunkist girls diving into the pool at Coral Gables, Florida. "By gum, you're right; that woman has been taking me for a ride."

3

Glenn was looking for number 332. He arrived at the door of a big old frame house with a porch and a mansard roof, set back from the street behind a ragged grassplot and two small ailanthus trees, and hemmed in by new brick apartments on either side. He felt dusty from the long traintrip and his arms ached from carrying his two heavy suitcases from the subway station. His raincoat, the pockets stuffed with books, hung round his neck. Sweat was running down his face from under his new felt hat. He rang the bell beside the peeling green door and waited, mopping his face and neck with his handkerchief. When he got tired of ringing the bell he began rapping with his knuckles. The door swung open. He found himself in a dark hall full of closed brown doors looking up a stairway covered with a worn red carpet held down by brass rods. On the post where the curving stairrail ended stood a marble lady swathed in too many draperies all of bronze and holding up a lamp. Glenn brought in his suitcases and yelled up the stairs, "Anybody in? Say, Boris . . ."

A girl's voice came in an answering whoop from an upper floor. A minute later the girl herself came sliding down the bannisters with her knees flashing white from under a tight black skirt. She wore a red blouse and her hair was bobbed; she must be Boris' kid sister. "I'm

Gladys Funaroff," she sputtered, laughing. "We slide down because the carpet's so treacherous. . . . Haven't you always wanted to live in a house where you could slide down the bannisters?"

Glenn stammered that he had, well, to be truthful he never had, but was Boris in. The girl said in a rush, no, Boris was at the lab but that she knew all about him, he was young Spotswood come out of the West, and she was disappointed; she thought he was going to be one of those great husky blonds, a real nordic beast, she was crazy about blonds, probably because she was so dark, that's why she and Boris had gotten married, wasn't it conventional of them, but Boris wasn't really blond at all. . . . Boris had talked so much about him and she was delighted he was going to live with them, all they ever saw was intellectual jews, and scientists who were all reactionaries at heart, and she'd thought he'd be a big blond coalheaver who'd keep them in touch with the masses. While she talked Glenn couldn't keep his eyes off her long curved black lashes and the sharp modelling of her very red unrouged lips. She had a little stilted way of talking that wasn't exactly an accent; he thought she was the prettiest girl he'd ever seen in his life.

She started to lift one of his suitcases and drew her slender black eyebrows together in a frown, her red cheeks got redder as she took two hands to it and lifted it. Glenn tried to take it away from her but she said women could carry much heavier burdens than men and started staggering up the stairs with it. Halfway up the carpet slipped out from under her feet and she fell on top of the suitcase.

Glenn dropped his own suitcase and grabbed her by the elbows, saying jeez, he hoped she hadn't hurt herself. She'd cut her stocking at the knee and gotten a little scratch from the buckle of the suitcase. She sat down deadly pale on the stairs. "Go on up, it's all the way up. Our domain is the entire top floor, you'll see it's palatial."

"But are you all right, Gladys?"

"Leave me," she said solemnly. "I always faint when I see blood."

Glenn took the suitcases up to the top landing and came back for her. She was coming up the stairs a step at a time, quite pale and with her mouth in a pout like a little child that's just been spanked.

He followed her into the front room on the top floor, a big attic room with bookshelves around the walls, and a low table in the middle piled with dusty books and, in one corner, an easel with charcoal nudes scrawled one on top of the other on the same piece of paper. In front of the window was a big square couch with an orange cover on it where Gladys lay down flat, whispering, "A pillow under my feet," and closed her eyes. "A cold compress in the bathroom . . . quick . . . no, not on my face, on my knee . . . roll the stocking down . . . oo, it's chilly. Thanks, you have very gentle hands for a coalheaver. Now bring me a pillow for my head and sit down beside me," she patted a place on the edge of the couch, "and tell me everything about yourself, and what kind of a girlfriend have you got."

Glenn sat down a little gingerly and said he hadn't been heaving coal and he didn't have any girlfriend, he'd been working on the Survey all summer and now he was back for a tough grind to try to finish up his course in three years and it was great of Boris and her to take him in like that.

Why did he want to finish up his course in three years, she asked, what could he learn in a capitalist college that would be of use to him in the struggle? Glenn said he hardly knew, but he had to make his living, didn't he? He could get better jobs if he had a degree, couldn't he?

She sat up and took her shoes and stockings off. When the washcloth fell away from her knee, he saw that the scratch had stopped bleeding. She said she felt lovely now, she always went barefoot in the house, it was more natural. She'd put on stockings just because Boris had said he was coming, wasn't that conventional of her?

Glenn took the opportunity to get to his feet. Sitting so close to her made him nervous. She lay back on the couch, curling and uncurling her toes like a baby, speaking drawlingly and looking into his face, but why should he be so nervous when he was so tanned from life out of doors, he must be very strong, she hoped he was welldeveloped physically, he must pose for her. One of the reasons she'd married Boris was to have a man to draw in the nude; but poor Boris was so skinny he looked like a birdcage.

Glenn didn't know what to say to that. Gladys jumped to her feet laughing. So he was shocked, was he, proletarians were so conventional. Glenn felt himself getting red and said he wasn't a proletarian exactly, he didn't know what he was.

She said they must all learn to be good proletarians, it was more important than taking silly degrees at capitalist colleges, but she must be a good landlady and show him his room.

He followed her through the square hall under a cobwebby skylight, past the bathroom with an oldfashioned boxedin tub and a two-burner gasstove where they cooked, into a small hall bedroom with a window over the backyard and no furniture except a hospital cot and a kitchen table. Next to it, she pointed out the locked door of Boris' private lab.

There were no curtains and everything was very dusty, but on all the bare walls there were glary heads, in orange and red crayon with violet shadows, drawn on brown paper and fastened up with pins driven into the yellowed checkerboard wallpaper, that hung loose from the plaster. Gladys said that Boris was a clever carpenter and that he would build Glenn bookcases and furniture next Sunday and she would decorate it beautifully and he'd be very comfortable. But now he must come out with her while she marketed for supper, because Boris was always so cross if he came home and found supper wasn't ready. It was his middleclass family training.

Glenn stood uneasily in the door, not knowing what to do with his hands while she combed out her dark wavy hair and shoved it under a red woolen tamoshanter that she wore on the side of her head, then she put on a black leather jacket she said was Boris' and solemnly slid down the three sets of bannisters to the front door. She stood watching Glenn come down after her, laughing at him and saying he was very awkward. She and Boris were experts. Glenn said didn't the other tenants complain if they made so much noise in the hall. Gladys said no, the other tenants must all be counterfeiters because they never showed their faces.

They walked several blocks to an avenue clanging with traffic and streetcars, and turned along a row of Italian grocerystores and markets and kosher delicatessens, back of a broad crowded sidewalk full of fat women with baby carriages. Gladys ran from one store to another buying rye bread and butter and red caviar and cartons of potato salad and vegetables in sour cream and ham and bologny, while Glenn followed her around with the packages. She hadn't any money, she said, so he'd have to pay.

On the way home they heard running steps through the crowd behind them; it was Boris with a broad grin on his face coming from the subway. He said, "Welcome, parlor boarder," and scolded Gladys for putting Glenn to work the minute he arrived. They trooped up the stairs and Boris took off his coat and vest and put on a yellow Russian blouse that Gladys said was hers, wasn't it awful to have a boyfriend who was so little he could wear your clothes? Then they cleared the books off the table so that they could eat off it. Gladys made tea and fried up the ham on the burners in the bathroom. The girlfriend was a great cook, Boris said, she thought hens laid softboiled eggs.

She answered, as she brought in some orange candles in battered brass candlesticks, that under socialism it would all be done by experts in public kitchens. He said that wouldn't do them any good if they starved to death betweentimes during the period of war communism because they didn't know how to peel a potato. Gladys said he needn't talk and sat down and cut and buttered the bread and they fell to. The Spingarns sure were fast eaters. They each of them drank four or five glasses of weak tea that made Glenn feel a little sick at his stomach.

After they had eaten Gladys lay at full length on the couch smoking a Russian cigarette, with her head in Boris's lap, and the three of them argued for hours about whether the time had come for a revolutionary movement in America yet. Gladys said that the ruling class was beginning to commit atrocities like the Sacco-Vanzetti case and that was a sign that they were on their last legs, and that as things in Russia got better and better and they solved their economic problems, the American worker would turn more and more to the leadership of the Party.

Glenn said he'd been around some among the American worker; most of the guys he knew thought the present setup was great, couldn't wait to scrape up a little cash to speculate in something, and if they weren't successful felt it was their own damn fault. That was the Geographic Survey, Gladys said scornfully, government jobs gotten by pull in Washington, bureaucrats, not the real proletariat.

He said sure, but the more proletarian the guys he'd known were, the more leary they were of foreign ideas. Chauvinism, cried Gladys, sitting up and tossing back her hair, the next war would teach them that chauvinism was for the capitalist. Sure, Glenn said, all he was saying was that they hadn't learned yet.

Boris yawned. What worried him was that so little was known about human behavior; Marxism was all right as a description of things as they were now, but its plans for after the revolution were too darn sketchy. Now suppose you were going to build a bridge over a river to take the place of an old bridge that was falling down, you wouldn't start by tearing down the old bridge; you'd build the new bridge beside it so that traffic could keep on getting across the river. Gladys jumped at him and started rubbing her knuckles in his head, saying she'd heard about that bridge before, maybe they wouldn't want a bridge in the new day, people would be strong and free and able to swim across any river. She loved to swim, didn't Glenn?

In Russia a good many of them sank, Boris said gruffly; he'd had uncles there through the revolution and he knew they weren't lying. The trouble was they tore down the old bridge before they had the plans for the new one all set; it wasn't entirely the fault of the revolutionary parties because you could say the old bridge fell of its own rottenness.

"Old Russia was hell," Gladys cried out in a tense voice. "Capitalism made life a hell."

"New Russia has been hell for a great many," said Boris, getting to his feet and walking back and forth across the room. "We haven't been there but we ought to know. Your mother's people were from Odessa, weren't they? My uncle Aaron was there all through it."

"Merchants, bourgeois adventurers . . . it's just your bourgeois prejudices won't let you see things as they are. You just won't understand. . . . Oh, I hate you, Boris. You are just a social democrat." She hunched up in the middle of the couch and began to cry.

Boris folded his arms and stood with his feet apart puffing on a cigarette. "Nervously unstable," he said, and walked out of the room. Glenn heard him unlock the door of his workroom and close it after him with a bang.

Glenn stood looking at Gladys' narrow shaking shoulders without knowing what to do. At last he went over and gave her a couple of pats on the top of the head. "Don't cry, you're too pretty to cry." She got up and rubbed her face with a towel. "I feel things too much I know. I must learn to be cold, a steel instrument."

"Oh, I wouldn't do that," said Glenn.

"Poor Boris," said Gladys. "He is tortured by skepticism. Still he has done much valuable work for the Party. I tell him he's a fellow-traveller. He would be with us when the time came."

"Well, I don't know what I am," said Glenn, and guessed he'd better go to bed.

"You are a very nice boy and I'm glad you've come," said Gladys. "You represent the confused ignorant masses of America. . . . Here is my hand." Glenn shook her hand a little awkwardly and went into his room to unpack his stuff. But there wasn't anywhere to put anything and no hooks to hang his clothes on, so he left everything in his bags and went to bed. As there was only one sheet on the bed, he had to sleep with the blanket over him.

Next day the college routine started. All that fall and winter it seemed to Glenn that he was spending all his time in the subway. It took him an hour and twenty minutes to go and come from Brooklyn. He left the house at seven every morning and rarely got home before nine or ten at night. He always had books to read or work to go over in the subway, but often he was too sleepy and just sat there drowsing, watching the people pour on and off at the stations, envying the young men with girls in the evening, wondering where they came from and where they were going. He'd about decided Marice Gulick was right, that he was a thoroughly inhibited customer, but he was too busy to do anything about it. Mike had gotten him a job sorting material in the stacks, and that was just like being in the subway. The only time he got out in the open air was crossing from building to building to go to lectures, and Sundays.

Sundays Glenn and Boris and Gladys would take long walks. The trouble was it took half the day to get out any place away from pavements and cars where they could breathe a little country air, and then it wasn't real country. Boris kept saying that what they needed was a motorcycle and sidecar that would get them out to the country quick. In the afternoon they'd always have to hurry coming back because Gladys had a meeting she just had to go to. Boris would grumble that he believed in the proletariat at work or on strike all right, but that proletarian hot air made him sick, and often wouldn't come along. Then Gladys would take Glenn's arm and say he'd have to come, and he'd go all soft and silly inside, and pay the carfare and cough up for the collection and spend the evening standing around in the backs of halls, because they always got to the meetings late. All the young guys crowded around Gladys; it made him feel sheepish somehow, when she introduced him as an I.W.W. comrade from the harvest fields.

The night of the great Lenin Memorial meeting, Boris came along for once. The three of them stood crowded together in the back of the gallery dazzled by the floodlights on red bunting and massed faces, and feeling to their bones the heady throb of the speeches and the beat of the cheers and clapping. When they played the Revolutionary Funeral March Glenn felt Gladys' small hand tight in his, her other hand held Boris' hand; tears made a little glimmering streak on her high beautifully modelled cheekbone right in front of Glenn's right eye. In the stuffiness of the hall, and the heat of packed bodies sweating with feeling, he could catch the smell of her hair. His head was reeling; they were comrades, he told himself, the three of them, comrades in the great army of workers ready to fight for a better world. Lenin was dead but the workingclass of the world was alive.

With the *Internationale* lilting in their ears they ran down the steps ahead of the crowd. In the exit they found three friends of the Spingarns, redfaced ponderous Sam Berger and Milton Rafaelson and his wife. The Rafaelsons said let's hurry, they were afraid of a riot on account of all the cops. Gladys pulled off her tamoshanter and tossed back her hair and said scornfully, "Let's link arms and sing," and started off on the *Internationale* again. The street was darkening with people tightening into singing knots. Mounted police moved slowly forward on their sleek horses amid boos and cries of "Cossacks."

"Come along," said Boris, taking Gladys' other arm and pulling them fast through the crowd, with the Rafaelsons who were middle-aged and stoutish panting after them, and across the avenue, packed with traffic in a snarl of horns and klaxons, into quieter streets where the groups on their way from the meeting, all moving in one direction, began to melt into the helterskelter crowds of the theatre district.

Gladys was still singing at the top of her lungs in spite of the grins, and the kidding remarks about Russian reds going back where they came from, of the people they passed; but the rest were only humming. At last at a corner Milton Rafaelson grabbed Boris and Glenn by the lapels and said in his quiet smiling way for everybody to stop demonstrating and he'd take them all where they could have a glass of wine and a broiled steak to celebrate this great occasion.

They were too many for the taxi so Glenn said he'd walk. He was so excited he wanted to get a little air in his lungs. All the way over to the East Side he walked fast. Streets, dark stores, restaurants, lettered signs, office buildings had a temporary provisional look to him. All these ruins were going to be swept away. A new world was going to be built on the ruins of the profit system. He and Gladys would be part of the new world Lenin had discovered the way Columbus discovered America.

When Glenn got to the Rumanian restaurant, all aglow, and ran down the steps from the street, the first thing he saw was that Gladys was dancing with a yellowhaired young man he didn't know, dancing with her head thrown back and her eyes half closed. Glenn sat down glumly next to Boris near the end of the long table. Redfaced Sam Berger sat at the head presiding over a welter of big plates of steak and frenchfried onions and chopped liver and pickles, shouting stories that kept the squarefaced Rafaelsons laughing, over the din of the threepiece orchestra.

Boris was being stubborn about something, he was insisting that the waiter bring him butter, muttering under his breath what was the use of having a revolution if a guy couldn't have butter with his steak just because he was with a bunch of jews. When the waiter, who was a sourlooking elderly man, at last brought the butter, frowning and shaking his head, Milton Rafaelson smoothed him down by kidding him in Yiddish. Boris laughed at what Rafaelson had said to the waiter and explained he'd just brought the matter up as an illustration: if we couldn't get over a slight prejudice about fats, how could we get over the much more profound prejudices about the property system?

"But once the economic causes are removed," shouted Sam Berger, and they all began to argue so loud that, when Gladys came back to the table with the guy she'd been dancing with, and introduced him as Ted Handley, who'd been to art school with her, and started talking to him in a low voice at the end of the table, Glenn couldn't hear what they were saying. In a lull Boris turned to him grinning, waving a longnecked bottle, and poured him out a glass of wine. "We must remove the economic causes," he said, mimicking Sam. Glenn didn't often drink, but tonight he drank down the sweetishsour stuff as often as Boris filled his glass.

When the music started again, he asked Gladys roughly if she'd dance with him. She gave him a funny look and nodded her head. Glenn wasn't much of a dancer and the dance was a waltz and he kept getting out of step and Gladys ended by whispering in his ear that she was starved and her steak was getting cold, and that, besides, he had no music in his soul.

When they got back to the table Sam Berger was roaring everybody down about sex, saying that for a real revolutionist there was only one test of any act, physiological or otherwise: did it help the working class in the struggle? Sex was a refreshment that no comrade should deny to a comrade who needed it. If a girl got a man all stirred up, she ought to let him soothe his nerves in the only way possible.

Rafaelson held up his hand with his fatcheeked smile, saying wait a minute, his experience as a lawyer had told him that sex tended to produce divorces and social contracts between participating parties, take alimony for an example, and what about children and homelife? Homelife under capitalism was no better than prostitution, growled Sam Berger with his mouth full of fried onions, capitalist society was a brothel.

But people did lead happy married lives, spoke up Mrs. Rafaelson shrilly, look at her and Milton, married eight years and never a regret. No, decidedly not; economic problems were one thing and homelife was another, wasn't that so, Milton? Rafaelson wiped his lips with his napkin and gave his wife a loud smack on the cheek. "Speak for yourself, my dear," he said.

"For a revolutionist," Sam Berger went on, pausing between his words to give them weight, "the sexual act is a mere refreshment, like a glass of water."

Boris was in great good humor, giggling to himself as he poured out the fresh bottle the waiter had just brought. Glenn was listening to what they said without paying much attention because Ted Handley was dancing with Gladys again and he didn't like the way he was holding her and once he looked over and caught him giving her a quick kiss on the neckline of her blouse. In the din of violin playing and talk, and the smell of broiled meat and onions and dill pickles, the restaurant began to swirl, a revolving cloud of stained mirrors and faded gilt fixtures round his head. The more of the wine he drank the colder and stonier he felt inside.

When the party broke up Boris called a taxi in a lordly way and said he'd set up any Brooklynites to the ride home. Glenn felt himself scowling into Ted Handley's blueeyed laughing face, but it turned out he lived in the Village. The Rafaelsons and Sam Berger were headed for the Bronx, so after a great many good nights, Boris and Glenn were sitting back in the speeding cab with Gladys between them saying oh, she felt wonderful, hadn't it been a wonderful evening?

Glenn growled something about how he didn't like that artist guy, and Gladys threw back her head laughing, he was just a boob, a Greenwich Village boob, just one of her boobs and Glenn was one of her boobs too. She let her head drop on his shoulder and all at once Glenn found himself looking down at her lips poked up at him. The lights in the empty streets and the tiers of dark windows sweeping by gave a swoop in his head as he leaned over to kiss her. Then she said Boris was the sweetest boob of all and made him kiss her.

They were crossing the bridge. Boris told the driver to stop so that they could look down at the sleek river far below and the dark wilderness of buildings on either side, shadowy cubes and tall oblongs outlined from below by the streetlights, and breathe-in the sharp wintry air of the harbor, that had a little rasp of coal smoke in it from a tiny black tug, showing red and green and yellow pinpoints of light, that had just passed under the bridge. Gladys hugged them both. "Oh, I love it so, I love it all." All the way home, first one then the other, she made them kiss her.

When he got out of the taxi in front of their house, Glenn's head was still reeling. He felt himself stagger a little. While Boris was paying the driver, he gasped out stiffly that he'd have to walk round the block to get some air, goodnight. As he started to walk, carefully spacing his steps, he felt the drunken feeling wearing off. When he came back sober and tired after a long trudge through the streets every window in 332 was dark.

After that Glenn didn't feel so shy about drinking. Boris occasionally brought back a pint of grain alcohol from the laboratory that they made up into various concoctions. Several parties they gave in the Spingarns' room turned out such a success that Gladys sometimes talked about moving over to the Village so as to be nearer the center of things. Glenn began to get behind in his college work. His marks at midyears were the worst he'd ever had. The report discouraged him so he decided to throw the whole thing up and get a job. He went around to Mike Gulick's office to ask his advice about it.

Mike leaned back in his chair behind his desk and stretched his long arms and poked out his adamsapple the way he had and roared out, "Rubbish."

Glenn said he didn't feel he was getting anywhere, and suppose he got his degree, what good would it do him? He held opinions that would bar him from teaching economics or anything like that. Mike said take it easy, he wasn't very old himself, but even in his time things had changed more than he could have imagined, people could expound theories openly now that they'd been ready to crucify poor old Veblen for a few years ago.

Glenn drew himself up and said that the exploiting class and the producing class could never have anything in common. Mike asked, how could you disentangle them? Glenn said that was just liberal obscurantism, his place was on the side of the workers. Fine, said Mike, bursting out laughing, but for cat's sake not to go off the deep end, he wouldn't do the workers or anybody else any good by getting to be a soapbox fanatic.

Glenn ended by admitting he might as well finish out his course, and Mike asked him to come around for tea that afternoon and to bring his radical friends; Marice had been asking about him only the other day. When Glenn called Boris up at his laboratory, Boris said he was busy but that he'd deputize Gladys to make him a report on how the other half lived.

Glenn met her at the drugstore next to the subway station on Broadway. Walking acrosstown Glenn caught himself wishing she hadn't worn that tamoshanter and didn't have that stilted way of talking. It wasn't a jewish accent exactly, but it would sound funny against the middlewestern drawl of Mike and his friends, and Marice's Westchester patter. The thought made him blush and he put his arm around her narrow shoulders and gave them a warm apologetic squeeze as he piloted her up the steep brownstone steps of Marice's house.

Marice looked wonderful in a red dress with her Japanesy bob, but Glenn didn't like the sharp appraising stare she gave Gladys out of her small black eyes. The Whites were there with their mousy redeyed look, and a couple of people Glenn didn't knew. The conversation was a little bumpy. They sat around drinking tea among the heavy red velvet hangings. Glenn felt awkward and wished Gladys wouldn't say things so emphatically. He wished Marice didn't have that rich look sitting there behind her silver teaset in her red silk dress on the old-fashioned horsehair sofa.

It was a relief when Mike came in and started to hold forth about child labor. He and Gladys had a hot argument about reform. Gladys said what was the use of making reforms when the whole system had to go, reforms were just a sham to deceive the workers and tighten their chains. Mike said that society was based on habits: people's habits could only be changed little by little in the direction of social consciousness. Gladys said that if you freed people from the oppression of a wrong economic system their habits would change, people didn't like to behave like wolves, but to tell them they could behave any differently under the present system was deception and lulled them into security and put off the inevitable hour of the victory of the working class.

Marice said that new discoveries about character and personality gave a hope of gradual change as individuals got rid of their complexes and inhibitions. Gladys said working girls in sweatshops didn't have complexes, they only felt tired and hungry and oppressed. Man didn't live by bread alone, came back Marice snappishly, psychoanalysis could liberate forces inside the individual.

"You just say that because you've always been rich. You don't know how the workers feel." Gladys jumped to her feet. "Now I've been rude and it's time for us to go home."

Marice got quite red and said she wasn't so childish as to take arguments personally about impersonal subjects. Gladys said she was a child, she hoped she'd always be a child and say what she felt. Mike smoothed them down saying that there was no use climbing on the barricades until they were built, in this country at least we didn't know what the lineup would be yet. "I know," said Gladys, tossing back her head and fastening the belt of her leather coat.

When she got out on the street she was shaking all over. "It was stifling. . . . Why did you take me among such people, all those buts and ifs and howevers, it was like reading the New Republic." Glenn couldn't help laughing at that and so did she. As they went into the subway, she said contentedly, "Now I have been rude to your high hat friends. I am a savage."

"Maybe you were jealous of Marice's red dress," said Glenn, kidding her a little. She gave him a furious look, pulled her arm away from his and ran through the crowd into the front car of the downtown express. When he caught up with her after the train had started she wouldn't speak to him. He sat opposite making faces at her and trying to tease her into a smile all the way to Brooklyn. When they got to their station she ran ahead of him up the steps and along the street through the evening crowd. He caught up with her at a corner where she was trapped by the traffic.

She was laughing and breathless. "You can run faster than I can, but that woman is a maneater. I hate maneating women and I am never jealous. No revolutionary worker can be jealous. Jealousy is the meanest thing about pettybourgeois psychology. That woman is jealous as a cat, you can see . . . ." That was one thing she could say about her and Boris, neither of them were jealous. Boris was ideologically unformed like all scientists and thought he was a superman and all that, but he was too noble to be jealous. "Well," said Glenn, as he pushed the door of their house open for her, "I guess I'm about as lowdown a capitalist as there is, at least when I see you dancing with that artist guy."

She turned from the foot of the stairs smiling at him with her lips

JOHN DOS PASSOS

parted and her eyes so wide that her curved lashes brushed her cheeks, red from running. "Even of Boris?" she asked in a whisper.

Glenn didn't answer.

Boris bought the motorcycle he'd been talking about, with the hundred dollars his family gave him for Christmas. The first Sunday the weather was anyway decent, he and Gladys went out on it to explore Long Island, they said. Glenn felt lonesome puttering around the empty top floor of 332 in the Sunday quiet.

In the afternoon he went to the library to catch up on some reading, and later went around to call on the Gulicks. Mike said he was looking thin and had better stay to supper and let Marice fatten him up a little. They were just sitting down to the table when the telephone rang and Marice came back and gave Glenn a funny look and said it was for him.

It was Gladys. Her voice sounded shaky. They had had an accident. Boris was hurt. He'd broken his leg. She didn't know how badly until they took the X-ray. He was in awful pain. No, she didn't have a scratch. She'd bounced off into somebody's shrubbery, a very soft shrubbery. Didn't Glenn think she was smart to have known where he'd be? A case of Marxian analysis. It was his pettybourgeois side. But wouldn't he borrow twentyfive dollars and come right on out. They were at the Bayside Hospital. He'd have to take the Long Island Railroad to Bayside.

The Gulicks were swell about it. Mike walked around to the drugstore and cashed a check for him for fifty dollars, said not to worry about it unless the Spingarns were well off. Glenn had to wait a long time at the Pennsylvania Station for a train, so it was nearly midnight before he got to Bayside. He took a taxi out to the hospital.

Gladys was waiting for him in the vestibule, looking very forlorn with her breeches covered with mud and a scratch on her cheek. Her eyes were red but she wasn't crying. It was a compound femoral fracture and they were waiting for Dr. Stein to come out and set it. "Put your arm around me, I'm trembling so," she said. "He wants to see you."

Boris' broad brown face was flushed on the pillow but his lips were pale and pressed tightly together. "Hello, kid, sweet of you to come," he said. "Silly . . . just a case of infantile leftism. . . . Better take Gladys home . . . I'll be here for some time. I'm damn lucky it wasn't the hip. . . . Got a pencil?"

Glenn got out his notebook and put down the list of books Boris wanted brought out tomorrow. "And if you forget my notebooks, Gladdo, I'll wring your neck. . . . Don't call the old people until tomorrow. They go to bed at nine." Just then the night nurse came in with an injection of morphine and said they'd better leave the patient alone so that he could rest and Glenn left him forty dollars to put in his wallet and they said goodnight and tiptoed out through the empty dimlylit halls of the hospital.

It had started to sleet so they got their feet soaked walking to the station, where they had to sit around for a long time waiting for a train. Gladys was shaking so from cold and nerves that Glenn had to keep his arm tight round her shoulders. Her hands were icy cold so he rubbed them for her to get them warm. Going home in the cab from the Atlantic Avenue station she fell asleep in his arms.

When they got up to their top floor, he made her some hot tea with gin in it. While he was heating the water, she was undressing in the dark corner of the room. She sat up in bed, huddled in Boris's flannel bathrobe, sipping the tea, with her cheeks very red. Then she said she was starved. Glenn brought her rye bread and cheese sandwiches and sat next her on the edge of the bed eating one himself. "You are a very useful boy," she said. "Now Boris is a chemist but he won't help himself in anything. If I didn't get him his meals he'd starve to death."

Poor Boris, he'd be all right in a week or two and it would be a good rest for him. They'd been very lucky. A trolleycar had suddenly come around a corner. They'd had as much chance as an individual in the capitalist system.

She still had fits of trembling, so Glenn made her more tea with gin in it. She leaned hard against him as he sat on the edge of the bed. He had one arm around her. With his free arm he was stroking her head. She said it was very soothing, Glenn dear, he had such soothing hands, he was a wonderful comrade. Boris was a wonderful comrade. She was lucky to have such wonderful comrades. She'd been such a silly innocent little thing when she'd married Boris, she'd hardly known how babies were made. Funny to think that was only six months ago. She was innocent now, anybody who was completely honest was innocent. But then she'd been so ignorant. Why, the first night she spent with Boris after they got married . . . they'd had to get married on account of Boris' old people who were conventional orthodox jews, that's where Boris got his pettybourgeois weaknesses, it wasn't that they believed in their religion, they just lived like that on account of race prejudice. The first thing a revolutionist had to do was cleanse himself of prejudices and stand naked and unashamed before the world. Glenn must get rid of all his small town middle-western American prejudices and be more free. But she was going to tell him about the first night she and Boris had spent together, to show how her parents had brought her up in reactionary ignorance. They were very ignorant people in Boston. She'd heard a rustling in the bed and thought it was Boris taking the paper off chocolate peppermints, since she'd been a little girl she'd loved to eat candy in bed and was quite mad at him because he wasn't giving her any. She really hadn't known about contraceptives. The rustling was a thing to keep from having babies, wasn't that absurd?

Glenn felt his heart pounding so hard he got to his feet and walked to the door, but she said in a trembling voice not to go, couldn't he put out the light and lie down beside her for a minute, she was so upset she didn't think she'd ever get to sleep. He lay down and she snuggled her cheek against his, whispering that the human body was always beautiful and innocent, we mustn't be afraid of the beautiful impulses of our bodies. Glenn tore off his clothes and slipped in under the covers beside her.

The next morning he woke up with a start to find himself in bed with a girl for the first time in his life. Red winter sunlight was pouring in through the front windows. Gladys was still asleep.

Glenn got up feeling flushed and full of life and took a cold bath. Then he went out into the frosty morning street where the ashes over the icy patches crackled underfoot, and ran to the corner drugstore to call up the old Spingarns and Dr. Gordon, an old friend of Boris' whom he asked to go out to take a look at him to make sure the surgeon out there knew his job. By the time Gladys was awake he had a breakfast of scrambled eggs and bacon ready for her. It was his whistling as he worked over the gasburners in the bathroom that woke her up.

"Hello, cheerful," she called to him from the bed, "is there any hot water?" Neither of them said anything about last night.

Glenn cut all his classes that day. The old Spingarns were already out at the hospital when he and Gladys got there, breathless from having hurried so all the way from the station. Boris's father was a small handsome old man with a neatly clipped white vandyke beard and gold pincenez. His mother was a severe small stout lady in black who evidently couldn't see Gladys for dust. The two of them were hovering over Boris like a pair of birds over a nest, while Dr. Gordon and Dr. Stein looked at the X-ray pictures of his leg. Boris was feverish and miserable but he wanted to know everything that was going on and was delighted he'd had a chance to look at his leg through the fluoroscope. When they decided to operate and tie the bones in place with kangaroo tissue he said the kangaroo was an animal he had always had a strange sympathy with, from now on he was going to be part kangaroo. There was nothing for Gladys and Glenn to do but stand around with their backs to the white wall of the hospital room and keep out of the way.

After the operation, upon which Dr. Stein and Dr. Gordon made each other elaborate professional compliments, old Mr. Spingarn invited everybody out to have something to eat at an oldfashioned German-Jewish restaurant he said he knew in Jamaica. There was nothing more to do about Boris who hadn't come out from under the ether yet, so Dr. Gordon drove them all over there in his shiny new Ford sedan. Glenn didn't like it much that Gladys sat in front on Dr. Stein's knee while he sat in back with the old Spingarns. They all sat at a round table in a mustysmelling old beerhall, and drank what seemed to be real beer, and ate roast goose with dumplings, while Mr. Spingarn held forth in a German accent to which he knew how to give a comical twist now and then, on the virtues of oldfashioned social democracy and on the absurdities of the younger generation, who he said were all for speed and slogans. But every time he brought out a crack against the Communists he gave his daughterinlaw a sly look and sighed, ach, what could you do when they were given so pretty?

Gladys and Glenn hung around the hospital a while in the afternoon, but there was nothing to do so they took the train in to Brooklyn. When they got in Gladys said she was too nervous to do anything useful so Glenn said why not go to a capitalist movie.

All through the double feature bill he held her hand. When they came out a wet snow was falling, filling the streets full of traffic with hurried white blobs that faded in black slush on the pavements. Running home, Gladys was like a kid, scooping up snow off stoops to throw at Glenn and stamping in puddles to splash him. In the yard in front of their house where the snow lay white and untrampled, they had a regular snowfight and rubbed handfuls of it in each other's faces. Just as Glenn was going in the door Gladys poked a great gob of slush down the back of his neck. Once they were on the stairs she straightened herself up and put her hand over his mouth and said hush, they must be respectable. They went each to his own room, but after he'd turned in on his own cot Glenn felt so tormented with the thought of her lying there so near that he got up and tiptoed across the hall. At first she said he must get out, she was sleepy, but in the end she let him in.

Boris was in the hospital eight weeks, most of the time with his leg stretched out in a frame. Glenn had made up his mind he'd have to tell him frankly, but he never seemed to get a chance to talk to him alone. He and Gladys spent every Sunday with him, but there were always friends coming in and out.

One afternoon Glenn cut his work at the library and went out to Bayside especially to see Boris and have it out with him. Boris was very cheerful and said this accident had meant everything to him because it had given him a chance to get ahead on his math; a chemist without math was just a laboratory attendant. Glenn kept trying to switch the subject to Gladys but Boris was bent on explaining symbolic logic, and then Sam Berger came in with the radical papers and held forth about politics, so Glenn had to go back to Brooklyn without having said a word.

He tried to talk to Gladys that night about what they ought to do about Boris but she was full of a strike meeting of furworkers she'd been to, and said she was going to help them in their publicity and design posters for them and that Glenn must take off his shirt and pose for her because she had to have a male torso right away while she was still full of it all, she wanted to get the revolutionary ardor of the workers into her art.

Finally Glenn told himself that he just couldn't afford to be going out to Bayside all the time, he wouldn't have enough money to get through college as it was, he'd have it out with Boris when he got back. For a while he managed to quiet his qualms with Sam Berger's glass of water theory. But the glass of water theory collapsed entirely when Boris came home from the hospital, stumping around on crutches, pale and hollowcheeked but full of zeal for symbolic logic.

Glenn began to admit to himself that he was crazy about Gladys and that it was agony to have her with Boris all the time. The Spingarns had a lot of parties to celebrate Boris's recovery and five hundred dollars the old man had given him when he'd promised not to ride a motorcycle any more. Glenn kept away from 332 as much as he could, saying that it was because he was studying his head off for a thesis he had to write, but at night he'd lie on his cot in the back room, hearing their voices and the sound of laughing and arguments, and feel as if the top of his head were blowing off.

Then one Sunday, when Boris and Gladys had gone out riding with Herm Gordon somewhere, he suddenly couldn't stand being there any more. He packed his bags and pulled out, leaving the Spingarns an affectionate note saying he had to sleep over in Manhattan to be near the scene of operations during his last two months' grind. He arrived with his bags at the Gulicks' house in a heavy downpour of cold rain, feeling like a wet cat locked out of the house.

Marice opened the door and seemed quite taken aback to see him there with his dripping bags asking if he could have his old job back, but she was very nice about it and said he'd have to sleep in the attic because all the rooms were going to be taken by a sending of Mike's relatives from Ohio.

She looked at him sharply under the light in the hall and said he looked like he'd been burning the candle at both ends, and maybe he wasn't as inhibited as she thought. He felt himself getting very red and said no, no, nothing like that, at least not for quite a while, it was the midnight oil that was bothering him. As usual Sunday nights there were a lot of people in the parlor and diningroom, so Glenn asked could he go right up there now because he needed a shave and felt antisocial.

Marice followed him up the stairs with some sheets and towels and showed him which of the big old walnut beds standing up there in the dust among hooded pierglasses and wardrobe trunks he'd better sleep on, and helped him rig himself up a table and reading light. He asked her please if anybody called him up, no matter who it was, not to say he was there. "Aha," Marice said, "the plot thickens," and he could hear her rippling society laugh as she went down the stairs.

Hell, he kept telling himself, as he took off his wet clothes, this summer he was going to quit this parasite's existence and get him a real job and live like a working stiff. But right at that minute there was nothing to it but to settle down and review his lecture notes in that course in French utopians he'd nearly flunked in at midyears, because he'd thought he knew more than the prof did about it. He'd been a damn fool to spend three years monkeying around a college, just to please Dad and the Gulicks.

He stayed on at the Gulicks' until the final exams, working his head off. After he had passed his oral and knew that he was going to get his sheepskin cum laude, he felt his brain begin to go blank. He couldn't keep his mind on anything he read, and he couldn't get into an argument with Mike or Marice without losing his temper and having to walk out for fear he'd be rude to them, though he loved them both dearly. He developed a twitch in his left eyelid that made him scared he was going crazy. Most of the fellows he knew were running around to shows and speakeasies and baseball games and throwing parties, but Glenn never had a cent in his pockets. He owed money to Dad and the Gulicks and the college office and the laundry and when he wasn't worrying about Gladys he was worrying about how he was going to pay it back.

Except when he was going to courses and taking exams, he didn't know what to do with himself. He took long walks around the city. Half the time he'd find himself walking back and forth on one of the bridges leading to Brooklyn. It got to be that he couldn't see a Flatbush

Avenue express in the subway without having something leap like a jumping fish inside him.

One night he walked all the way over there, and finally found himself with his feet sore and his shins aching standing in the brick path in front of 332 and looking up at the light in the Spingarns' top floor. He stood there about five minutes in shaky indecision. Then he opened the front door gently and ran up the stairs as fast as he could.

The familiar grimy smell, like old raincoats, of the creaky stairway gave him a twinge of pain. The door to the Spingarns' room was open. Gladys was lying on her stomach on the bed, reading, with her bare feet in the air. She was wearing Boris' brown flannel dressinggown. She rolled over on her elbow and looked up at him.

"Why such a hurry after staying away so long? We thought you'd forgotten us."

He could smell the paint from her easel and the slick smell of the turpentine she kept her brushes in, and a little whiff from her clothes, and the close smell of tea and cigarettes the room always had. He couldn't keep himself from yelling at her, "It's not that I haven't been thinking about you . . . I've been busy. How's Boris?"

She sat up crosslegged on the bed, tucking her toes under the edges of the dressinggown, saying Boris was all right, but now he must tell her everything. Was he still going around with all those social fascists?

"Where's Boris?"

"He's working nights now as well as days. He's crazier than ever. How do you like my portrait? Turn the shade up so you can see it."

Glenn turned her reading light onto the wall behind the easel, where hung an unframed fresh oil painting of a girl's thin face built up out of flakes of lilac and white. He said he thought it was terrible, who'd done it?

"Ted Handley."

"I thought so."

"Well, Glenn, you might as well sit down and act like a human being."

"I'm not a human being. I'm crazy about you. Gladys, I'm almost crazy."

"Almost?" she asked, laughing cosily.

He sat down beside her on the bed and tried to put his arms around her. She drew away from him a little without moving. "You've been filling your head full of reactionary ideas over there in that capitalist college." She sat there beside him nodding her head and smiling as if she were talking to a child. "I bet she got you to go to a psychoanalyst."

"Gladys, I want you to leave Boris and to come and live with me."

She shook her head. Glenn jumped up and started to walk up and down the room. "You're a darling, Glenn, and I love you very much . . . I love everybody, but I like to live here," she said.

"All right," he said suddenly. "That's what I had to know." He ran down the stairs again and out the front door.

He didn't feel tired any more. He didn't feel the blister starting to rub on his heel where he had a hole in his sock. There was a kind of sick, numb feeling all over him. He walked fast along the street without looking to the right or the left. After a while he found himself in a subway station. He was in front of the turnstile before he remembered that he didn't have the carfare. He searched through his pockets to make sure; not a nickel; he'd damn well have to walk home.

Crossing the bridge he stopped and looked out over the river. The tall buildings downtown sparkled with bright strips of windows where the offices were being cleaned. From deep in the canyons between, streetlights sent up a rosy haze into the mild spring night. The air felt rainy, almost smelt of wet gardens. Down below towboats and barges, a little sideways from the current, drifted by on the glazed blackblue water, shiny here and there with the reflection of lights. Glenn suddenly felt so sorry for himself his eyes blurred with tears.

An electric train clanged past under him. He leaned his elbows on the rail of the footwalk. Suppose he were to climb out on a girder and let himself drop off the bridge. There was nobody to stop him. It would only take a second. It would be like turning in to bed to sleep, only for always.

He leaned on the rail without moving while little pictures formed in his head of himself lying white and drenched on a marble slab at the morgue, Gladys lying flat on her face on the orange cover of the square studio couch crying, Dad's pallid halting manner as he went to the ticketwindow to buy himself a ticket to New York, Tyler's red face and scornful voice saying well, that the kid always was a little sissy, as he read about it in Dad's letter, Paul Graves' black brows drawn together in a puzzled frown, George Dilling shaking his head and muttering it was the natural end of blasphemy and atheism, the smirk on Boris' thin mouth when he remarked, emotionally unstable. To hell wid 'em, a tough voice seemed to say in his ear, what's the use of bumping yourself off if you can't be there at the funeral?

Limping from his rubbed heel he walked on across the bridge. Inside his head he was standing on a platform in a great crowded hall hung with red bunting, making himself a speech: Wasn't it about time Glenn Spotswood stopped working himself up about his own private life, his own messy little five-and-ten-cent store pulpmagazine libido. Suppose it had jumped off the Manhattan bridge, a damn fool cum laude grind who'd broken down from overwork and sexfrustration, to hell with it, let it go out on the tide past Sandy Hook with the garbage barges, a good riddance like the upchuck when you've had too much to drink. The new Glenn Spotswood who was addressing this great meeting in this great hall was going on, without any private life, renouncing the capitalist world and its pomps, the new Glenn Spotswood had come there tonight to offer himself, his brain and his muscle, everything he had in him, to the revolutionary working class. Hands clapped, throats roared out cheers.

He came to suddenly on the cobbles under a clattering El structure. A streetcar's yellow headlight was bearing down on him. Scared, he jumped forward right in the path of a taxi. For a splinter of a second he thought he was gone. The shiny silver radiator, the staring headlights, the popping eyes of the driver, were right on top of him. He managed to throw himself forward over the muddy cobblestones. The taxi was past, leaving behind the driver's scornful yell out of the corner of his mouth: "There'll come a day . . ." Glenn was leaning panting against the iron pillar of the El. You damn fool, you don't want to die, he said to himself, and started to laugh. The taxi's red taillights were halfway down the block.

He felt full of life. Noting with amused distant interest, as if out of somebody else's eyes, the streets, the dark storewindows, the faces of men slumped outside of flophouses, the drunk flopped like a dropped bananapeel on the sidewalk, the lively glare of uptown streets where young men and women were coming out of movies, buying papers at streetcorners, crowding into jazznoisy supperplaces past doormen in fancy uniforms opening the taxicab doors, looking carefully into drugstores and the big plateglass windows where the latest models of cars were on show, lit by trick lighting that glinted richly on chromium fittings, he walked on uptown with a steady swinging stride. With the last of his strength he climbed the brownstone steps and the thick-carpeted stairs of Marice's house, pulled open the door of his room and twitched off his clothes, to fall, worn out, into bed and to sleep fourteen hours at a stretch.

4

The day after his last examination, without waiting for Commencement, Glenn took the noon train down to see Dad who had written, enclosing the carfare, that he wanted to have a heart to heart talk with him before he made any decision about the future. As he lugged his suitcase across the Union Station to the pay telephones to call Dad up at his office, he felt a shiver go up his spine; the last time he had walked across that station had been the afternoon Dad had met him at the train to tell him Mother was dead. For a moment he felt everything the way he'd felt it then, even to the wet spot where the snow had leaked in through the hole in his shoe. The feeling wore off as he stood hesitating in the phonebooth with the nickel in his hand. When he finally screwed himself up to calling Dad's number it was more or less of a relief to be answered by a woman's voice he didn't know saying she was Mr. Spotswood's secretary and that he'd left word for young Mr. Spotswood please to meet him at sixthirty at the Forum Club.

Glenn walked across the city that had a familiar forlorn look in the late afternoon sun, with its empty white buildings and its glary reaches of treelined avenues, with strings of yellow streetcars shuttling down the middle of them packed with government employees going home in their shirtsleeves. The smell of hot brick and softening asphalt and sunbeaten leaves brought back ways he had felt as a kid going to school.

Once inside the revolving doors of the club it was cool. Elderly men moved around quietly on thick carpets in shuttered rooms. The whitehaired colored attendant whispered that Mr. Spotswood was in the library. Glenn felt his heart begin to thump as he stood in the tall doorway looking in at the bookcases and the redleather chairs and the neat ranges of magazines on varnished mahogany tables. The faint whir of electric fans seemed to add to the quiet. Sitting by the fireplace that was hidden under an arrangement of ferns in brass pots, there was Dad, with his glasses on, reading. He wore a blue shirt and a white suit and had a pale spruce look Glenn didn't remember. His neatly clipped mustache was almost white.

Dad saw him coming and got to his feet holding his forefinger in his book to keep the place and pulling off his tortoiseshell glasses with the other hand. He had to fumble a bit to get the glasses into his breast pocket. Glenn stood there with his hand stretched out teetering on the balls of his feet. They shook hands awkwardly.

Dad's bulging gray eyes, a little redrimmed as always, were looking into Glenn's eyes from either side of the thin lopsided nose that showed the red marks the glasses had left round the bridge. Glenn leaned forward to kiss him, but Dad had dropped his eyes and was sitting down again with his book open on his knee. "Sit down, Glenn," he said. "Well, sir, you are to be congratulated . . . very much to be congratulated."

Glenn sat down on the edge of a heavy chair and started mopping his dripping face. "Dad, you're looking well," he said.

"Washington suits me . . . always did . . . even in summer. . . . Well, Glenn, what do you propose to do now?"

Glenn sat listening to the purring of the fans in the corners of the room. Dad looked down at his book and seemed to be making a mental note of the number of the page. Then he closed it as if reluctantly and laid it on the smokingtable beside his chair.

"That's the big question, Dad," Glenn broke out when he couldn't stand the silence any more. "Teaching's out . . . I couldn't teach what I didn't believe and what I do believe would get me in a jam right away, like the jam you got into at Columbia."

Dad seemed to wince. "I still believe I was right," he said haltingly, "but perhaps I might have tried to insinuate my ideas more tactfully; there's a certain selfindulgence in extremism, which I am coming more and more to distrust."

Glenn looked down at his scruffed black shoes that he'd forgotten to get shined at the station. "I don't see how you can talk against extremists when the whole capitalist system is tottering on the brink."

"Suppose we leave the capitalist system to the speculators in the stock market, who seem to be doing rather well if you ask me." Dad leaned back in his chair laughing a little creakily, and looked Glenn up and down. "Glenn, you need a new suit of clothes."

"But honestly, Dad, prosperity is an illusion that can't last. The contradictions of capitalism . . ."

"Won't keep us from eating a nice hot supper, son," Dad interrupted, getting to his feet with a vague smile. "I have a very nice letter from your Uncle Mat Avery about you. He and Aunt Harriet are delighted with what you did at college. . . . We may not agree with Matthew's ideas, and I for one don't get along with him very well, but he's a man of growing power and influence in his own state, and I guess he's a pretty goodhearted fellow at bottom. He's certainly been very nice to Tyler."

Dad was leading the way to the diningroom. Glenn followed, feeling the thick carpets, the discreet expressions of the colored waiters in their white jackets and the correctly set tables with their starched white cloths and their little shaded lamps, all tightening into a numbing mesh about him. "I guess I'd better wash," he said suddenly, his voice sounding too loud in the purry quiet.

When he came back from the washroom with the smell of liquid soap on his hands, Dad was reading a letter over two little glasses of fruit salad set in bowls of ice. "Here, form your own opinion of it," Dad said, passing it over to him. It was a typewritten letter on the stiff watermarked stationery of something called the East Coast Corporation from Uncle Mat offering to find Glenn a job in Horton in a local bank. Glenn felt the life ebb out of him into his shoes as he read it. "Gosh, Dad, that ud be an awful life . . ."

Now look here, Glenn, Dad began, before he made up his mind he had to listen to a few considerations: in the first place twentyfive dollars a week was remarkably good pay for a young man just out of college and he mustn't forget that his first obligation was the debts he'd contracted for his schooling. No matter what a man's political ideas were, the first thing he had to do was to make his own way in the world without being under obligation to anyone.

Glenn answered hotly that there were other ways of making your way than by getting to be one of the exploiting classes yourself, he believed the way Eugene V. Debs did, his ambition was to rise with the working classes and not from the working classes.

"But, Glenn," Dad said, holding his glass of iced tea in front of him, and drinking it in little sips. "You don't belong to the working classes. If there's such a thing as the professional class, that's where we fit."

"I feel different about it, Dad," Glenn said bitterly.

For a while they ate their lamb chops and baked potatoes in silence. Then Dad pushed his plate away from him and began scraping his breadcrumbs into a little square with his knife. Maybe Glenn could think of it this way, he started in a low voice without looking at him; he must remember the men Moses sent to spy out the land of Canaan for Israel; now mightn't it be the best thing he could do, from his own point of view as a socialist? Here was an unexampled opportunity to see what things were like on the capitalist side of the fence. Mind you, he would never try to induce any son of his to do anything at which his social conscience rebelled, he only wished more people felt as he did, especially Tyler, who had no more social conscience than a foxterrier, or any other kind, he feared.

Glenn said hurriedly that he wasn't a socialist, the socialists were full of democratic illusions, it was the socialists who'd done the work of reaction by putting down the workers' revolution in Germany, now they were busy selling out the British working class.

Dad laughed and said all right, all right, he wasn't either, no use whipping a dead horse, but he didn't feel that a man who wanted to do some good in the world had to limit his field of endeavor. For himself he'd chosen the field of propagating every argument against the use of war in international relations. It seemed a pretty hopeless task sometimes, sowing grains of mustardseed, often it was hard to keep his faith in humanity.

"After all, Dad, I suppose if I find the job too tough for me I can always get out," Glenn drawled, feeling himself weakening.

"Most assuredly," said Dad cheerfully, "we all have to try out a number of things before we can find the right career for ourselves. You can live at Aunt Harriet's and save up your money." Dad went on, as they drank their coffee, that it would be a great relief to him to have Glenn settled in a job, as things might so turn out, he couldn't say for sure yet, but they might, that he might have the privilege of being sent to Geneva as the representative of several American peace societies.

"But, Dad, only the revolutionary working class, following in the lead of the Russian working class, can really give us world peace."

Dad threw down his napkin and started walking to the diningroom door, saying in a low angry voice that preaching violence and hate was a funny way to work for peace. He believed reasonable methods of arbitration were just as much needed to negotiate away the causes of wars between classes as wars between nations. Dad was so agitated he forgot to sign his check and the colored waiter had respectfully to run after him with it.

"But, Dad, how is it that whenever there is any arbitration the workers get sold down river?"

Wasn't that rather jumping at conclusions, Dad asked sarcastically. Glenn suddenly said, good night, Dad, he was taking the nineforty train to Wilmington to go spend a month with Paul Graves, who'd rented a cottage at the shore, he'd write Uncle Mat telling him he'd take up his proposition. Glenn saw a wince of disappointment on his father's face; "Well . . . very well, Glenn . . . I'd rather hoped we could be together a few days, I'd fixed you a shakedown in my study." Glenn started fidgeting with his hat. "Gee, Dad, I'm afraid Paul will be expecting me tomorrow."

"Very well. Have you money for the trip?"

Glenn nodded. "I bought a ticket right through to Wilmington. Paul'll meet me there."

Walking back to the station Glenn couldn't help remembering how solitary Dad had looked standing there in the doorway of the club after they had said goodby. He half wished he had stayed over. They might have gotten to talk about things without getting each other sore. All the same it was a relief to be out in the treeshaded streets that had a sluggish underwater swirl in the hot night. The station looked empty and big and colorless. Sitting in the waitingroom waiting for the announcer to call his train, a panicky feeling of loneliness came over him. The brawling voice echoing through the station calling his train was a big relief. He grabbed up his bags in a hurry.

It made him feel great next morning when he piled out of the daycoach hoteyed and gritty from sitting up all night, to see Paul Graves' tall blackbrowed figure swinging long tanned arms in rolledup shirtsleeves, striding towards him up the platform. "Well, if it isn't the wildeyed radical himself, Glenovich Spotswoodski?" Paul squeezed his hand hard with his long hand and snatched up his bag. "Come ahead, we'll get out of Wilmington, it's hotter'n the hinges of hell."

As they climbed into Paul's Model T, Glenn said did Paul remember the time they'd met at a station once before? When they'd started the red revolution up at Winnesquam? Paul sure did and he let out one of his oldtime heehaw laughs that made Glenn feel warm all over. They drove out through uncrowded streets, shaded by big trees, with big old white houses, that most of the paint had worn off from, leaning back on green lawns, set here and there with groups of big shinyleaved magnolias that poked up huge white leathery blossoms at the ends of their branches. Even in the city mockingbirds were singing.

Paul stopped at the edge of town to get gas. A lean young man in a torn shirt shambled to the door of the new white stucco filling station still unfinished inside, said, "Howdy, Paul," and disappeared again.

Glenn leaned back in his seat and took off his coat and necktie and put them in behind on the suitcases and rolled up his shirtsleeves so that the warm sunlight stroked his arms and said, yawning, "Gosh, things smell good down here."

After a while the young man with the torn shirt came back to fill the tank up and Paul asked him how things were going, Sport. Sport scratched his head and said, fineanddandy, he was hoping to make a

little killing soon and buy out the joint; stock market; he was following Auburn, Christamighty, it had horseracing beat all hollow. "See,"
said Paul, laughing as they drove off, "us tarheels are right up to date."
"Hurry back," Sport called after them. "And the joke is," added Paul,
after one of his great laughs, "that his given name really is Sport."

They drove on through pinebarrens and patches of parched farm-
land, where unpainted shacks stood up drearily at long intervals on
stilts, sometimes with a few skinny yellow children scratching round
the doors with the chickens, under a tall blue sky full of brightwhite
clouds, while Paul talked about his work at the state experimental
station, growing corn. He was after the cornborer, he said, either to find
something to make the cornborer sick or else to develop a borerproof
strain; of course he had some of the professors crazy because they
claimed that if you were an entomologist you were out of bounds
studying plant heredity, but he told 'em if you were studying a plant
you had to study all around it, biologically, chemically, environmen-
tally, and every which way. For the first time in his life after all this
schooling and farting around he felt he had got something he could
put his teeth in.

Glenn cocked his head and said he could put his teeth in an ear of
corn right now. Paul laughed and said he sure would before long even
if they had to get it out of a can.

When Paul reached the end of the surfaced road through the pines,
he turned into a shell track that crossed the end of a salt marsh, from
which three white herons rose like on a Japanese screen as the car
went by, and wound through scrubby dunes till it stopped in a sand
pit behind a string of bungalows. When the motor stalled they could
hear the pound of surf on a beach beyond. Dragging Glenn's bag and
a carton of groceries Paul had bought in town, their feet sinking in the
sand at every step, they trudged over the first dune to a little cottage off
by itself at the end of a rickety plank walk.

The blackeyed girl in a loose pink smock who held open the screen
door for them was Peggy, Paul's wife. As Glenn shook hands with her
in the livingroom, tiny and dark after the seashore dazzle, he noticed
that she was going to have another baby. He asked where the son
and heir was, and Peggy said in a singsong voice that the little rascal

was asleep, and were the boys going to take a dip before their dinner, because if they were they had better hurry. Glenn and Paul went into the narrow bathroom to put on their bathingsuits, as the baby was asleep in the only bedroom.

When they had bobbed in and out of the stinging salt breakers and dried off for a while in the roaring glare of the white beach, where the sun burned down from overhead through the haze that came off the surf, they went blinking into the house and filled up on the fried chicken and corn fritters and cowpeas and rice Peggy had laid out on the table. As soon as he'd eaten Glenn began to feel sleepy in the heat of the bungalow that was close with seadamp and the reek of the oilstove in the kitchen that Peggy had kept on to heat up the coffee. When he couldn't keep his eyes open any more he asked if it was all right if he turned in on the cot in the livingroom. They gave him a sheet to put over him and he pulled it over his head and fell fast asleep.

When he woke up the sunlight was slanting in through the back door. He heard water being poured, and, along with Paul's and Peggy's quiet voices as they moved round the room, a cooing babbling noise. He turned sleepily so he could look out from under the sheet. The baby, pink and plump with a little gold fuzz on his head, was sitting in a whiteenameled basin in the patch of sun on the floor. Peggy's heavy figure, on thin legs with big breasts and belly, showed through her smock as she leaned over to soap him with a washcloth while Paul, sunburned and hairy in his bathing trunks, stood over them with a sponge and a water pitcher.

Glenn lay there watching them, feeling a smile grow on his face. The baby had Paul's black eyes and straight brows; all three of them had the rangy black look of the same Scotch-Irish stock. Paul leaned over and cooed back at the baby as he sponged the soap off him and lifted him into the towel that Peggy held up. The three of them saw Glenn at the same moment, as he sat up from under the sheet. The baby gave a yell and started crying and Paul jiggled him up and down laughing.

"Meet the boss," he said. "Call that southern hospitality, Paulino?"

Peggy gave Glenn a quick unsmiling stare and took the baby roughly from Paul to wrap him in the towel. She stood with her legs apart rocking him in the hollow of her arm and making clucking noises at him. Glenn got to his feet and looked down into the baby's knotted face muttering, "Well, well, well." Soon the baby was smiling again and reaching for Glenn's eyes and saying Da. "Why, I guess he likes you," Peggy said gravely. "He knows you and Paul were buddies. . . . Well, excuse us, I guess it's his meal time." She carried the baby off into the bedroom with a last halfembarrassed black glance at Glenn.

"Why, he's a dandy," stammered Glenn.

"We've got another under way, a slight miscalculation, but once he got started we thought it was better to go ahead . . . I'm all for production, you know." They both tittered awkwardly.

After a while Peggy's voice screeched to Paul from the bedroom. Paul went in the kitchen and came back with a feeding bottle that dripped from the warm water it had been standing in. When he came back he closed the bedroom door saying softly that Paulino was going to sleep, about all he did was sleep and eat. Glenn sat at the table turning over the pages of a copy of Science. It tied you down though, Paul went on, raising stuff tied you down. Sometimes he wished he was a rolling stone like Glenn; but if you were going to raise stuff, corn or stock or babies, you just had to stay put. Bejabers, he liked to raise things.

"Makes me feel like I didn't have a friend in the world," said Glenn.

"Boy, don't you worry, some girl'll be putting her hooks in you before you know it."

Glenn shook his head.

That night after supper he and Paul took a long walk down the beach. The tide was out. The hard sand, shimmery from the bright shine of a low halfmoon, was cool under their feet. Glenn got to talking about how he felt he'd wasted the last three years, taking all that trouble putting himself through college just because nobody of the whitecollar class could think of anything better to do. And all the time what he'd really wanted to be doing was beat his way around the country living like working people lived. The whitecollar class was all washed up. It was in the working class that real things were happening nowadays. The real thing was the new social order that was being born out of the working class. Of course, some things had been real, there had been a girl named

Gladys. But gosh, it was hard to keep your life from getting all balled up. What he'd decided was to hell with your private life. He'd live for the working class. That was real.

Paul said so far as he was concerned he thought private life was great, of course it was hell's own business living on seventyfive dollars a month, that was all he was making and babies sure were an expensive luxury. Why didn't Glenn keep on in sociology? That branch of fake science sure did need a few guys with brains to straighten it out, a simple uptodate textbook now would be a mighty useful thing.

Glenn interrupted; a fat chance he had of holding a teaching job, the interests would never allow it, his textbook was the Communist Manifesto.

Paul laughed and said he was willing to have them try that experiment out in Russia, after twentyfive years we'd be able to see what was in it. Glenn said angrily there wasn't time; capitalism was headed for a smashup before that.

Paul stopped in his tracks and started to scrape his initials in the sand with the big toe of one foot. The moon had set. They could see tiny phosphorescent flashes where he scraped the wet sand with his toe. He was drawling that a man could live a thousand years, just studying the biochemistry of those pesky little phosphorescent jellyfish. No, the way he'd figured it out was that no matter what kind of a social system they had, people would need science and improved varieties of field corn and would want to get rid of the cornborers.

But if the bosses went on enslaving the workers, what good would it be, Glenn argued, wouldn't the scientists be slaves too? What did monopolists care about science except speculating on its products? Now in a true socialist society science would have a real chance.

Paul said that was all hot air and came from associating with longhaired men and shorthaired girls up there in Greenwich Village.

Glenn tried to keep his temper: anyway he was bound for Texas now to take a job in a smalltown bank, he wanted to see the whole picture. Paul let out a hoot and said that was great, those damned eastern colleges didn't know there was anything west of the Hudson River, pumped you full of highsounding ideas and no facts to back them up. Glenn said that was just what he'd meant all along.

They walked back to the shack without saying much. Glenn had been looking forward so long to the talks he'd have with Paul that he felt let down.

They stood on the porch a while looking out over the sea quiet under the stars. The tide had turned and each small wave came hissing a little further than the last one up the beach. A few mosquitoes whined around their heads. Well, the only thing he could do, Glenn said in a voice that sounded halting in his ears, was look the country over as much as he could and see how things were. The only thing, Paul said, yawning and shaking the sand off his feet on the porch, was not to make up your mind before you began the experiment. If you really wanted to find out facts you had to take your preconceived notions and put them in a tin box and lock them up in the safe.

"But even scientists use a hypothesis. Marxism is a hypothesis, God damn it," Glenn shouted.

"Don't wake the baby," said Paul and yawned again. "Let's turn in, that damn youngster wakes up at the crack of day just like a rooster."

Glenn didn't stay so long with Paul and Peggy as he had planned to. The shack was a close fit for the three of them. He began to feel it was too much trouble for Peggy, getting his meals and everything, although he did wash all the dishes and kept out of the way as much as he could. When he got a letter back from Aunt Harriet saying that she and Uncle Mat were looking forward to seeing him and that she hoped he hadn't gotten too sophisticated for them after all that eastern schooling, he decided he'd better pull out and start making a living. As it was he had to borrow money from Paul to make up his trainfare.

Aunt Harriet and Lorna were there to meet him at the station in Horton in a big new Buick towncar. Aunt Harriet had the same cheerful cosy slim look Glenn remembered, but Lorna had grown up into quite a beauty with her dark eyes and her curly brown hair. She was all dressed up in a rakish straw hat and a silk dress and talked in a loud opinionated voice.

Well, Glenn, she shouted, when he'd kissed them both, it was a relief he hadn't come down wearing hornrim spectacles, she had thought he'd get off the train wearing hornrim spectacles with a book under his arm. Did he play golf? She was crazy to take him out to the new eighteenhole course they were just finishing out at the country-club, everybody said it had the best greens in the state. My, it would be wonderful to have an extra man in the house again, they'd had Tyler for a while, but all he did was play pool and drink hootch with the political gang. All the girls were crazy to meet Glenn, collegeboys from eastern colleges were rare in these parts; if he couldn't play auction, they'd line him up and shoot him against the courthouse wall, she declared they would.

Lorna drove them, past an unpainted welter of shacks, through a street of small lawns and white houses with vinecovered porches, into the business district, and stopped in front of the big arched entrance of the East Coast Building in the middle of a block of new tall cream-colored officebuildings. She said for Glenn to go up and get Uncle Mat, tell him lunch was on the table; if they all went up they'd never get out of there, the colored boy would tell him where the office of the legal department was.

The elevatorboy's teeth shone and the brass coats of arms on the new elevator shone and the floors shone in the offices he went through before he was ushered in to Uncle Mat. Uncle Mat had put on weight since Glenn had seen him and had a round shiny look in his cream-colored Palm Beach suit. He was dictating a letter to a pretty dark-haired stenographer and took Glenn's hand and pressed it warmly without losing track of a sentence. After he'd said, "That'll do, Miss Read," and the girl had closed her notebook and trotted out the door on her high Spanish heels, he cleared his throat and said, "Well, boy, I'm glad you've come. What you think of our new business block? What do you think of the office? Ever seen anything to beat it on Fifth Avenue? I bet you won't believe it when I tell you, but it's the gospel truth that ten years ago the site where this building now stands was old Silas Riggs' corral where he used to brand his stock. Then young Riggs built him a cotton warehouse here during the war boom and now . . ." Uncle Mat gave his arm a wave around the room. "I tell you, Glenn, this is the place for a young man right now; my soul and body, I'd give my right hand to be your age . . . well, we can't keep 'em waiting."

On their way through the bright outer office he introduced Glenn to several young men in their shirtsleeves who were all very cordial and smiling. On his way down in the elevator he put his arms around two big flabbylooking men in light gray suits and said, "I want you to meet my nephew from the East." In the lobby they met a tall stoop-shouldered old man with a mass of cottony white hair whom Uncle Mat greeted respectfully as Judge Green. "Looks like you knew everybody in town," said Glenn.

"I guess there may be some I don't know, son," he said with his sluggish grin.

Several young men were standing round the car, bareheaded in the sizzling sun on the broad sidewalk, talking to Aunt Harriet and Lorna. There were more introductions and handshakings.

Uncle Mat got in the back seat and Glenn got in with Lorna. "All right, let's go," roared Uncle Mat, but Lorna was still talking to a slender young man who wore his blue shirt open at the neck and who had patent leather hair and an olive skin. "Sorry, Jed, dinner's getting cold," said Uncle Mat sharply.

The young man showed a set of very even teeth in a smile, and bowed and stepped back with a vague wave of the hand. Lorna put her foot, in its pump with a red bow, on the starter, and, as she drove slowly down the street she turned to Glenn. "Looks like a Mexican, don't he? Mother claims he's a halfbreed."

"He didn't need to try to climb into the car," said Aunt Harriet from the back seat.

"But I think he looks like the sheik," Lorna went on over her shoulder at her mother. "I wouldn't touch him with a tenfoot pole," snapped Aunt Harriet.

"Old Judge Farrington," came Uncle Mat's deep voice from the back of the car, "was one of the most respected old men on the bench, the Farringtons owned a big block of Horton in the old days. Half the south end was built on the old Farrington ranch."

"But, Daddy, that was a long time ago," said Lorna.

"It must have been their own fault that they couldn't hold on to anything," Aunt Harriet added cheerfully, "and the way Jed's carrying on it doesn't look like he was going to build up the family fortunes."

"Oh, but, Mother, he's so handsome," Lorna squealed.

"As far as I'm concerned the less you see of Jed Farrington the better," growled Uncle Mat. "He's the kind of troublemaker we don't need in this town. If it weren't for the respect people have for the old man's memory, he'd have been run out of here before this."

The car was drawing up in front of one of a row of big new Tudor-style houses set far out in a field of red clay, that hadn't yet been graded into lawns. "Well, Glenn," said Uncle Mat. "Here's the ancestral mansion of the Averys. We just moved in three months ago and that darn cloudburst washed out our front yard. As the old Mexican landowners used to say, Welcome to your house."

A lanky black woman in a white apron opened the screen door. "Miss Harriet," she was yelling in a shrill cross voice, "you all is so late the biscuits burned." Uncle Mat laughed. "That's how I like 'em, Sally . . . now you show Mr. Glenn his room and we'll be ready before you can say Jack Robinson." Aunt Harriet was shaking her head and whispering, "My, how they love to grumble."

Right after lunch, while Glenn was still a little wuzzy from stuffing down all that fried chicken and biscuits and icecream amid the brightvarnished shine of the new shell pink diningroom and the cut glass and the flat silver, and from Lorna's shrill kidding chatter in his ears, as she rowed with her parents about which car she was going to use to take the Mexican children out to the Junior League picnic that afternoon, Uncle Mat drove him down to the office of the East Coast National Bank.

He and Jeff Stoat played golf every afternoon, Uncle Mat was saying, one of the smartest men in the state, likely to show those New York bankers a trick or two before he was through. While they were waiting outside the groundglass door, lettered in gold: MR. JEFFERSON DAVIS STOAT, Uncle Mat went on to explain in a low hurried voice that of course he could have given Glenn a job himself in his own office, but that he didn't believe in it, wouldn't be fair to the other boys working their way up, wouldn't do it not even if he was his own son.

Mr. Stoat opened the door on them suddenly. "Come on in, Mat. They're ridin' me pretty hard today. . . . Is this the nephew? . . . Glad to meet you. . . . Well, we'll see if he's got what it takes. At least he'll be getting that booklearnin' out of his head. Have a cigar, Mat?"

"Doctor's got me down to three a day but . . ." began Uncle Mat, reaching out a freckled hand; but Mr. Stoat was already putting the box away in the side drawer of his desk. He was short and stocky, with thin lips over tobaccostained teeth, and had a big triangle of black hair like a crow's wing that kept flopping over his dead white knobby forehead. He reached for one of the nickel phones on his desk and talked into it in a fast mean voice. "Mr. James, please . . . all right, Eddy, I got a new college boy for you . . . renowned eastern university . . . Mat's nephew, nice refined boy and all that, you know. Maybe he don't know much, but he might be just what we need for those country schoolteachers, investment trust prospects. I don't need to tell you, Eddy . . ." Mr. Stoat put down the telephone, and his eyes dropped to some typewritten sheets on his desk. "All right, Mat."

"Thank you, Jeff . . . I'll be looking round the lockerroom for you about fivethirty."

"Maybe next week some time," said Mr. Stoat, without looking up.

A sour wrinkled look came over Uncle Mat's round face as they walked back into the outer office. "Well, I'm late for an appointment, Glenn," he said hurriedly. "You go in and see Eddy James and talk to him man to man. . . . You see we don't hem and haw around this town. We want results and we want 'em quick." Uncle Mat gave Glenn a slap on the shoulder and left him.

Eddy James was a baldheaded young man with a long pink face and a sugary Louisiana drawl. He said for Mr. Spotswood to sit down, he was just going to send across the street for a cocacola, maybe he'd join him, meanwhile they'd have a cigarette. Glenn said thanks, he didn't smoke. "You should indeed," he said seriously, "takes the formality out of interviews like nothing else on earth."

Then he leaned back in his chair and asked if Glenn had ever sold anything. Glenn said sure, he'd sold books and subscriptions to magazines when he was working his way through college, but he'd never gotten much out of it. Eddy James laughed and said he needn't worry, this wasn't soliciting, this was a job. The bank didn't employ solicitors, but they had been forced into this investment business by the number of flybynight jew brokers who were taking people's money away from them. For the protection of their depositors and potential depositors, they'd been forced to do some canvassing on their own account, of course in a thoroughly dignified way. Now first he was going to let Mr. Spotswood familiarize himself with the situation. He handed Glenn a pile of typewritten sheets clipped together with some illustrated booklets. By that time a colored boy in a white jacket had brought the cocacola. Sucking at the straw in his bottle, Glenn sat there reading while Eddy James leaned back yawning and stretching in his chair.

Glenn felt called upon to say something. "Why, it certainly looks as if you were offering people a great opportunity to make a little money," he said, feeling his face getting red.

"Well, we believe in it," drawled Eddy James, "if we didn't, we wouldn't offer the service. In this world you have to believe in things to be able to make other people believe in them. That's all there is to salesmanship. . . . When do you want to go to work, Mr. Spotswood?"

It turned out that they expected him to have a car, so the first thing Glenn had to do was to get Uncle Mat to go on his note so that he could start payments on a secondhand Chewy that had just had a new paint job. Lorna teased him about the car, said nobody but a Baptist minister would drive an old jalopy like that, but Aunt Harriet stood up for him and said he was wise not to get an expensive new car before he could afford to pay for it. Glenn made them laugh by saying he couldn't afford to pay for a child's scooter for that matter.

Evenings when Uncle Mat was out at some businessman's organization, Glenn would have a cosy time telling Aunt Harriet and Lorna funny stories about his prospects. After supper one hot night of dusty wind, Lorna was pretending to be sore because Glenn wouldn't go out to the countryclub dance. The boy she'd been going with had just broken his leg playing polo down at San Antonio. Glenn didn't have any clothes and he had to be out of the house by six next morning, he was driving two or three hundred miles a day visiting investors, he kept explaining. Finally he said why didn't he drive her downtown for a soda at the Palace of Sweets?

Outside the sodafountain they ran into Jed Farrington. "Hello, Jed," Lorna said. "Meet my northern cousin." Jed shook Glenn's hand hard. "I sure have wanted to meet you," he said, showing even white teeth in a smile. "Lorna makes out you're another dangerous red."

"Now if you two get together and blow up anything around here, Daddy'll blame me for it," said Lorna, laughing. They ate some icecream together and it ended by Lorna teasing Jed into taking her to the dance, though he said she'd have to protect him if they tried to lynch him out there, he was ratpoison to that crowd since he'd taken that case for those pecanshellers.

The next time Glenn met Jed Farrington was on the broad pavement in front of the bank when he'd just gotten through work one evening, and Jed asked him to come up to his office to have a drink. Glenn said he wasn't much of a drinker, but he walked up the street with him to the old brick Lone Star Building. On the ground floor in back was an oldfashioned suite of dusty lawoffices packed to the ceiling with calfbound volumes. "This is where the old man used to hold forth . . . I'm afraid I'm not keepin' up the tradition as well as I might." Jed leaned over to open the rusty old safe and brought out a bottle of whiskey and two glasses. They sat down in two deep chairs of worn leather and Jed Farrington started to talk.

He said he read the liberal weeklies and stuff like that and tried to keep up with what was going on in the world, but now he'd gotten into something he didn't know what to do about. Well, like most trouble he'd gotten into it through a woman.

There was a cute little Mexican girl he'd been messing around with and she'd come to him for help when the police landed her father in jail. They all worked in one of those pecanshelling sweatshops where they had the life worked out of them for four cents an hour. Well, a young feller had turned up from old Mexico who had big ideas and he told the local Mexicans they ought to go on strike until they got a decent wage. They had all marched around in a picket line, women, children, oldpeople, and everything and naturally Logan, he was the chief of police, beat 'em up and put 'em in jail, and threw away the key. They let out the women and children after a while but they held the men on ten thousand dollars bail, charged with riot and mayhem and what have you and they were planning to send 'em up for long terms, just so they'd know who was boss around here. It was such a raw deal Jed had felt he'd ought to take the case and now the Mexicans all thought he was God Almighty, and the case had him half crazy because he knew damn well they'd be convicted in the local court and the only chance was in an appeal. He'd tried to interest the local A.F. of L. boys and nothing doing. He wanted to know whether Glenn knew any organizations or independent radical unions like the Unity League that would send an organizer down, or raise a stink in the press, or do something to help the poor bastards out. There was nothing he could do for 'em openly except as a lawyer and he'd do all he could for 'em but, Jesus Christ, his law practice was small potatoes and few in a hill as it was, and this case would probably put the quietus on it.

Glenn got to his feet. Gosh, they ought to do something, he said, maybe he could write friends he had in the labor movement in New York who might take the case up, but gosh, he didn't want to lose his job either now that he was just getting started, because he thought he had a chance of making a little money and he needed it to pay his debts.

Not a word about debts, said Jed, pouring them each another slug of whiskey, he had more debts than you could shake a stick at. But this deal was too damn raw, these Mexicans were the most harmless people in the world and somebody sure ought to stand up for 'em. Anyway he'd taken the case and it was his intention to fight it through if he had to take it to the Supreme Court. After all there was such a thing as a bill of rights in the Constitution.

Glenn called up Aunt Harriet that he was detained on business and wouldn't be home for supper; then he and Jed, getting to feel like old friends, had a couple more drinks before they went down to a Mexican restaurant the other side of the railroad station to eat. While they were eating their chili con carne Jed asked the waiter in Spanish if Frankie would be around that evening. The waiter, who was a short frogfaced little man in a very frayed white jacket, grunted, "Cómo no?" but narrowed his eyes as he gave Glenn an uneasy stare. Jed waved his hand. "He's okay . . . old friend of mine."

A few minutes later a slight young man, with dead white skin and a prominent nose and teeth and black curly hair on a long head, came in quietly from the kitchen and asked if he might draw up a chair at their table. He had a very low voice and a smiling elaborately polite manner. Jed introduced him as Frankie Perez. Glenn said he had an idea he'd seen Frankie before somewhere. Frankie smiled and bowed. Sure, he'd cut his hair at the East Coast barbershop. He spoke English correctly but with a strong accent as if he'd learned it out of a book. After they'd sat talking a few minutes he suggested that perhaps it would be more convenient if they all went to the Morenos' house where he boarded and where they would not be observed by Meester Logan's stoolpigeons, then the gentleman could see how the Mexican colony lived in Horton and why it was necessary in the name of humanity to assert their rights.

Glenn was feeling his whiskey and said in a loud voice that he wasn't a gentleman, he was just a workingman who happened to be working for a bank. Frankie Perez gave him a half friendly, half suspicious look out of his very bright black eyes and said quietly, all the better, perhaps they would discover they were compañeros.

Frankie lived in a threestory frame house with wide brokendown porches. They had to step carefully across the holes in the rotten boards. Inside, the house looked as if it had been gutted by a fire and then whitewashed. The place was full of low voices coming from behind flimsy partitions, and the smell of burning charcoal and drying clothes and chile. They climbed over a group of little ragged blackeyed kids sitting up playing solemnly with a few torn cards as they followed Frankie up the stairs into a big room with several beds in it, lit by one electriclight bulb that dangled from the ceiling. Under the light was a round table where sat an old woman with very Indian features huddled in a darkblue shawl, and a handsome girl who looked very much like her, except that her complexion was pink and olive and that she was very straight and slender, and a young fellow in a pink shirt, obviously her brother. As they came into the room three pairs of dark eyes looked at them questioningly from under similar brows.

Frankie introduced the girl as Guadalupe and the boy as Luis. They dragged out chairs with many apologies for the accommodations. Meanwhile Frankie was saying that they were progresistas but this was how they lived, and that many of their friends were worse off. American people said it was good enough for the greasers to live like pigs, but they were American citizens, and Meester Logan, when he wanted to run for the legislature would be coming around with big talk about flowers of Spanish-American culture; but now they had had enough, they were going to show that they were conscious of their dignity as men. Then he brought out a bottle of Mexican mescal and some little glasses and poured out a drink all around. They drank to workingclass solidarity. Glenn couldn't keep his eyes off Guadalupe.

On the way up the street back to the restaurant where they had left their car Jed told about Frankie, said he was one of the best read boys he'd ever talked to, had read all of Kropotkin, Tolstoy, Henry George, Dickens, everything you could think of; called himself an anarchist, but he talked like an oldfashioned Jeffersonian democrat; funny how your attitude towards a man's political opinions depended on whether they had a nicesounding name or not. But it certainly had given him pause to get to know a boy like that who was only a barber and had never had an advantage in the world; and here he himself had had all the schooling his old man could buy and had studied for the bar and everything, and all he could think of was raising hell.

Glenn couldn't help asking Jed if that was the girl. Jed shook his head, laughing, and said, no, no, Lupe was a good little girl, he didn't like 'em good. When they got into Glenn's car, Jed suggested they go around to a place he knew to have a nightcap. Glenn said he was sorry but he had to pile out at six. Jed said in that case he guessed he'd have to go to see Marie, it was too early to go to bed, and Glenn left him under a windblown poplar at the corner of a dark street of little identical bungalows.

Lorna teased Glenn unmercifully about getting so thick with Jed Farrington, she said if there was one quicker way than another to get in wrong with folks in this town it was to be seen around with Jed. Glenn said well, what about herself, hadn't she let him take her out to the countryclub? But she tossed her head and said that wasn't any of his business, they'd been raised together and anyway that was because she was mad at a certain somebody.

Glenn guessed that must be Joe Stockton, a lanky towheaded young fellow in a second lieutenant's uniform who turned up on crutches as soon as he got out of the hospital and was always around the house, not saying anything but following Lorna's every move around the livingroom with sulky blue eyes. Lorna treated him like dirt, but he was

Aunt Harriet's favorite and she used to make him go downtown with her in the morning when she went down to watch the stockmarket announcements on a big blackboard in the branch office a New York brokerage firm had opened in the East Coast Building.

Aunt Harriet's flyers made Uncle Mat so mad he couldn't talk about it. It was the main subject of their rows at meals, when Aunt Harriet usually would end the argument by saying it was her mother's money and if she lost it she could always bake cakes for the Gentlewomen's League. The day that Lorna came out with the fact that Mother was consulting a hindoo, Uncle Mat got so mad he threw down his napkin and left the table.

Lorna got the giggles and Glenn and Joe Stockton sat there eating their Brown Betty and not knowing where to look. Aunt Harriet threw back her head and cried out that Daddy made her tired, she knew it sounded silly, but everything that hindoo had told her about the market had come true so far, and he only charged five dollars a sitting, and you'd be surprised the high class people she met in the waitingroom, she'd met Emma Stoat down there only day before yesterday.

The only answer was the slam of the front door. Lorna gulped down a glass of icewater. The tears were running down her cheeks from giggling. "Poor Daddy," she spluttered, "he's gone down to the Elks to sulk."

Glenn was surprised himself a few days later to see in front of Mr. Stoat's desk at the bank a white turban and under it a sourlooking tobaccocolored man in a carefully pressed lavender suit, with a big stone that looked like a diamond in his necktie. As Glenn walked past, Mr. Stoat's secretary came out and ushered the hindoo into Mr. Stoat's private office. That afternoon Glenn found Eddy James in a very good humor, because he'd just heard he was in line for a vicepresidency, and asked him what the hindoo was up to. Eddy James laughed and said not to ask him, all he knew was that that hindoo ran a powerful big account. Glenn asked if that was a real diamond and Eddy said at least that was what the girls all said and they usually knew.

Then Eddy sent out for his afternoon cocacola, and leaned over his desk talking very slow, and said, Glenn my boy, he wanted to talk to him. It was kind of a delicate matter and he had been wondering for some time how he could get around to talking about it, now first thing he wanted to say was he thought Glenn deserved a raise, he was making good allright, Mat Avery said his dad had been a preacher at one time and that was probably where Glenn got the gift of gab, anyway he thought he could arrange for a ten dollar a week raise, that showed how much they thought of him, and he mustn't forget that he himself would be moving on soon and this department would need a new manager. . . . Now Glenn was well connected around this man's town and the prospects were mighty good for him, but there was just one thing . . .

Eddy James drained his bottle and put it back on the tray and lit himself a cigarette and started to blow smoke rings. Glenn stirred uneasily in his chair. From across the partition came the rattle of a typewriter. Glenn said vaguely he sure did appreciate Eddy's talking open and aboveboard like this.

"Well," drawled Eddy. "It's Jed Farrington . . . ." Now he knew the boy had a heart as big as a church and if he didn't hit the bottle so hard he'd be a brilliant trial lawyer and, with his name, there was no office in this state that he couldn't aspire to, but all this Mexican business, stirring up these poor ignorant creatures, hardly any better than niggers, and at least niggers weren't treacherous, no, sir, that would not do.

"But suppose I agree with him?" Glenn asked in a low voice.

"If you do, don't tell me about it . . . I'm no father confessor. . . . All I'm tellin' you is, that boy's goin' to get in so wrong around here one of these days he's goin' to have to leave town quick, he'll be lucky if he don't leave it ridin' on a rail."

Glenn jumped up laughing and said he'd think about it. Eddy James got to his feet and put his hand on Glenn's shoulder and said not to get him wrong, he wasn't for downtreading any man, white, colored or caféaulait, but that's the way things were in this town, and now how about getting down to that report for the directors' meeting, thank God he at least had somebody in that office who could read and write. Glenn said, grinning, how about digging into his jeans a little for Jed's Mexicans, and without a word Eddy forked up a ten-dollar bill. Glenn kept feeling himself smiling as he settled at his desk to go over the papers.

The next time Glenn went around to Jed's office after supper for a meeting of the defense committee he found himself slinking in by the back door. When Jed met him in the outer office with his quiet mysterious manner Glenn couldn't help thinking to himself how much like a Mexican he was. Jesus Christ, he said in his slow colorless voice, he was glad Glenn had come, the laborleader was here and full of big ideas, too full, he was talking to Frankie in the back office now; they'd been at it for three hours about whether Marx or Bakunin was the grand old man and he was about ready to have 'em go back where they came from, both of 'em. When he argued the case next week the grand old man was going to be Robert E. Lee, if there was one thing in the world he understood it was a Kendall County jury.

As soon as Jed opened the door of the back office he could hear a loud Brooklyn voice saying, "We must turn every courtroom into a school for the workers." A thin young man with closecropped hair and goldrimmed tortoiseshell spectacles was walking up and down with his necktie flying. "It doesn't matter if we lose one case or a hundred cases as long as the workers are made to realize the significance of revolutionary Marxism." Frankie Perez was shaking his head gloomily as he leant back against the wall. He had a haggard look of fatigue on his face and violet circles under his eyes. "Mr. Silverstone," broke in Jed in a businesslike tone, "meet our treasurer." The thin young man turned around with a jerk, gave Glenn a piercing look through his glasses and shook hands. "Irving Silverstone's the name," he said. "Comrade Spotswood, I hear you are rallying the support of the whitecollar workers ... what I am telling these comrades is that their historic position must be explained to the workers of Horton. They must be made to see the significance of this strike as the awakening of an exploited colonial minority, and as part of the daily struggle of the world proletariat against the encroachments of the exploiting classes. We must flood the city with leaflets. Mass pressure ..."

Frankie's English was worse than usual when he broke in to say haltingly that his people did not need to be told about exploitation, they felt it in their skins, you understand, but they would not allow the trial to be made a demonstration for the Marxist interpretation. . . .

The committee's work was one thing: to raise money to get the compañeros out of jail.

Glenn noticed that Guadalupe was sitting in the dark of the room, nodding approvingly as Frankie talked. Comrade Silverstone, he said, if Jed could get these boys off by talking the kind of language the jury understood, wouldn't it make it easier the next time? As he spoke he felt the girl's big eyes fixed on his face. "Please," she said in her low gruff voice, "we gotto gettem outa jail." A sulky disgusted look came over Silverstone's face as he let himself drop into the swivelchair. "Opportunism," he said, spitting the word out like something sour. "It is the Marxist politicians who are opportunists," said Frankie gravely, "not the anarchist workers."

"Gentlemen, gentlemen," entoned Jed and dove down in his safe for his bottle of whiskey. Silverstone wouldn't drink, so Glenn decided he shouldn't either, and Frankie and Guadalupe only took polite sips, but Jed poured himself out half a tumblerful. "My folks sure didn't educate me right," he said soothingly. "You've got my head spinnin' around with all this Karl Marx dialectic. . . . Now let's talk about how we're goin' to raise the money for the appeal."

"Comrades," began Silverstone, after clearing his throat. "I have been sent here to express to the Mexican workers the solidarity of all the downtrodden masses . . . ." Then they argued for another two hours. When Guadalupe said she ought to go home to her mother, Glenn said couldn't he give her a lift with his car? She nodded.

As she settled back with a sigh in the front seat she said Mr. Spotswood must make beeg money to have such a nice car. Glenn said he hated to have people call him mister, he never called anybody mister unless he didn't like them.

She said oh, she was so tired, on strike it was more tiring than at work, for three families she made meals and fixed the kids, and her feet were so sore, she had to walk so far going to all the Mexican people to collect dimes and nickels for the relief fund, she had bought a new pair of shoes for two seventyfive at Goldstein's and now they were wore out.

"Poor little girl," said Glenn, and put his arm around her shoulders. She let her head fall into the hollow of his neck. A warm quiet feeling came from her. His fingers touched the edge of her full breast. Would she let him take her out in the country for a ride sometime, he whispered. They were turning the corner of the street where she lived. She pulled herself gently away from him. "Como no?" she said.

When Glenn got back to Uncle Mat's house on El Dorado Avenue, he found Uncle Mat and Aunt Harriet in the livingroom going at it hammer and tongs about the stockmarket. Uncle Mat had been out some place to dinner and was walking up and down in his boiled shirt with his coat off and his blue silk suspenders hanging over the seat of the pants of his evening clothes. Now Harriet must be reasonable, he was saying, puffing blue smoke out of his cigar, this was more than a bear raid, he had inside information there was something funny happening up there on the street, he'd sold everything he held on margin that afternoon and if she didn't do the same she was going to get stung, after all there were plenty of good investments right there in their own home state, and as for that damned hindoo. . . . Aunt Harriet interrupted that she'd made twentyfive thousand dollars out of that hindoo. "You haven't banked it yet," shouted Uncle Mat.

Glenn had been standing first on one foot and then on the other in the middle of the parquet floor. Uncle Mat caught sight of him and said, "Glenn, have you heard any news?" Glenn said no, he hadn't, but Eddy James didn't seem worried and he ought to know.

"Well, if you want my opinion, two people are going to get run out of this town. One of them is that hindoo and the other one is Jed Farrington," Uncle Mat said in the tone of a man trying to pick a fight.

"He said he saw oilwells," said Aunt Harriet, "fields of oilwells like a forest down the old range road."

"Who did, Jed?"

"No, Mr. Punjabi, darling."

Uncle Mat threw his cigar down into the unlighted gaslogs under the cement renaissance mantel and said oh, what was the use, he was going to bed.

Aunt Harriet ran over and picked up the cigar and mashed it out on a brass ashtray and started bustling around tidying up the room, saying of course to anyone who didn't know Mr. Punjabi it did seem preposterous, but couldn't it be possible that some people just had a gift of second sight, and Mr. Punjabi was the most scrupulous, most cultivated man, he said his powers would leave him the moment he let himself think of profit or business and that they demanded absolute selfeffacement.

But, Aunt Harriet, Glenn pointed out, that hindoo had a bank-account and was all the time around the bank in conference with Mr. Stoat. That proved it, cried Aunt Harriet; there must be something in him. Jeff Stoat was the keenest businessman in the eastern part of the state, of course he'd been accused of sharp dealing but everybody had enemies. . . . "Glenn, I think you ought to save up a little money and put it into stocks each week. A young man like you has got to be think-ing of the future."

"I haven't paid for my car yet, Aunt Harriet."

At that moment Lorna came in from the hall swishing a yellow evening dress and trailing her ermine cape in her hand. "Why, what's the matter, Lorna?" Aunt Harriet asked. "We didn't expect you till all hours." Lorna dropped down in a chair.

"Mother, I declare I was so worried I just got in the car and came home to talk to you and Daddy. I was dancing with Teddy Honeywell. He just flew down from Baltimore in his plane. He says the market break is just the beginning. He says we're in for a regular crash."

"He's probably interested in selling short," said Aunt Harriet coldly. "Mr. Punjabi warned me about thinking dark thoughts."

"Mr. Punjabi'll land us in the poorhouse, that's what he'll do," screamed Lorna. "Where's Daddy?"

"Your father's gone to bed. I wouldn't stir him up if I were you."

Well, it looked like we were beginning to feel the contradictions of capitalism, Glenn kept saying to himself up in his room with the door closed. He found himself whistling as he undressed.

Next morning everybody had a long face around the bank. When Glenn went out to lunch he noticed a big crowd outside the brokerage office in the vestibule of the East Coast Building. In the afternoon as he made a tour of his prospects he had tough sledding assuring them that East Coast was the Rock of Gibraltar, and no matter if they did have a few failures on Wall Street, that would just squeeze the unhealthy speculative element out of the market and improve the prospects of sound conservative business.

The next day was Sunday. In the afternoon he drove Lupe around to scattered Mexican shacks on the edge of town while she gave out some loaves of stale bread she had talked one of the bakeries into donating to the strikers' children. Afterwards he drove her out in the country. It was a warm afternoon of premature spring. They left the car in a little grassy sideroad and walked across the corner of a field through the rows of dry skeletons of last year's cotton to a clay riverbed behind a dense fringe of bushes.

"Glenn, what you tink, Judge lettum outa jail?" she kept asking. "Don't worry," he said, and drew her to him. "We're doing the best we can. . . . Let's not worry for just five minutes."

They sat down on a clay bank that had little spears of fresh green grass coming up through it. Out of the wind the sun was hot. As they stretched out in each other's arms her body felt hot and firm and quiet to him through the cotton dress that smelt of the washtub.

After a while Glenn began to talk, while she listened gravely. She must understand, he was explaining, that this work for this lousy bank, whooping it up for the stockmarket, was only temporary for him, he wasn't going to keep it up a minute longer than he had to to pay back the money he owed for his schooling. He was a spy in the camp of the enemy. He was going to pull out and live like a worker, he wanted to be part of the masses in their great upsurge towards a new world.

"Twentyfive dollar a week job awright, ten dollar a week job not so good," was all she'd say to that. There was a trace of teasing in the tone of her low voice.

"But it's all so dishonest, I hate it."

She laughed and stroked the hair off his forehead. He lay beside her without saying any more, looking up at the bright fuzz of new green against the blue sky full of a herd of small silveredged clouds, breathing in the smell of wet clay that came from the creek.

That night when he got home he noticed a big Packard touring car with the motor running standing at the curb. He was hardly inside the front door when Tyler came towards him down the hall looking husky and redfaced in a new tweed suit. Tyler grabbed him by the arm and started talking fast with his mouth half closed, "Come on, kid, I've been waiting for you. I got the car there." He pointed to the Packard with a jerk of his thumb out the door and got his hat and coat from the hall closet. "I drove over from Austin to have a talk . . . ."

That puffy look came from drinking too much, Glenn was saying to himself. He tried to make his voice sound cordial. "Sure, Tyler, I'm darn glad to see you . . . you look prosperous."

"Oh, I'm allright . . . hop in." Tyler put the car in gear and they slid slowly down the street in the late dusk behind the smoothly purring motor.

"Well, a fine mess you've gotten into, Glenn, old boy. You gotto get outa here pronto."

"Tyler, you have your ideas and I have mine."

"This ain't a question of ideas, bo . . . Uncle Mat and Aunt Harriet have treated you square, fixed you up with a good job and everything. Now you gotto treat them square and pull out while the going's good. The KKK's going to run all the damn lousy reds out of this town and you're one of 'em. . . . It ud look fine for Uncle Mat's practice to have 'em burning a fiery cross outside his house."

"How do you know?" Glenn tried to keep his voice from shaking.

"Legion's been investigating subversive activities, see, and I'm in on it. We sent an investigator down here to find out who was stirring up the pecanshellers and first thing I know there's my cute little kid brother listed as a leading agitator . . . nice for me, I'll say."

"All I did was take care of their funds so that they could have a break in the courts."

"You did plenty, and how about getting this New York Christkiller down to stir up trouble?"

"How do you know that?"

"We know plenty. . . . What you expect? Half your little greaser friends are stoolpigeons. Give 'em a couple dollars they'll tell you anything you want to know. They can get you for immoral practices with a Mexican girl who's a minor if they want to be real dirty."

"She isn't a minor." Glenn felt the cold sweat breaking out on his neck.

"You damn fool, they look thirty and they turn out to be fifteen.

Wiser guys than you have been framed on that proposition. . . . Anyway, there isn't going to be any framing. . . . These guys know I'm regular and they don't want to embarrass me any more than they want to embarrass Uncle Mat. All you got to do is kiss that twentyfive a week goodbye and take a trip north for your health. . . . Later on if you get over your radical pipedream we'll see what we can do to fix you up with a meal ticket. . . . I'll take care your name gets left out of the report."

"Suppose I don't go."

"Kid, you're going and don't you forget it. . . . If you don't resign it's easy enough to tip 'em off at the bank so that they'll give you your walking papers. Good Christ, I been working my head off to make this thing easy for you and to keep it outa the records. . . . Don't you ever try to think what Mother would have wanted you to do?"

"That's hitting below the belt, Tyler, and you know it."

The car was back in front of the house. Glenn jumped out on the sidewalk and stood glowering at his brother with his fists clenched. Tyler started to laugh in his throat. "All right. I'll cut the sob stuff . . . but that's how I feel about it." "Well, I guess you mean it well," Glenn said. "Are you staying over night?"

Tyler shook his head. "I got to be at my desk in that office at nine o'clock in the mornin'. . . . If you want to I'll send you a telegram signed Dad saying come to Washington."

"No use lying about it. . . . So long, Tyler." Glenn turned his back on him and went into the house and up to his room and closed the door. When he looked out of the window the Packard was gone. He pulled off his coat and necktie and sat down on the bed to think.

Down at the office bright and early Monday morning it turned out he didn't have to resign; he found a note on his desk saying that due to unusual circumstances the bank would have to dispense with his services . . . to take effect immediately. He was still staring at it when he felt a hand on his shoulder. It was Eddy James. "I did the best I could for you, old man," he said. "Anyway you're bein' fired in style." Glenn got to his feet. "Oh, well, it had to come," he said.

Say, drawled Eddy as he settled himself at his desk, had Glenn ever thought that maybe banking wasn't just his field? . . . Had he ever thought of studying law or the ministry? In Eddy's opinion he was just a naturalborn reformer.

Glenn laughed cheerfully. Already a plan was in his head to go to New York and see Gladys. Well, he said he guessed they'd give him that week's pay. Of course they would, said Eddy, and asked him to sit down and list his prospects for the next guy they put on the beat; he'd take him out and set him up to lunch while he still had change in his pockets; because if the stockmarket had another week like last week, he wasn't going ever to be able to set anybody up to lunch again.

At noon Glenn drew his pay from the personnel department, said goodby to a couple of young fellows he'd gotten to know, and walked out of the East Coast National Bank for the last time. Then he drove his car around to the dealer's he'd bought it from to ask him to try to sell it for him and walked around to Tony's Spaghetti Parlor, a little dump where Eddy said he was sure they wouldn't meet anybody they knew. Eddy had brought down a bottle of gin and they went into a back room so that they could drink the Martini cocktails that the waiter, who seemed to know Eddy of old, made up for them.

Glenn just sipped at his drink but Eddy wolfed his. After the first two cocktails he started talking fast; he knew the whole story and he thought it was darned outrageous the way things were going in this country, that conditions were frightful and banking was unsound and the politicians were crooks and the sooner the crash came the better. He told Glenn he was proud to have known a guy who had the nerve to try to do something about the miserable rotten system; he'd never be able to stand up against anything because he had a wife and kids and a mortgage on his home and margins to cover. All he could do was to stand by and see injustice done, instead of joining up with boys like Glenn and Jed Farrington who were trying to make this great country of ours a decent place to live in. He thought Glenn was a twofisted feller and straight as an arrow even if he was a red.

He had a third cocktail and said that Glenn old boy was damn lucky to be out of the banking business, what it did to you was to make you a big mealymouthed hypocrite, and the biggest mealymouthed hypocrite of the bunch was that rat Jefferson Davis Stoat. He hoped he'd get his in this panic on the Street . . . he'd be almost willing to be thrown out on his can himself if he could have the satisfaction of seeing Jeff Stoat wearing stripes, right now he was using investment trust funds to cover his personal margins. "You know there's only one letter divides speculation from peculation."

Eddy began to giggle drunkenly at that. Then he straightened himself up and leaned across his plate of spaghetti he hadn't touched yet, and shook his finger under Glenn's nose and said when he read in the papers that Jeff Stoat had gone to jail he must remember that it was Eddy James over his gin told him it would happen.

Eddy had another cocktail and began to get gloomy. No, he'd never have the satisfaction. Old Jeff was too slick for 'em. Then his face lit up with a grin. "Did I tell you about the hindoo?" Glenn shook his head. Eddy got to laughing so he choked.

He said that in the fifteen years he'd known him, Jeff Stoat had never met his match at any kind of horsetrading proposition until that hindoo came around. That hindoo had put it all over old Jeff Stoat, that hindoo was the smoothtalkingest bastard he'd ever seen, he'd been making money hand over fist with that clairvoyant parlor he had, must have oiled up somebody to get around the police. You couldn't trust that boy Logan with a plugged nickel, it was probably him. Anyway, naturally he'd put his take in the market, and last week he had to cover his margins like everybody else. It was something to hear him hypnotizing Stoat about how this was just profittaking and the prelude to hitherto unfathomed heights, the old line; that hindoo knew all the answers. He got hold of Mrs. Stoat, who between themselves and the gatepost never did have the sense of a guinea hen, and got her all coked up with the idea that he had mysterious powers that could discover oilwells. Well, last week he'd come around to Jeff with a bunch of oilleases and hypothecated them for funds to cover his margins. Meanwhile he drew out all the cash he had in his checking account after a lot of tall talk about how he was on the tail of some options on property along Old Range Road and how that test well Sterrett put his last nickel in was going to come a gusher, all of it wrapped up in the highfalutinest talk about reincarnation anybody ever heard. Well, over the weekend Stoat got worried and hired Sterrett, who knew the oil situation in the eastern part of the state better'n any man living, to make him a report on the hindoo's leases. This morning the report was on his desk. Eddy's voice rose into a shriek. "N.g., old suckerbait that had been layin' around this town for years. Glenn, you ought to have seen his face. If you're hopin' for the collapse of the capitalistic system it would have done you good. We call up the hindoo ... phone disconnected. We send a confidential operative around ... Hindoo dematerialized, leavin' old Jeff Stoat sittin' on his can in his office holdin' the bag. Hindoo's probably across the Rio Grande by now!"

They were sitting there laughing like fools when the waiter came in with the coffee. Eddy's face was crimson. He mopped his face and head with a handkerchief and said for Glenn for God's sake never to repeat anything he'd told him, there were times when you just had to blow off steam if you didn't want to end in a straitjacket. Then he looked at his watch and said, Jesus Christ, he had to go, Glenn ought to be glad he was out of it and didn't have to go back to that accursed office to pick up the pieces. They shook hands and wished each other luck outside of the restaurant.

There was nobody at Jed Farrington's except an old colored man who was sweeping up dust into the streaky afternoon sunlight that came in through the grimed windows. He said Mr. Jed was in court right now; so Glenn hurried around to the courthouse as fast as he could.

On the broad pavements in front of the seed and agricultural instrument stores opposite the whitedomed building, groups of Mexican laborers were standing around in their overalls, talking in low voices. There were none of the usual loafers sitting on the courthouse steps; three motorcycle police had parked at the curb in front of the main entrance. As Glenn was stepping out to cross the street the traffic cop motioned to him nervously to stop, and he noticed that the cars were being held back on the cross street.

A line of closed cars packed with men in white pointed hoods drove by fast while the cop held up traffic for them. On the back of each car was a lettered banner: AGITATORS BEWARE. The crowd of Mexicans turned as one man as the cars passed them. Nobody said a word. A couple of men leaning out of an upper window of the courthouse clapped. There was no sound from the Mexicans or from the men in the cars. About ten cars passed. Then the cop waved to the traffic to come on.

Glenn had a funny feeling in his knees as he crossed the street. Walking past the policemen at their motorcycles he thought several sets of eyes looked into his face sharply and followed him up the empty white steps of the courthouse.

Jed with his black hair mussed and a frown on his face was coming out the broad door. He took Glenn's arm. "Come on over to the office," he said. "Just been in chambers with Judge Green. He's granted Joe Wilks a change of venue . . . allegation that radical agitation will intimidate witnesses. That puts us right back where we started. Joe, he's prosecuting the case, has got a stack of affidavits a foot high. Your friend Comrade Silverstone did that to us with his damn leaflet and a speech he gave down at the colored Oddfellows hall last night. . . . One thing though, Judge Green has reduced the bail to one thousand dollars each. He told me perfectly frankly he'd do anything on earth to keep this case from being used as a pulpit for radical doctrines."

It was a relief when they got through the dingy vestibule of the Lone Star Building and closed the door of Jed's office after them. Too many eyes had been following them down the street.

"Where's Silverstone?"

"He sashayed off the minute the judge left the courtroom, had a telegram to go keep 'em from lynching some niggers in Alabama. I'm glad I'm not in that boy's shoes."

"Now the question is," said Glenn, trying to be practical and cool, "can we raise the bail?"

"Frankie's already raised it. He's a boy that gets results. . . . He's lined up all the Mexican storekeepers. . . . Hell, let's have a drink."

Glenn shook his head and started telling about his talk with Tyler last night. "God damn it," Jed growled over his tumbler of whiskey. "It's enough to make a feller go on the wagon . . . I'll tell you one thing if those buzzards think they're goin' to run me out of town they got another think comin' . . . I belong in this town. . . . There are as many decent liberalminded people in Horton as in any town of its size in the country. What are you goin' to do?"

Glenn felt himself getting red. Under the circumstances he said he didn't think he could stay, he was going to get into the labor movement somewhere, he guessed he'd go north to New York while he had the carfare, there were people he wanted to see there.

"Female people?" asked Jed.

Glenn nodded. "I want to get married," he said. "And have kids and lead a normal life. I'm sick of helling around."

"Why, Glenn," said Jed, "you lead the life of a plaster saint." But speaking of helling around suppose they went to New Orleans for Mardi Gras? Glenn said he'd be glad to have a lift that far but he'd head north right away. "Fine and dandy," said Jed. "Let's pull out right now." Jed wrote *Back Friday ten A.M.* on a piece of scratch paper and pinned it to the outside door of his office with a thumbtack, got his hat and coat and put a pint flask in his pocket and pushed Glenn ahead of him out the door. It was already dark. There was an old Buick touring car with a sleepylooking colored boy in the front seat waiting at the opposite curb. "Remnants of past glory," said Jed, pulling Glenn along by his elbow. "Buck," he said to the colored boy, "do you think you could drive us to New Orleans tonight?" "I reckon we could start out, Mr. Jed."

First they drove around to Jed's hotel to get his bag and then out to the Avery house on Eldorado Avenue to get Glenn's things. It was a relief to Glenn to find that Uncle Mat and Aunt Harriet and Lorna were all out to dinner. Glenn packed his things in a hurry and left an affectionate note for Aunt Harriet saying that his job had petered out and that he'd been forced to leave suddenly for New York and thanking them for all their kindness.

When he got back in the car Jed was just taking a nip out of his pint. "Did you say goodby to the lovely Lorna. . . . You know, Glenn, if I had my way you and me ud be cousins. I swear she's the smartest little girl in east Texas." Glenn laughed nervously. "Oh, hell, let's forget it," roared Jed. "All right, Buck, on to the Mardi Gras."

They lay back in their overcoats under a big bearrug that Jeff said he'd shot himself, while the colored boy drove them back, through the brightly lighted downtown district, past the skyscraper block that had East Coast's big building in the middle of it, and through the Mexican shantytown, and out the concrete highway that shot out straight for miles across the flat coastal country. Everything looked hard and cold, with sharp definite edges.

At the sight of a broad darkeyed Mexican woman standing in a lighted doorway Glenn thought of Lupe. Then he thought of Gladys, the way she'd looked when she had walked along singing the *Internationale* coming out of the big Lenin Memorial Meeting last winter. Then he remembered the quiet lowering beaten look of the Mexicans on the pavement in front of the courthouse all looking one way at the cars going by full of hooded men, all looking one way without any expression like a bunch of cattle in a field staring at a stranger.

"By God, Jed, we've got to do something to stop this kind of thing."

Jed didn't answer. He had dropped off to sleep. Glenn snuggled down as far under the rug as he could because his overcoat was too thin. It was a night of cold gusty wind that blew in swirls across the road. Beyond the telephone wires a little shrivelled moon huddled in clouds was riding along with them.

5

Tatters of cloud hurried across the sky that sagged low over the square. Glenn stood hesitating a moment on the box beside the small American flag. His breath caught in his windpipe as he looked out over the soggy caps and felt hats and heads of the streetmeeting. The dark mass of people in overcoats, with a woman's dress making an occasional brighter patch, filled one corner of the square and thinned out along the curved asphalt path, where under the scrawny trees, men were slouched in rows on benches, or talking in knots, or walking hurriedly past. On the street beyond, cars and trucks moved in a shine of enamel and metal against the plateglass showwindows full of bright colors of cheap clothing stores, capped by biglettered signs that cut across the outlines of gawky old dingywindowed buildings. He couldn't stand there like that. "I've come to tell you," he gasped out, "what I know about the great fight the underpaid Mexican workers are making against the sweatshop system in the state of Texas."

His voice rasped hollowly in his ears. They weren't looking at him. Youngsters and girls were chattering and giggling at the edge of the crowd. He had to make them laugh.

"When the pecanshellers complain that four cents an hour isn't a living wage the bosses say they don't need any more because they eat so many nuts." Several people laughed.

The caps and hats turned up now, he could see the white blur of faces, eyes were looking in his face. The crowd was all faces now. Glenn found himself picking out one face, a youngish ruddy face of a curlyhaired man who seemed to be going along with him, and talked straight at it. When he got to the part about the heroic fight the women and girls were making he told it all to a blackeyed jewish girl in a green hat. He ended up with something about how nobody was going to help this poor and exploited foreign language group except their fellowworkers all over the country who must never forget that an injury to one was an injury to all. About half the people clapped when he stepped down.

It was beginning to drizzle. Glenn stood mopping his face while Irving Silverstone hurriedly announced a big meeting for the benefit of the pecanshellers' defence that night. A gust of sleety rain swept across the square and the crowd began to scatter. Walking away along the path littered with wet sheets of newspaper, past the searching stare of a brokennosed dick from the bombsquad, Irving took Glenn's arm and said it had been pretty good, but why on earth had he used that old I.W.W. slogan about an injury to one was an injury to all?

Wasn't it true, asked Glenn. Sure, said Irving, but it was bad tactics to remind the workers of the I.W.W., the I.W.W. was a thing of the past. Anarchosyndicalism was all washed up; and why hadn't he brought in something about John D. Rockefeller?

Glenn said, laughing, he couldn't see the connection and he didn't believe in personalities. It was the system that was wrong, wasn't it? It wasn't anybody's fault, was it? You had to put things concretely for the workers, muttered Irving.

Somebody was running after them through the driving rain calling Glenn, Glenn. It was Gladys, rosyfaced in a green raincoat. She threw herself into Glenn's arms and kissed him on the mouth. He'd been wonderful, Irving, hadn't he been wonderful? Here she was thinking Glenn had gotten to be a regular southern kukluxer and lyncher and she'd stopped to listen to the meeting and there he was talking to the workers. "Sure," said Irving patronizingly, "we can make a speaker out of him, if he'll only get over his petit-bourgeois ideology."

Then Irving said he had to go to a conference and, after telling Gladys to make sure that Glenn turned up at the meeting that night ready to speak for twenty minutes, he ran across the street dodging through the traffic and left the two of them standing there on the curb in the rain. "Let's go somewhere and talk. I want to talk to you about things," Gladys said in a businesslike tone. Glenn answered without looking at her, feeling his throat stiff. "Anywhere you say, Gladys. . . . Say, how's Boris?"

"Oh, he's fine. . . . No, he's terrible. Come along, I'm getting soaked."

They crossed the street and scampered acrosstown two blocks through crowded pavements, halfblinded by the rain as they hurried along with their heads lowered into the east wind, laughing and apologising when they bumped into people. "Boris is more of a socialfascist every day." Gladys spluttered out the words. "I'll tell you about it when we get inside. Let's go to the Royal and eat cheesecake."

It was warm and cigarsmoky inside the restaurant full of mitteleuropa-looking people talking fast at round tables with stained white tablecloths. After they had ordered coffee and cheesecake of a gray elderly waiter Glenn sat at the table feeling his feet cold and wet, thinking of nothing, staring out in front of him without seeing anything, while she went to the ladies' room to fix her hair that had been sticking wet and spiky to her forehead and ears. She came back looking tidy and smiling, her face glowing with the color in her lips and cheeks and in the pink tip of an ear that showed where she had combed her wavy short hair back over it. "Now tell me everything you've been doing."

Glenn mumbled that there wasn't much to tell. His uncle had gotten him a job in the bank down in Horton and he'd been fired for acting as treasurer of the pecanworkers' defence committee, and as soon as he'd hit town Irving had taken him in tow and made him go to see Elmer Weeks, and Elmer Weeks had made him a big speech about how he was the man to go down and organize the Mexican workers, but Glenn had said he didn't know Spanish and he didn't feel he had enough preparation. "But you've got the courage . . . you know the system is rotten . . . all decentminded people agree with you. What more do you want, Glenn?"

"I know, that's what Elmer Weeks said, but I couldn't make out whether he was kidding himself or kidding me."

"He was telling the truth, Glenn," said Gladys, reaching over and squeezing his hand that lay on the table beside his coffeecup. "Isn't Comrade Weeks wonderful?"

Then she laughed and said, tossing her hair back, "I bet that bank's failed already."

"The contradictions of capitalism are beginning to stick out like a sore thumb," Glenn said. "But what's the matter with Boris?"

Boris was one of them, she said with a pout, she thought maybe she ought to leave Boris for a while and give herself up to party work. Glenn twisted his hand around and grabbed hers. The words were out of his mouth before he knew it. "Come and live with me."

She didn't answer, but her eyes looked very big and dark. She beckoned to the elderly waiter, who turned his facefull of sour disappointed wrinkles from one to the other, and ordered some more coffee and cheesecake. The waiter was thinking of something else and had to be told twice. Her voice trembled when she spoke. "I'll wager he's a social democrat," she said after he'd gone. "I hate tired old jews."

Under the table Glenn felt her leg brush against his. He tried to catch her foot with his feet but she pulled it back. Her eyes, so big and so dark, were watching his lips. "Gosh, it would be the most wonderful luck," he said lamely.

Then he began talking his head off. What he was going to do was get a job in a mine or mill or something, he wanted to get plain hard laborer's work, live, eat, sleep like a worker. He was sick of this whitecollar business. He hadn't any interest in the owning class, he was through with being a parlor pink. He was sick of it. It disgusted him. After this he was going to say what he thought and to hell with everything. "And what about the Party?" asked Gladys, reddening. Glenn clenched his fist and pounded on the table. He was going to join the

Party as a worker and not as a whitecollar slave. When he was an honest to God worker he'd join the Party all right.

"I'm not a meeting," said Gladys. The little worried pout of her lips relaxed into a smile. "You talk just like I was a meeting." They both laughed and Glenn said, gosh, he'd better go and write his speech for tonight, why didn't she come and help him with it, he had a furnished room around the corner, he thought he could sneak her past the landlady. "I had things to do," said Gladys, "but I've forgotten what they were. . . . Oh, Glenn."

They walked, talking about politics in a brisk, businesslike way, the two blocks around to the tall brownstone house with pursedup windows and a blistered green door where Glenn had a furnished room. Inside, the hall was hot and smelt of stale cabbage and roach powder. They held their breath as they tiptoed up the creaky stairs to Glenn's hall bedroom. The room was dark and dense with the smell and hiss of steamheat. He closed the door gently behind them, shot the bolt and reached out his arms to her. She turned away from him, she seemed to be shivering. "Poor little girl," he whispered. Very gently he turned her head around until her lips were under his. She let him kiss her, and her arms tightened around his neck.

They raised a hundred and eight dollars at the meeting that night, although the hall was small. Afterwards, when they had gotten away from the others and were walking to the subway, Gladys said she'd have to go home to talk to Boris. Glenn asked hoarsely whether she thought he'd better go. No, she said, they were too good friends, it would be too great a strain on their comradeship. Boris would understand that she couldn't go on living with him and having him sneer at everything she believed in. Glenn made her feel strong like a real worker; it was terrible how scientists and engineers couldn't get over being the lackeys of capitalism. And poor Boris was such a sweet boy.

They took the East Side express together. Glenn held onto the strap with one hand; their arms were linked and she held on tight to his other hand as they lurched with the train closepacked in the crowd that pressed their two bodies together. "Gosh, we are going to be happy," Glenn whispered in her ear, "when we shake off our stiff old skins." "We'll go out to the country someplace and lie in the sun," she said in a little singsong voice. "And change our skins like snakes," he said, his lips touching her ear. "Oh, I'm scared of snakes." She giggled. "I don't believe in being scared of anything . . . especially not in the spring," said Glenn gravely. It was hard to talk above the clatter of the train.

Glenn went all the way to Brooklyn with her, though it was torture to sit beside her on the seat, after the crowd thinned away, with only their thighs touching and the edges of their hands, when all the time he wanted to have his arms around her. It was worse pacing up and down the empty draughty platform waiting for the train back to Manhattan after she'd given him a hurried peck on the chin and had run off up the steps.

When he went to bed he couldn't sleep. He was worrying about having only thirty dollars in his wallet, that meant he'd have to get a job mighty soon; and the bedbugs that the landlady had promised him only that morning she'd get rid of, had begun to come out and bite him; and he was racked with memories of Gladys, how Gladys' cheeks and Gladys' lips and Gladys' neck had felt under his lips, and the smell of her hair and the sound of her voice. At last he couldn't stand lying there any longer and dressed and went out.

The first gray of dawn gave a ghastly red flare to the streetlights. Garbage cans stood in groups between the unswept brownstone steps of old houses, with here and there a scrawnynecked cat scuttling out from between them. In the entrances of tenements the electric light shone wanly on tarnished rows of mailboxes. In the nightlife section on the West Side there was still a little stir; a few young drunks, a screaming girl in an eveningdress being helped into a taxicab, hackdrivers with their coatcollars turned up standing around outside of a busy bright whitetiled lunchroom in front of a row of freshpainted yellow cabs, shuffling panhandlers, and newsvendors flapping their arms over bundles of morning papers. Glenn walked around until it was day. Then he bought himself a cup of coffee and went back to the room and let himself drop on the bed with his overcoat on and went to sleep.

A knocking on his door woke him. He jumped to his feet. The landlady was standing at the foot of the bed grinning at him. She was a tiredlooking woman, with violet rings under sharp eyes in a face soft and wrinkled as a halfspent toy balloon, who wore her gray hair, dyed henna at the tips, in an oldfashioned pompadour. "Young lady to see yez," she said, squinting at him with her head on one side. "I says to her she's got to wait in the hall till you gits dressed and comes down. . . . Too bad, but I can't afford to allow no . . . no social life in my rooms, ye never kin tell where that sort of thing'll end. A house gits a bad name and first thing you know the vice squad comes around to shake you down for the protection."

"Yes, I understand," interrupted Glenn and closed the door on her to keep her gimlet eyes out of his face. He threw his things into a suitcase in a hurry and ran downstairs.

Gladys was sitting in the hall on the oak settee under the mirror with a little wicker suitcase beside her. She had been crying. He grabbed her and kissed her and said for God's sake they must get out of this town, they must have one day of living like human beings without feeling everything filthy and stinking around them. "That's what we're going to change, Glenn, all this dusty sordid life," she said in a funny coaxing tone, then she put her head on his shoulder and whispered, "Take me someplace, Glenn."

Fred Dyer had offered to lend Glenn his stone cottage up on the Delaware River for a weekend, so the first thing they did when they got their bags over to the Penn Station was to call him up. Glenn left Gladys sitting in the station reading while he went down on the subway to get the key from Fred at his office.

When he got back he ran breathless across the station. He was sure she'd be gone. But there she was sitting quietly where he'd left her. She was reading and eating a chocolatebar. She gave him a kiss that tasted of chocolate and said the station was the only place she'd ever found where she could read without people disturbing her. After this she was going to do all her reading in railroad stations. People on the benches around were beginning to stare at them, they were acting so excited, so they grabbed up their bags and hurried to the ticketoffice. A train was just leaving. When they clambered puffing into an almost empty daycoach, and felt the wheels begin to move under their feet, Glenn cried out, "Now I know I'm not dreaming."

146

They settled themselves and their bags and coats on two seats. "Did you tell Irving you'd come in for the meeting Saturday?" asked Gladys. "I'll write him to wire Jed Farrington to come up. . . . He'd come up quick as a flash if we asked him to."

"Isn't he a degenerate?"

"That's all Irving's talk. He's an honest liberal lawyer who drinks too much. . . . He's a bright feller too." Gladys screwed up her face. "Sounds like a reformist politician trying to get ahead on the backs of the workers to me."

Her hands were in her lap in front of him, making a little wringing gesture as if they were moving without her knowing it. He put his hand over them and squeezed them tight. "Don't be unhappy, Gladys," he said. "Please don't. Don't think about anything except us. We're starting from the ground up, see. Nothing's ever happened to us before. We're going to come back from the farm and get us jobs and work our way up with the workers."

Glenn moved over from where he was sitting opposite to her and sat beside her. She put her arm around his waist and held him tight. He put his lips very close to her ear. "We've got to live real complete rounded lives. We ought to have kids. . . . God, I feel happy."

The train came out of the tunnel. Over the violet flats misty with smoking garbage dumps a thin spring sun shone pink over the girderwork of bridges, distant factory chimneys, silver oil tanks. They crossed a black river strung with rusty freighters with great patches of red on their hulls. Between rows of warped and smokegrimed wooden houses here and there a tree stood up in a pale flare of green. "Oh, there are flowers already," Gladys said. "Look at the yellow ones. I'm so glad I brought my painting things."

Glenn felt a chill go through him. "The first thing we want to do is live really human natural lives ourselves, before we start telling other people what to do." His voice sounded hollow in his ears. "Hell, that sounds cheesy, like the head of a boys' camp where I used to work, but you know what I mean." Gladys nodded quickly with her lips pressed together. He found himself stammering, "I've just led half a life . . . without anybody . . . you know what I mean. . . . Jesus, we need whole men at a time like this."

It cost them two dollars and a half for. the taxi to go out to Fred Dyer's cottage, but it turned out to be a little stone house by a brook with a view of the river and daffodils in bloom in the grassy front yard. When they went in staggering under cartons of groceries with the longnosed taxidriver following them with their bags, Gladys shivered. "Oh, it's cold.".

There was no wood chopped, so Glenn had to take off his coat and go after a pile of logs in the woodshed with an axe. He was awkward with the axe because it was a long time since he'd used one, but Gladys, who was standing around in the sun in front of the house with a blanket pulled over her shoulders on top of her overcoat, seemed to think he was wonderful to get the wood chopped at all.

It was only when he had the range started, and a roaring fire in the big fireplace in the old whiteplastered livingroom, that she'd come in out of the slanting afternoon sun. The air was already beginning to get chilly. She crouched shivering on the hearth with the blanket still around her and her damp shoes and stockings steaming beside her. He rubbed her feet to warm them. She couldn't seem to stop shivering.

When he made her some hot tea she felt better. By the time he had gotten ready their lunch of steak and boiled potatoes and fried onions, blue dusk was crowding in the windows. The room began to feel warm and cosy with the smell of the steak. There was no electric light and they'd forgotten to bring kerosene for the lamps so they had to eat by firelight.

Afterwards Glenn went out to bring in as much small wood as he could find in the dark while Gladys stacked the dishes and tidied things up. It was a clear chilly liquid spring night full of stars. Peepers and little frogs sounded like sleighbells from a pond down in the hollow somewhere. As he rummaged around in the dark woodshed he could see Gladys' slender little figure passing and repassing in front of the window lit pink by the firelight. When he came stumbling in the back door with his arms piled high she ran to him. "Oh, Glenn, I was getting scared; suppose there's a spook in the cottage." He let the wood drop with a thud in the woodbox. "That'll scare him away," he said, laughing.

There didn't seem to be a double bed in the house, so they got hold of two mattresses and laid them together in the middle of the floor in front of the fire. Rather solemnly they tucked in the sheets and spread the blankets. They sat side by side in front of the fire and gradually undressed. Suddenly Glenn pulled her to him and kissed her all over her face and neck. "Now we're not ashamed of anything, are we?" he whispered, very low. She jumped up. "There's nothing in life to be ashamed of except silly ideas and maybe bedbugs," she said oratorically. He laughed out, "You're right, by God, you're right." He stood up with his bare feet wide apart on the warm stones of the hearth and lifted her off the ground as he drew her to him.

In the morning Glenn was the first to wake up. He got up and after tucking the blanket carefully around the sleeping girl, pulled on his pants and shoes. Outside it was raining hard. A raw gust from the open window slapped him in the bare chest and arms. He built a fire in the range, put on coffee, and, taking off his shoes again so as not to wake her, made up the fire in the fireplace. The wood began to crackle. He couldn't help whistling as he worked around the stove after he'd washed himself all over at the kitchen pump. He cut some bread and put it on the hot stove to toast and started to sizzle some bacon in the skillet.

The rain stopped. Except for the roaring of the fire in the living room and in the range, the house was so quiet he could hear the drops drip off the eaves and the throaty gurgle of the little brook outside. A robin was whistling somewhere behind the house.

Beyond the stone wall he could see a hillside curve up vivid green with winter wheat. The smell of wet clay came in through the window and through it the smell of hot toast and coffee and frying bacon rose in streaks. "You're the only boy I ever knew who was the first up in the morning," came Gladys' voice. "It shows a very fine character." She was sitting up crosslegged on the mattress in front of the fire combing her hair.

After breakfast they put on rubbers and went out for a walk. Glenn felt so good he couldn't keep his pace down and kept running ahead of her, up muddy roads, past stone farms and fields full of last year's stubble where they heard quail calling. He made her laugh by whistling bobwhite bobwhite at them and making them answer.

The sky cleared and the day became sunny and hot. They found a little pool in the brook back of the house deep enough to take a dip in. They dared each other to go in. The water was icy and they had to run back to the house with their clothes bundled in their arms and their shoes in their hands, to dry themselves in front of the fire. That gave them a raging appetite for lunch so they ate up everything they had in the house. After lunch they washed the dishes and swept the floor and made up their bed, and then walked down to the village to buy some groceries. On the way down Glenn began to talk about getting a job on a farm around there.

Next day he left Gladys painting watercolors and walked around to several farms and asked if they needed a hired man. The farmers were dutchmen mostly and seemed to think it was a great joke; no, they never hired outsiders. Then he went down to the boxfactory he'd seen behind the freightyard in the village. Nothing doing; they were laying off hands every day. A couple of days later he went over to Bethlehem on the train, and walked around to the employment office of one of the steel companies. He'd no sooner gotten in the door than he caught sight of a lettered sign on the bulletin board saying NO USE ASKING FOR JOBS. THERE AREN'T ANY. THIS MEANS U.

After he'd bought some groceries and started up the hill with them slung across his back in a canvas laundry bag he counted out his money and found he had two dollars and sixtyeight cents, not enough for their fare back to New York even if they'd wanted to go. Hell, he told himself, tomorrow he'd have to wire Paul or Jed Farrington for a loan. Gosh, Paul couldn't spare a cent he knew, he had two kids now and Peggy had been sick. Jed seemed an openhanded guy, but you never could tell. Boris would loan them the money soon enough, but Christ, he couldn't ask him.

Glenn was tired and his feet were caked with redbrown mud when he got to the door of the stone house. He stopped to wipe his shoes on the long grass around the big millstone that served for a doorstep and turned to look for a second at the yellow sunset laced with slender salmoncolored bars of cloud behind the bulging purple and green hill of the wheatfield.

There were voices in the house. Somebody had come to see Gladys.

Glenn opened the door and walked in and set his bag of groceries on the livingroom table. For a second he couldn't see who was there on account of the dusk and the dazzle of the sunset in his eyes. "Hello, Glenn," said Gladys in a stiff voice. "We need some more wood. We're freezing."

She was sitting on the mattress in front of the dying embers of the fire. Somebody was stretched out on the mattress with his head on her knees.

Glenn felt his whole body stiffen. He struck a match and lit the lamp on the table. "Boris has come for me . . . I'm going home with him. He's been very unhappy," Gladys was saying in a dreamy impersonal-sounding tone of voice.

Glenn took a step towards them to put the lamp behind his back. Boris was stretched out with his eyes closed and his head on her lap. She was gently rubbing his temples with her fingers. "He's got a splitting headache. He's been working too hard," she said in the same low cooing tone as if she were talking to a child. "I'll go get some wood," Glenn said and walked out of doors.

As he chopped at the tough old pine boughs in the woodshed, he began not to tremble so. Walking back to the house, with his arms full of the resinsmelling wood, he found it was hard to keep his knees from knocking together. He went in by the kitchen door and stood looking at them.

He still had the axe in his hand. Gladys was sitting in the same place but Boris had gotten to his feet and stood with his back to Glenn whispering something to Gladys he couldn't catch.

Glenn felt his right hand tight round the axe handle. Boris' round skull with the curly hair cropped close on it was right in front of him. Glenn stood there feeling the sharp new axe heavy in his hand. Boris's big head looked fragile as a big egg on his small body. The axe was swinging a little in Glenn's hand.

Glenn found he was biting his lips. He turned sharp and put the axe outside the kitchen door. Then he went back into the livingroom without a word and began putting wood on the fire. Cold sweat had formed round the neck of his flannel shirt. When he'd gotten the fire going he turned and, standing on the hearth, with his hands that were still icy and trembling in his pockets, said in a controlled voice, "Hello, Boris, I thought you'd gone to Germany."

"I may go yet," said Boris, without moving a muscle of his face.

"Not without me," said Gladys with a hysterical titter. Boris ran his tongue over his lips. "You see she's done this before. . . . We might have known she'd get over it." Something warm and confiding came into his tone. "She's always gotten over it before in about a week."

Glenn cleared his throat. He was so relieved about the axe, he was thinking, he didn't give a damn about anything else. "Well, I guess it's up to me to butt out."

"Oh, it's beginning to rain. Isn't this weather horrid?" cried Gladys shrilly.

"Look," Glenn said, feeling the blood coming back into his arms and legs so that they felt less like wood, "you people take the key back to Fred Dyer when you're through with this little . . . this little lovenest."

"Yes, indeed," said Boris seriously. "I've got his address. That's how I found where Gladys was."

"Oh, but, Boris, I wrote you," whined Gladys.

"I had to know how to find the damn place. . . . As usual you didn't put any address on your letter, Gladdo, artistic temperament I guess."

"Be sure to lock everything up," said Glenn. "The axe is outside of the kitchen door. Don't leave it out in the rain."

Nobody said anything while Glenn walked back and forth across the room, collecting his things and stuffing them into his suitcase. Without looking at either one of them he put on his hat and overcoat, picked up his bag and left the house.

III. THE MOMENT OF CHOICE

I

THE ROAD GREW STEEPER as they wound up the mountain. There were patches of mist and, higher, the rain began to turn to sleet and to freeze on the windshield, so that Glenn had to lean forward over the wheel with his eyes screwed up as he drove, to try to see the curves. Even in low the motor of the old touringcar strained and knocked. Now and then he had to stop dead when his headlights flattened out suddenly in a wall of mist, and it was hard getting started again on account of the thin scrim of ice on the road. All the while he could hear Less Minot's hoarse voice beside him mumbling on and on about how this was a tough proposition they were going into, these here mountaineers would just as soon shoot a man as not. Warn't no more than taking a bite out of an apple. Suppose they missed the comrades who were going to meet them in the gap and rode right on into town and landed in the arms of the deputy sheriffs, that would be the end of the pair of them. At least they'd ought to had a couple drinks before they started. It was all right for the central committee sitting around with a map and a lot of mimeographed statistics in a nice warm office, but not one of those comrades understood what an organizer was up against in a proposition like this. "Sure they do, Less. . . . Have a heart,"

Glenn said, without turning his head. "You're the toughest organizer the American Miners have got. Hell, their deputy sheriffs can't be any more dangerous than their mountain scenery."

Glenn's hands were icy in the wet cotton workgloves he was driving in. On one curve the car took a skid that brought his heart right up into his throat. He kept her in the road but couldn't get her started up the hill again until they had piled out to put stones behind the rear wheels. At last they were grinding along a straight gravelly level. "Less, I bet you we're up in the gap," said Glenn.

"Well, you needn't sound so cocky about it. How do we know some stoolpigeon ain't tipped off the company guards? A night like this you could shove the car and us in it out over the edge of one of them places and nobody'd be the wiser. . . . By God, there's a light."

Ahead on the road there was a dim red glow. Glenn put his foot on the brakes and the car slewed around. He pressed on the gas to give headway to the spinning wheels and managed to bring her to a stop sideways across the road with the front fender dug into a glistening claybank.

"Whoa, there," came a voice. Somebody was holding up the lantern and peering into the car.

Less Minot was out on his feet in a second and his voice was firm and hearty. "Who are you expectin'?"

"Brothers," came the voice.

"I'm Less Minot, are you Joe Kusick?"

"Sure; glad to meet you, brothers. This here's Pearl Napier. He's secretary to the Muddy Fork local. . . . Well, you made it right on the dot, boys, we sure didn't expect to see yous this night."

Glenn was leaning out from the car straining his eyes to see. He could make out the red outline of the flame in the lantern and two white faces, one very young and smooth, and one wrinkled and lobsided. "Meet Comrade Crockett, Sandy Crockett," said Less. "He's an eddicated feller but I'd trust him before I'd trust most people."

Glenn wasn't quite used to his party name yet, so he hesitated a moment before he stuck out his hand. Two hard hands gripped it in turn. "Say, brothers," he said, "give me a hand to push us back on the road, will you?" They jumped at the car and lifted the front axle right off the ground. "Thataboy," said Glenn, laughing. "Gosh, you fellers are hefty." They were all laughing, silly with relief.

"Don't you fellers want to ride?" "No, we'll walk ahead with the lantern to show you the way. Hit's hard to find," said the younger man. "Hit's good you boys came. Half the brothers was sayin' you dassent."

"Why?"

"Hit's a rough country acrost this here gap."

"Well, we been in some tough spots before up in the Pittsburgh district, ain't that so, Sandy?" bawled Less in his deep voice.

"Did you bring plenty litrachur?" asked the younger man.

"Sure, the whole car's stacked with it."

"The boys is hongry for it."

Driving slowly in low Glenn followed the swinging lantern down the road. After the first bend the men struck off down a steep deeprutted wagontrail. "Do you think we can make it?" whispered Less nervously. "Sure," said Glenn. "Gee, I like those guys."

At the bottom of the gulch they had to ford a stony creek and almost stuck. The car charged out the other side with the motor sputtering. The headlights cut out a rail fence against the mist and two black figures leaning over to take down the rails to let the car through. Then Glenn was driving over the grassy ridges of what had once been a cornfield, towards the faintly lit blur of a window.

He stopped the car and turned off the switch and the lights and followed the others round the edge of a shack. He could smell woods and there was the warm sweet reek of a cowbarn and the sound of something fourlegged treading on cornstalks.

Then he was stepping through a low doorway into a room full of white faces outlined with coaldust lit by yellow flame from a softcoal fire in a grate under a toppling stone chimney. "Comrades and brothers," said Less in his deep voice. "We bring you the greetings of the American Miners Union."

"Oh, boy," whispered Glenn as he brushed past Less, pulling off his wet gloves, "let me at that fire." Pearl Napier followed him and put his arm round Glenn's shoulders as he stood opening and closing his hands in front of the flames to get the blood back into his fingers. "We was fixin' to have somethin' hot for you all to eat," he whispered in Glenn's ear in his slow, serious voice, "but we just ain't got nothin', that's all. We been livin' on the mercy of the people sence we started this here strike. . . . Joe Kusick, he's got a lil store, he'll feed ye up strong when he carries you all down there tomorrow."

Less and Joe Kusick were already getting down to business, sitting on two stools in the middle of the room, while the miners round the walls watched them silently. The black dust in their eyelashes and eyebrows and in the hollows of their cheeks gave them the look of being made up for the stage. Sure, Joe Kusick was explaining, they'd oughta waited till they got their charter to pull out Muddy Fork but the boys was right mad since the company had brought in them gunthugs swaggering around and treating themselves to the best of everything and the boys swore they warn't agoing to wait for no charter, and now everything was ready to pull out Slade's Knob at the break of day. "Jesus Christ, you don't need no agitators in this neck of the woods," roared out Less. "What you boys need is moderators."

"Our agitators is honger an' the flux an' High Sheriff Blaine," said a solemnvoiced, bent old man who'd just come in the door of the cabin. "Amen," said the miners along the walls. As the old man turned to bolt the door behind him Glenn saw that he had a gun slung over his back. "Amen to that, Pappy," said Pearl. "But ain't you posted for sentry?"

The old man walked slowly over to the chimney and hung up his gun on a hook. "There won't none of Caleb Blaine's gunthugs dast come out this night," he said. "I want to listen to the meetin'."

Less got to his feet and said he had the charters right out in the car and asked Glenn to go out and bring in his satchel. Somewhere in the dark end of the cabin a child had begun to cry.

Outside the night was full of driving sleety rain. Glenn found Less' satchel and grabbed an old piece of canvas out from under the seat to throw over the hood of the car to keep the ignition from getting wet. When he got back in the cabin Pearl was on his feet saying that as elected secretary of this here Muddy Fork local of the American Miners he moved this here assembly be duly constituted a meeting in accordance with the constitution and bylaws and he was going to give the floor to brother Minot, but first he wanted Pappy to say a few words of prayer. "Amen," said the miners round the walls.

The old man straightened up and stood with his back to the fire with his two hands lifted above his head. "O Lawd . . ." he began, his voice a deep rattle in his throat. A barefoot girl in a torn cotton skirt with her hair in a tangle over her face pushed her way out from behind the men. She was carrying a crying baby wrapped in a torn piece of patchwork quilt. She crossed the shaky boards of the floor with two long strides and crouched on her heels in front of the fire. The baby's cries died into a choking whimper. "Can't you make it hush, Wheatly?" whispered the old man, letting his hands with their bent knobbed fingers drop to his sides. "Hit's cold and hongry. Mom said she ain't got no milk for it."

"Hain't you got no sugartit, Wheatly?"

The girl's eyes flashed black under their tangle of hair that the firelight edged with gold fuzz. "Pappy, you know we ain't had no sweetenin' in this house sence they won't let us go to the store."

"Hush it as well as you can, Wheatly," said the old man wearily. The girl let her head drop and began to rock the child, moving her whole body from her hips. "O Lawd," the rumbling voice started again, "bless this here house and this here meetin' of the 'Merican Miners like you blessed the Mineworkers in the old days before them organizers got to be traitors an' scallywags an' sold us out to the oppressors. . . . O Lawd, we need bread an' meat an' clothin' for our children, that's terrible sick of the flux an' can't sleep because they's so cold an' hongry, an' can't go to school to learn to be good citizens because they's so naked, an' they's likely to grow up the worst trash is ever been seen in these mountains. O Lawd, the operators an' Miss Nancy Pringle the postmistress, who gits the Red Cross relief an' keeps it all to herself, tries to tell us hit's sinful to jine the union an' that the 'Merican Miners is the sinfullest antichrists an' rednecks in these mountains; but ain't it true, Lawd, that poverty and wretchedness is the highroad to sin and damnation? An' in the old days of the Mineworkers we used to make a livin' in these mountains an' now the coal operators won't let us live and has sent in foreigners and gunthugs to oppress us an' Caleb Blaine, that we went down to the polls to elect for sheriff, has hardened his heart against us, an' he won't never git another miner's vote in these mountains . . . ."

"Amen to that," shouted the miners round the walls.

The old man lifted his shaky hand for silence and went on, his voice filling the cabin. "An' ain't it gospel true, O Lawd, that if the 'Merican Miners was red Rooshians or the devil hisself, we'd do right to jine with them to git food for our chillun, an' stand up agin the oppression of the Law with our guns in our hands, because nobody else in this world's ever come forward to help us. . . . An', O Lawd, set thy blessin' upon this meetin'." As the miners roared, "Amen," Glenn untied a bundle of newspapers and handed them around. The miners stood holding the papers reverently in front of them. The thought flashed across the back of Glenn's head somewhere that it was like handing out hymnbooks at a revival meeting.

Less Minot got up and said that the American Miners was affiliated with organizations all over the country that was working to overthrow the rotten capitalistic system that kept the working class down to starvation wages with guns and grafting officers of the law, and that if that was being a red, he was glad to be called a red, and as for the Rooshians, he didn't know much about them, but so far as he could hear tell the working class had overthrown its capitalistic oppressors over there under the leadership of the Marxist-Leninist Communist Party and was running the country in their own interests and was ready to help the workers in other countries to do the same.

Then Glenn told about the soupkitchens the American Miners were going to organize and how the Workers' Defense was already shipping in clothes and flour and groceries with a girl comrade, Jane Sparling, who was a doctor and who'd tend the sick and ailing children as long as the strike lasted.

Then Pearl Napier stepped into the center of the floor and said, "Brothers, I ain't much a one to break down an' cry, but I tell you brothers I was all broke up with thanksgivin' when I stood up in that gap in the rain an' the sleet an' saw the lights of that automobile an' knowed that these here brothers, or comrades like they say, had come away from their homes an' their families an' given up their jobs if they had 'em, to come an' help us poor people up here in these mountains. Now don't let 'em tell you that these boys is furreners. When you're facin' the coal they ain't no furreners in the mine, only your buddy by your side. Now we're facin' High Sheriff Blaine an' the Slade County

Coal Operators' Association an' there ain't no furreners 'xcep' the gun-thugs that wants to kill us. I vote the meetin's adjourned with heartfelt thanks to Comrade Minot an' Comrade Crockett. All in favor say Aye."

While the miners were crowding round Glenn and Less to shake hands, Joe Kusick said boys, hadn't they better get a couple of winks of sleep because they was going to march before day while the gunthugs was all asleep drunk in their beds in the Appalachian Hotel down to McCreary. Pearl Napier came back from the dark end of the cabin and whispered in Glenn's ear he'd have to apologize they didn't have no bed to offer them; the old woman was mighty poorly and she and the children was asleeping in the bed, but he reckoned he could scare up a coverlet and they'd be right warm in front of the chimbley.

As the men settled themeslves to sleep in a row across the floor, Glenn noticed that some didn't have any shirts on under the old army tunics shiny with grime most of them wore. He and Less wouldn't take the clean patchwork quilt Pearl brought them but said to lay it over the children who must need it.

They took off their shoes and put them on the stone hearth to dry and stretched out side by side in the place the others left for them near-est the fire. When the cabin had quieted down to the heavy breathing and snoring of crowded sleepers Less began to whisper in Glenn's ear that Jesus Christ, if they marched on Slade's Knob it would be a mas-sacre, but they were in for it now, there was no holding them back. For one thing it was up to Glenn to see the miners didn't carry their guns, because there'd be shooting sure as fate, and if the miners shot back the Governor would have in the militia and the strike would turn into a lockout before they could get any locals organized and they might as well have stayed home. Glenn said sure, he'd talk to Pearl about it as soon as he woke up, and lay back with his head on his arm and closed his eyes.

He couldn't sleep. He lay on his back staring at the flicker of the firelight among the cobwebs that hung looped from the rafters over-head. Cold spurts of wind came in through the chinks in the boards under his back. Excitement made his heart thump and made the skin round his eyes feel tight; his face had a scalded feeling from the long drive through the winddriven rain. The baby cried at intervals all night and the girl walked back and forth, stepping across the sleepers with her long barefooted stride, rocking it as she went. Glenn watched her through halfclosed eyes. When she leaned over with the child on one hip, to put a fresh hunk of soft coal on the fire, he could see the points of her firm breasts and the flat curves of her belly and thighs through her skimpy rumpled dress. He had a pitiful tender feeling as he watched her, as if he'd known these people in this shack in these mountains all his life. He thought of the other shacks in these mountains and the crowded rooms in slums, and working people asleep in shacks and crowded barracks all over the world. Now he was one of them for keeps, part of them, like a povertystricken kid asleep in bed with his brothers and sisters.

The noise of men shuffling about and talking hoarsely woke him. The rain and wind had stopped, but mist sagged like a blob of wet cotton in through the door of the shack whenever it was opened. Somebody had brought in a bucket of cold water with a dipper in it; that seemed to be all the breakfast there was.

Glenn was stamping around outside the cabin, tightening his belt after he'd taken a leak, when he bumped into Less Minot. "Say, Less, oughtn't I go on this march?"

"Nuttin' doin', Sandy," Less said. "Your business is soupkitchens. You go down and see what you can do with Mrs. Kusick. We got to have somepin' for these guys to eat when they're through marchin'. Then we'll have a big organization meetin' down to Bull Crik. Jane's comin' up to Kusick's from McCreary today. You got to be there to make contact, see. . . . Hell, I wouldn't march myself except the boys ud think I was a yellowbelly if I didn't." Less' voice dropped to a shaky whisper. "If they get me, Sandy, you'll go see the old woman, won't you, Sandy? . . . And git up a fund so's she can buy a little house or somepin."

"Less, there's nothing going to happen."

"Who said there warn't? This here operators' association means business, I tell you. . . . What about the guns?"

"Pearl's talking to the boys about 'em now. He's going to make 'em put away every gun they got."

"That's the stuff. I wanted it to come from you and not from me, see. Pearl's a smart kid . . . there's a firstclass workin'class leader in that boy if the bosses don't git him."

"How would they?"

"Jesus Christ, man, they shoot to kill around here, and then there's other ways: jail, money, a woman, a good job, liquor. I seen many of 'em go to hell. Well, so long, Sandy, it's got to come sometime. . . . I'll carry the flag, God damn it." He grabbed Glenn's hand and shook it. Glenn was surprised that Less' hand was cold and sweaty and trembling.

The miners faded off into the mist that was beginning to churn overhead with faint rosy light. Everything was suddenly very quiet. Old Napier had led a skinny swaybacked cow out of the cowshed and was standing in front of the cabin waiting. The cow had a halter around her neck and stood placidly moving her lower jaw from side to side. Old Napier said he was going past Joe Kusick's place and would carry Glenn on down there. First Glenn put the car in the cowbarn that was still sweetly steamy with the cow's warmth, and closed the door on it. He asked old Napier if the kids would keep their mouths shut about its being there. They wouldn't talk to nobody but their own folks, not if they was Napiers, old Napier answered proudly.

They started down the slippery path that zigzagged between brokendown rail fences into the valley. They had to hop from side to side to avoid the little clear stream that ran down the middle of it. Glenn asked old Napier where he was taking the cow and the old man said he reckoned he was going to sell her, she didn't give no milk no more, too bad after they'd fed her corn all winter, but he had to do something to even up his store account.

They came out on a rough macadam road winding up the side of the mountain and turned down it. The mist was beginning to lift from the valley floor. It was almost day. Old Napier pointed with a crooked forefinger to where the railroad curved through the valley in front of the black hunched buildings and inclined trestles of a mine. "Look yonder," he said.

A piece of wet road caught the light where it curved up over a clay hill beside the tipple. Up the road moved a black crawling mass of men marching. At the head of it fluttered a tiny pink and white patch. "Yonder's the flag." Glenn and old Napier stood still in their tracks watching the mass move up the hill, blotting out the wet gleam of the road. Then the flag dipped out of sight over the ridge of the hill.

Glenn's tongue was dry in his mouth. A long freight pulled by two engines slowly puffing white steam was toiling up the line on the valleyfloor. They started walking again with the cow ambling behind them.

At the next curve the mine was hidden by the wooded flank of a hill already sifted over with spring greens. "Hit's been a hongry winter," said old Napier, shaking his head.

Where the road came out onto the highway beside the railroad tracks, there was a small unpainted clapboard store plastered with Moxie and Coca Cola and Chicken Dinner signs. A stumpy gray-haired woman stood in the door with her hands in the pockets of her apron looking fixedly down the empty highroad toward's Slade's Knob. "Ella," said old Napier, "this here's the furrener Joe said to carry down to you all. . . . I'll be on my way."

The woman's brown eyes, set in a mass of little wrinkles, searched Glenn's face. "So you've come here to help these poor creatures? I don't know where you've come from or why you done it, but come inside . . . I'm crazy worried about Joe. He told me he wouldn't go with that march, and now he's gone and done it. I thought I heard shootin' while ago. Right now I'm goin' to show you a place to hide in case the Law comes along because if they find what they call a foreign agitator here, there's goin' to be trouble."

Talking his ear off all the time she showed Glenn how to climb on a packing case in the middle of the little dark storeroom that opened back of the counter and to push up a trapdoor that led up into the loft overhead. Then she asked him if he'd had anything to eat that day. Glenn said he was about starved.

She took him in the kitchen in back, that was hot from the roaring range, and fried him up some fat bacon and brought some hot biscuits out of the oven and some weak coffee off the back of the stove, all the time telling about how there'd been a time when her and Joe lived pretty well, but now nobody could pay their store account, and the companies made the poor creatures trade at the commissaries, charging thirty per cent more than the ordinary store prices, and if her and Joe did scrape up a little something to eat, Joe gave it away to those poor creatures. What folks didn't know outside was that the poor creatures in these mountains was hongry and it was right pitiful the way the little children died with the flux and the lack of proper feeding.

Glenn sat there, eating away on the biscuits and bacongrease, feeling like a pig to be eating so much. As she talked Mrs. Kusick kept watch down the road out of the back window. Suddenly she said, "You git up there quick, here comes a earful o' Law." With his mouth still full Glenn shot into the storeroom and up through the trapdoor and into the little loft that was piled with woodshavings the carpenters had left. He lay out flat across the rafters and tried not to breathe.

From below he could hear Mrs. Kusick making a great clatter with her dishes in the kitchen sink. Then he heard a car stop with a screech of brakes outside the store, and heavy steps and voices. Somebody was grumbling hoarsely that there'd been trouble up to Slade's Knob and some of those damn hotheads from Sladetown had gotten in the way of some lead slugs. Glenn could hear Mrs. Kusick's voice pipe up shakily to ask if Joe was all right. He was all right now but he sure wouldn't be for long if he didn't keep his nose out of all this sedition and conspiracy, answered the other voice gruffly. Why didn't Joe mind his own business?

Mrs. Kusick quavered that there warn't no business to mind, the poor creatures didn't have no money to spend no more, that was the trouble with this country, Sheriff Blaine. These here jew agitators from New York must think they got some money yet, roared the sheriff's voice, because they was two of them come over the gap last night. He said he had a mind to search the premises. Mrs. Kusick's voice rose shrill. "Caleb Blaine, you ain't got no warrant . . . you can't search my place without a warrant."

There followed confused angry talking and heavy boots tramping and Mrs. Kusick's voice in a shriek. "The first sonofabitch steps into my kitchen I'll scald him with the teakettle, by God and by Jesus I will."

There was a pause. The sheriff's voice rose in a pacifying tone saying he guessed her and Joe must have liquor stowed away somewhere, and other voices laughed and the car drove off down the road.

Glenn lay there for a while and then he pulled up the trapdoor and peeked down. "You kin come down now, they won't be back," Mrs. Kusick said in a shaky whisper. "They're off for McCreary to the grand jury to swear out warrants hellbent for election." Glenn let himself drop to the floor and stood in the kitchen brushing the dust and shavings off his clothes. "I reckon I kinder forgot to talk like a lady but Caleb Blaine makes me so goddam mad apokin' his dirty face into my kitchen. I wisht I'd ascalded it. I'd ascalded it plenty if he'd taken one step further, I wouldn't acared if they'd sent me to the chair. That lowdown lowtalkin' ole piece of nothin'. Warn't so long ago he was hangin' around here tryin' to git him a job tendin' store. That was before he got in with the Operators' Association and messed in county politics. Well, if you heard me not talkin' quite ladylike I sure must apologize."

At that moment a truck stopped in front of the door and Glenn, peering nervously out over the counter, saw Jane Sparling jump out from the front seat. She was wearing a print dress like the miners' wives wore, with a motheaten fur coat over it. "Where's the American Miners' soupkitchen?" she asked. "Hello, Sandy." She strode in the door in her jaunty flatfooted way.

"Mrs. Kusick, this is Dr. Sparling from the workers' relief. She's come up with some food and she's got some funds." Mrs. Kusick looked Jane up and down with her small sharp eyes. Jane walked up to Glenn and asked again, pushing her untidy graying hair back under her hat with her big hand, well, where was the soup kitchen, the truckdriver was in a hurry to unload and get out of here, he seemed scared to death about something, what was the trouble, she couldn't see anything to worry about.

Glenn had a time convincing Mrs. Kusick that Joe had said they could use the brokendown cabin on the lot behind the store for a soupkitchen. They backed the truck up there over the soft grass and unloaded the crates of groceries; as soon as Jane paid the colored man who drove it, he was off in a hurry.

When Glenn could get a word with Jane out of earshot of Mrs. Kusick he said severely, "Jane, please remember Less and I are underground. You don't know us any more than any other union members. There's the worst reign of terror here you ever saw."

"Well, I don't see anything to be scared of," said Jane, lighting a cigarette. "If you can get me a stove you can have about ten gallons of nourishing soup to distribute by noon. That's more useful than conspiratorial monkeyshines."

Joe Kusick came back walking alone down the road from Slade's Knob with his whole lobsided face wrinkled up in a frown. Things was bad. They'd shot two boys dead and wounded some more, but the mine was out all right. Hadn't nobody gone to work on the morning shift but the superintendent and a half a dozen niggers.

Joe knew where there was an old cookstove and sent a couple of miners, who were standing around waiting for something to do, over to get it. They got some boards and a hammer and nails and by noon they had a counter and some long tables fixed up and had propped up the walls of the old shack and were on the roof patching up the gaps in the curly chestnut shingles. Jane had tied an apron around her rawboned hips and had a big washboiler of soup started while daylight was still coming in through the roof overhead.

Glenn was at work handing up shingles while Joe Kusick tacked them down, when somebody tapped him on the back. It was Pearl Napier who made a gesture with his thumb over his shoulder and walked away fast. Glenn followed him. "Hit's Less," Pearl said as he leaned over to crank a rusty Model T Ford without any top parked beside the store. "You an' him's got to meet some feller from the higher degrees. . . . Say, how deep are you in this business?"

Glenn grinned and said, all the way, he guessed.

"Me too," said Pearl. "I'm in up to my neck."

As he drove Glenn down the main road towards McCreary he talked about the union, he said this here shooting this morning would bring the whole county out, the miners up in these mountains was sick and tired of being herded like cattle and shot down like niggers, this would bring them out all right. Now if they could have the right kind of support from the outside, food to keep the chillun from dying like they was and litrachur to eddicate the boys up a little, they'd have the grandest union in Slade County that had ever been seen in the minefields; but right now there wasn't a miner's shack in these mountains where they had a cup of flour from one day to the next, most of them was living on the mercy of the people. They had to have help from a national organization.

"Well, that's what Less and Comrade Sparling and I are here for. We bring you the support not only of a national but of an international organization." "Hot damn," said Pearl. "You and me sure is goin' to be buddies, Sandy."

They were driving down the valley, crossing and recrossing the great loops of the coffeecolored river, through meadows and patches of red plowedland, past barns and white farmhouses with fruittrees in bloom around them. Then they went under the tipple of another mine and came out among the crowded rows of little unpainted shacks set on stilts of a coaltown. The car rattled over the cobbles past a filling-station and a couple of brickfront stores and stopped in front of a frame building with staring black windows. Over the door the word ROOMS barely showed through the grime on a cracked electric globe.

They got out of the car, gave a quick look up and down the street, where the wind was blowing little whirlwinds of black dust, already dried out by the hot spring sun, between rows of weath-erbeaten parked cars. Nobody seemed to be watching them, so they went in the house. Pearl led the way up a back stairway and knocked on a door with a white enamelled number eight on it. Less Minot's voice said, "Come in," and Pearl slipped away saying he'd be back presently.

Less and Irving Silverstone were sitting on the rickety iron bed with a satchelful of papers between them. A tall welldressed redfaced man in a tweed cap was walking up and down the room. "Comrade Crockett, meet Comrade Stong, he's getting the story for the party press. Also he makes the report," said Irving in a cold voice without getting to his feet.

Irving was stouter than when Glenn had last seen him. He still wore his hair cropped close and his goldrimmed tortoiseshell spectacles. There was more authority in his manner and he had a way of lifting his forefinger when he spoke.

"Well, soupkitchen number one is started," said Glenn, squeezing in beside Less on the bed. "And there won't be a load o' coal goin' out of the county by the end of the week," added Less, pushing his thick grizzled hair, that grew low in a thick cowlick on his forehead, back with a stubby hand.

"I'm staying here," Irving said. "Stong's going back tomorrow. Now the first thing I want to bring up is this O.B.U. local. These workers they killed belonged to their bunch."

"Well, they're from Sladetown. The Sladetown local seems to be joiners," drawled Less. "They're an old Mineworkers' outfit. Then they took out an O.B.U. charter and now they've asked us for a charter too. . . . Those boys want action."

"Politically immature."

"I guess so . . . I been talkin' to 'em about mass pressure and all that all mornin'," said Less, "but they're all so mad they can't see straight."

"We've got to put on a meeting to show them what mass-pressure looks like," said Glenn.

Irving got to his feet suddenly and walked up and down with pursed lips. "Here we have a chance to organize a group of absolutely untouched militant American workers. It's the start of a series of real revolutionary industrial unions. These miners drink the class struggle with their mother's milk." Irving threw his head back and looked from one face to another.

"That's about all the kids get these days," said Less, looking at his feet. "They are great boys, but it takes a treasury to win a strike. . . . What will the party do to back us up?"

"We organize the whole Appalachian coalfield into one great union. Why not?" Irving let his voice ring out.

"You tell us," said Less sullenly, sitting with his broad shoulders hunched over his chest and his short legs apart. "The O.B.U. boys are militant as hell."

"As district organizer," said Irving, in precise tones, "it's up to you to bring them in."

"Well," said Glenn soothingly, "is it all set about the meeting at Bull Creek Sunday?"

"Suppose they shoot it up?" asked Less.

"We rouse the liberal elements all over the country." Irving lifted his finger to the level of his glasses as he spoke.

"Sure," drawled Glenn. "Free Speech, Freedom of Assembly, the U. S.

Constitution suspended in Slade County . . . We ought even get a decent play in the capitalist press."

"The O.B.U. confuses all the issues. . . . Outworn opportunism." Irving began to pace up and down the narrow room.

"As a national organization they don't amount to a hill of beans," said Less. "But the boys are all right."

There was a knock on the door. Irving walked over to the window with his hands in his pockets. "Who is it?" growled Less. "Hit's me," came Pearl Napier's voice. Glenn opened the door.

"Well, comrades," said Pearl as he stepped into the room. "Cornorer's jury asettin' on those two boys found person or persons unknown. . . . They found they was atrespassin' on company property and didn't make no recommendations to the grand jury."

"Gosh, they didn't lose any time about it, did they?"

"Coal Operators' Association don't lose no time."

"Well, we were just talkin' about the big protest meetin' we're goin' to have up to Bull Crik Sunday, they can't stop that without infringin' our constitutional rights," said Less.

"They can't stop us from buryin' our brothers," said Pearl.

"That's it," said Irving, coming back suddenly from the window. "A mass funeral for the two classwar victims."

"Look, brothers," said Pearl, drawing Less and Glenn over to the window that looked out on a roundhouse and the rows and rows of tracks of the trainyard. "See them coal cars. They's empty. If they was aworkin' up the valley, they'd be acomin' down full. . . . Them empty gondolas says more'n the best kind o' speakin'."

Next Sunday turned out to be a sunny spring day. Glenn was so busy fixing in his mind what he was going to say to the miners when his turn came to speak that he hardly knew what was going on all morning. Birds were singing in the red swampmaples back of the Bull Creek Missionary Baptist Church. The Reverend McDonnell, a tall man with sunken eyes under thick black brows, who'd been a miner himself when he was younger, read the service over the two pine coffins in the church. Meanwhile miners kept coming; men and boys in carefully brushed clothes and clean shirts frayed by much scrubbing, and their wives and little girls in starched threadbare cotton dresses, piling out of old crowded Fords and Chevvies or walking in long silent straggles up the road or down the footpath that curved over the brow of the hill past the minetipple. The crowd got so big Less decided they'd have to conduct the speakin' outside the church; so Pearl and the boys from the Muddy Fork local, all in their best clothes and wearing red armbands, started to build a speakers' stand on four flourbarrels. Meanwhile people kept coming until the whole grassy space between the ranked parked cars and the little pointed white church, that the paint had almost worn off of, was mottled black and white with a tense closepacked quiet crowd.

Pearl's boys with the armbands kept a lane open to the church porch that had a little crooked steeple over it where swallows had built their nests. All through the services the swallows kept up a great twittering, flying in and out. After the services the boys carried the coffins up into the graveyard that was in a grove of great dead silverybranched trees that had once been chestnuts. The thin voices singing "Nearer, my God, to Thee" as they lowered the coffins into the graves had hardly died away when the first speaker started exhorting from the stand in front of the church. It was old Napier who got up to say he'd been a voter in this county for fiftyseven years and a Republican, but he felt he had to say that these terrible things that was happening in this county and no one putting out a hand to help the poor people of these mountains from the terror of the gunthugs had made a Democrat out of him.

Then a tall man who stamped back and forth so hard he almost brought down the flimsy platform, gave a hellroaring talk, making his points by thumping his right fist into his left hand, saying he'd been a miner thirtythree years and things had gotten worse instead of better, and now with these here hellhound criminal syndicalist laws a man didn't even have no right to complain of his condition. If things went on the time would come when a man would have to go out with a gun to rob and murder and steal to keep his children from starving. And, if they wanted to know, he loved the flag of the United States of America and he loved our government, if it was handled right, but he loved his children ten thousand times better than he loved the President of the

United States or the High Sheriff of Slade County. The coal operators
said that was being a Roosian red; maybe they was right but to his way
of thinking a man who wouldn't stand by his children was worse than
an infidel.

Pearl, who was chairman, sang out he couldn't imagine why it was
they called us poor miners reds and rednecks unless it was because we
was so thin living on pinto beans and bulldawg gravy that if you set one
of us up against the sun you could see daylight right through him. And
as for him and his folks, pappy, grandpap and greatgrandpap, they'd
been in these mountains so long, longer than these here coaloperators
who was foreigners nobody knowed where they'd come from, that if
you went fur enough back you'd mebbe find some Cherokee injun
blood, and that was red all right. Then he called on Glenn. "Comrade
Sandy Crockett who risked his skin to come up outa Pennsylvania into
these mountains and help organize us poor sinners before we starve to
death aworkin' for coallight and carbide."

Glenn climbed up on the stand and looked around at the closepacked lean gray faces eagerly strained to listen that filled the space in
front of the church. At the edge of the crowd he noticed a shiny new
touring car with the top down full of prosperouslooking men in felt
hats. Beside it stood a thin man in black with a notebook and pencil taking everything down. Out of the corner of his eye he noticed
other burly figures with bulging hips skulking about the outskirts of
the crowd. He felt a funny taste like iron in his mouth. He took a deep
breath and began to talk.

The one way the working people of this country, he said, could
make it so that their friends and brothers who'd been shot down for
standing up for their rights as citizens hadn't died in vain was to organize solidly, he didn't mean only coal miners but all the workers. . . .
He was talking slowly. He could feel the people listening; his voice
seemed to fill the quiet sunny afternoon, the little graywhite weathered church and the graveyard with the gaunt branches of the dead
trees spreading over it, and to surge over the patch of scraggly woods
and beat against the black tipple of the Bull Creek mine and the ruddy
mountains patched with sprouting green beyond. His words soared
easily and hovered in the sunlight and the quiet over the big listening

crowd. His body felt easily balanced on the balls of his feet so that he could hardly feel the shaky boards of the speakers' stand. They were listening to every word. When he paused there was a roar of cheering and clapping. He was through.

Less grabbed him by the arm as he climbed down from the stand and hauled him round the corner of the church. "Sandy, you and Pearl git. . . . Carry as many of the Muddy Fork boys as you kin with you. . . . There's two carloads of deputies down the road. We got to handle this right or we'll have a fight. The reason you boys got to go is the C. C. Johnson Company up to Muddy Fork is ready to sign up with the union. You got to be there to see they don't put nuthin' over on the boys."

"But I don't like to pull out now."

"Ain't no two ways about it." Less climbed on the platform and took over the chair from Pearl and introduced the Reverend James Breckenridge, an Episcopal bishop interested in social conditions and the criminal syndicalism laws. The bishop was a grayhaired man in knickerbockers and golfstockings who started to speak in a smooth easy voice. To hear him carried Glenn back to chapel at college; no, nothing could happen while the bishop was there.

Pearl was puzzled but he said he reckoned old Less knowed what was what. They got together four boys from the local and his sister Wheatly, who looked very pretty in a green wash dress with her reddish brown hair combed back from her forehead and neatly plaited in a pigtail down her back. As they got into the car the boys took off their armbands and tucked them under the seats.

Down the road in front of the mine they passed three carloads of deputies who stared hard in their faces. No guns were showing. The deputies stared and the miners stared back without a word. After they had gotten past them Pearl said he'd regret it till his dying day if it came to a shooting and here he'd run off home.

Glenn said he'd guarantee old Less could handle the situation, he had the coolest head in a pinch of any man he'd ever known, and the most important thing now was for the Muddy Fork local to sign that contract and get to work. That would make it hard for the Operators' Association to keep the small mines in line. That would be the first victory of the American Miners in these mountains. "Anyways," said Pearl, smiling, "you all kin spend the night at my house an' Wheatly too. Hit'll be too late for her to go on up to Pappy's."

Halfway up the valley they got a flat and had to pile out on the side of the road to fix the puncture in the inner tube with one of the patches Pearl carried in a little tin box in his back pocket, so it was dark before they got to Muddy Creek village, which was a square of company houses down in the gulch just below old Napier's cabin where Glenn had slept the first night after coming over the gap. They crossed the swollen creek, full of fast brown water from melting snow over the mountains, on a narrow swinging footbridge. In the moist air of the deep gulch the coalsmoke of the fires hung low about the little ramshackle cabins set on stilts.

Pearl's was the first cabin they came to. Glenn noticed as they stepped on the porch that the creaky floor had been repaired with fresh lumber. Two skinny towheaded kids, with puffed bellies sticking out from under their grimy little shirts, ran to meet them in the doorway, and Pearl picked up one in each arm and carried them into the house with him. Glenn and Wheatly and two of the boys who had driven back with them followed him in.

"Jessie," Pearl said to his wife, a tall skinny girl with pouches under her blue eyes, who came to meet them wiping her hands on her apron that bulged ahead of her very big with child, "this here's Brother Crockett, or Comrade Crockett like we say now. Sence the way he's acted and the way he talked at Bull Crik this afternoon, he's a big man in these mountains."

"Was there any shootin'?" asked the girl in a flat whining voice. The men all shook their heads. The girl turned back to stirring something in a saucepan on the edge of the little grate. "I can't seem to git these beans soft," she said peevishly. "Well, let's eat," said Pearl. "I'm hongry."

The two men who had come in with them said good night and went out. Jessie brought out three tin plates and two bent spoons and a fork and Glenn and Pearl and Wheatly sat on a rough bench in front of the fire eating the beans. Pearl and Wheatly had pulled their shoes off, and as they ate were toasting their feet, grimed with coaldust where they were chapped round the ankles, at the fire. Meanwhile Jessie shuffled around the cabin trying to get the children to bed.

Glenn asked her if she'd eaten. She said yes, she'd eat bakersbread and 'vaporated milk with the children, Miss Sparling had brung it around, she sure was a nice lady, she'd brung some to every house and said she was going to organize the women in a ladies' auxiliary to the union, and she thought it was wonderful getting the women together, because they suffered more'n the men did from conditions in these coalcamps, seeing their children blue with cold and without no shoes to go to school in. Wheatly looked up with a black flash of her eyes and said women and children had been a drag on men sence time began, by God she wisht she was a man. "Wait till you git gone on one of these boys around here," said Jessie. "You'll be right glad you're a girl." "Suppose I am. Don't do me no good," said Wheatly, her face turning red in the firelight. "My, you look pretty when you blush like that," said Glenn. Wheatly started to giggle and ran out the door.

Pearl set down his plate and took a dipper of water from the bucket and said well, the first thing he was going to do when they'd signed that contract with Mr. Johnson and was getting some money payday was buy him a shotgun so's he could go hunting. They'd fared right well, hadn't they, Jessie, when he'd had his gun and been able to buy shells and bring home a rabbit or a fat 'possum sometimes. Even if he could clear a dollar a day it would be something, he knowed conditions was bad all over the country and operators warn't making no prices for their coal, but now that they had the union, they'd see they had to let the miners live. Next thing he'd like to get him some kind of little old car, that old flivver belonged to Joe Kusick who let him run it on account of the union, poor ole Joe, he just had to be interested in the union because the miners owed him so much on their store accounts that they just had to have wages to pay him back. "I been a workin' man all my life. I git to feel ornery jus' hangin' around."

"Hain't it work organizin' the union?" asked Wheatly, sticking her head in the cabin door.

"Not like cuttin' coal."

"Hit's a blame sight more risky," said Wheatly.

"How old were you when you first went to work in a mine, Pearl?" Glenn asked.

"Nine years old."

"How old are you now?"

"I'm acomin' on twentyone, ain't I, Jessie?"

"That's what they tell me," said Jessie. "Pearl's a year and two months older'n me."

"And you got two kids?"

"An' one acomin'," said Pearl.

"Gosh," said Glenn. "I'm twentyeight and I'm not even married yet." "You better git busy," said Pearl, laughing. "Up in these mountains we don't have nothin' to do but work and git chillun. Do we, Jessie?" Pearl stretched out his arm to grab Jessie around the waist but she slipped away from him and went into the end of the cabin where the whimpering of the children in the bed had risen to a choking yell.

Pearl stood up in front of the fire and stretched himself and yawned. "Sandy, if you and Wheatly was married, we could let you an' her have the other bed, but thisaway she got to sleep with Jessie an' the chillun. I guess me an' you won't fight if we sleep in the narrow bed. Hit's got clean cornshucks in the tickin'. I fixed it myself for Jessie when she was sick."

Glenn stepped outside. Except for the swashing clatter of the creek the valley was dark and quiet. A little piece of moon was shining over the rim of the steep hill opposite through the stiff bare branches of a thicket of sapling oaks. Glenn found he was shivering.

Pearl was already in bed, lying against the wall. The cornshucks rustled when Glenn sat down on the edge to take off his shoes. "We ain't got much cover but we'll keep each other warm, Sandy," Pearl whispered. "If we sign that contract, tomorrer's goin' to be the happiest day the boys in this coalfield has seen for many's the year. I'm askeered somethin's agoin' to happen. Hit's so long sence things come our way."

"Nothing's going to happen. I bet you inside of a week all the independent companies'll sign up."

"That's what I'm aprayin' for." Glenn suddenly felt warm and secure lying next to Pearl on the narrow mattress that rustled whenever either one of them moved. He fell asleep.

A flashlight shining in his face woke him. Something hard stuck in his ribs. "Put up your hands, the both of you," a voice shouted. Tottering and dazed Glenn and Pearl got to their feet. The cabin was full of men in heavy boots. In the circle of light from another flashlight Glenn caught a glimpse of Wheatly running forward with her hair over her face and Jessie sitting on the edge of the bed trying to hush the children's crying. Glenn and Pearl stood up with their arms over their heads while big hands ran expertly up their sides and felt all their pockets. Meanwhile a man stood in front of each of them poking them in the stomach with an automatic. The other flashlight was travelling over all the corners of the cabin. "What's the trouble, Mr. Blaine?" asked Pearl coolly.

A large man was leaning over the fire warming his hands. Glenn caught sight of his bigjowled blank face in the yellow light of the coal as he turned. "We got a warrant for criminal syndicalism for you boys an' it looks now like we'd slap on murder an' conspiracy to murder."

"Hain't nobody been murdered around here."

"It's too bad to disturb a pretty li'l alibi." The sheriff drawled in his rumbling voice, "But there was two deputies killed in the gunfight after the Bull Crik speakin'."

"We ain't been in no gunfight."

"Sure, I know, jus' sat around the patch all day and went to bed early and the womenfolks'll swear 'emselves blue in the face hit's the gospel."

"Caleb Blaine," shrieked Wheatly, running out into the circle of firelight, "I never told a lie in my life."

"All right, boys, put your shoes on an' come along," said the sheriff. "You'd oughta thank me for takin' you to jail. If those there company-guards from Bull Crik git aholt of you I swear they'll tear you to pieces. Hit's my duty to the people of this county to see that everythin's done legal and orderly and so help me God . . ."

"Don't say it," cried Wheatly. "We don't want no falseswearer struck by lightnin' in our house."

While Glenn got his clothes on, the deputies were ripping open the two mattresses and turning out the drawers of the dresser. He was handcuffed and led across the swinging bridge over the creek and set in the back of a car between two deputies who kept their pistols poked into his stomach. He heard them putting Pearl in the other car and the sheriff calling back to the men still in the house to be sure to bring along anything that had writing on it. Just before the car drove off a face was pressed into his suddenly. It was Wheatly. She gave him a smacking kiss in the corner of the mouth and was gone. The two deputies laughed. "Don't we get no kiss too?" They yelled back into the darkness as the car drove off.

When they got out on the highway, Glenn asked the younger of them what the devil had happened at Bull Creek. The man in the front seat turned around and said seriously, "Boys, I wouldn't talk to him. Sheriff says how he's a Rooshian red. Hain't our kinder folks."

Down in the rivervalley the heavy mist slowed them up. Glenn's clothes were thin; he couldn't help shivering from the chill. In McCreary the two cars stopped for a while in front of the courthouse while the sheriff and some of the deputies went in. There was a group of men with newlooking sawedoff shotguns on their shoulders standing around under the light at the door of the jail. Two men were opening a packingcase and pulling our black metal objects that Glenn guessed were takendown parts of machineguns.

"How did you like the ride, Sandy?" came Pearl's voice cheerfully from the back of the other car. "Fine," sang out Glenn, trying to keep his teeth from chattering.

While they were waiting they saw miners being herded along out of the darkness and shoved in through the door between the men with shotguns. The deputy who had been in the front seat came back strutting importantly, with a batch of papers in his hand. "Boys," he said, "we're takin' these here down to Bluegrass. Sheriff's got the jail so full o' rednecks they're standin' up edgewise."

The mist was getting gray with dawn as they drove out of McCreary. It was broad daylight when the car stopped in front of a pretty little redbrick courthouse with white columns set in the middle of a little square lined with old brick houses used for feed and fertilizer and agricultural implement stores, and a few dwellings with whitecolumned porches. They were hurried in through a stone passage under the courthouse and taken into a neat bright greenpainted office.

A whitehaired old man with a big gray felt hat on the back of his head was seated behind the desk smoking a cigar. Glenn felt a pair of steelgray eyes looking him up and down. The deputy pointed at Glenn with his thumb. "This here's the furrener," he said and leaned over the desk to spread his papers out in front of the old man, who sat looking down at them peevishly for a while without a word. Only his mouth moved, chewing thoughtfully on the end of his cigar. "I don't want 'em but I guess I got to take 'em. Blaine called me up," he said. "Look here, son," he looked up in Glenn's face, "I don't know who you are. But in my jail every man who acts right gets a square deal. If he don't it goes hard with him. . . . Understand? Turn out your pockets and take off your belt and necktie."

Making out the commitment and fingerprinting him and itemizing his possessions seemed to Glenn to take an endless time. Then he was led up an iron stairway into a small block of cages painted peagreen with a space for exercise in the middle. Sunlight was coming in through dusty windows on the other side of a passage. On the whole the place didn't look as bad as Glenn had expected.

The air was hot from steamheat and dense with the greasy smell of slum cooking somewhere. The fat turnkey, who was wheezing from dragging his lame leg up the steep stairs, showed Glenn into a cell with four iron bunks in it and a gloomylooking toilet seat in back and told him he could walk around in the space between the cells until he got his dinner. He'd get a mattress later.

Glenn took off his coat and laid it on the bunk and sat down on the steel slats. Through the light green bars that looked quite gay where the sunlight struck them, he could see the eyes of the other inmates looking him over. After a while Pearl came in smiling, saying it was right nice they let them bunk together sence they sure was buddies in misfortune now, and sat down beside him and told what one of the deputies had told him about the gunfight.

The guards at Bull Creek had been drinking that afternoon and started driving their car fullspeed up and down the road when the boys was going home from the speaking. They'd run a woman down and somebody had gotten so hellfired mad he'd started shooting, at least that was what the deputy said, and some of our boys had been hurt but nobody knowed how many, and now the county prosecutor claimed that the union boys had made a conspiracy to shoot up the gunthugs and they was agoing to lock up every redneck union agitator in the penitentiary. That was what the deputy said. What about Less, was the first thing Glenn asked. Deputy hadn't knowed nothing about Less.

During the afternoon the little jail began to fill up with miners. Most of the boys who were brought in were from the local at Sladetown. With them came Harve Farrell, who said, hell, he warn't no organizer, One Big Union boys organized themselves, he'd just come on down from Chicago to give the boys a little advice about keeping out of jail, well, he guessed it hadn't taken. Harve was a stocky bullnecked Irishman with a red face and red hair nearly turned white; he said he'd spent eight years in Leavenworth for resisting the draft. The minute the barred door clanged to behind him, he began to pick on Glenn and call him the comical commissar.

That made Pearl sore at first, but after a couple of days Glenn could see that Pearl thought Harve Farrell was all right. From the time they were let out of their cells in the morning until they were locked up again in the afternoon, they were at it hammer and tongs, starting with the row between Marx and Bakunin, through the Knights of Labor and the Western Federation of Miners right down to the Sandhills Convention. The other men played cards and checkers and told stories or passed around the one local newspaper the lame turnkey brought into the cage each day, but Harve and Glenn never seemed to get through arguing. At first Pearl sat listening to them, with his black eyes fixed on one, then the other, but gradually he began to get gloomy. He took to spending most of the time lying flat on his back on his bunk with his hands clasped under his head, and began to say how he wished they'd try him quick and convict him so's he'd be quit of the whole goddam business.

Pearl and Hank Davis, who was the only other miner from the Muddy Fork local in that jail, got to sitting off in a corner by themselves and talking low with their heads together. The days dragged on into a week and still no word had come to any of them from the outside. Harve and Glenn pestered the turnkey half to death telling him they were going to sue him for false arrest. When the warden, always with his cigar and his broadbrimmed hat, made his daily rounds to inspect the cells they all crowded around him asking when they were going to be brought up in court. "Boys, all I can say is that you're better off here than you would be in the penitentiary," was all he'd answer.

Harve and Glenn got to be good friends finally. Harve said Sandy was the only comical he'd ever met who even looked straight, and they shook hands on the proposition that their job was to organize union locals and let the other guys do the wrangling. A raise looked just as good to a miner if it came wrapped in a syndicalist or marxist line of talk. The fancy work came in when you had to choose what kind of piecards to pay your union dues to.

That afternoon the turnkey hobbled up the stairway and called Harve out, said they were taking him back to McCreary for trial. Harve went around and shook hands with the boys and said whatever happened to him the defense committee would be working their heads off to get 'em out of jail, if they were bringing him up for trial that meant he could see a lawyer and get in touch with his outfit. Last thing he went up to Glenn and held out his hand and said he hoped he could get his people to cooperate fiftyfifty on these cases. Glenn shook his hand and said sure, he'd do everything he could.

Next morning Glenn was standing in line with the other guys waiting to get to the faucet to wash up, when somebody called his name. Irving Silverstone was standing in the passage outside the cage with the warden and a tall man with a mane of steelgray hair. Glenn couldn't help running over and grabbing Irv's hand through the bars and pumping it up and down.

Irving was making out not to know him more than anybody else, and waited until Pearl and Hank Davis and the rest of them came over, to make a little speech, introducing the tall man as Colonel Ferris, a prominent attorney from McCreary who was going to take the cases for the Workers' Defense. Then Colonel Ferris said he reckoned you all were pretty sick of being cooped up in there but he was going to get every last one of you boys out if he had to take a habeas corpus clear up to the Soupreme Court of the Younited States.

"It's this way, comrades," said Irving, "we have held a conference of the workers' organizations involved in this strike and we have decided that all the cases should be handled together. This way we can pool all our efforts and get the best legal advice available in this state and make the heroic fight of the miners of Slade County tell as part of the class struggle."

Pearl was frowning. "Say, how about these boys from the Sladetown local? There's only Hank an' me here from the American Miners."

"All they've got to do is sign a paper retaining Colonel Ferris as their counsel. Of course, we'd like to see their local come into the American Miners." The boys from Sladetown were putting their heads together and whispering. "Can't you see, comrades," said Irving, his voice breaking, "that what we want to do is get you boys out of jail as soon as we can."

"We can't do nothin' until we know what the boys at our local wants. Harve Farrell, our secretary, and the Prisoners' Defense up in Chicago is takin' care of us," one of the miners answered.

Irving Silverstone's face looked pale and thin through the bars. He was sweating so he took his glasses off to wipe them. Without his glasses his bulging gray eyes with their slight cast had a vague girlish and innocent look they didn't have behind the flashing goldrimmed spectacles. The thin bridge of his nose had red marks on either side and the blond eyelashes grew out sparsely from redrimmed lids. He began to talk fast, whispering with his mouth close to the bars. "Comrades, I don't like to sling mud at anybody who's not present but we have a definite suspicion, backed by confidential reports from our Pittsburgh office and general headquarters in New York, that this man Farrell may be a provocator."

"A what?" asked Pearl, his black brows knitted in a frown as if he were trying to make out a small object very far away.

"Well . . . a stoolpigeon. We can't say for sure of course but anyway the conference of allied and affiliated workingclass organizations feels that you comrades will be better defended by the American Workers' Defense that is in a position to use mass pressure and to put this struggle in its true light as part of the international movement of the working class."

A blackjowled husky from Sladetown with long arms and big fists pushed his way through to the bars and said if he wasn't in this here birdcage he'd knock the block off any man who said Harve was a stoolpigeon. The other miners started backing away from the bars and went and sat on the bench scowling at their feet.

"Well, I guess it's only Crockett and Napier and Davis at present, but I'm sure you comrades will accept our defense when you see what a good job we've done raising bail." Hank and Pearl were both looking Glenn hard in the eye. "Sandy . . . What do you think?" they asked in unison.

Glenn felt himself turn red. "Well, I think we'd better all stick together with the American Workers' Defense and the American Miners. That don't mean I don't think Harve Farrell isn't a perfectly straight guy . . . I just think he's wrong."

"Boys," said Pearl. "I'm for stickin' together. . . . Us miners we don't want no different lawyer from the Sladetown boys. We better stick with our own folks."

"Name callin' don't git nobody outa jail," went on Hank Davis. "We've had union officials up here in these mountains git all our dues an' then go to Jacksonville an' sell us out to the highest bidder. We had plenty piecards up in these mountains. One thing about that Farrell I know, he come down here an' gits him a job drivin' a coaltruck. He ain't no swivelchair piecard."

"Well, come on, we can't argue all day," said the warden in a cross quaver. "Crockett, you can come along." Pearl and Hank had turned their backs and walked over to join the bunch of miners sitting along the bench. The warden hurried Glenn off so fast that he didn't get a chance to say goodby, and once he got outside in the car with the deputy and Irving and the lawyer he forgot everything in the sweet taste of the spring morning. The trees, that had been just budding the last time he'd seen the valley road, were almost in full leaf. Three bluebirds flew out of a green appletree that he'd remembered in bloom in front of a brokendown barn where the road curved into McCreary.

Irving didn't say anything on the whole drive, but the lawyer who sat beside Glenn with the deputy in the back seat said Sheriff Blaine was releasing most of the miners under their own bond to keep the peace and only holding a few that County Prosecutor Prout was going to charge with murder. He'd had a talk yesterday afternoon with Herb Prout and he felt that old Herb was beginning to take a more reasonable attitude, he was a ver' reasonable feller; for one thing he was going to nollepros the C.S. cases.

"What's he got me charged with?" asked Glenn. "Well, we're goin' to have a li'l conference about that, Mr. Crockett, in Mr. Prout's office, as I say he's willin' to take a ver' reasonable attitude." Irving hadn't said anything. As they were getting out of the car in front of the courthouse in McCreary Glenn noticed that Irving was holding up in front of him a notebook with a corner of white paper sticking out of it. On it was written, *Terms: low bail leave state: we accept.*

Glenn couldn't help feeling his insides turn over wetly with joy; he'd been trying to accustom himself to the idea of a fiveyear sentence in the pen, that was what the boys in jail at Bluegrass had decided they'd get if they came up before Judge Crawford in Sladetown because Judge Crawford's wife and brotherinlaw owned controlling interests in half the mines in the county. All the time the lawyer was talking to County Prosecutor Prout about the details of posting the bailbond, Glenn couldn't pay much attention to what was going on; all he could think of was that it was a fine spring day and he didn't have to go back to jail.

He and Irving and the lawyer had a good lunch of steak and fried potatoes at the Appalachian Hotel with the Coal Operators' Association guards glaring in at them through the door from the lobby. Then they drove over the gap to Slocum in the adjoining state for a meeting of the Slade County Miners' Defense Committee that was held in a room on the tenth story of a big metropolitanlooking hotel.

The first person Glenn saw when he stepped out of the elevator in the hall was Less Minot. They shook hands and slapped each other on the back in high spirits, old Less saying well, Sandy, he sure hadn't expected him out of that jail for twenty years. Glenn asked how come they hadn't picked Less up. Less said he didn't know; all he did was keep on talking and talking on the principles of unionism, dullest talk he'd ever made in his life, he'd gone rambling on and on with the court stenographer taking down every word of it, and all the time the folks were melting away, lighting out for home, getting their wives and kids out of the way; for some reason he had an idea the gunthugs wouldn't try to start anything while the speaking was still going on and it turned out he'd been right; the trouble had all been down the road. He'd talked and talked till there wasn't nobody left but him and the bishop and the Baptist minister, and the bishop had driven him in his own car down to Joe Kusick's and then out to Slocum; they'd driven right past the deputies about ten times, sure, they'd seen him, but they didn't seem to have the heart to pick him right off the seat next to a bishop. "Oughta seen me stickin' to that bishop like I was glued to him."

Still laughing, they knocked on the door of the room where the meeting was. Elmer Weeks himself opened the door for them, smiling at them under his neat mustache. "Comrades, I congratulate you," he said, shaking their hands stiffly with his schoolteacher manner. Then he walked them around the room and introduced them to everybody. The delegates from the liberal organizations made a particular fuss over Glenn because he was the one that was fresh out of jail. That seemed to put old Less' nose out of joint a little. Even Jane Sparling was polite to Glenn; she introduced him to Mark Burgess of the League for Citizen's Rights as one of the nerviest damned organizers we've got.

During the meeting somebody called up Glenn from downstairs. It was Harve Farrell. Harve said he'd just come in on the bus and wanted to come up and put some propositions before the meeting. He'd just had the Sladetown local on the wire; they said the prosecutor had let everybody go except eight miners, and he was holding them for murder, six of 'em were his Sladetown boys and the other two were from Muddy Fork. Glenn couldn't keep the tremble out of his voice when he asked was that Napier and Davis? What was the use of asking; he knew it already.

Glenn put his hand over the receiver and beckoned to Irving Silverstone. Irving went over and whispered to Elmer Weeks and then came tiptoeing back to Glenn and said on no account to let him come up, Comrade Weeks had deputed him and Crockett to talk to him downstairs.

They found Harve walking nervously up and down in the lobby. His short stocky frame looked ready to burst out of his rumpled storesuit that showed a gap of grayish shirt between the vest and pants; his face was gray and he had pockets under his eyes as if he hadn't been sleeping recently. "Got a room? We better go up because the house dick won't take his eyes off me."

"We'll go in the writing room on the mezzanine," said Irving in a cold firm voice. "All right, have it your own way. . . . So they turned you lose, Crockett?" Glenn nodded, grinning as he shook Harve's hand. "What charge did they bring against you?" he asked Harve.

"Bandin' and confederatin', but they turned me loose on a thousand dollars bail like they did you, Crockett . . . I guess they want us to jump it."

"Who put up your bail?" asked Irving, blinking his colorless eyes behind his glasses. "J. P. Morgan, of course," said Harve and laughed, as he settled himself on the stained red upholstered sofa in the little stuffy writingroom that was curtained off from the hall where the elevator doors were. He pulled out a package of Luckies and passed them around. Irving shook his head. Glenn took one. "Conolly did."

Irving's thin lips tightened into a line. Glenn cleared his throat and finally broke the silence. "You mean the old Mineworkers' state president?"

Harve nodded. "Seems a damn good thing to me, though he's a parasite from way back, maybe we've made enough stink so that the Consolidated Mineworkers'll come in and help. . . . That's what I want to talk to you guys about. I want you to go with me and see Conolly and see if we can't all get together on this."

"That social fascist," said Irving, getting to his feet. "If you want to help him sell out the workers you can; that's not what we came down here for."

Harve's face was getting red. His big fists clenched the knees of his shiny pantlegs. "Your outfit came down here to raise a big political stink and git yourselves a new crop of martyrs to raise money for . . . for your own mealtickets." Harve got up with his fists tight and ground his cigarette out under his foot on the green carpet. "Well, you can go f—k yourselves." He hitched up his pants that were too short for him and walked out.

Glenn hadn't said a word. When Harve had gone he said suddenly, "How about going to talk to Conolly . . . he's probably got political influence . . . after all, Burgess is a social fascist too, isn't he, and all the namby pamby liberals, and we're cooperating with them, aren't we? They tell me Conolly and Prout have always been thick. Prout used to be the Consolidated's attorney. We got to get those boys out, Irv . . . particularly Pearl Napier. That boy's got the makings of a real laborleader."

"They're all of them politically undeveloped," said Irving as they were going back up in the elevator.

"I'd rely on Napier anywhere."

"I know," said Irving in a doleful tone. "Real proletarians . . . lovely people . . . but they lack marxist preparation. There's too much of the artist in you, Sandy. You are sentimental."

When they went back into the room where the meeting was going on, Mark Burgess, who was a middleaged blueeyed man with steelgray hair and a broad freshlooking pink and white face and a knowall manner like a country doctor's, came up to Glenn saying, Crockett, the committee had just decided he was taking a speaking tour for them under the auspices of the League for Citizen's Rights to tell the people of this country just to what degree constitutional rights had been suspended in Slade County.

Two weeks later Glenn started his tour; sometimes he had a couple of miners with him in their black caps with little lights on them, or Mary Lou Napier, a cousin of Pearl's who sang mountain songs about the strike, or a liberalminded newspaperman who had a report to make about conditions in the coalfields, or the bishop who had turned up at the speaking at Bull Creek. The first chance he got he wrote Pearl a letter explaining that everything possible was being done to get the boys the best legal talent they could find. After he'd closed the envelope he sat there at the writing desk in the noisy hotel lobby, smelling again the greasy smell of slum and seeing again the greenpainted bars of the little jail at Bluegrass. "Irv's right. I'm too damn sentimental," he said so near aloud that he felt his lips forming the words.

One night after Glenn talked at the Y.M.C.A. in a southern collegetown he was amazed to see Paul Graves in the group of people waiting to speak to him after the lecture. Paul looked older; his skull seemed to have gotten bigger and his eyes to have sunken into it under the dense black brows. Paul grabbed Glenn's hand as he hurried out of the hall. "Paul, it can't be you're beginning to get red," Glenn said in a voice that sounded unnecessarily sarcastic in his own ears.

"I always used to be kinder pink, an outdoor pink, didn't I?"

"Gosh, Paul, I wish I had time to chew the rag . . . I've got to go along to a conference about raising some money for the miners."

"I'll go by your hotel afterwards. I saw your picture in the paper and drove all the way over especially to see you."

"All right, it's the Mountain View, room 21, the dump across from the station."

When Glenn got back to the hotel at midnight deadtired from the speaking and the conferences, there was Paul waiting for him, smoking a pipe in the grimy little lobby with its moosehead over the desk and its old brass spittoons under the tables piled with last week's newspapers.

When they got up to Glenn's airless room, with its gangrenous green wallpaper, Paul pulled a pint of corn out of his back pocket and set it on the nighttable and let himself sink down on the brass bed that jingled with his weight. "First thing, Glenn, I want to ask you about this alias . . . I think what you're doing's great, but why can't you do it under your own name?"

"Plenty of reasons, Paul, lots of the time we're underground, particularly in the South."

Paul poured himself a drink in the only glass. Glenn had refused one, saying that his kind of work and drinking didn't mix. "Don't you kind of forget who you are, who your folks were, all that sort of stuff?"

Glenn felt his face getting red. "I believe in it, the lack of a name . . . our folks are the workingclass . . . can't you see?"

"Well, Glenn, I'd rather you'd kept your identity, after all you were quite a friend of mine . . . and don't forget that the cells that make up your carcass contain the same chromosomes whether you go under one name or another."

"Paul, I gotto go to bed, I pull outa here on a bus at six-thirty."

"I just wanted to know if you ever went to the Soviet Union."

"Not yet."

"Well, I'm going this fall taking Peggy and the kids, we got four now, you oughta see 'em. I've got a job running one of their new agricultural experiment stations for a year. I thought it would be a chance to make a little dough and to check up on how the great experiment's going."

"You lucky bastard," said Glenn. "Meanwhile I'll be going back to get my block knocked off in the Slade County minefields."

After Paul had gone Glenn noticed he'd left the pint of corn. First Glenn thought of putting it in the wastebasket but then he decided he'd better take it with him. This was the kind of thing they framed radicals on. Why the hell had Paul brought it? He went to bed feeling vaguely sore at Paul, though he'd been glad to see him; here he had a nice wife and four nice children and was getting a rep as an agricultural expert and was going to make big money going to the Soviet Union, and Glenn didn't have anything in the world, no wife, no children, he'd even thrown his name overboard. He went to sleep feeling cosily sorry for himself; as sorry for himself as he remembered feeling sometimes as a small boy.

He still had Paul's pint of corn with him the night he met Less in Slocum to go back over the gap to see if they couldn't straighten things out among the locals. Less was full of bad news and even gloomier than usual. About half the locals had gone back to the old Consolidated Mineworkers after the boys at Bluegrass had been convicted for the Bull Creek shooting and sentenced to twenty years. The lawyers were up at the state capital arguing an appeal right now.

Old Less sure was glad to get the corn after the comrades who'd driven them over to the gap had left them halfway up the mountainside. They'd decided to walk over by the old trail for fear the operators might have guards posted on the road. "This time," Less kept saying, "they'll pump us full of lead and ask no questions."

"But they won't dare do anything to us in Colonel Ferris' office at the state capital," said Glenn. Less drank down the corn in about two gulps. "We won't git to no state capital. We got to go around to see the locals first to tell 'em what's what, see? Well, you can't tell me they ain't got some stools in some of them locals."

"Well, it's too late to back out now," said Glenn, beginning to get sore.

"That's what I'm tryin' to tell you, Sandy," said Less in a hoarse voice, and pitched the bottle away from him down the mountainside. They both stopped still and listened for its crash on the rocks below. The hillside was absolutely silent and already bluedark, although the sky overhead was still rosy with long streamers of afterglow from the sunset the other side of the range. "Well, we'd better hurry if we're going to make it by dark," said Less in an even kind of tone. They both picked up their grips heavy from being jammed full of copies of party newspapers that told about the campaign for the boys in jail, and started toiling up the steep rocky trail again.

It was pitch black by the time they reached the gap. They found the highway and walked cautiously down it, stopping every now and then to listen. Once they heard a car coming up and hid flat on their faces in the deep shadow of a culvert until it drove past them. At last they found the wagonroad through the woods that led to old man Napier's cabin, just in time because the moon that was almost full had risen back of the range and all the contours of the mountains began to show up dripping with milky light.

Down below in the valley they began to see the scattering pinpoints of the lights of Muddy Fork, and the strings and tangled rectangles of lights halfhidden in smoke, of Sladetown. They caught a little rough taste of coalsmoke in the air from the cabins down in the gulch.

Less got across the creek all right over the slippery stepping stones but Glenn's foot slipped and he went splashing in, both legs up to his knees in the cold water. The water squudged in his shoes as he walked across the grassy ridges of the old cornfield. When they came up to the cabin they first thought it was empty because no light was showing from the window, but around in front they saw a chink of light from the door and knocked. "Who's that?" came a girl's voice. "I bet that's Wheatly," said Glenn. The door opened a crack at a time.

Wheatly looked more filled out than when Glenn had last seen her. She let him and Less in and closed the door and barred it behind them. For a moment it looked as if she were alone in the cabin. Then a pair of feet in heavy black boots shot down from the rafters above and Joe Kusick was standing in front of them sheepishly wiping the cobwebs off his arms. Meanwhile two of the boys from Muddy Fork were crawling out from under the bed where Wheatly's mother and the little children were fretfully asleep.

They stood around in front of the fire looking at each other and laughing a little in their throats. "Looks like there might be some trouble around here, boys," said Less.

"Trouble," said Joe Kusick. "Juss wait. They blowed up the soup-kitchen last night . . . Caleb Blaine and Judge Crawford, they say they're out to run every redneck out of this end of the county and it looks like they could do it. He's so afraid of that appeal that he wants to scare any of the miners outa testifyin.'" Joe stopped and took a long breath and then he grabbed one of their hands in each of his and shook it. "Well, boys, I'm glad you come. They's been a lot of old time walkin' delegates in here of the old sellout variety tellin' the miners if they'll give up this here comyounist business and go back to the old Consolidated Mineworkers everything'll be hunky dory. They all said you two had yellered out on us."

"Jesus Christ, what do you think we been doin', takin' the cure at Atlantic City? We been shouting our lungs out raisin' money for you bastards," said Less. Wheatly had been looking hard, first in his face, then in Glenn's. She gave her head a toss. "I seen plenty preachers shout and ain't brung no rain . . . I hain't seen Pearl and Hank gettin' outa jail yet."

"Honest, Wheatly," said Glenn, his voice breaking, "we're doing everything we can. We hope we can get 'em out on this appeal, or at least get new trials."

Wheatly started to laugh. She put her hands on her hips and laughed till her face was red. "Fell in the crik, did yer? Well, you'd better take them pants off and let me dry 'em." "Look out there, Sandy," said Less, giving Glenn a poke in the ribs with his elbow. "When a pretty young girl starts takin' a man's pants off first thing . . ." "You shet your dirty ole mouth before I shet it for ye," said Wheatly, still laughing. "Hain't nothin' new to me in how God made a man."

While Glenn was blushingly taking off his wet clothes, Joe and Less were deciding what to do. They'd have to move quick, Joe would drive Less down to Sladetown so that he could talk to the boys before they went home after the shift changed, then Joe'd drive him right on through to Bluegrass and he'd be out of the county before them gun-thugs was outa bed at the Appalachian Hotel. Then Glenn would be checking on the Muddy Fork and Bull Creek locals and walk over and stay in Joe Kusick's store till the next night when Joe would drive him straight out to the state capital. When Joe gave Glenn the key to the store he had to put it in the pocket of his jacket because he didn't have any pants on to put it in; Wheatly, with her brow furrowed like a little girl doing a difficult piece of schoolwork, was carefully toasting them over the flaring coalgrate.

"Say, Joe, I always meant to ask you," Less was saying in a casual kind of voice. "How come Sheriff Blaine don't never pick on you none?"

Glenn found that both he and Less were staring hard in Joe Kusick's lined lobsided face. For a second everybody in the cabin was so still they could hear the roar of the draft in the chimney. Joe pointed with a thumb to a masonic emblem he wore in the lapel of his old O.D. coat and said in an easy voice, "Caleb Blaine's been beholden to me for a lot of things. He's a yellow dawg but he ain't so crooked as some. . . . If I could'a' sworn on their alibi I know Pearl and Hank would be free men this day."

"Why didn't you, ye little old man?" Wheatly strode out from the fireplace waving Glenn's steaming pants under Joe's nose.

"I was down to McCreary all day . . . the old lady wouldn't let me go to the speakin' . . . I never saw either one of them from sunup to sundown. Yesterday I carried the old lady down to stay with her sister in Bluegrass. There's nothin' those coal operators won't do now. This strike's beginnin' to pinch 'em where it does the most good."

"Sure," said Less, "that's why we just had to come in and talk to you boys. If we can hold the union together for another two months they'll be eatin' out our hands; if we don't, the miners in this county'll be down on their knees before the operators every time they want a drink of water. You know that. . . . Price o' coal's goin' up. That's what you want to tell the boys. . . . Well, so long, Sandy, have you got the program straight? We'll go along. You better follow along as soon as the lady lets you have your trousers." All their hands shook Glenn's and the door closed behind them.

Glenn and Wheatly stood looking at each other in the flicker of the firelight. From the bed at the end there came heavy snoring and the intermittent sickly whimper of a sleeping child. For a corner of a second Glenn remembered another fire, and Gladys, as if it had been in a different world; then he was thinking of the first time he'd seen Wheatly in that cabin last spring. Wheatly hung his pants over a stool and went to the cabin door and went out. Glenn followed her.

Outside the high moon was brimming the valley with light and shimmered over the flat mist that covered the coaltowns below like over the surface of a lake. The girl was facing him standing right up against him so that her firm breasts touched him. When he grabbed her to him and kissed her upturned mouth she began to sob. The jagged door of the old brokendown cowshed cut off the moonlight with blackness. A pile of dry cornstalks crackled and rasped crazily under them.

He was lying beside her stroking the warm curve of her shoulder that had broken out through her torn dress when suddenly she jumped on him, with her thin knees on his chest, and started to choke him. Her long hands were very strong. He had to use all his strength to tear them away from his throat. "What the . . .?" He went into a fit of coughing.

"I'm achokin' you so you won't forgit me or brother Pearl rottin' in that penitentiary. You go git him out, do you hear, if you don't I'll take an axe an' split your skull right in half an' spill your brains out on the highroad an' tromp on 'em. . . . No boy kin ever go around asayin' he had my ass for nothin'." She started to pummel him blindly with her fists.

He broke away from her and ran panting back to the cabin to put on his trousers and shoes and stockings. Then he took the bundle of papers out of his suitcase. She came in and grabbed him by the arm just as he was leaving. "Hain't you goin' to sleep none? Hain't no call to be down there before day." Glenn shook his head. "I might forget what I came for. . . . Keep the bag and stuff for me, will you, Wheatly?"

His head was spinning as he walked slowly down the rocky path into the valley with the bundle of newspapers on his shoulder. As he walked down the trail the sound of the creek below got louder. He went through streaks of cool and warm air, here and there tinged with the sulphury reek of coalsmoke. In one place there was a strong smell of honeysuckle.

He stepped out on the valley road, white and empty in the moonlight, and walked up it to the footbridge that crossed to the Muddy Fork patch. Opposite the bridge he halfcaught-sight of the glint of metal of a car parked under some trees. Anyway he couldn't go back. He had to get across. As he stepped on the swinging bridge a voice behind him said in a low conversational tone, "Put 'em up, Buddy, let's see who you are."

Glenn dropped his bundle and stood staring into a flashlight. The lights of a car went on full behind him at the same moment. There was nothing to do but stand there dazed.

"Boys," shouted a voice, "we got one of them visitin' reds and he's got enough litrachur to set red Rooshia on fire." Glenn's arms were pulled behind his back and handcuffed and he was shoved into the back seat of the car. They didn't take him far, but it must have been to the Bull Creek mine, as he saw the tall shadow of a tipple cut into the moonlight overhead as he was hustled into a building. Down the passage was a little room that had a cot and a barred window. They took the handcuffs off him and slammed the door to. There was nothing left to do but try to get some sleep.

When he woke up he was sitting up on the cot. Daylight was filtering grayly through the bars. Less Minot was standing over him scratching his grayblack head with his stubby hand. "Well, Sandy, I have to hand it to you, there you go sleepin' like a baby and these gorillas is plannin' to kill the two of us dead." "How do you know?" "I know," Less said in a tired voice and sat down on the bed with his head in his hands.

After an hour or two they began to want to go to the toilet and knocked on the door until a guard came with a big automatic in his hand. As he walked Glenn down the hall to the stinking watercloset Glenn asked him what they were going to do with them. The guard said he could tell them one thing, they was going to be quit of troublemakers round here from now on, they was a pair of thoroughbred reds he could see that and they was going to be quit of them. A little later the same guard brought them in a couple of tin cups of coffee and some stale hamsandwiches wrapped in oiled paper.

That night just when the barred window had gone black, four men with shiny sawedoffshotguns and big pistolholsters came stamping in and told them to get a move on. Glenn could smell whiskey on their breaths. He noticed that they talked loud and wouldn't look him in the eye. He was piled into the back of a car between two of them and they were off at sixty miles an hour.

Instead of going into McCreary they turned off on the road up to the gap. Nobody spoke. Glenn could feel the car laboring on the grade. Now and then the four tall men in the car passed a flask around. As the car zigzagged up the incline to the gap, Glenn could feel the pounding of his heart grow louder and louder until he was scared the gunthugs could hear it. He managed to keep his lips very still, just meeting in front of his clenched teeth.

Overhead was pitchblack under an even blanket of clouds; for some reason Glenn kept wishing the moon would rise. The car rounded the last curve and drew up with a shriek of brakes in the loose gravel of a parkingplace on the highest point of the gap. The men on either side of Glenn started poking him in the ribs with their guns. Their voices were thick. "Redneck, unload."

As Glenn stepped out on the gravel another car drove up facing them and in the place where the headlights crossed he could see a big man sparring at Less who'd just been pushed out from the car. "Any you rednecks want to fight?" the man was yelling as he shadowboxed around in a circle.

Less was about half his size. He put up his fists and stood waiting for him. Glenn saw another guy creep up from behind and land an uppercut on the side of Less' jaw that almost bowled him over, but he managed to keep his feet, spinning around, protecting his head with his short arms.

Just then something hard came down on the back of Glenn's skull and felled him to the ground. He came to with lights flashing around him and heavy boots kicking him. Somehow he managed to wriggle out of the circle of light just as a big stone grazed his shoulder. He felt the rocks at the edge of the parking place and dragged himself over the edge. There was a red flash from a gun and a bullet zinged overhead.

He'd let go and was rolling down the mountainside in a whirl of loose stone and dirt. "Now I'm done for," he had time to think. He had caught in a clump of bushes. It wasn't hard to lie still; he was almost out. Overhead he heard yells and curses and shots.

Everything was silvery around him. He was drenched and shaking with cold. When he moved he had a knifelike pain in his ribs. One side of his face throbbed. He managed to get up in a sitting position in the clump of bushes. He spat out a mouthful of blood. The whole hillside was full of bright moonlight; through the forested valley below a stream curved in loops of silver wire. From the bushes he crawled along a ledge out over a turn in the road. It seemed to take him hours to let himself down little by little to the parapet of the road below. He sat there with his head and his whole body throbbing with pain. When his strength seemed to come back a little he got to his feet and called out, "Hey, Less, where are you?" a couple of times, but his voice didn't carry. Didn't seem much use. Then he started limping down the road in the early dawn still silvery from the setting moon.

2

For a week Glenn had been flat on his back with his ribs strapped up and his jaw in plaster of Paris and his head swathed in itchy gauze. Through the daze of an aching stiff sickness he remembered stabbing pain and brilliant morning sunlight and two colored men picking him up and putting him in a truck and the agony of the joggling on his broken ribs. They had brought him in and laid him in the carbolic-creeking entry of the hospital, and some nurses and a doctor in a white coat had come out and made a big row and said they wouldn't take him. He must have passed out again because he next remembered ether and the sharp pain when they were setting his jaw, and Jane Sparling being there and quarreling with the orderly who wouldn't let her smoke in the ward. She'd gone off leaving Glenn some Workers' Defenders to read, saying that she was late, and had a hundred miles to drive in two hours, to meet a delegation of liberal writers on its way in from Slocum to try to distribute food, because the striking miners were in bad shape now that the second soupkitchen had been blown up; she sure hoped Sheriff Blaine would beat up a couple of the prominent stuffedshirts on their committee because dollars to doughnuts that would get them a senatorial investigation.

The hospital people wouldn't let her leave before she'd paid the hospital bill; he remembered hearing her and the matron rowing about the anaesthetist's charge. The ward was seedy and smelt bad; nobody paid any attention to the patients, and a gaunt man in the cot at the end kept Glenn awake all night retching and coughing. Then one morning when the nurse came up to tidy his bed he noticed something different in her manner. She said a lady who was a relative of his was coming in to see him, a Mrs. Gulick, and he must comb his hair. For a minute he couldn't think who it was. It was Marice.

Marice came sailing into the ward with her bracelets jangling, wearing a mink coat and a red hat shaped like the prow of an old-fashioned battleship, spreading a mist of sandalwood perfume, and saying that Glenn was a hero and she'd just found out who he was, and she never imagined he had it in him, and she was going to get him out of this filthy hole before he could say Jack Robinson and he wasn't safe from arrest here anyway. She was as good as her word; by afternoon she had him in a drawingroom on the train to New York.

As the train rumbled through the night she sat up beside him, holding on to a jar of roses that kept falling off the little table of the drawingroom onto the floor, telling him how she and Mike had separated, they were still good friends but they couldn't help nagging each other and had decided it was better for the children if they lived their own lives separately. She thought the horrid old capitalist system was on its last legs and she had been so interested in the Slade County miners and when Mike called her up and told her that Sandy Crockett, the heroic leader of the miners, was their old star boarder from Ohio who'd always seemed so quiet and mousy and inhibited, she declared she hadn't been able to believe her ears. She decided one thing she could do to help was to give him the best medical and legal care. The minute she'd laid eyes on him in that hospital she had decided not to leave him there another day but to take him up to New York where she'd put him in the hands of the best specialists Dr. Blumenthal could recommend. The next morning she took him right from the train to the hospital in an ambulance. It made him feel like an ass to have so many doctors and nurses fussing over him. But he was in so much pain he didn't care what happened.

When he was able to walk around, and the knitting bones gave him a stiff ache instead of sharp agony, Marice made him move to her house, saying that she was alone there with the children and it would be good for them to see what a real labor leader looked like, and that she had every intention of spoiling him, because he was still shaky from the concussion, and it was much better for her to spoil him than to spoil the children, and maybe give them complexes.

It was a funny feeling for Glenn, after the rough life he'd been leading, to sleep between fine linen sheets and on boxsprings, and to have a bath of his own with plenty of hot water and soap that smelt of almonds and big thick monogrammed towels, and to feel the rumble of the city coming in to him through the heavy silk draperies of the old brownstone house, and to have his meals brought to him by a colored maid and to have Marice barging into his room at all hours with her silk negligee with blue and red poppies on it floating out behind her. Sleeping with Marice, once he'd gotten rid of his casts and felt like a human being again, seemed so much part of the picture, he hardly knew when it started up. She told him he was a very satisfactory lover.

What did embarrass him was to have Marice tell the twins, who were towheaded nineyearold boys by this time, that their Uncle Sandy was mother's lover; but she said she believed in the most absolute frankness about those things, especially with children. She invited Mike, who was still teaching at Columbia, to come over and have dinner with them, and Glenn certainly felt a fool shaking hands with old Mike, although he was darn glad to see him at that. Marice didn't let them stick for very long to general conversation. She had made very strong cocktails that went to her head, and she started to tease them both for acting humorous and civilized about the situation, until Mike flared up and said the only choice was between being humorous and civilized and beating her face in with the leg of a table; and that he wasn't going to continue humorous and civilized if she made a public scandal of this thing because that would cost him his job and he didn't have the income from Grandpa's nut and bolt factory to live on like she did, and had to make his living, and besides he had his academic career to think of. He was going to get a divorce, that's what he was going to do. Oh, why did we all have to act so conventional, Marice kept whooping.

Once dinner was announced things were better because the soup sobered them and Marice shut up in front of the housemaid. Glenn got to telling Mike about the setup in Slade County and they all talked about what could be done to help the national campaign to free the eight miners who had been framed for the shootings at Bull Creek. As they talked Glenn caught himself wishing that things were the same they had been the last time he'd had dinner there with the Gulicks, when he was still in college; he couldn't imagine how it had all happened so fast. When Mike left them to go home to his bachelor quarters Glenn and Marice stood at the open door saying goodnight, while he walked down the steps from the stoop. Marice had an arm tight around Glenn's neck.

Glenn didn't know what Elmer Weeks would say about the situation, he knew he and Irving must be wise to it, because Marice was all the time answering the phone for him, and drifting in and out of his room when they came up to the house, while he was still in bed, to confer about what tactics the Party should pursue in the minefields now that the American Miners' locals had all been driven underground in Slade County. He made up his mind to bring it up the first time he went downtown to headquarters and got a chance to talk to Elmer Weeks alone.

It was a fine fall afternoon. Marice called him a taxi and made him take five dollars and told him to be sure to be back in time for dinner. He sat there leaning back in the taxi, wearing the new suit and new tan oxfords and the new light overcoat Marice had had sent up to the house for him, looking out at the hazy glitter of afternoon traffic and wondering what the hell he ought to do next.

Elmer Weeks was waiting for him in his cramped little office, seated at his rolltop desk, smoking a briar pipe in a last ray of sunlight that came in through the dusty windowpane. He pushed back a pile of reports on yellow paper, smiled broadly at Glenn from under his mustache and whispered into his telephone, "Comrade Silverstone, please . . . Irv, step across the hall, will you?" Then he gave Glenn another broad grin and said, "Glad to see you on your feet . . . hope you're ready for some speaking . . . my, you look the prosperous capitalist."

Glenn felt himself getting red as a beet. "I don't know what to do about it."

"In the first place," said Irving in a brisk tone, who had just stepped in through the glass door behind Glenn, "private morals are no affair of the Party's. . . . We're only interested in social morals. In the second place, there is always the danger of being contaminated by the decadence of the liberal bourgeoisie . . . after all, that's probably your sphere. Your class origins."

"Aren't strictly kosher," said Glenn agrily.

"That sort of remark, verging on antisemitism, proves my point . . . it's a remark no true worker . . ."

"Mrs. Gulick," Elmer Weeks interrupted soothingly, "inherited part of the Obadiah White fortune, if I'm not mistaken."

"She's very much interested in the Slade County situation. She's a very goodhearted intelligent woman." Glenn felt he was talking too eagerly.

"We can never transcend our class origins," said Irving in a condoling tone. "That doesn't mean that petitbourgeois radicals can't be useful to the movement."

"I've done a hell of a lot more manual labor than you have," broke out Glenn.

"What's the use? Personalities," said Irving with a shrug of his shoulders.

Elmer Weeks was looking thoughtfully at the smoke of his pipe. "We mustn't let ourselves look at things from too narrow a standpoint," he began. As they talked Glenn found he had more and more trouble keeping their minds on the minefields. They talked about more money for the party press, posters for campaign rallies, hiring halls and the chance the Party had of polling a considerable vote in the presidential elections, on account of unemployment, the disillusionment of the whitecollarworkers and intellectuals, the lack of leadership in the old line trade unions. . . . Glenn kept saying that if they could get those miners out of jail and keep the American Miners' Union together, they'd have a real mass basis for a labor movement. He still felt too weak and shaky to get any conviction into his voice. Finally, Elmer Weeks shook his pipe out in the wastebasket and got to his feet saying he had to speak up in the Bronx and must be off, anyway it wouldn't hurt letting Comrade Crockett see what he could do with a liberal committee. "Under proper direction," said Irving. "Perhaps."

As he went out the door of the office Elmer Weeks, with a gray tweed cap on his head and a briefcase under his arm, turned back and shook his empty pipe at them. "Comrades," he said in the staccato voice he used when he gave orders, "we must keep one thing in mind. Our function is to educate the American workingclass in revolutionary Marxism. We are not interested in the fates of individuals."

Glenn asked him if he thought he ought to go back to the minefields now he was on his feet again. Elmer Weeks stepped back into the office and pulled the ground glass door to behind him, and stood there a moment stroking his mustache with the forefinger of the hand that held the pipe. "Just at present it looks to me as if you could do more for the movement right here in New York than anywhere else."

"You've been beaten up for the movement," said Irving nastily. "You oughtn't to complain of an uptown assignment." Glenn had an impulse to punch Irving on the end of his pale sharp nose. "Okay," he said. As he limped off in a hurry down the grimy hall, brushing past several comrades with briefcases who were waiting to see Comrade Weeks when he went out, he could hear Irving's voice rising in denunciation, behind the door that had closed again. That fellow doesn't like me any more, he told himself.

When he got back to Marice's house he found a childishly addressed letter for him that had been forwarded from the American Miners' office in Pittsburgh. It was a scrawl in pencil from Wheatly:

*Comrad Sandy, we just got to git Pearl and them boys out. Pappy
he went and talked to Caleb Blaine the blackhearted old buzzard and Caleb Blaine says those boys stays in jail juss so long
as them furren rednecks keeps messin up things in the minefields
and wont mind they own business and that they was all a theists
so now Pappy's hellroarin around everywhere about how the reds
aint our folks and our folks ought to stick together but Sandy you
and me is the same kind of folks and all night I'm awishin you
was hear and us ahuggin and kissin and things it aint proper to
write like We did . . .*

Glenn crumpled the letter up and dropped it in the wastebasket.

"What's the matter, Sandy?" Marice asked. She had just come into
his room all dressed for dinner with a little shaker and two cocktail-
glasses on a tray. "Lost your last friend on earth?" Glenn stooped
over with difficulty, as his back was still stiff from the cast, and picked
Wheatly's letter out of the wastebasket and tore it into small pieces.
"Marice, I got to get back there before they begin to feel I've run out
on them."

"Why can't Less Minot go back?"

"He's all bunged up too. . . . He's back running the Pittsburgh
office."

"But, Glenn, you know perfectly well they'd shoot to kill this time."

"They did last time."

"I know how you feel. . . . But everybody agrees you can do a better
job for those miners outside the state than in. We need you to testify before the senate investigating committee, we need you to make
speeches . . ."

"I know the arguments," said Glenn.

"But aren't we having fun together?" Marice said suddenly, stammering and casting her eyes down like a little girl. He took her by the
ears and pulled her mouth to him and kissed it. "Sure thing," he said.
"Suppose we get Mark Burgess and that lawyer up here tonight and see
if we can get 'em to start something."

"I'll call Mark up right now . . . maybe they can come for dinner,"
said Marice, running out to the hall to the phone, suddenly all excite-

ment. Glenn was rubbing her greasy lipstick off his lips with the corner of his handkerchief.

Mark Burgess rang the front doorbell promptly at seven, looking very spruce in his lightgray suit with a blue necktie the color of his eyes. He was delighted to see Glenn again, asked about his injuries and introduced him enthusiastically to the tall man in baggy tweeds, George Hurlbut Cramm, who had come with him. Marice came swishing out from the diningroom carrying a new tray of cocktails and wearing a black spangly dress with red slippers and a noisy red necklace. She had a great deal of rouge on her cheeks and turned her round black eyes up under Mr. Cramm's chin and sighed that now that the ablest lawyer in the New York bar was interested in taking the cases she knew those poor boys would get out of jail.

Mr. Cramm made a deprecatory gesture with a large white hand and said dear lady, just for the present all he could afford to contribute to the good cause was advice. They had a number of cocktails and sat down at the big diningtable with its stifflycreased linen tablecloth and its glitter of cutglass and silver. While Marice carved the roast beef, Mark Burgess brought out a looseleaf notebook and began to map out a new campaign for the miners' defense to be organized by the League: speeches, moneyraising, legal fees, etc. They had just gotten started when the maid said somebody wanted Mr. Crockett on the phone. It was Jane Sparling, she said if they didn't mind she was coming right up, she felt the Workers' Defense should be represented.

Marice had a place set for Jane, but she said she'd eaten. Jane's voice was dry and her manner was scornful; the first thing she wanted to know was why a new committee was needed, why the old defense committee couldn't handle the new trials too. Glenn put down his napkin: in the first place they had to have a broader base and a nonpartisan group who wouldn't be immediately branded as reds. After all, this wasn't a political issue, it was a matter of civil rights, Elmer and Irving agreed with him, he'd just been talking to them this afternoon, and in the second place there was the fact that most of the miners wanted to be defended by the O.B.U. Now a liberal citizens' committee wouldn't encounter ideological difficulties. "After all the main thing is to get those boys out of jail, isn't it, Jane?"

"Of course," said Jane impatiently, getting to her feet and walking around the room, "but we don't need to break up the union to do it."

"The American Miners has a hell of a lot better chance in the coalfields if we get those boys out of jail," said Glenn, "than if we leave them there to rot. The new trials are our big chance."

"But how can there be any question?" asked Marice, leaning forward from the end of the table, her round eyes shining.

Jane pushed the untidy gray hair off her square face and said, "It's no use arguing with people who don't understand what we're talking about."

"Now, Jane dear," said Mark Burgess with mock humility, "we are ideologically unformed little liberals from the outer darkness, but we want to learn . . . we're listening to teacher."

Jane couldn't help joining in the laugh, but Glenn noticed that she and Marice were giving each other sharp looks. It was a relief when Mark Burgess said in his smooth pulpit manner: "Now I think there's a way out of this little difficulty. My old frend George here hasn't admitted it yet but I know what he is going to do."

"Gosh, Mark, I don't see how I can afford the time at this moment . . . I have the traction company case pending and I may have to argue a brief before the Supreme Court in January."

"George," said Mark Burgess gently, "you know you will. . . . You always come through. The head says one thing but the heart says another."

"I wish you could see those miners," said Glenn. "Honestly, they are wonderful guys. The state Superior Court has granted new trials. . . . It's our great chance."

"Well," said George Hurlbut Cramm, "I suppose we can get some of the youngsters in my office to prepare a brief amicus curiae if nothing else . . . ."

"As for expenses," said Marice, who had been paying attention to mixing the salad in the big wooden saladbowl, "Mark and I can put our heads together. We can get things started anyway."

"Attagirl," said Burgess. "Now we are doing business."

George Hurlbut Cramm leaned across the table. "Mr. Crockett," he said, "I hear that you can testify on the alibi of two of the miners . . . ."

"That's one reason they tried to rub me out of the picture," said Glenn, laughing.

"Well, they won't try anything like that this time. There'll be too much publicity."

"Well, I can't be here all night . . . I've got to go back to the office," said Jane suddenly. "Comrade Crockett, I hope you won't forget you are dealing with political irresponsibles." "Who, us, Jane?" asked Mark Burgess, rolling his eyes up. "No, of course not," she said crossly, "I mean those O.B.U. miners," and went out.

That night the phone rang just as Glenn and Marice were climbing into bed. Yawning he shuffled into the hall in his bare feet. It was Elmer Weeks telling him that the Central Committee had just thrashed the matter out and decided that the thing to do was to concentrate on getting out the two American Miners' boys; outside of that the trial was an educational demonstration and to be treated as such by the liberal lawyers: and as for cooperating with the O.B.U. he had every reason to believe it would be a mistake, after all we knew none of our boys had shot those deputies, no use trying to defend irresponsible elements, no time for Quixotic gestures. Comrade Crockett's business was to go to Bluegrass and convince Napier and Davis that their cases were separate. "But it won't be any use," Glenn found himself yelling into the phone. Elmer Weeks' voice became very dry and crisp. That was the decision, he said. Of course, he'd have a right to take the general principle up before the plenum, if he thought the movement had anything to gain from that sort of discussion.

"What on earth are you talking about so long?" said Marice who had followed Glenn out into the hall with her quilted red Chinese robe thrown over her shoulders. "Well, goodnight," said Glenn hurriedly and hung up. "Headquarters," he added to Marice, with a tart laugh, "telling us where to get off."

It was a sparkling blue November morning when Glenn and Marice drove up in front of the rambling mansarded frame building of the Bluegrass Hotel. In the back seat of Marice's Chrysler Imperial, wrapped in a plaid blanket and hemmed in by suitcases, was the lumpy redfaced figure of Dr. Blumenthal, who had come with them to study a labor situation from the psychoanalytic point of view, and also, as Marice whispered to Glenn when they were leaving New York, to act as a sort of chaperon, Glenn knew how unimaginative people were in the sticks.

Driving down the main street, between two lines of parked mud-flecked cars, Glenn had hardly recognized Bluegrass. There were old cars of every model, weathered to colors like bluebottle flies, teams of mules drawing big wagons with oldfashioned round covers over them; there was even a yoke of oxen. The streets were full of miners and countrypeople in their best clothes. Lanky men with black felt hats on the backs of their heads were standing along the curbs chewing and spitting and passing the time of day. A colored man in a white jacket was selling hot dogs and pop at a little stand on the courthouse lawn. There was a fairground feeling in the air as if a calliope might start playing at any minute.

The hotel lobby was full of talk and cigarsmoke and the smell of fried ham from the diningroom where the outoftown newspapermen were eating breakfast. Glenn pointed out County Prosecutor Herb Prout to Marice as they were walking over to the desk to register. He was leaning back with his thumbs in his vestpockets looking the crowd over with the appraising air of a theatre manager watching a line waiting for tickets at the boxoffice. While the bellboy was bringing in their bags they stood a moment talking in singsong ceremonial voices to George Hurlbut Cramm and Colonel Ferris, the local attorney for the American Miners.

Harve Farrell was standing in the diningroom door; he beckoned Glenn over and introduced a skinny young man with coarse black hair as the Honorable Jim Ellis who was taking the O.B.U. cases. Harve looked the same as ever and still wore the same creased suit that didn't meet in the middle. "Well," he said, "you birds are puttin' on a big show, but what do those big boys care about the workin' class. . . . They care about words . . . that's what you'll get, a big talkfest and the boys'll stay in jail." "How else can you educate people, Harve?" "We'll eddicate 'em by gettin' our boys out of jail."

Glenn walked back over to where Marice and Dr. Blumenthal were talking to Prosecutor Prout and Judge Crawford from

Sladetown. Marice was making a great hit with the local boys. Everybody was elaborately polite and full of old southern hospitality. Everybody seemed to be having a wonderful time. A funny feeling like seasickness began to take hold of Glenn. He stood there with his ears ringing, looking at the people and the cigarsmoke and the crowds passing in the street beyond the broad dusty window of the hotel lobby, that was flanked on either side by rubber plants and flowering begonias, and that had a row of brass spittoons along the bottom of it, as if he were looking at it all from a dark quiet room through a keyhole. Among the faces outside the window he found himself looking at old man Napier's white mustaches and his broadbrimmed felt hat, and Jessie and Wheatly in new blue and pink gauze hats that were very unbecoming to them, standing kneedeep in all the little towheaded Napiers; or was it just another mountain family that looked like them.

It was a relief when Cramm put his big soft hand on Glenn's shoulder and said what about talking to their clients. They walked down the street to the jail without meeting any miners Glenn knew. One big fellow in khaki, who looked like one of the Sladetown gunthugs, had been standing in the hotel entry; he gave them a dirty look and started slouching after them through the crowd.

The old warden was very polite and greeted the lawyers warmly and even offered them cigars. He and George Hurlbut Cramm had a little chat about racehorses and whiskey and the fine fall weather. Then he called to the lame turnkey, who gave Glenn a great friendly wink, to bring down Napier and Davis and politely left them alone in his office to talk.

Glenn felt a second's embarrassment on account of his new suit when Pearl came in, but Pearl and Hank strode over to him and pumped his arms and said he looked right pale and must have been powerful poorly and he sure must have been light on his feet to dodge them bullets. That made him feel better. Their faces looked paler than when Glenn had seen them last, and they were beginning to get a bluish bloat under the eyes. He introduced them to George Hurlbut Cramm who said that the procedure was going to be to try the boys separately and not together like at the last trial, that was what the superior court had ordered and they were going to take full advantage of it to bring out every bit of evidence there was.

Pearl mumbled that whatever the Union thought was all right, was all right by him, he didn't care no more. Glenn told him to cheer up, but Pearl shook his head and pulled him into a corner and whispered in his ear that they had brung in Jessie to see him that morning and he was all broke up, he could take it for himself but it sure was hard on the women and the children. Them operators had gotten in a mountain preacher who sure had been working on the poor people up above Muddy Fork about the sinfulness of the rednecks and infidels and now they had Pappy all worked up agin the union and going around saying it had been the ruination of the Napier connection. Pearl said Pappy never did have a bit of sense, but now it looked like old age had done dried up his brains, and like as not he'd testify and there was no telling what he'd say. "But, Christ, he can't testify you were in on that shooting because you weren't." Pearl's brows stiffened into a frown. "Pappy won't be fixin' to do us no harm," he said.

The warden came back and said Judge Purdy was just entering the courtroom and that he thought the Napier case was third on the docket. They shook hands all around, and Glenn and the lawyers walked out through the courthouse into the bright sunlight outside.

On the steps they found Jane Sparling bustling around in a great stew, saying she was being followed everywhere she went, and that gunthugs from Sladetown were intimidating witnesses. The rest of the day, while the jury was being chosen in the courtroom, Glenn spent driving Jane around in Marice's car to round up defense witnesses. Jane was full of dark forebodings about a sellout. She said Harve Farrell and his lawyer were in cahoots with Prout to pin the red flag on Napier and Davis and to convict them, and then to get the O.B.U. boys off. She said Glenn's idea of trying to cooperate with the O.B.U. was criminal. He'd see when it was too late that he'd been conniving in a sellout.

Glenn asked her what she'd do if they got her on the stand and asked her if she were a radical. "I'd give 'em an earful about conditions in Slade County, that's what I'd do; flux, starvation, terror. . . . If that's radicalism let 'em make the best of it."

"You and Patrick Henry."

"Sure thing." Jane laughed and brushed her stringy gray hair off her forehead. They were just climbing out of the car after their last trip. Marice came out of the hotel to meet them. She said the jury was picked and she thought they looked splendid, all honest farmers. Jane stopped in her tracks, looking Marice up and down with her sour angry stare. "I suppose you know," she said, "farmers are the worst thing you can have in a labor case."

Maybe it was the concussion had made his head funny, but all next day sitting in the stuffy courtroom, listening to droning voices, Glenn kept having the feeling that it was all happening somewhere far away. It was all happening so fast. He couldn't seem to catch up with the way things were happening.

The small colonialstyle courtroom was packed with lank, intent faces of country people and mountain people. Judge Purdy sat up in the center of everything, with ample gray hair drooping off his head, and with big jowls and mouth, drooping at the corners, like a cartoon of a judge drawn to look like a bloodhound in a radical paper. Lawyer Cramm was urbane and Lawyer Ferris was full of fair play and oldfashioned kindly southern cheer and Prosecutor Prout strode back and forth across the floor and pointed the accusing finger.

Glenn didn't like to look at Pearl Napier's furrowed brow as he tried to follow what was going on. Glenn could see that Pearl had the same feeling of not being able to catch up that he had, of not being there at all, maybe.

County Prosecutor Prout was doing a good job; hour by hour Glenn watched him building up a story, in spite of the objections and the sarcasms and the scholarly exceptions and big city ways of George Hurlbut Cramm. Glenn could see the jurymen eagerly following the story that came out as clear and simple as if Prosecutor Prout were writing it up on a blackboard in a large round hand. At the meeting at Bull Creek the American Miners' leaders had been infuriated because the sheriff's deputies were taking down their seditious speeches for evidence in criminal syndicalism indictments, and planned to ambush them after the speaking and so destroy the evidence; that was why several of the miners, including the chairman of the meeting, Pearl Napier, had left in the middle of it with anger in their hearts. Many witnesses testified to that. Witnesses testified that it was late at night when Pearl Napier and the other three men in the car with him reached his home at Muddy Fork. Everything linked up. Where had Napier been all afternoon? Lying in wait with a gun with anger in his heart and murder in his brain, lying in ambush waiting to maim and kill High Sheriff Caleb Blaine and his deputies who were proceeding on a lawful errand, doing their duty to protect the homes and the property of the citizens of Slade County in accordance to the oath they had sworn before God.

That part brought a chorus of exceptions from the lawyers and a burst of clapping from one corner of the room that made Judge Purdy threaten to clear the court.

The defense began parading its witnesses. Before he was ready Glenn found himself changed to an actor in the play. He was on the witness stand. All the pairs of eyes were turned on him. His head ached and his forehead was dripping with sweat. He still had the illusion that he was looking out at it all from out of a black humming room. He wiped his face with his handkerchief. Gradually the mist of faces cleared round him. He could see Cramm distinctly. They were talking in a friendly leisurely way. Cramm was asking him about his health. Glenn said he'd just recovered from a severe beating at the hands of . . . Prout was on his feet howling for an exception.

Cramm went back genially to the story of Glenn's activities in the minefields and especially to the drive home with Pearl Napier the sunday of the speaking at Bull Creek, how they'd left the speaking in fear of their lives, how they'd had a flat tire, their late supper at Pearl's house with his wife and children. The story that had seemed so plausible when they'd rehearsed it with the lawyers, began suddenly to sound hollow and false in Glenn's own ears. He began to wonder if he could be lying.

He looked in the two rows of quiet attentive hick faces in the jurybox; it was so simple, they must believe it. They were kindly hardworking outofdoor men, the kind of people he got along with. Suddenly he felt at ease in the courtroom, for the first time everything seemed gentle, cheerful, almost jolly.

Prosecutor Prout was asking him questions now.

"Do you believe in God, Mr. Crockett?"

Glenn felt himself getting red. The lawyers were on their feet waving their arms. The Judge waved them back into their seats with his limp hand. Glenn was looking in Cramm's face.

"That's a complicated question."

"Answer me, yes or no."

"No."

"Do you believe in the future life promised us by the Good Book in which we shall be punished for sins committed in this world?"

"No."

The lawyers were seething. Judge Purdy consented to listen to their arguments. The jury was sent out. The Judge held that the Prosecutor was in his rights asking questions to establish the credibility of the witness. When the jury came back their faces were grim and their jaws were set. All the time Glenn had stood there with empty, aching head. Nothing to do now but go on and give them the works.

Prosecutor Prout started up just where he'd left off. "Then it's not the fear of God that makes you tell the truth?"

Glenn felt blind anger rising in him. "I tell the truth because I don't believe in lying . . . because I believe in the dignity of man," he shouted.

"Do you believe the present socalled capitalistic order of society is right and just?"

"No."

"Do you consider the Russian system of communism as practiced in red Moscow more conducive to the dignity of man as you call it than belief in the Gospel, the sacredness of the home and private property and the Constitution of the United States?"

"Yes."

"Then you prefer the red flag of anarchy to Old Glory?"

"That's not a fair question."

The lawyers were on their feet again. The jury was sent out again. Cramm asked for a mistrial. It was denied. Glenn stood leaning on the bar of the witness stand feeling sick and shaky like he'd felt as a little boy the first day in a new school when he didn't know the lesson. Judge Purdy announced the court was in recess and went into chambers with the lawyers. That was all that day. When Glenn walked over to the hotel people made a lane for him to pass through as if he had a contagious disease. Nobody looked him in the face but he could feel black looks piling up behind him. He went up to his room and lay down on the bed.

Dr. Blumenthal, with whom he shared the room, came in rubbing his hands and saying it had been most interesting to observe the purely automatic reactions of the jurors to ritualistic words and phrases. Glenn sat up on the edge of the bed and said well, he supposed it was just as well in the long run, you had to tell the masses the truth. Blumenthal took a little comb and combed his silky white whisps of mustache in front of the glass, then he turned to Glenn with his silly English giggle and said, "Quite the contrary. I never believe in telling anybody the truth, least of all the mahsses."

"But you can't build a great political movement on lies."

"You can't build it on anything else if you ahsk me," Dr. Blumenthal said, jauntily walking back and forth on his bandy legs.

Glenn was kneading his aching head in his fingers. "It's not fair," he said. "We've got to smash it, by God, we've got to smash it."

"What?"

"The whole hideous system."

"I'm very much afraid, my young friend . . ." Dr. Blumenthal's accent, that often had a slight cockney twang, became very Oxonian, "that this time it is the system that will do the smashing."

"Oh, Sandy, you were magnificent . . . it was the greatest emotional experience of my life," said Marice, sticking her head in the door. "How about a little teeny drink? Poor boy, you need it. Mamma's got a flask in her handbag."

"Splendid, my dear," said Dr. Blumenthal, rubbing his hands. "This trial is most interesting."

"Marice, for chrissake this isn't a picnic," said Glenn, brushing past her out the door.

It was dark. He walked out the rutted country road back of the hotel. Behind a hedge he saw sparks going up in the starry fall sky. Mountain people were sitting around a little fire at the rear end of a wagon. Pink light followed the curve of the canvas cover on the cart and splashed on faces and shirts and cotton dresses. Glenn leaned over the rails of a gate watching them for a while before he recognized who it was he was looking at. Then he whistled and called, "Wheatly, come here a minute." She left the others and came walking across the field with her long stride, her face stuck forward to peer into the darkness. Before she got to the fence she stopped in her tracks. "That's who it is," she said. "Hain't none of us talkin' to you, but if they send that boy to the chair I'll git me a gun and blow the top of your head off an' watch you squirm till you die."

"Honest, Wheatly, we're doing our best, all of us."

She had already turned her back and walked away towards the fire. Glenn went back to the hotel. In the lobby he found Jane sitting coolly reading the New York papers while two big huskies in khaki sat chewing tobacco and scowling at her from the opposite side of the lobby. "Things may look bad here, Sandy," she said cheerfully, "but from the national angle we couldn't do better."

"The trials are cooked," muttered Glenn, dropping into the chair beside her and staring into the palms of his hands that had lost all the calluses they used to have.

"I talked to Comrade Weeks over the long distance," whispered Jane. "He pointed out that this was a war. No army can expect to win a battle without losing some effectives. He says we got to get you out of here before they re-arrest you for something. He wants to save you for speaking. . . . Say, let's go upstairs to the lovenest and talk to the fair Marice. . . . Those bozos are getting my goat."

"Jane," said Glenn, "I don't care what happens . . . I feel that everything I've ever tried to do was a flop . . . ."

"Petitbourgeois defeatism, my dear," said Jane airily.

Next morning Dr. Blumenthal, saying that after all he had a duty to his patients, left on the early train for New York. The jury had been out an hour, when Colonel Ferris came over to the hotel shaking all over, to tell Glenn he didn't think he and Cramm would be safe in Bluegrass another minute. There'd be nothing gained by staying and getting a bullet in them. They'd better pull out right away.

Marice was great. Her round eyes were shining and her cheeks were pink without any rouge. She said she'd stay as long as they liked, but Cramm started muttering about chartering a plane because he needed to be in his office that afternoon; so they packed their bags and were off, leaving Jane Sparling to handle the defense. Marice drove the Chrysler. She hit sixty as soon as she got out on the highroad. "My, this is exciting," she kept saying. "Sandy, sign me up in your revolution. I think it's great. . . . Why, even that cat Jane Sparling . . . I know she hates me . . . but think of her nerve. We go in and out but she stays there in the minefields all the time."

When they stopped at a crossroads gasstation, a big touringcar full of deputies, with gun barrels sticking out in all directions, whizzed past down the highway going hellbent for election. Marice asked the attendant for a map and plotted out a route, following the roadlines with the sharp point of a glossy pink manicured fingernail. Then she started out due west along the highroad. George Hurlbut Cramm sat all huddled up holding on to his knees in the back of the car, now and then casting a look backward and giving a low groan, but nobody caught up with them. Marice never let the car below seventy. When at last a motorcycle cop crowded them to the side of the road, they were all puffing with relief. They could tell by his uniform that they'd crossed the state line. Marice kidded him so coyly and was so cucumber cool that he let her off with a reprimand.

They drove into Pittsburgh in the late afternoon and, while Marice was driving George Hurlbut Cramm to the station, Glenn went over to the office of the American Miners to get in touch with Less Minot. There was nobody in the office but a little jewish girl all smudged and inky to the armpits from trying to mend a brokendown multigraphing machine. She shook her head sadly and said he was at home ill, but the minute Glenn told her his name she said, "Comrade, go over to Donovan's Saloon on Monocacy Street. You'll find him in the back room; maybe you can straighten him out." "Will they let me in?" "Sure," she said, "this is a wideopen town."

Less did look terrible. He was slumped over a glass of beer at a small wooden table, wet with spillings, in the corner of the back room, with his hair over his face, that was swollen and grimed with dirt. He mumbled, "Hello, Sandy, old cock, have a drink." He was tapering off on beer, been tapering off for a week.

Glenn asked what the hell was the matter. Less said everything was the matter, American Miners was f—d to hell and back, the boys in Slade County was f—d and now here was this christbitten hellhound party line f—g them proper. No more dual unions. What the hell had we been getting our blocks knocked off for, and letting the boys get their blocks knocked off for, but our own party union. Now the story was go back and be good little boys and bore from within the good old Mineworkers. . . . No, Mr. Conolly wasn't a crook or a socialfascist labor faker any more, he was a noble progressive fellow traveller, and we were going to work to bore from within him. Give him the order of Lenin. "Kerist, I won't dare show my face in any coalcamp in the Alleghanies."

"I'm just about through," said Glenn.

"No, you're not," said Less and started to get to his feet. "Give a hand, legs not good, wanna wash my face." Glenn grabbed one of his arms and yanked it across his shoulders and pulled him, swaying and lurching, through a passage that stank of stale beer, into a toilet where there was a tap of cold water dripping into a scaly red sink. Less stuck his head under the tap and held it there for a long time. Then he sent Glenn out to get a towel from Angelo the barkeep. After a few minutes Less had pulled himself together enough to walk back one step at a time to his table and to sit up and drink his beer. He pushed his wet hair back with his black stubby fingers and screwed his face up in a knot in an effort to look Glenn in the eye.

"No, you're not through, Sandy . . . you won't give up the fight. . . . Party does some things right, some things wrong. . . . Ain't nuttin' else strong enough to lead the workin' class outa captivity. The bosses can beat us up, shoot us, jail us, do anythin' they damn please, only the Party says no . . . mass pressure . . ."

"Suppose the Party gets separated from the masses?"

"It can't while they got me . . . I'm the masses. . . . Kerist, I've had every raw deal since I was that high. . . . I been jailed an' beat up an' rolled an' gypped an' deported an' sandbagged an' shot at. They ain't hung me yet but they will. . . . Hey, Angelo, another whiskey. . . . Say, Sandy, got any dough? My credit's low."

"I got ten bucks."

"Jesus Christ. Angelo, make it a quart and put the rest down on account."

"Say, Less, don't you think you ought to lay off?"

"Shut up, Sandy, before I spread you out over the pavement." Less' voice was getting thick again. "When a guy's been f—d he's been f—d, ain't he? What you want me to do, go down to headquarters and bust up the office furniture?" He shook his head hard, and started off again in a singsong tone. "No, I don't do things like that . . . I'm regular . . . Less Minot's always been regular . . . Less Minot was regular when your mammy was still wiping the snot off your nose. . . . You be regular, Sandy, or by God I'll knock your goddam block off."

It took Glenn a couple of hours to get away from Less. Then he left him sitting there staring with eyes that had a blue glaze on them at the halfdrunk quart. It was a relief to get out in the air. He jumped on a streetcar to the hotel where he'd told Marice he'd meet her. She was all settled in a room, but Glenn asked her would she mind his driving her into New York tonight, there was something he had to attend to at the office. She yawned. Sure, she said, she was game but he'd have to drive because she was too sleepy. Coming out of the hotel they went by the newsstand. The papers all had the verdict in headlines.

MINERS GUILTY *Jury recommends mercy* Miners get twenty years in slaying of deputies *Farmers' jury finds all miners guilty* UNIONISTS CONVICTED.

It was dark. Without waiting to get anything to eat Glenn drove out of Pittsburgh with his teeth set.

The dawn was over and done with and the morning was a strong gray glare in their eyes that were redrimmed and staring from dust and fatigue, before the concrete fourway highroad, with its always increasing stream of traffic, began to shake itself loose from the frame houses, and the vegetable stands ranked with squashes and pumpkins and demijohns of cider and baskets of apples, and the brightcolored fillingstations all the time closer together, and the lunchwagons and hamburgerstands and dining and dancing joints of the Jersey towns, and to shoot out straight across the broad russet marshes, smoking from dump piles, towards the tall whitepointed angular cutout of Manhattan that rose suddenly through a rosy haze among the piled clouds beyond the flat heights of Weehawken. The car, already part of a continual parade of fast traffic, lurched through tangles of construction-work and at last dove into the clean, evenly lit concrete tunnel. "My," said Marice, as they came out into daylight again. "It makes me happy to drive into New York in the fall."

As soon as they got uptown to the house, after a tiring jerky drive through the city traffic, Marice rushed upstairs to see the kids. Glenn found himself staggering sleepily about the lower hall with a pile of phone messages in his hand. The phone was ringing. Without taking off his coat and hat he answered it. First a woman's voice answered; then Irving Silverstone's. He'd been calling all morning. Where had Sandy been all morning? Didn't he know about the dinner a group of liberal intellectuals were giving him that night? "Who?" Glenn yelled into the phone.

Sandy Crockett had come to symbolize Slade County, Irving insisted. It was a very important occasion because a number of influential writers and journalists had promised to be there. Why, even the capitalist press in New York had been full of editorials deploring the Slade County verdicts. It was a very important occasion. Liberal opinion was very much stirred up. It had been even suggested that Sandy ought to wear a dress suit, but it had been decided that wasn't necessary, perhaps unwise, a plain business suit, preferably dark blue would be all right. "We've got to show them we are not hooligans. . . . It is very important."

But, Christ, answered Glenn, he'd driven all night to come down and make a report to the Central Committee. Tomorrow would be time for that. It seemed to Glenn that Irving's rapid voice had an unusually impatient hiss to it. This dinner meant a real widening of support among intellectuals; it was in accord with the new thesis.

Glenn found himself yelling into the phone, "Why the hell, if you'd decided to collaborate with the old unions, couldn't you have decided to collaborate with the Mineworkers in time to get them in on the Slade County trials? Don't you know that if you people had gone around to see Conolly and told him you were going to lay off, he might have influenced the prosecutor not to step on the murder charges? Jesus Christ, we might have gotten those boys out of jail."

Irving answered in his hurried whisper that he couldn't discuss it over the phone and that Glenn must go get some sleep because he had to make the speech of his life at the dinner.

The dinner, in a big private diningroom with salmon pink hangings and filet mignon and waiters in dress suits, went off very well. Several hundred dollars were cleared after the expenses had been paid. Glenn's looking so tired and haggard made a great impression on the welldressed men and women at the long tables arranged in the form of a U. When he felt people were listening to what he was saying he couldn't help feeling good about it. The women all kept their eyes on him. Marice's round dark eyes never left his face.

He couldn't help feeling good too, because, though some of them were younger, Marice was the bestlooking woman there and much the best dressed. After dinner he smoked a cigar and was slipped a glass of scotch and soda, that he sipped while he chatted with several nationallyfamous writers and artists. One doughyfaced little man in evening clothes came up to him and wrung his hand and said his speech had been one of the big moments of his life. "We write the stuff but you live it," he said, looking up at him with wet dog's eyes.

Glenn never did get around to having it out with the Central Committee because the speaking tour never gave him a moment. After two weeks speaking twice a day at meetings around the five boroughs, he went to the Coast, and started working his way back across the continent again. A hardworking young woman, Sylvia Freund of the Workers' Defense, attended to all the details and kept track of the collections. Everywhere it was applause in halls crowded with faces of working people and professional people, and handshakings and little gatherings of comrades and sympathizers after the meetings or parties arranged for leading intellectuals by liberal hostesses. Only in a few places the police made things difficult by forbidding meetings, or American legionnaires made trouble for the reds by picketing halls.

Glenn was coming out after a meeting in Chicago one snowy night of whipping zero wind with a group of comrades who had invited him to eat spaghetti with them in an Italian restaurant when he noticed a headline in a bulldog edition of a morning paper that an old man had

for sale in a little shelter beside the entrance to the hall: RED SLAYER
KILLED IN JAILBREAK.
He bought a paper and shoved it into his pocket. At the restaurant he looked at the paper. He had just taken off his coat. He felt he
couldn't control himself. He put his coat on again and asked the comrade who had the car to drive him around to the hotel. He explained
he felt too tired after speaking to eat, he hoped the comrades would
excuse him.
When he got up to his room he yanked the paper out and read it
again:

> Pearl Napier, 22, Slade County miner convicted of the mur-
> der of a deputy sheriff during recent labor disturbances, was
> killed at 4:30 this morning in a daring attempt to break jail
> at Fort Pleasant Penitentiary; Hank Davis, 30, an accomplice
> convicted of the same crime, was severely wounded and Fred
> Russo, 42, a prison guard, was slightly wounded . . . .

The phone was ringing. Glenn walked up and down, letting it ring
and ring before he answered it. When he picked up the receiver a thick
but vaguely familiar voice he couldn't quite place asked for Sandy
Crockett. The man must be drunk. The voice said this was Harve Farrell and that if that was Sandy Crockett he was coming up to punch his
face in. Had he read the news? Yes. Well, did he know who was responsible for that guy's death and the holy mess they made of the defense,
well, he was, the sonofabitch, and if he was a man he'd come and get
his dirty lying face smashed in. . . . And what was he doing now with
all his speeches in defense of the classwar prisoners, the snarling voice
went on breathless; who was getting the money? The prisoners or his
organization? Who was in jail? The working stiffs. Who was riding
around the country staying in the best hotels making speeches and
passing the plate? The comical commissars. "That's a goddam lie,"
Glenn yelled into the phone. Harve Farrell began cursing back and
the operator cut them off. Later Glenn tried to trace the call but it had
been from a booth in a tobaccoshop and the party had gone.
Glenn walked up and down that hotel room all night. In the morn-

ing he called up Sylvia and told her he'd have to cancel his next few meetings and she'd have to find somebody else to speak, he was going back to New York on the first train.

"But, Comrade Crockett, don't you think you had better wire for instructions?" Her voice rose shrill so that the receiver went flat and twanged in his ear.

"No, there's something very important come up . . . that I have to discuss personally."

"Are you sure you think it's advisable, Comrade Crockett?"

"You'll understand when you see the morning papers."

"But who'll speak at the meeting?"

"Search me. . . . Goodby, Sylvia." Glenn hung up. His hands were shaking as he rolled up his toothbrush and shaving things in his pyjamas to shove them into his grip.

3

Glenn came out of the office and closed the groundglass door that had DO NOT ENTER lettered out on a piece of paper and pasted under the almost obliterated gilt PRIVATE. For a second he stood there with his hand on the knob, not able to think what to do next. Then he threw his shoulders back and walked down the grimy uncarpeted hall. A fairhaired young man in rolledup shirtsleeves was standing in the door to the next office. When he saw Glenn he started to smile. Then his face stiffened and he turned away so as not to meet Glenn's eye. At the end of the hall Glenn saw Irving Silverstone's familiar glasses and teddybear haircut coming towards him. He began to fix his mouth to say Hello when suddenly Irving had turned off and a door was closing behind him. Glenn started down the dark stairs. Just before the ground floor he bumped into one of the editors of the Defender, trudging up the stairs with some proofsheets in his hand. "Hello, Joe," said Glenn. The man gave a noncommittal grunt and hurried on up with his eyes on the stairs.

Glenn stepped out onto the street into a spray of spring rain, turned his coatcollar up, and started out with his head bent and his chin pulled down into his chest. He'd reached the corner and was waiting for a chance to cross the avenue through the dense noontide traffic when he heard heels clicking on the pavement behind him and a breathless girl's voice chirping "Comrade Crockett, Comrade Crockett." It was Sylvia, in a black man's slicker. "Oh, I've been back for weeks. . . . I wanted to talk to you. I know all about it. They are going to bring up your expulsion." She was panting.

"Not before I put this thing up to the plenum," said Glenn savagely. "What did Comrade Weeks say?"

"He said I was all wet. He said publishing income and disbursements would be playing into the hands of the reactionary employers."

"Come in and have a cup of coffee. . . . Oh, I didn't sleep a wink all night." She was almost crying.

"All right," said Glenn. "I don't seem to know anybody round headquarters any more. . . . I guess they've got the skids under me all right."

"I shall resign from the party," said Sylvia, tossing her head back.

They went into a crowded cafeteria on the square. As they walked through into the back a stumpy man, who looked like a garment worker, jumped up from the end of the table and stood beside them pumping Glenn's arm. "Comrade Crockett," he said and choked, grinning with sudden embarrassment. "More power to you." Glenn noticed out of the corner of his eye that he had walked back to his table with quite a swagger and was pointing him out to the men and girls he was sitting with. Glenn wondered what meeting he'd met that guy at. "The workingclass comrades still think you're wonderful," Sylvia whispered timidly in his ear. She had taken off her glasses and was wiping them on her handkerchief. Her gray eyes, that squinted a little, had an oddly helpless unprotected look without the glasses. "Wait till they read the party press," said Glenn.

When they'd each gotten a cup of coffee and a ham sandwich they found themselves a corner to sit in and Sylvia settled back in her seat and looked up in Glenn's face and said, "Now tell me everything."

"When I tell 'em we've got to stick until we get those boys out, they tell me I'm a sentimentalist and putting my own individual feelings ahead of the party. After all it was my individual feelings that got me into the party. . . . If we're not for the workers, who are we for?"

"Shush," said Sylvia. "Don't talk so loud."

"We had a yelling match and I got out. . . . I'll bring it up before the plenum."

"You'll never get to do that."

"Why?"

"Democratic centralism."

By the time they had finished their sandwiches the sun was shining on the square. As they walked out of the cafeteria several young men and girls said, "Greetings, Comrade Crockett," in warm admiring tones. "The leadership is losing contact with the masses," Sylvia whispered in Glenn's ear.

Outside all the wintry look had left the sky that was pale blue, ranked with soft yellow and pink clouds. Pigeons flew over the sign-littered roofs in the sunlight. Glenn suddenly put his hand on Sylvia's shoulder and said would she walk around with him a while that afternoon; suppose they went up to the zoo and walked around and looked at the animals and the people in the park. "How can we take the time, Comrade Crockett?" asked Sylvia, quite flustered. Glenn said nonsense, people had to take time out sometimes, and anyway he had to think out what he was going to do next. She was still protesting she had too much to do, she ought to go back to the office, when he bundled her onto a green uptown bus.

Sitting up there, looking down at the mixed crowds moving parti-colored up and down the sidewalks that were drying fast after the rain, Glenn found himself talking about how when he was a kid he used to take courses in taxidermy and butterflies and things like that and think he was going to be a zoologist when he grew up. He wondered what it was had put him off the track, maybe it was moral indignation; his father had studied for the ministry and ended up as a pacifist lecturer, he was in Geneva now helping anaesthetize the workers of the world with the League of Nations. Must be in the blood. Here he was now at loose ends like a methodist preacher without a call.

Sylvia shook her head and made a little clucking noise with her tongue. She hadn't known that, she'd thought his people were workers.

Glenn didn't pay any attention, but went on and on about how it was probably from his old man he got the gift of gab, maybe that had been the ruination of him; the trouble was that he couldn't help feeling responsible when he talked people into committing acts that ruined their whole lives, silly scruples he supposed, but that was how he felt. Now if it hadn't been for the gift of gab he'd have led a happy life studying bugs or some goddam thing like his old friend Paul Graves, whom Sylvia would have to meet sometime; he was running an agricultural station in the Soviet Union, no, not as partymember, as an expert, the lucky son of a gun.

"But what about our political work?"

"It's the workers are going to do it anyway," said Glenn, "not a lot of soapbox sobsisters."

After they had climbed down off the bus, Sylvia looked up at him uneasily through her glasses as if she thought he'd lost his mind. He could see her deciding not to let him out of her sight. She let him walk her all round the dilapidated little zoo.

First he stared for a long time at a shopworn Bactrian camel with two limp humps, then at an American buffalo or bison, *Bos Americanus*, as lifeless as an old fur rug. The bright perky eyes of a single raccoon were looking out from his hole in a box at the bottom of a dead tree. Inside a little smelly building there was a civet cat, two agoutis and a coatimundi and a lot of little cages where the animals had burrowed their way into the straw until all that could be seen was an occasional bunch of fluff. In an outside pen there was a badger, broad and lowslung, who toddled back and forth with his slightly turnedup nose close to the ground and his beady little eyes looking out with comical hick suspicion from his piebald face. Glenn was talking so loud the badger took fright and scuttled into his hutch. They watched the door until they caught sight of him again. This time he was curled up securely inside; as he looked out at them he opened his long mouth and showed them a pale pink tongue and palate in a slow bored yawn. Even Sylvia couldn't help laughing.

Glenn's talking jag got worse and worse. He jabbered on that it made him happy, he didn't know why, to look at animals, he wished he could go round the world looking at people like that, just like they were looking at the little animals now, observing them and noting down their characteristic feeding habits and habitats and protective coloration, all kinds of people; workers, farmers, fishermen, sailors, capitalists, finks, scabs, prostitutes, bureaucrats. He loved the sonsofbitches. That was why he'd never make a real party organizer. That was why they were putting the skids under him, parties and politics were built on hate. A good political leader hated everybody. "Don't look so worried, Sylvia, I'm not drunk or mad . . . I'm just getting it off my chest because you are such a sympathetic listener."

Sylvia blushed crimson and cast down her eyes. She put her hand out and grabbed Glenn's hand and squeezed it; then she dropped it as if it had burned her. They were looking at a cage of rhesus monkeys that, screeching, scratching, twitching, leaping, had always the same sad eyes set too high in small tearstained faces. Glenn was telling her a story about when he'd gone to see his friend Paul Graves, years ago, down in North Carolina and they'd met a woman selling a tonic for female complaints who was crazy to get hold of a Venus's Flytrap, that was an inseceating plant that only grew in the Carolinas, to send to her sister who was bedridden so that she could entertain herself feeding it flies, and see it eat like a critter. Sylvia shuddered and said the story made her feel quite sick and so did the smell of the monkeyhouse. "But that's the real naturalist's urge, Sylvia, curiosity, morbid, prurient curiosity. I guess I didn't have enough of it and just get morally indignant."

When they got out in the air the afternoon had clouded up again. Big purple rainclouds had piled up over the gleamingwindowed buildings round the park. "Well," said Sylvia, planting her feet firmly on the asphalt path, "it's going to rain, and don't you think we ought to make up our minds what to do next?"

"Don't worry, Sylvia, you don't need to call an ambulance, I feel much better. Let's go call up Cramm."

"You look like a nervous wreck," said Sylvia. He had lit out across the curving path that led to the other side of the park; she trotted after, finding it hard to keep up with him on her short legs.

By the time they had ducked into a drugstore the rain was pouring again. Sylvia's feet were wet, and she was saying she was sure she'd caught a cold in the head. She waited outside the booth while he called up Cramm. He was able to get through to him right away; his voice was friendly and reassuring. The only thing left to do, he said, was to try for a pardon from the new governor who had the reputation of being a goodhearted kind of a man, of course this jailbreak attempt was the devil. Glenn had better come around to the office in a day or two to talk about the procedure.

"Gosh," said Glenn after he'd hung up, "I wish I was that badger in the zoo. . . . Man makes things too damn hard for himself." Sylvia gave him another puzzled look and then said she had to go home. She took his hand and squeezed it and said very fast, "You can count on my solidarity, Comrade Crockett. For years now since they silenced the opposition I have doubted the correctness of the party line." They went down into the subway and took trains in opposite directions. She waved at him, smiling tearfully through the glass door, as her express pulled out.

When Glenn got home to Marice's and opened the frontdoor with his latchkey, a warm buttery smell of dinner cooking cosily tickled his nostrils. As he took his coat off in the front hall he could hear the kids yelling in the playroom upstairs. The house was quiet and warm. The carpet was soft under his damp feet. In the front parlor a coalfire was burning. The heavy red velvet curtains had been drawn across the windows. The evening papers were laid out on a table. On the bench in front of the horsehair sofa stood the silver teaservice and a cocktailshaker and some plates of thin sandwiches and little cakes. Two cups and two glasses had been drunk out of. The big silver ashtray was stacked with butts of Russian cigarettes. Glenn couldn't help wondering in a furtive, unhappy kind of a way who it was had been having tea with Marice, and telling himself, as he had a hundred times in the last months, that he'd have to get out, he couldn't go on living like this.

When Marice came in from the diningroom, her eyes followed his eyes and all at once he knew she'd guessed what he was thinking. "Oh, Glenn," she shouted extravagantly, "you missed meeting the most wonderful Russian . . . Stanov . . . the humorist . . . we got along famously. He doesn't speak a word of English, just broken French and German . . . he says he's learning the Indian signlanguage." She was still bubbling with laughter in recollection. "Anyway, he's going to be at

Jane Sparling's tonight and he said he'd cry his eyes out if I didn't come. He said you must bring me.... What's the matter?"

"Nothing," said Glenn. He couldn't help feeling how pale his face was.

"Glenn." Marice grabbed his hand and made him sit down beside her on the sofa. "You need a rest. You've been worrying yourself sick about those miners.... I know. And, then you don't feel about me the way you used to ... I've been talking to Dr. Blumenthal about it." She looked up at him with her black eyes round and coyly cocked her head. "You know I've been having some most extraordinarily interesting dreams lately ... maybe I'm effecting a transference. But you've got to get away somewhere for a rest ... Dr. Blumenthal says you are heading for a crackup."

"Sure I've been worried," stammered Glenn. He patted her gently on the back of the hand. "Marice, you've been swell." Suddenly she started to blubber. "I know you despise me for a silly rich bitch." Glenn hugged her. "Honest, Marice, I've always thought you were great.... You know all you've meant to me." He could hear his own voice as if it were somebody else talking.

She looked up at him smiling through her tears like a child. "Then promise you'll take me to Jane Sparling's. If you bring me, it'll be all right."

Glenn's throat stiffened. "She didn't ask me ... I saw her yesterday.... All right, what the hell?" He pulled her to her feet. "What time do we go?"

"Stanov said to be there at nine o'clock. He wants me to take him to Harlem afterwards. Glenn, he's a scream ... he'll make you laugh your head off."

Glenn said soberly he'd go upstairs and clean up, he'd had so many things on his mind he'd forgotten to shave that morning.

All the way downtown in the taxi he was trying to think of a way of explaining to Marice how things were between him and the Party; but maybe it was all imagination, maybe Sylvia was just a hysterical woman who'd always been secretly an oppositionist anyway; putting things into words made them happen. Marice kept complaining about Glenn's looking so glum: she said she guessed he was ashamed of her, ashamed to take her out among his real friends. Well, she didn't care, she found she always got along with everybody just by acting perfectly natural.

Jane Sparling's apartment was downtown on the west side in an old brick tenement house that had been isolated from its street by the cutting through of a new avenue and stood up forlornly in a triangular lot amid the rubble of torndown buildings. There was a paper over the bell saying, *Come on up buzzer out of order.* Marice was tittering with excitement as they climbed the steep stairs of worn and grimy marble. They could hear the buzz of talk before they got to the fifth floor. A little girl with a sleek black bob opened the door, and looked sharply in their faces as if trying to recognize them. Glenn didn't know her. "Come in, comrades," she said, and showed them where to put their coats. "Comrade Sparling's in there somewhere." She pointed through a narrow door into a closebacked mass of backs. At the end of the room somebody they couldn't see was singing a cowboy ballad to a guitar. A little man with a large head covered with closecropped curly black hair was blocking the door. As they started to push past him he turned. It was Boris Spingarn.

"Well, well," he said with a dry laugh. Glenn introduced him to Marice. "The revolution's looking up . . . I'm organizing a league of unemployed scientific workers and the Soviet Book Corporation has sent us down a big jar of real beluga caviar."

"You mean you are in the . . . the movement," stammered Glenn.

"You remember my old bridge that used to make Gladys cry? Well, a lot of water's gone under it, a lot of unemployed water."

"Has Stanov come yet?" asked Marice breathlessly. "Let me lead you to him, Marice Gulick." He took her arm and began poking her gently sideways through the crowd.

Glenn stood in the doorway looking at people's backs. When the guitarplaying stopped people began to move around and he began to see faces he knew. Nobody looked his way.

He walked down the hall to the other door. A small diningroom had been cleared of furniture and people were dancing to a phonograph set on the floor in the corner. Against the mantelpiece stood Gladys Spingarn, still looking very pretty, talking to a tall blond young man who looked Russian. She was tossing back her hair and kicking out her legs as she talked. Glenn could see her moulded lips moving emphatically over the words but he couldn't hear what she was saying. The young man was laughing. When they started to dance she threw back her head with her eyes closed.

The next door opened into the kitchen. There a table had been set with a punchbowl and bottles and glasses, and another with plates of sandwiches. A tall yellow man with a completely shaved head was pouring vodka into a tumbler and handing it to Marice who was looking up at him laughing with her mouth open. Behind them Jane Sparling, in a gray dress falling off one shoulder that was almost an evening dress, was busily slicing a ham. Glenn walked up to her with his hand out. "Well, look who's here," she said with a snort and went on with her slicing. "Since we crashed your party, I wanted . . ." began Glenn lamely. Already she was sailing off with a plate of sliced ham held above people's heads towards the other room.

Glenn went back out into the hall, since everybody in the kitchen seemed too busy talking and drinking to notice him. Clear at the other end a bedroom door was open. People were sitting on all the chairs and dressers and were packed on the bed with drinks and cigarettes and sandwiches in their hands, listening to Irving Silverstone, who squatted turkishfashion on the pillows at the head of the bed, and held forth about the international situation.

The historic role of fascism, he was saying, spacing his words carefully, was to prepare the way for the triumph of the communist parties by destroying the democratic camouflage by which decaying capitalism deceived the masses. The state became in actual fact the executive committee of the ruling class, reformist and liberal elements were swept away, and the workingclass was left facing the naked exploitation of monopoly industrialism. Chauvinism and the economic contradictions inherent in fascism, which was no more able to solve any of these problems than democracy, resulted in war. In the universal disillusion following a second world war there would be nothing left but for the Party to lead the masses, now in full revolutionary temper and free from demagogic influences. . . . Irving had looked up and was looking Glenn full in the face as he said that. He turned his head away as if he hadn't recognized him.

Glenn went to get his coat and hat. He had to go back into the room where they were dancing to tell Marice. A space had been cleared in the middle of the floor; she was teaching Stanov the Charleston while everybody stood around smiling and making suggestions. Glenn pulled at Marice's sleeve and said in her ear, "I've got to go . . . I'll explain about it later."

Marice's cheeks were very red and her eyes were snapping. "I'm having a wonderful time, Glenn," she cried out. Then, as he turned towards the door, she ran after him whispering excitedly, "Why, they are all perfectly lovely. I knew they would be. . . . It's the nicest party I've ever been to in my life . . . and I promised Stanov . . . isn't he wonderful? He's just like an enormous baby . . . to take him dancing. And you almost didn't let me come." She gave him a sudden kiss on the ear and pushed him away from her.

"Well, goodnight, Marice."

Glenn closed the apartment door behind him, shutting out the cigarettesmoke and the smell of drinks and the dancemusic and laughing and chatter of the party. He took a deep breath and started walking slowly down the stairs. The door opened and closed again above his head and steps tramped fast after him. At the street door a man in an overcoat and muffler, wearing a flat foreignlooking cap pulled down over his eyes, caught up with him. A heavy squarish face with thick lips was turned to him with a halfsmile. "How about having a little drink, Crockett?" he said. "I'd like to hear the full story of Slade County." Glenn looked at him suspiciously with puckered brows. "No, thanks," he said. "I'm going home."

The man followed him out on to the street. "Mind if I walk a few blocks with you?" He talked like a middlewestener but there was something else to his accent that made Glenn wonder if he weren't a Scandinavian. "All right," he said. "You don't remember me," the man said, "I'm Bernard Morton. I met you in Pittsburgh."

"Is that where you come from?" asked Glenn. The man nodded with a confidential kind of smile. "That and a town on the Baltic. . . . But now just for my own information, what would your attitude be . . . if you parted . . . er . . . company with the Party?"

Glenn looked at him with narrowed eyes. They were walking up the avenue, that was already fairly empty of traffic, in the cruel north-west wind that had come up and blown away all the moist spring airs of the afternoon. "You wouldn't come into a bar and have a couple of drinks?" Glenn shook his head. "Old Less was talking about you just the other day. He thinks a lot of you. He's a bighearted fellow. This will distress him. If we had a few thousands more like him in the lower cadres of the party our way would be easy." Glenn put his chin down in his overcoat and walked fast. "The same applies to you . . . but you understand the Leninist conception of a monolithic party."

"Lenin meant monolithic in action. . . . He believed in the fullest discussion before a policy was decided on. I can't get anybody to dis-cuss anything. They just expect you to take orders like a zombie."

"The comrades have feelings," Morton let the words drag, "like everybody else. It is impossible to look at passing events as coldly as theory demands. . . . What are you going to do?" Morton's voice was suddenly hard as a traffic cop's.

"Keep on as best I can outside. After all, the majority of the workingclass in this country is out of reach of the party." "And you will make it your business to keep them there?" Morton's voice grumbled in his throat. "Goodnight," he said sharply as if it were an insult.

Next morning Glenn was eating his breakfast with the twins when Marice came in with green circles under her eyes. He couldn't get much out of her except that Irving Silverstone had gone to Harlem with them and acted funny as a crutch, she'd never thought he had a sense of humor, but Stanov just made everybody funny, and that she'd had the time of her life and was going to bed to sleep for a week.

At noon he met Sylvia at George Hurlbut Cramm's office. Cramm had been in touch with friends of the governor-elect and said that if Glenn could come with him to St. Louis where he had to go on busi-ness that night, he thought he might be able to arrange an interview to give Glenn a chance to tell him the actual story of the Bull Creek shootings, in an informal way. Perhaps he could be induced to hold hearings after his inauguration. The laborunions had supported his campaign. Glenn said the main question was carfare. He didn't have a cent. What about Marice, asked Cramm with a sidelong smile. Glenn blushed. No, he had reasons for not wanting to ask her. Sylvia spoke up excitedly that she had some money in a savings bank. She could furnish that, maybe it could be paid back to her later after they had their nonpartisan workers' unity committee established. "I suppose you know," said Glenn, "that I won't be representing any party or organization in this . . . I am entirely on my own."

"All the better . . . all the better," said Cramm, rubbing his hands. "After all, it's an errand of mercy."

A week later Glenn got back from St. Louis thoroughly discouraged. He'd been taken to see the governor-elect at his hotel and had tried to explain things, but the governor-elect, a pinkjowled cordial sixfooter with sparse red hair, had been so full of rye whiskey and backslapping and had had to be so folksy with so many people who had kept breaking in on them that Glenn was afraid he hadn't remembered a word. Glenn managed to put in his hand the story reduced to headings on three typewritten sheets, but all he could get out of him was a promise to confer with his advisers and to investigate all influences subversive of the proper course of justice. The governor-elect had tried to remember how the quotation went about the quality of mercy is not strained, but had fallen down on it, and his secretary had too. Of course, George Hurlbut Cramm had known the whole piece; after that the governor-elect would talk of nothing but the beauties of Shakespeare and the contemptibleness of contemporary literature, so there was nothing left to them but to say what a pleasure and privilege it had been to meet him, and leave. Coming back the train had been held up by a blizzard and was hours late, so that it was three o'clock in the morning before Glenn got into the Pennsylvania Station. On the way to the subway, he passed a phone booth. Something told him he had better call up Marice's before he went up there.

After a lot of ringing a man's voice answered the phone. It was Irving Silverstone. He started to stutter a little when he recognized Glenn's voice; then he asked coldly did Comrade Crockett want to speak to Comrade Gulick? For a minute Glenn couldn't think who that was. Then he said please, yes. Marice seemed a little flustered and vague, said she hadn't expected him, but he'd better come up and get some rest.

When he got up to the house, after having to wait twenty minutes for a subway train, Marice came to the door herself looking flushed and with her eyes shiny bright, in a red eveningdress cut very low, and said, my dear, he ought to have been with them, all Harlem had been there, she'd given a benefit for the victims of southern lynch law and had raised two thousand dollars and he ought to have heard John Henry singing *Swing low, sweet chariot.*

They were standing in the hall. Glenn was so tired he was groggy. He let himself drop on the settee without taking off his overcoat. "Marice," he said, "I've been having a hell of a time."

"Better have a little bacon and eggs before going to bed . . . Irv and I were just having some."

Glenn followed her into the big livingroom that was littered with paper napkins and festooned with Chinese lanterns and colored paper garlands hung from the chandeliers to the corners of the room. There were palms in the corners and soiled glasses all along the mantelpiece and on all the tables. On the horsehair sofa a skinny palechocolate-colored young man was fast asleep with his mouth open. Marice giggled. "Don't wake him. . . . He's the king of buck and wing . . . he passed out a little. . . . It was the most wonderful party." Glenn followed her back into the diningroom, where plates and dishes with remnants of icecream and chicken salad and cake were stacked up on the big mahogany table, and through the gutted pantry into the kitchen, where Irving Silverstone with his shirtsleeves rolled up on his skinny arms was stirring scrambled eggs over the gasstove. It seemed to Glenn that Irving hesitated for a moment whether to shake hands with him or not. "We're having scrambled eggs and bacon," shrieked Marice shrilly. "Better have something." Glenn stammered that he was too tired.

"Well," said Marice in a businesslike way, "the bed in the third floor front bedroom is all made up. You better go up there. Don't go in back because you'll find yourself in bed with the children's nurse and it would be a shock to both of you."

The stairs seemed endlessly steep. Glenn found the room and turned in. The next morning, before anybody was up, he got his things together and walked the streets of the upper west side until he found himself a furnished room.

4

The meeting was in a huge dimly lit hall. He was speaking; closepacked faces were ranked in circles around him, spiralling up tier on tier until they faded into a swirl of smoke above his head. He was going through all the motions of speaking but his throat had turned to wood; no words came out. He could see the worker men and women in the nearest rows cupping their hands to their ears and leaning forward. Their heads stretched towards him on long necks, their eyes were staring out of their heads like metal knobs, their bigknuckled hands, cupped round their ears to hear, spread out enormous and gnarled. No words came from his wooden throat. Already he could hear the shells from the big guns the bosses had trained on the hall: shriek, sizzle, shriek, sizzle: there was no explosion. His throat was wooden, no sound came out of it to warn the workers they were being shelled with gas. Suddenly a loud alarum bell started ringing in his throat. The tocsin, the tocsin, the faces yelled as they whirled past him like spiralling smoke. He woke with his alarmclock going off beside the bed.

Seventhirty; he'd be late. Glenn jumped to his feet, as he put down his window he glanced out at the grimy roofs streaked with yellow-pitted snow. He sponged himself off at the washbasin, pulled on his pants and hurried out to the bathroom to shave. All the time he was thinking he must shake off that bad dream. Then as he was shaving, looking in the speckled mirror at his own face pale and lumpy as suet, with its colorless eyebrows and hair not quite red and not quite brown, he began to remember that it wasn't all a dream. He really had been in a hall last night at a meeting to protest against the bombardment of the workers' apartment houses in Vienna. Good Christ, it was worse than his dream, he told himself, as he hurriedly scraped the safety-razor down that upper lip of his that still had an immature childish pouting look he was pretty sick of. The meeting had broken up in a fight between Communist and Socialist party workers. As he drew the razor up the stubble on his neck . . . gosh, he was getting to look skinny and white as a mushroom, ought to get more outofdoor exercise . . . he began to work out an editorial. *The complete lack of sincerity*

of the leadership of the official Communist Party was again proved by
the lamentable events that took place last night in Madison Square Gar-
den . . . proved or proven? Dabbling his chin with a piece of toiletpaper
to staunch the blood where he'd cut himself he ran back into the hall
bedroom to finish dressing.

The room hadn't warmed up. He put his hand on the radiator; there
was a tiny bit of warmth at one end. No use complaining to the landlady, all she'd say was why did you insist on opening your windows, for
three dollars a week you didn't have a right to fresh air when you slept,
not in these hard times. He hurried shivering into his clothes and ran
out of doors.

It was a raw foggy morning of winter thaw. At all the crossings
there were deep torrents of slush. Hell, he kept forgetting to buy him
rubbers. By the time he got to the cafeteria his feet were soaked.

At the corner stand outside he bought the morning papers, then
he took a green ticket from the machine on the white metal turnstile
that rang a little gong with a cheerful ting as he passed, and went up
to the counter to order the fifteen cent combination breakfast. He was
just coming away with his tray when he found himself face to face with
Sylvia Freund, the small dark girl with a thick hooked nose and squat
hips who helped him edit the paper. "Now what?" she asked him, staring ardently up into his face through her thick glasses across the cracked
wheat and orangejuice she was going to make her breakfast on.

"It's the worst thing that's happened yet."

"It's so wicked. How can they be so wicked with the blood of the
workers not yet cold in Vienna?"

"The united front from below," snapped Glenn as he sat down at
a table.

"From below decency," she said as she slipped into the seat beside
him.

He laughed sourly. "Anyway I suppose there's some advantage in
hitting the bottom . . . nothing worse than this can happen to us," he
said.

"I looked everywhere for you at the meeting," she said in her timid
breathless pushing way.

"I was upstairs in the gallery."

"I went home to Mommer and cried and cried. She thought it was because I was thwarted in love."

"Poor kid," said Glenn.

"You don't think I'm sentimental?"

"I think you're the best revolutionary worker there is. . . . Gosh, we've got to hurry if we are ever going to press." They swallowed the rest of their breakfast and, still chewing, hurried past the cashier, each paying his own check, and rushed out into the crowded street. At the first corner Sylvia looked down at Glenn's feet. "You naughty boy," she said. "You ought to have rubbers." Glenn made a face. "I can't seem to remember to buy any."

"I'll buy some for you today, but you must come and try them on."

"Remind me after we've put the paper to bed." They were running up the three wooden flights of dusty stairs to the little office they split with the Acme Novelty Company, which consisted of another desk at which sat an elderly gloomy stout man in a derby, Mr. Golden, who this morning was already at his desk chewing his always unlit cigar, and reading his mail. They shouted Goodmorning to him, and Glenn slid into the chair at the typewriter by the window that the partition cut in the middle. He shoved in a piece of yellow paper and began: *In the name of the class war prisoners and the long list of martyrs of the workingclass in their long heartbreaking fight for a decent society where a worker will get the true value of his labor . . . we protest against the disrupting and heartbreaking incidents that were provoked by the Communists last night . . . .*

"Glenn," Sylvia was shoving an old telephone book under his feet, "take your shoes off and let me dry them on the radiator. . . . Put your feet on this."

Glenn had just taken off his shoes and had put a new sheet of yellow paper in the typewriter, after tearing up the old one, when there was a loud tramping on the stairs and a voice shouting, "Is Mr. Spotswood's office here?" He heard Mr. Golden's voice saying sharply, "Next office, please."

"Sylvia, see who it is," hissed Glenn, without looking up from his typewriter, "keep him outside. *We protest in the name of the working class*," he began again.

Sylvia was back. "He insists on seeing you . . . he says he's an old friend." Right after her came Paul Graves holding out both hands. He wore a lightbrown tweed suit and looked tanned and tall and prosperous; a little sprinkle of gray hair on his temples and in his beetling eyelashes gave him a dignified professorial look. "Well, for crying out loud," he said, "old Spotswood's the hardest man in New York to see . . . how are you? My gosh!"

Glenn felt silly hopping around in his socks with holes in them that his toes stuck out of. "Say, Paul, could you come back in a couple of hours. I've got to put the paper to bed so that Sylvia . . . this is Paul Graves . . . he's about the oldest friend I've got . . . Sylvia Freund. She takes it to the printer, but I got an editorial to write."

"I bet I know what it's about," said Paul cheerfully. "Vienna."

"It's worse than that. It's a row happened in New York last night between the workers' organizations at the protest meeting."

"I want to talk to you about all that, Glenn. Come on up to the hotel and have a drink and forget the editorial. . . . We just stopped off to see you . . . we're all there."

"Who?"

"Peggy and Graves' travelling circus. . . . They'll tell you about the Soviet Union."

"Of course, the kids . . . I'll come up in two hours."

"Come up to lunch . . . Miss Freund, can I trust you to deliver this young man at the Biltmore Hotel in time for lunch? My wife would be most delighted if you'd come," said Paul, dropping into his southern gentlefolks manner. "I'm afraid I couldn't," said Sylvia, giving him a sideways look through her glasses. "I have to take Workers' Unity to the printers, but I think Comrade Spotswood would go if he could find time." "Sure," said Glenn, starting to pound at his typewriter again. "I'll be there."

It was nearly two before he got up to the hotel. It was so long since he'd been in an uptown hotel that he felt awkward going past the doorman in his shabby raincoat and his shoes that left little rings of water wherever he stepped on the marble floor. Paul met him at the door of a large bright room that had a round table set with knives and forks and plates and things under silver covers in front of the window. "Peggy and the young had to eat but I said I'd wait for you if I waited till Christmas."

"It's not Easter yet," shouted a little girl with silky gold hair, coming out from the next room. "This is Bettina," said Paul.

"Slushet Pavl . . . Gheorgh ciudah," he called. Two tall sharpeyed blackhaired boys came in, and after them Peggy, who had grown into a big handsome fullbreasted woman. She had a goodnatured look that Glenn didn't remember, in spite of the overdressed fussiness there was about her silk blouse with puffy white sleeves. "Hello, Glenn," she said, shaking his hand. "My, I'm glad he found you. . . . He nearly drove me crazy coming over on the boat, whenever we'd start talking about anything he'd say: Gosh, I'd give anything in the world to talk to old Glenn about that."

"And these," interrupted Paul, without paying attention to what Peggy was saying, "are Paul and George, they are regular sovietzkis and this is Oliver . . . ." A pinkfaced towheaded youngster of about two came out frowning from behind his mother's silk dress. "And now everybody get out while I give the tovarisch a little shot of vodka . . . it's a special kind flavored with oakleaves. . . . It's what the boys in the Kremlin drink." He reached a bottle and some glasses from the shelf in the wardrobe. "You all eat some lunch," said Peggy, gathering up a child in each hand. "I'll be trying to get these hooligans to sleep for their afternoon nap." "Bolshoy skandal," yelled the two older boys.

Paul closed the door on them and went to the telephone to ask for a waiter. "Well, here's how . . . vashezderovia . . ." he said, pouring the pale yellow spirit into two little glasses. He smacked his lips on it. "That's what makes 'em forget Marx and Engels," he said. Glenn took a sip and choked. They sat down at the table and Paul uncovered some relishes and bread and butter. "The Russians always tell you you've got to eat something with it . . . have an anchovy?"

"Paul," said Glenn with his mouth full. "My gosh, you're looking well. . . . How was it over there? How's the five-year plan? Is it going to work?"

"It'll work if Red Joe has to starve every miserable peasant in the Soviet Union to death to make it work. . . . But tell me about yourself, Glenn . . . at least you're sailing under your own name . . . I can't tell you how this alias business used to make me sick . . . I don't know why."

"They threw me out of the party," said Glenn, trying to keep his voice casual.

"Chort. I thought you were their most loyal adherent."

"Couldn't swallow the party line."

"What are you doing now?"

"Running a little paper for working class unity . . . and campaigning to get guys out of jail that everybody else has forgotten. Have you heard about the splinter parties? Well, I'm a splinter."

The waiter came in and Paul ordered up a broiled porterhouse steak and frenchfried potatoes and a pitcher of imported German beer. "Gosh, Paul, you must be prosperous," said Glenn after the waiter had gone.

"Never had so much money in my life. . . . They paid me in gold. . . . I made more out of it than they did . . . good Christ, in every way. They gave me everything in the world but as soon as I'd get a station started the goddam party line would come in and they'd shoot my best guys or put 'em on forced labor and send me off somewhere else . . . I could have stayed on but I got sick of it and came home . . . damn good thing too . . . the New Deal's got the five-year plan knocked for a row of red squares as a social experiment . . . I began to hear the eagle screaming." He filled up the glasses again. "It's a great little antiseptic," he said, coughing behind his thin long brown hand that had big veins on it under the black hairs. "Say, Glenn, why don't you give up all this agitation and get a real job? You could make a living teaching in a college."

"Got too many commitments . . . comrades who've gotten in jams on account of me . . . workers who been framed and put in jail."

"Well," said Paul, "I've only been home four days but it seems to me that the country's changed a hell of a lot. . . . The whole setup's different . . . I think we are going to have the kind of country where guys like us can do useful work, see what I mean. . . . The revolution's happened; kid, it's all over."

Glenn felt his face tightening with disappointment. He didn't want to get into an argument. He cleared his throat: "What are you going to do, Paul?" he asked quietly.

Well, Paul said, his voice dropping into a drawl, first he was going home to see the folks and park the kids and then he might go to Washington to see if he could chisel something out of the Department. He'd worked out some ideas about agricultural experiment stations and the government was sure shovelling out the money. Maybe they would set him up in a small way and let him do his stuff. He could have done a lot more in Russia if every new variety of corn hadn't had to spell out the Communist Manifesto. In the last year it had gotten worse yet, you couldn't raise a patch of cowpeas without having Red Joe's picture on every pod.

The waiter came in with the steak. A cosy broiled meat friedpotato smell filled the warm room. Glenn felt himself settling back comfortably in the deep chair. They began to eat. "Is there really an opposition?" Glenn asked, chewing.

"You don't ask your best friend a question like that in the Soviet Union. He might be a spy or just turn you in for your job or your wife or your apartment or a cake of soap. . . . You don't know what it's like there, boy. . . . Lemme tell you something, I never been so happy in my life as the day I got the bunch on the Italian steamboat at Odessa to go to Alexandria. We went to Egypt to get a little sun on us after the great Russian fog."

"I still believe in the workingclass," said Glenn grimly.

"They got 'em working, all right," said Paul. "The rest of the European dictatorships are comic opera, but there's nothing comic opera about the Soviet Union. . . . Don't get me wrong, Glenn, I think the Russians are great people. Lenin was a great man, but the old Russian revolution is in a bad period. Every great movement in history has its bad periods."

"That's why the first duty of every revolutionist is to fight the Communist Party."

"When you can get a good beefsteak like this you don't need to fight the Communist Party."

"In an uptown capitalist hotel; what do you expect? But the unemployed workers are starving, really starving. Haven't you read about the hunger marches?"

"The President is fixing 'em up, isn't he?"

"He's buying their votes for a program of reformist illusions . . . he's the real social fascist."

"He's getting 'em fed though . . . at least he's trying to feed 'em," said Paul, slowly putting down his knife and fork on the table and looking out the window. Glenn's eyes followed his and he stared out at the tops of the buildings in the steely latewinter sunshine and the high solid clouds above them in the blue varnished sky. "In Russia they've starved 'em deliberately. There's no way to explain it to anyone who hasn't seen it . . . I don't know what the real figures are, but I seen 'em . . . what's left of them . . . trainloads of 'em being shipped to Siberia."

"You mean collectivization?"

Paul nodded with his face still turned away. He cleared his throat. "Can I order you up any dessert? They're bringing coffee."

Glenn shook his head and got to his feet and walked back and forth on the deep carpet of the room.

"It couldn't be like that here," he said in a low strained voice. "We won't let it be like that here."

Peggy came in and drank coffee with them and little Paul and George came in and showed off their Russian. Glenn felt wellfed and cosy and relaxed. He liked the kids. It made him feel good that Paul still seemed to think he was a great guy.

Before he knew it it was late afternoon. He and Paul were telling the kids about how they'd been counsellors at a summer camp and gotten fired for teaching the kids to play the Red Army game. Peggy had the radio going. Paul was saying he wanted Glenn to stay to supper and go on with them to see a musical show and some New York hotspots, when the phone rang.

It was an outside call for Glenn. He went to the phone still laughing at Paul's hayseed talk about big city nightlife. It was Sylvia. "Oh, Comrade Spotswood, have you forgotten about the meeting? It's the restaurant and hotel workers. It's seven o'clock; we just have time to make it. I didn't call up. I didn't want to disturb you and your capitalist friends. I've been waiting in the drugstore on Fiftyninth Street where you said you'd meet me and go up together, I've been there thirty-five minutes already . . . ."

"All right, Sylvia, I'll be right over . . . I forgot the time. We were talking about the Soviet Union."

"Of course, dear." There was a changed note in her voice. The querulous squeak had gone out of it. "I understand."

Glenn couldn't help a certain stiffness getting into his manner while he was shaking hands with Paul and Peggy and the boys. He went off in a hurry saying he'd forgotten that he had to speak at a meeting.

5

Over the outside door of the office was a strip of white bunting on which red letters had been sewn: ORGANIZE. The door was ajar. Glenn pushed it open and walked in. He was in a big unfurnished room full of automobile workers in their storeclothes standing in groups, smoking and talking with their hats on the backs of their heads. Glenn worked his way through to the other side, where he spoke to a young man in a football sweater who was poring over a card catalogue on a deal kitchen table. The young man pointed over his shoulder with his thumb through the door behind him. Glenn walked on through a room full of young women typing and pushed open a groundglass door that said PRIVATE. At a mahoganyfinished desk in a small office with two bright windows, was a squareshouldered man with a thick stubble of gray hair growing low on his flat forehead who was leaning over some papers sucking a pencil. As Glenn walked towards the desk the man looked up. It was Less Minot.

Less jumped to his feet. "Why, you old sonofabitch, I didn't know you were out here."

"I been here for a year working around. I worked at Ford's until they got wise to me and laid me off."

Less gave a kind of roar and slapped him on the back. "Why, you old sonofabitch, you'd ought to be damn glad they didn't lay you out in your coffin. . . . Want to go to work organizin'?" Glenn nodded. Less went back and sat behind his desk and began to drum on it with a short tobaccostained forefinger. He pulled two cigars out of the pocket of his doublebreasted jacket and poked one at Glenn. "Smoke, Sandy?"

Glenn shook his head. Less' face had gotten a little thick and jowly but he hadn't changed much. For a moment they looked at each other without speaking. Then Less cleared his throat and said in a furtive low voice:

"Are you through with all this opposition crap?"

"Now, Less, you know I never had anything to do with any opposition. . . . All I've done is say when I thought policies were wrong."

"I know you used to be straight, Sandy, but Kerist, if half the things they wrote about you . . ."

"Skip the ancient history, Less . . . our job is to organize the workers . . . you and me used to dream about industrial unions up in the Pittsburgh district."

"I know. I know. . . . Look here, are you a member of any party now?"

"We tried to get up the Workers' Unity League but it flopped."

"That was a bum steer. . . . Kerist, Sandy, I don't know what to do." Less took a big wooden kitchen match out of his pocket and struck it with his thick thumbnail and lit his cigar. "I know you're regular . . . but the first thing I know you'll be getting diarrhea of the face . . . you got too much eddication for an organizer. How do I know you won't bore from within? How about applying for readmission to the Party?"

Glenn shook his head. "I can't, Less . . . I don't believe in a lot of what's going on."

"Shush," said Less almost unconsciously. Then he went on in a whisper, "But that means you're still opposition, don't it?"

"Less, I'm an American workingman who wants to help the boys organize."

Less got to his feet again and came over and put his arm around Glenn's shoulder and started talking fast into his ear. "We need guys like you, Sandy, in the Mechanics' and Metalworkers' . . . you're the kind of guy who'll go right to the top. . . . You could be one of the top labor leaders in this country . . . but I can't give you a job unless you promise me personally you won't go back on the Party . . . neither by word or deed no matter what happens . . . I know if you say you'll do it you'll do it. It's takin' a big chance for me personally but I think you're worth it. . . . You can go places I never could. The bosses started beatin' up on me too soon . . . skull's too thick. You got brains, Sandy."

Glenn went and looked out of the window with his hands in his pockets. Less sat down on his desk swinging his short legs and started puffing coils of blue smoke out of his cigar.

Down the street beyond the gleaming tops of two streams of moving automobiles Glenn could see a little segment of the grass of the park littered with squares of newspaper. On every square was stretched out the figure of an unemployed man. A few pigeons were fluttering overhead. He wasn't thinking of anything. He turned back.

"Less, it's no use," he said.

He walked out of the office of the new union and went down in the elevator. On a bench in the park he found Sylvia. As she looked up at him with anxious eyes, the sunlight caught on her spectacles and lit up a series of bright edges inside the thick glass. Glenn sat down beside her and said, "No go . . . I saw Less, he's gotten to be quite the big labor-leader, cigar and all. . . . No oppositionists need apply."

"But we're not." Sylvia burst out crying and took off her glasses to wipe them. Glenn took her gently by the hand and gave her knee little soothing pats. "Well, I guess we'll have to go home and get on the W.P.A.," she said, sniffling. "We can get on in Brooklyn . . . Popper's a kind of foreman."

"Sylvia," said Glenn, "you can do useful work on the Spanish workers' committee." She started to cry again. "Oh, there's so much to do. The workers being defeated and murdered everywhere and they won't let us help."

"If you say the same words over too often, you get so you don't believe them," drawled Glenn, leaning over and looking down at his hands that hung between his knees.

"You're too honest for them," she said, her voice petering out into a whining sigh. She was looking up at him with an embarrassing doglike gleam in her eyes.

"Too big for my boots, I guess," said Glenn with a laugh that rasped in his own ears. "Anyway I feel terrible."

That night he kissed Sylvia and put her and her battered suitcase and typewriter on the New York bus, saying he wanted to hang around Detroit for a day or two more to see if there was some place he could fit in. Next time she saw him, he said, laughing, maybe he'd have joined the wobblies or the old Communist Labor Party, she'd better get ready for shocks. The bus moved off; the last he saw was a tearful smile behind her glasses, behind the doublewindow of the bus that reflected the glare of floodlights of the station.

For several days he'd been keeping an address on an old envelope folded in four in the breast pocket of his coat. As soon as the bus went off down the street he walked around there. It was a frame fourfamily tenement. He rang the bell under the name of Lopez and toiled up the three flights of stairs. A small grayhaired man opened a door for him. "State your business, please," he asked in a clipped meticulous English. "I want to enlist," said Glenn. The man gave him a hard look out of his gray eyes for a moment, then he smiled and asked softly, "Volunteer or mercenary?" "Volunteer," said Glenn.

The man shook his hand and let him into the stuffy little parlor with oldfashioned indiaprint draperies lit by a stained glass lamp. "Come in, comrade," he said.

"I'm not a partymember," said Glenn. "I'm not a member of any party."

"We are all comrades . . . all of us who want to fight against . . . the enemies of the human race," the man said. "Where did you work last?" "Ford's . . . they fired me because they heard me talking union in the washroom."

"Ever thought about tanks?"

"I'd rather drive a truck . . . or an ambulance," said Glenn.

"Anyway you want to fight."

"It's the one thing we all can agree on." The little man gave Glenn a sharp look and then called to somebody through the dusty curtains that divided the little room from the next. "Dr. Wiseman . . . here's another customer . . . right through the curtains, comrade."

The bedroom beyond had been fixed up as a kind of doctor's office. Behind a kitchen table with white oilcloth tacked over it sat a man in a white Russian tunic, who had a long thin face, and a thin white crooked nose on which a pair of noseglasses were set a little askew. "Haha," he shouted jauntily in a high voice. "More cannon fodder . . . take off your upper clothing and loosen your belt and please urinate in this glass . . . you can go in the back of the room if it embarrasses you. . . . Well, I don't mind telling you I think you boys are all great. You know it's no picnic over there. I'd be going myself as a doctor if I didn't have my wife and children and the old people to support. . . . The defense of Madrid . . . it's a great crusade . . . I do what I can . . . I give all my evenings. When you boys come back I'll give you free medical service." He gave a rasping chuckle. "What more can I do?" As he talked he went over Glenn's chest, thumping with the ends of his fingers. "Never had anything tubercular, or syphilis that you know of? Good . . . I'd say sound as a dollar . . . or ought I to say sound as a soviet ruble?"

While Glenn was putting his clothes back on the grayhaired man stuck his head through the curtains. "You know, Comrade Spotswood, we have to have a few days to check on your statements," he said severely.

"I haven't got anything to lie about," said Glenn, laughing. "You guys better make up your minds quick whether you can take me or not, because I'm flat broke."

"Do you know about the onecent restaurant?" asked Dr. Wiseman. Glenn nodded. "Well, here's a coupla dollars to keep you going. Sure they'll take you . . . don't worry . . . Comrade, I'd give anything in the world to be in your shoes tonight."

"Even at the onecent lunch?" asked Glenn. They all laughed. They were still laughing when Glenn pocketed the two dollars, shook hands and walked out onto the street again.

6

When the train stopped Glenn stuck his head out of the window of the thirdclass compartment he had been sitting alone in all the trip to see if the others were getting out. It was raining hard on the glass roof of the railroad station. The gray platforms were empty except for two elderly redfaced porters in blue tunics who were slowly pushing along a handtruck with a battered muchcorded trunk on it. Down the train a couple of doors opened. Among the few countrypeople in dark clothes who were lowering themselves backwards down the steep steps of the oldfashioned cars, Glenn saw the little man with a rumpled yellow face whose language nobody understood who had been introduced to him in Paris as Peter, and Monty's tall overbelted figure with its ham actor look, and Saul Chemnitz's curly head without any hat on it bobbing from side to side. Glenn hoisted down the heavy box he'd been asked to carry across the border which they had told him was full of X-ray equipment, put his paper parcel of clothes under his arm and followed the straggle of people with bundles that crossed the empty tracks and platforms towards an iron gate with a blue enamelled sign over it saying: SORTIE.

When Glenn stopped to hand his ticket to a greenishgray bleareyed old official at the gate, Saul bumped into him from behind and said "Excuse me" in English. Glenn let his lips form the words "Shut up" and walked on down the scaling stucco passage that led out. At the exit he found himself looking through a curtain of rain at a stonepaved street bordered by a row of stone houses streaming with rain, and wondering what to do next. People brushed past him and hurried out under umbrellas to get into a small wet yellow streetcar. After the streetcar had gone jangling off Glenn set down his box and looked around him. Saul, tall and loose jointed with a jewishlooking nose and pink cheeks, was standing beside him making I'm sorry motions with his lips. Monty was staring out into the rain without moving a muscle of his face like a picture of a highlife movie star; Peter was lost in contemplation of the worn pointed shoes he wore on his feet. Everybody else had gone except a young fellow in mustardcolored corduroys with a dusty blue beret on the side of his head who was leaning against the yellowed printed notices on the wall, reading a paper and rubbing one sockless foot in a grimy canvas sandal against the other. As Glenn glanced in his direction he folded up his paper, and Glenn found himself looking into a pair of eyes green as olives set in an oval brown face that had a little light down around the chin and on the cheeks. The boy smiled and came forward showing very white teeth. "Abraham

Leencoln," he said very low. His breath smelled strong of garlic. They all four had their mouths open ready to speak. He shook his finger across his mouth and pointed to a big square black limousine that had just driven up in front of them. Monty nodded and opened the door and they all piled in.

As soon as they had gotten themselves and their boxes wedged in the back seats the driver, who was a sandymustached Frenchman with a halfsmoked cigarette in the corner of his mouth, leaned back and shook each of their hands in turn with a "Salut, camarades." The boy with the beret, who had climbed into the front seat, thrust his narrow brown hand back to them and said, "Salud, camaradas."

Everybody pulled a deep breath. "Greetings, comrades," shouted Saul, bubbling over like an opened bottle of pop. Monty took out a package of Luckies and offered them all around. Everybody started puffing out smoke.

Comrades, Saul was declaiming in his stuttering voice, he'd been getting the heebyjeebies. Monty tapped the driver on the shoulder and asked, "Espagna, Wee Wee?" The Frenchman shook his head. The boy in the beret turned around and tapped himself importantly on the chest and said, "Yo Antonio," and made two fingers of one hand ride horseback on the other. Meanwhile Saul babbled on, stuttering through his cigarette, asking everybody if they had ever done any mountainclimbing, saying he sure guessed they were going to get some mountainclimbing experience now and that he wished his stomach didn't feel all knotted up like it did.

Monty said that that was how a yellow streak felt but added solemnly that he mustn't worry, everybody had a yellow streak. Saul interrupted spluttering that he wouldn't miss the experience for a million, the comrades mustn't get him wrong.

After they got clear of the town, the road ran straight through the bottom of a green valley among treecovered mountains, hidden above the first slopes by lowhanging rainclouds. The Frenchman drove very fast. At the end of the valley they jolted over the cobbles of a stone village, shot through a rainwashed square with striped awnings over the storewindows and feathery trees and a babyblue bandstand and on up through small fields of vines and brightgreen patches of early crops. At the turn in the road they got a backward glimpse of the village hemmed in by stone castle walls piling up to a peak in a hunched stone church with a rustcolored roof that moss and shrubs grew on; beyond was the valleyfloor pale bluegreen and steaming with rain.

They had all settled down to enjoying the scenery when there was a whistle from the side of the road and the car stopped with a lurch. They were in front of a new unpainted sentry box that looked like a farmhouse privy from which a wooden bar stuck out across the road. A man with a broad black beard tucked into a rubber hood and cloak, under which was a blue uniform, came out and peered into the car. "Nonintervention," growled the driver in his throat and poked a folder of papers in the officer's face.

He looked at them, frowning and shaking his head, and beckoned the driver to go inside the sentrybox. As he left the car the driver made a downward gesture to the Americans, meaning keep your shirt on, with the palm of his hand. Monty cleared his throat elaborately. Not even Saul said anything. Glenn could imagine he could hear all their hearts thumping.

After what seemed hours, during which loud voices raised in French altercation came from the sentrybox, the driver came back grinning. After he'd climbed in he made them understand that the gendarme had telephoned the frontier and then shrugged his shoulders laughing as if to say what the hell did that matter. Monty passed around his cigarettes again and they all drew in deep sucking breaths.

The driver stepped on the gas and kept on zigzagging up the mountainroad skidding the car around the sharp curves. Then he jammed on the brakes suddenly in front of a field full of sheep all headed one way with their tails to the driving rain and turned under an arch through a mossy stone wall into the courtyard of a farm.

A lanky man in corduroys with a beret on the side of his head and thick black stubble on his lanternchin opened the door of the car with a brokentooth grin and a cheery, "Salud, camaradas americanos," and started hauling out the boxes. They all piled out, and stood around in the downpour watching the lanky man and Antonio fit the boxes into the big saddlebags of four wet mules that were stamping and fretting on the small slippery stone cobbles. Then the Frenchman shook hands all around, said goodby sharply in English to the Americans and drove off down the road.

"Well, Tony," said Monty, "where do we go from here?" Tony grinned and stuck out his forefinger like a kid playing gunmen at home and said, "España, boom, boom." Then he pointed to the lanky man and said, "Paco."

There seemed to be considerable hurry, Paco explained with elaborate dumbshow that they must climb on the mules on top of the backsaddles and set off leading the first mule. Tony followed after the rear mule yelling Arrhé. They started off along a trail that skirted the old stone walls of the squat farm buildings and cut across a squudgy pasture and then climbed over loose stones through a grove of firtrees. Once in among the firs they left the trail and started straight up the steep slope, Paco and Tony yelling and cursing at the mules in Spanish all the time.

The rain kept on falling and soon worked its way through Glenn's cheap raincoat. The low ragged sky was beginning to go indigo with dark. Glenn was shivering and slid off his mule to walk. It was tough going, slogging up the steep mountainside, where only an occasional rocky glen full of ferns with a brook in the bottom of it broke the monotony of regularly spaced firtrees, through the firneedles soggy underfoot.

It was dark before they came out on another trail that led them round the edges of a narrow valley filled with the roar of a watercourse somewhere below. Glenn found he was stumbling so on the sharp pointed rocks, and stubbing his toes and getting his legs soaked in the muddy pools between, that he climbed up on the mule again; not without Tony's help, who ran forward to grab the saddlebag from the other side. Tony and Paco were soaked to the skin, because their only protection was a narrow blanket pulled over their shoulders, but they were scampering back and forth, shouting merrily at the mules and singing. The Americans were all dead tired by the time they lurched around a spur of rock that jutted suddenly out into the path, and found themselves trotting over a rolling meadow towards the faint light of a doorway. The mules seemed to know where they were going.

"Espagna, Wee Wee?" shouted Monty at the guides. They laughed and yelled back, "Dormir Francia, dormir, compañeros."

Two big woolly white dogs came out to bark at them until a woman's shrill voice from inside the house called them off. The Americans slid off their mules and crowded into a small smoky stone room dimly lit by a lantern where a skimpy fire smouldered in a huge stone fireplace. An old man with straggling white whiskers and a bigbreasted blond woman got up from two canebottom chairs as they came in and stood silent, leaning against the wall, looking cannily at them out of sour gray eyes.

Paco made them a speech while Tony scuttled around gathering up sticks to liven up the fire. The old man went out and came back with an armful of bottles of wine that he set out on the oilclothcovered table in front of the fire. Paco had to bring a hundred franc note out of his fat wallet and spread it out in front of her before the woman would start sluggishly laying the table and stirring up supper. Meanwhile the Americans were huddled round the fire drying their shoes and everything they dared take off in the chilly room.

The woman ladled hot soup with bread in it out of a black iron kettle and set a loaf of bread and a stonylooking cheese on the table and they ate and drank the sour puckery white wine and began to feel a little better. The old man seemed to be kidding them for drinking so little wine. He made them understand that he was eightytwo years old and drank a bottle with each meal and one for breakfast, three bottles a day, that was why he was so healthy. Glenn had a French phrasebook out on his knee and was getting along famously with the old man, who was telling him he ought to get himself a wife and settle down here, they needed men up here in the Pyrenees, husky young men ought to be in bed with the girls getting children instead of going and getting themselves killed, when Paco tapped him on the shoulder and made the dumbshow of putting his two hands together against his cheek and closing his eyes with a seraphic expression on his face, and whispered *dormir*.

The woman took a candle and groaning at every step led them up a flight of steep tiled stairs to a chilly room with two beds in it. They turned in two in a bed on hard straw mattresses. It was tough getting to sleep because they were still cold and wet and the covers were too short for them. Glenn slept with Saul who kept going into nightmares and waking up screeching. When they finally did warm up and drift off to sleep, bedbugs came out and bit them. It didn't seem as if they'd been asleep a minute before Paco was standing in the center of the room waving a lantern and yelling *arrhé* at them the way he did to the mules.

Downstairs Tony was blowing up the embers of the fire to heat up a saucepan of coffee. They each drank a cup of the sweet watery stuff that tasted of woodsmoke and ashes, and started out into the raw mist already silvery with morning. When they asked where the mules were Paco laughed and said *feeneesh* which was the only English word he knew. The rest of the way was on foot. The six of them took turns carrying the heavy boxes of X-ray equipment.

They warmed up after a while. They were climbing a rocky trail. Soon sweat was pouring off them and they were breathing heavily. Paco and Tony didn't seem to feel the climb at all and kept disappearing in the mist ahead. The boxes became a torture. The periods he wasn't carrying one Glenn was dreading the next time it would come around to him. His feet got to feel leaden in his stiff boots.

They came out on a rocky ledge with patches of snow on it. A stiff sharp wind blew right through their soaked clothes and sent the mist scurrying past them. Now and then through a tear in the clouds a rolling silvery landscape opened up under their feet. At the top of the ledge they tried to rest in a little gully that was sheltered from the wind, but Paco kept yelling at them to hurry.

They were climbing up a narrow snowy gorge that ended in a sharp lip of freshfallen snow at the top. This must be the border, they were telling each other as they fought, wheezing, for breath. The guides dashed up through the soft snow, sinking in above their knees. Glenn was after them with the box gouging into his shoulder. At the top he paused. This couldn't be right. It seemed a sheer drop into a swirling crater of fog.

But the snow round him was already giving way. He was sliding down a steep soft slope holding onto his box for all he was worth. He stopped with a bang with his legs jammed in a rocky crevasse. Paco and Tony were crowded beside him laughing.

They waited until the others slid down to them and started off at a jogtrot zigzagging down the slope through a downpour of rain. The snow stopped and the hillside became slippery mud among big shaggy evergreens. Glenn was so tired he hardly felt the icy glassclear water of a torrent at the bottom when he plunged into it up to his waist. He struggled across, lunging and slipping on the rolling stones underfoot. The guides were leading them a crazy chase up the other side of the valley again. At last it was time to turn over the box to Monty.

This time climbing was easier because there was a wellmade zigzag trail, but Glenn found himself falling flat on his face several times before he got to the top. When he fell he lay still, holding onto the rocks until his strength came back a little. He didn't dare look at the others. The last steep lap up to the pass Paco and Tony had to make several trips to carry up the boxes; over the last rocky stretch the Americans were barely able to inch themselves up hand over hand.

Glenn felt sun warm in his face as he dragged himself up through a shaly runnel, he shook the sweat out of his eyes and lay there looking out at clear blue sky and a row of snowy rockbuttressed peaks stretching away on either hand. Ahead, looking past a few cottony speeding clouds, he could see, beyond green hillsides cut by deep blueshadowed canyons, a great expanse of country yellow and ruddy in the sun. Just below him on a little grassy ledge Paco and Tony were stretched out on their backs with the boxes in a neat row behind them.

Suddenly he felt very happy. When he started to move again his knees shook so he could hardly keep his balance, his whole body felt light and dizzy. He stretched out on the grass beside Paco. The grass was warm and dry from the sun. He closed his eyes and fell asleep.

When he woke up they'd all taken their pants and shoes and shirts off to dry them. Paco was handing around a small skin of wine he'd taken out of an embroidered bag he wore over his shoulder. Then he made gestures of putting food into his mouth and they all cried sí sí and started reaching for their phrase books. "Well, we're over the border, boys," yelled Saul, and gave out a whoop.

They had to drink the wine out of the little resinous skin; it took considerable aim to get the thin stream into their mouths. Their hands were so shaky they spilled it over their faces and down their necks.

That seemed a great joke to Paco and Tony. Only Peter seemed still to have a steady hand.

Then Paco rummaged in his bag some more and brought out a big round loaf of dense white bread and some sausages and cheese. Tony pulled an oblong of chocolate out of his bag and frowning with care laid it on a rock to divide up with his knife into six pieces. While they ate he stood on the edge of the ledge, his cheeks bulging with bread and chocolate and, with the air of a professor in front of a blackboard, pointed out villages and rivers and mountains in the sunburned distance. Then smiling he made a big sweep with his left arm and said, "Nosotros," and a big sweep with his right arm, frowning, and said, "Enemigos." Next he made a pistol out of his hand and pointed down the middle and said, "Boom boom . . . frente de guerra."

"Gosh," Monty said, "it looks like fine country . . . it's almost as good as the view from Mount Frazier." "Where's that?" asked Glenn and Saul. "California . . . of course, that's higher . . . and you can see the sea."

They laughed and Monty drew himself up with a sulky look.

"I tell you, comrades," stuttered Saul, "this walk is some experience."

"Augenblick . . . wonderschön," sighed Peter, opening his mouth for the first time.

"Gosh," said Saul, "the world would be a fine place if it didn't have war and fascism in it."

"Well, it won't have when he get through with it," said Monty.

They rested an hour in the sun and then put their clothes, that were stiff with caked mud, on again and dragged themselves to their feet. They were all limping as they started out. Glenn felt a sharp stabbing pain in the back of his ankle at every step.

For the first hour they crawled along a barely visible path on the shaly shoulder of the big snowmountain to the left. Now and then one of them slipped and started a little shower of shale off into the treepacked valley a thousand feet below. They were jittery with relief when they came out on a grassy upland pasture with stone huts where Paco made them understand shepherds came in summer. They trotted along, laughing and kidding at a great rate, over the springy gently sloping turf.

At the edge of a grassy knoll full of flowers that overlooked a deep valley ranked with chestnuttrees, Tony suddenly stopped frowning and looked up into the sky. He pointed with his whole arm. "Aviación," he said. Paco stood beside him looking up and frowning at a little V of silver specks crossing the sky far off to the southward. Monty tried to ask if they were ours or theirs, but the guides just shrugged their shoulders and walked on frowning. "Well, comrades," stuttered Saul, "that reminds us of what we are here for . . . no summer vacation . . . but it sure is an experience to see this beautiful country. We were letting ourselves forget our political position." "Don't worry," said Monty. "The Henkels won't let us forget it."

It was late that night before they saw the first houses of Spain. They were walking along a broad smoothpaved muletrail. Below them lights came in sight, flickering in the cool still air. Then they smelt the smoke of fires that had some aromatic herb burning in them. Then, in no time, they were sitting at a long table in a lamplit whitewashed room in a square stone house in front of a roaring fire while a handsome girl with an oval brown face and white teeth like Tony's and a purple and black silk handkerchief on her head, was pouring out thick red wine for them and setting out a big meal of eggs puffy and crisp brown from being fried in olive oil, and pork stewed in tomatoes, and beans and bread. At the end of the table sat a bland little roundfaced man in khaki who said in somewhat slippery English that he was the governmental delegate and had come to greet the brave American fighters for democracy in the name of the Spanish Republic and the workers of hand and brain of the Spanish masses who were fighting for their lives against a double fascist invasion and the perfidy of the other socalled democratic states of Europe.

The Americans were so tired they could scarcely eat, much less listen to the rounded and oddly accented remarks of the governmental delegate. After they had staggered around shaking hands with everybody in the room, the governmental delegate told off a brighteyed young militiaman with a springy step to show them up the stairs to a row of cots that had plenty of blankets, and even clean sheets on them. Glenn never remembered how he got his clothes off.

Next morning when he woke up and sat on the edge of his cot he was so stiff he could barely put his feet to the ground. He was in a clean whitewashed room with a vaulted ceiling. Sunlight was pouring in the windows, that opened clear down to the redtiled floor and had iron railings across them. He cleaned the mud off his pants as well as he could and pulled them on and hobbled to a window and stood in the sun with the tiles warm under his bare feet, looking down into a courtyard. A few chickens were pecking among the cleanswept stones. In a dark arched doorway a girl was kneeling fanning at a charcoal brazier with a little wooden fan. On the warm air Glenn could smell the charcoal and frying olive oil and the heliotrope that grew in a big pot in the corner of the courtyard. Glenn felt like whistling but he didn't because the others were still asleep. He shaved and cleaned himself up at a basin with a towel beside it at the end of the hall, and hobbled painfully down the stairs.

Several militiamen in various uniforms with big pistol holsters on their hips were drinking coffee at the long table. They all raised their clenched right fists in a salute as Glenn came in. Their rifles were stacked in the corners of the room. One of the faces was familiar; rather bulging bright eyes and curly hair cut close on an elongated skull; it was Frankie Perez whom Glenn had known back in Horton. He'd thickened up with the years and his skin was blackish bronze from the sun. He wore a red silk handkerchief round his throat. He stared at Glenn for a minute and then he jumped to his feet and came forward with his hand out. "Sonofabeetch, it's Meester Spotswood."

"Frankie Perez . . . Jesus, I haven't been mister for many a year."

"Compañero is better."

"Isn't it camarada?"

Frankie frowned. "Maybe . . . you join Brigada International?" Glenn nodded. "Communist Party?" Glenn shook his head. Frankie smiled and slapped him on the shoulder. "Drink coffee? Please seet down . . . Hola, Teresa, café," he called over his shoulder. While Glenn sipped his coffee Frankie talked. For many years now he'd been working as a barber in Barcelona, lovely city; at the time of the movement he had fought three days in the streets, then, boom, wounded, get better and again fight; then again wounded.

Glenn suddenly became conscious that the sleeve of Frankie's khaki tunic was empty: "Explosive bullet . . . and now I am delegate for barbers' cooperatives. . . . Did you hear how the barbers marched to the front when the soldiers had fled from Madrid?"

Frankie was watching his face narrowly. "Friend," he went on. "Here several different kinds of war. We fight Franco but also we fight Moscow . . . if you go to the Brigada you must not let them fight us. They want to destroy our collectives. They want to institute dictatorship of secret police just like Franco. We have to fight both sides to protect our revolution."

Saul had come limping down the stairs looking tousled and unwashed. After lifting his fist and yelling, "Salute, comrades," he had sat down at the table and was listening to what Frankie Perez was saying. Frankie gave him a sharp suspicious look and got to his feet. "I must go for business at frontera." He seized Glenn's hand and held it. "You Americans must not forget you come to help our fight for liberty, not for party business." He turned, saluted with his clenched fist and walked out of the door, swanking a big silver embossed holster on either side of his slim hips.

Saul wrinkled up his nose and started to splutter excitedly in Glenn's ear that this was just the type of provocation by uncontrollable elements they had been warned against; Comrade Silverstone in New York had told them many of the socalled anarchists were fascist spies. "Keep your shirt on, Saul, they can't all be spies," Glenn said with a forced kind of laugh.

He felt suddenly a chill inside him. A lot of things he'd forgotten in the excitement of the trip from New York and dodging across the border came up in his mind like bile from a sick stomach.

His hand shook so he could hardly get his match to his face to light his cigarette. He got up and went outside and walked up and down in the courtyard looking at the flowers and the chickens and the pigeons with rainbow breasts that were strutting and cooing on the stone balconies above his head.

As soon as he got hold of the governmental delegate to see about transportation to training quarters he asked him if he knew where Jed Farrington was. The little Texan? Of course, Farrington was a great man, he commanded a battalion. He would see him. Was he a friend of Farrington? Bueno, bueno. In the afternoon the governmental delegate saw them off in a truck with some more American recruits, fellows they had known on the boat, who had crossed the border at another place. That evening they saw their first bombed villages.

That night they slept in a barracks full of young Spanish peasant boys getting their first training who yelled greetings at the Americans whenever they saw them and crowded round them to give them chunky loosely wrapped Spanish cigarettes. Glenn felt the way he had felt when he had first gone over the gap into Slade County.

First thing next morning they were off again driving across a long red rolling plain misted with the emerald green of new wheat. The soil was red and the villages were red and the longfaced peasants and their mules were covered with red dust that blew in little whirlwinds on the sharp north wind. All day Glenn halfsat halfstood with the other guys holding on to the sides of the jolting truck, looking at the dry country and smelling the dry smells of straw and the herb they burned in the fires in the low earthcolored houses, and the smell of mules and dry turds that came from the village streets, feeling strange and lost, wishing he'd stayed home where he understood the language, where he had some way of doping out what things were about. He wondered if the other guys felt the way he did; some of them looked as if they did. He'd feel better when he saw Jed; it was years since he'd seen old Jed; old Jed would help him get his bearings.

Late that afternoon a blankfaced German orderly led him out of the village full of international troops where the truck had unloaded them, along a footpath through an olive orchard, to see Jed, who they said was at the brigade headquarters in the villa of a departed Spanish grandee. At first Glenn didn't recognize the bald brown stout little man, belted into a welltailored whipcord uniform, who was seated at the end of a long wooden table in a long room hung with portraits of longfaced darkeyed men in tarnished gold frames; but his dark

Mexicanlooking eyes and his voice were the same. "Why, Glenn Spotswood, I declare you haven't changed a bit," he drawled.

"Great grief, Jed," said Glenn, laughing happily. "Who would'a' thought you'd turn out a military man?"

"Sit down, Glenn old man," said Jed, pulling out one of the carved Gothic chairs. "I don't mind tellin' you that I'm happier than I've ever been in my life. . . . Haven't had a drink since Christ was a corporal . . . soldierin' sure does beat wranglin' in front of a Texas jury. . . . Ever played chess? Well, war's the greatest chess game in the world. At least it suits me down to the ground."

"I hadn't thought of it that way," said Glenn.

Jed didn't answer. Suddenly they didn't have any more to say to each other. Glenn found himself fidgeting in his chair. "Say, Jed," he said, clearing his throat, "who else do you think I've run into from Horton?"

"Some of those Mexicans I bet . . . we got some good Mexican fliers."

"Frankie Perez."

The smiling hospitable look faded off Jed's face. Glenn felt his black eyes boring into him. "Oh, I know all about him." Jed pushed back the big armchair he was sitting in and got to his feet. "What outfit are they puttin' you in?"

"I dunno," said Glenn. "I asked for truck or ambulance driving or repair work . . . I haven't got the taste for killing people you seem to have . . . at least not yet."

Jed shook his small outspread brown hand that had a silver bracelet watch at the wrist. "You make yourself think they're pawns, that's the trick . . . all a chessgame, see? But about this Perez or any of his kind . . . uncontrollables . . . for chrissake, don't monkey around with 'em. . . . The minute the fascists are cleaned out we'll have to clean out those boys."

"But don't they represent a good part of the workingclass?"

"Our business is to win the war . . . they are interfering with our winning the war, see? My only hope is we won't be forced to clean 'em out before we win the war. We've cleaned out some of the worst of 'em already."

Glenn felt again the cold, sick feeling he'd felt when he'd talked to Frankie Perez. He and Jed stood looking at each other. From an adjoining room came Spanish voices and the sound of a typewriter. "Come outside . . . I want to talk to you," Jed said suddenly. He let him out through an ironstudded door into a small stone courtyard with arches and columns. The sharp heels of Jed's wellpolished boots rang on the marble flags. As they went out the gate the sentry clicked to attention. Jed gave him a half salute, half wave of the hand.

They came out on a big terrace with huge old formally arranged box bushes. Below it the garden of elaborately scrolled beds of roses fell away to a row of poplars and a green swirling river. Beyond, across a wide valley cut into green rectangles by the irrigation ditches, rose jagged desert mountains crimson in the sunset. "My, this is the beautifullest damn country," said Jed. "And the greatest people in the world. . . . By God, we can't turn this place over to the wops and the squareheads . . . that's why we got to win this war."

"The Spanish workers have got to win it," said Glenn, his voice faltering in spite of him.

Jed turned on him savagely and stamped his foot on the gravel. "We got to win this war . . . us," he said. "Why did they throw you out of the Party?"

Glenn took a deep breath and squared his shoulders. "That's ancient history," he answered quietly. "I came here to try to help . . . I'll do any kind of work you people say, except tell other guys to go get their blocks knocked off. I'm fed up with that."

Jed looked down the valley. On the riverbank under the poplars there were clothes spread out. In the green water a couple of black heads bobbed. "I bet that water's cold," he said. He paused and took a deep breath. "If you went home now, what would you tell the folks back home?"

"The truth . . . that's what I've always tried to tell."

"You wouldn't try to make out these damn uncontrollables were martyrs of the workingclass?"

Glenn stood beside him with pursed lips without answering.

"I don't see why the hell they let you come," Jed burst out peevishly. "Haven't we got enough trouble with the fifth column?"

"Jed," said Glenn, "you've known me for years."

"Men change."

"Sure, but not like that."

"We happen to know they do . . . this is no time for the old friend stuff."

"But how can you tell except by how a guy's acted before. . . . How do I know you're all right?"

Jed turned and looked directly in his face with beady, narrowed eyes. "You haven't come all this way to tell me I'm a crook, have you?"

"Have it your own way," said Glenn, and turned and walked off. It was almost dark. He walked back under the olivetrees towards the house at the edge of the village where he was billeted. Overhead every leaf stood out sharp, cut out in tin against the flaming ochre afterglow.

Next morning he was up before daybreak with the casual detachment, waiting in line in a dusty yard hemmed in by adobe walls. The end of the yard was cut off to form a corral for sheep. As soon as the sun was well up the shepherds came, old men in rusty black cloaks and big flat hats, and opened the tall gates, letting a cut of brightness in across the steaming blue shadow and the crowded backs of the flock. Two little darkfaced boys and some wooly black and tan dogs helped drive the sheep out into the village street and off to pasture somewhere. Then the village bakery, in the basement of the building opposite, opened and women in dark shawls began to cluster round the door waiting for bread. As the shadows narrowed along the walls and the sunlight grew hot, there began way off a low hollow drumming hardly audible in the quiet morning. It was noon before Glenn's name was called. In the stuffy room that had been fixed up as an office, a Spaniard who spoke English and an American with one leg in a cast, who sat sweating in their shirtsleeves behind piles of typewritten papers, seemed puzzled about what to do with him. Finally they said they'd send him up the line to Jack Stern, and wrote him out a transport order.

Jack Stern was a thinfaced little man with a long nose and a greenish complexion who ran a repairshop and a gas station, in a stone village with a great ruined church with two towers that perched on a bare hogback where the main road climbed up the divide between two eroded rivervalleys. He spent his time worrying about the lack of spareparts and the ignorance of the local mechanics and the bad quality of the gas and his own stomachulcers. At first he was delighted to see Glenn, who at least knew one end of a screwdriver from another, but gradually, as he heard whispering about him from guys coming through, got so that he only talked to him about the work and then only in the short peevish phrases he used to the Spanish helpers. One day Glenn heard him talking to a truckdriver who'd stopped to try to pick up some sparkplugs. "And aint it just my luck," he was saying. "First time I get a guy who's a mechanic and not a muledriver, the bastard turns out to be a Trotzkyist."

Their mess, in the fat widow's house across the street, was a glum business, once they'd run out of the few phrases they could exchange with the Spaniards, because Jack Stern had an idea that every mouthful of food cooked in oliveoil he ate was killing him. Glenn passed the time putting down Spanish phrases in his notebook and keeping a diary, or when he was through work, he climbed to the top of the hill and sat there on a stone looking at the great sweep of country beyond the town, made up of closepacked walls of convents and stone mansions of hidalgos and adobe houses of peasants that seemed to have grown together into a great compact ruin. He could hardly tell which ruins dated from this war and which from old wars centuries ago. Up the road towards the front moved muletrains or great jungling twowheeled carts with canvas covers shaped like snailshells over the driver's seat, pulled by teams of three or four caparisoned mules tandem, often led by a little donkey with a string of blue beads round his neck. Then, as there got to be talk of an offensive, staffcars appeared, weaving in and out of the traffic, and newpainted French trucks packed with brown young men in fresh uniforms who looked at him with brown friendly eyes and clenched their fists in salute as they passed. One day for hours the road roared and clanked with a string of new tanks.

The tanks brought airraids and machinegun strafing and dogfights at the edge of the sky. Nobody had much confidence in the shelter so Glenn and Jack Stern would go on grimly working while the rafters of the repairshop shook with the rending crack of the bombs and the tiles clattered down off the eaves. Every day the guns from the front sounded nearer.

There began to be traffic on the road from that direction, trucks full of civilians, busses jammed with women and children, and then countrypeople driving loaded mules and donkeys, little handcarts stacked with crates of chickens, and household furniture, droves of steers, flocks of sheep and goats, old people painfully dragging bundles, staggering under heavy sacks, lost children. The guns sounded nearer. For a whole day something burned, sending up heavy volutes of smoke beyond the horizon to the westward. The ambulance drivers who stopped for gas said the front had caved in.

One night at midnight a brigade passed on foot going into the lines. The moonlight was bright as day and everybody was jumpy for fear of bombers. For hours Glenn stood by the gasoline pump watching the dustwhite hollowcheeked faces of the young men passing in the moonlight. They were not noisy and singing like most of the outfits that had gone up. Many of them limped. There were no lights, no glint of metal, only here and there the rosy tip of a cigarette passed from hand to hand.

Next day the ambulance drivers said the advance nad been stopped. About noon a staffcar of the internationals stopped for gas. In it Glenn recognized a Polish staffofficer and Irving Silverstone in civilian clothes. As he pumped in the gas he watched them eating sandwiches out of a picnic basket and washing them down with wine they drank out of little silver cups, and heard them talking about the campaign to lift the embargo in the United States. As they drove off Irving waved his hand at Glenn and said, "Thanks, comrade," without recognizing him.

When two bespectacled Germans who spoke English followed him out into the repairshop one morning when he was going to work, and whispered in his ear that he was wanted for questioning at the special brigade, he was hardly surprised. He'd been expecting something like that. He couldn't shake off a funny feeling that he was going through a play that he had rehearsed many times.

The German comrades marched him into a room back of headquarters, and then back through a stonepaved courtyard where stood a newlypainted gray truck that had been crumpled up by a bomb like a tin toy somebody had stepped on, in through a little door into a large square building with barred windows. In the passage, where some explosion had knocked off all the skyblue stucco from the walls, stood a sentry with his bayonet set in his gun. One of the Germans took a big key out of his pocket and unlocked an ironstudded door. "You vill take the place of a monk," he said with a low laugh.

As soon as Glenn had stepped into the bluepainted cell with only one small heavily barred window high up the wall, the door was slammed after him and he was alone. In the middle of the dirty tiled floor was a wooden pallet with a blanket on it, on which was set a greasy tin cup and plate. There was no other furniture. When the sentry came, keeping him covered with a revolver held in one hand, to feed him out of a bucket of steaming rice at noon, Glenn roared and shouted at him in English and what little Spanish he knew, but the sentry only shook his head with a stupid smile. He was a blueeyed, lighthaired, thicknecked young man with high cheekbones. Glenn gave up trying to talk to him.

Before he'd let Glenn eat, prodding him from behind with the revolver like a farmer driving an ox, the sentry pushed him out into the main passage and down it to a latrine where there was also a bucket for washing, stood patiently until he was through, keeping him covered all the time, and then marched him back to his cell.

That night there was another bombing, far enough away so that Glenn could distinguish the bumble of each circling plane, and the shriek of the bombs hurtling down and the deep rumbling snarl of the explosions. After the bombing this time there was the rattatat of machineguns, strafing the road probably; where the hell was our pursuit, or the antiaircraft battery back of the church, Glenn caught himself asking aloud.

Next day he tried to make the sentry understand that he wanted a shave and writingpaper and something to read, but the man shook his head with narrowed eyes and said mañana knowingly in Spanish. The next night was quiet. Glenn was asleep when the door, rattling open and banging against the wall, woke him with a start.

"Herous," said a mild voice. Glenn staggered up off the pallet blinking. A small figure in a neat uniform was pointing a rifle at him in the position of a man at bayonet practice. A smoky lantern at the man's feet threw both their shadows enormous and gesticulating on the walls of the cell above them. The man picked up the lantern with one hand and awkwardly shouldered the rifle and marched Glenn down the black passage outside his cell into a room several doors down.

The room was tall and white and brilliantly lit by an acetylene lamp that hung from the ceiling. Glenn found himself standing under the lamp in the middle of a floor littered with papers and cigarettebutts staring into three faces behind a board table that was piled with red cardboard folders. Their eyes were redrimmed and bloodshot and their cheeks were drawn in under their cheekbones. They looked as if they hadn't slept for nights. It was an instant before Glenn recognized the middle face as that of the man who didn't seem to understand any known language coming across the border, whom they'd introduced to him as Peter. The man to the left was one of the bespectacled Germans who had made the arrest, the man to the right, he couldn't be mistaken, he'd known in New York. "Say, aren't you Bernard Morton?" he said in a low, puzzled tone.

"Sure . . . we know each other," said Morton slowly, without changing the expression of his face. As he spoke he reached for a cigarette out of a pack on the table in front of him and lit it from the butt he took out from between his heavy lips without taking his yellowishgray eyes off Glenn's face. It seemed to Glenn that his cropped hair was whiter than when he'd last seen him. His broad face had a ruddy outofdoor look that was faintly reassuring.

Peter shook his finger impatiently in front of Morton and began to speak in slow precise British English; all the taut lines on his yellow face moved as he pronounced the words, shadowed by the glary lamp overhead like the lines on a reliefmap: "We are informed that you represent the Trotzky counterrevolutionary organization in America and were one of the channels of communication engaged in actively preparing the Barcelona uprising."

"Better make a clean breast of it, Spotswood," Morton interrupted in a not unfriendly tone. "The less you waste our time the easier you'll get off."

"Don't vorry, he vill not get off . . ." said the German, relighting a stump of a cigar that had gone out. "Ve have evidence enough to shoot him tonight." The German's bloodshot eyes rolled as his mouth made an Oh to let out a big blob of cigarsmoke.

"How have you communicated with Francisco Perez?" asked Peter, trying to stare down Glenn as he shook a stubby forefinger at him across the desk.

Glenn rubbed the stubble on his chin with the fingers of one hand. It shot through his head that they were all staring mad. "I have only seen him once, at that village we spent the night after getting across the border . . . you were there."

"I am in many places," said Peter, without smiling. "Naturally there you established contact with this movement of counterrevolutionary wreckers and spies?"

"It was a coincidence," said Glenn. "I hadn't seen him since years ago in Texas. I helped him with a pecanshellers' strike."

They all threw back their heads and laughed drily, drowning out his words.

"Skip it . . . coincidences don't happen," said Morton, writing something down on the pad he had in front of him.

"And your notebook," asked the German, "is that a coincidence too?"

"Very interesting," said Peter. "A literary gentleman."

Glenn felt himself coloring up. "There's nothing in that of military significance. I just wanted a record . . . Jesus Christ, all the guys keep diaries."

Morton lit himself another cigarette. "Not to use as a basis of an attack upon the party leadership," said Morton.

Glenn recognized the little black shiny oilcloth book he'd bought in Paris. They were passing it from hand to hand, pointing places out to each other with their pencils, rolling bloodshot eyes, with dry cackling chuckles, taking notes on the pads in front of them. Glenn tried to remember what he'd written, but his head was empty.

Morton leaned back, yawning and stretching. "They threw you out of the Party, didn't they? They had good reason. . . . I came here to try to get you off . . . but if you won't talk, what the hell?"

"There's nothing to talk about . . . I've done absolutely nothing outside of my work. There are plenty of people who know all about me. . . . Ask any oldtimers. Ask Jed Farrington, or Irv Silverstone if he hasn't gone home yet."

"Hum," said Morton, "so you know Comrade Silverstone was here? That little visit was supposed to be private."

Peter nodded his head gravely. "We have the reports of the comrades."

"It's no use trying to shield anybody," said Morton. "I don't suppose you know that Perez was shot for armed resistance in Barcelona the third of May."

"But I don't know anything. You people have kept me rotting in this damn repairshop," said Glenn.

"Put him back on ice for a couple of weeks," said Morton, yawning again. "Maybe he'll remember something." He lit himself the last cigarette in the pack and crumpled the paper up and tossed it into the corner of the room.

"Look here, comrades," said Glenn, "how about dropping all this nonsense and letting me go to the front? I applied to go to the tank school two months ago."

Peter got to his feet. "We are not the comrades of Trotzkyist-Bukharinist wreckers. . . . We are a court of inquiry."

"Unless we're damn lucky we won't need to go to the front. The front'll be right here looking for us," said Morton and shoved back his chair and started striding heavily up and down the room, puffing smoke as he went. Peter walked up to Glenn and put his pale face close to his. The pupils of his eyes were dilated and had a little jerky motion from side to side. Glenn felt the sour smell of his breath through his yellow teeth. "When did you last communicate with the opposition?"

"What's the use of my talking if you won't believe what I say?" yelled Glenn. Up to then he'd managed to keep his voice steady, but now his nerves were beginning to go. In spite of him his hands were clasping and unclasping.

"Snap it up, comrades," said Morton, "we got to go to bed sometime . . . we won't do anything till we get orders in answer to our report, anyway. Take him away, Fritz . . . ."

Back in his cell Glenn was taken with a fit of shaking. He rolled himself up in his blanket and lay face downward on his board pallet and tried to think. Up to then he'd thought he didn't give a damn, but now he knew he wanted to live, he wanted to be free, he wanted to go home. Crazy plans for escaping began to race through his head.

The barred window was silvery with a new day. Through it on the fresh morning air came a smell of charcoal, then a smell of coffee, then a smell of frying oliveoil. Outside, Spanish soldiers were cooking breakfast. The early morning smell was cosy and foreign; he couldn't share their breakfast. Why the hell had he come over anyway. He remembered the dry unfamiliar smell of the country, the strange voices, the odd taste of the smoke, the dusty villages, the smell of men's dung behind walls.

Suddenly he heard a boom, followed by a distant loudening shriek like a piece of goods being torn and then a shattering crash. This wasn't aviation. This was shelling. They must have the bead on the place from a battery somewhere. The front must be a whole lot nearer.

Suppose they captured the village, would they shoot him? Maybe not as an American. Hell, they shot first and asked questions afterwards, when they didn't rip you open and wind your guts round your neck. Another came in, another, another. Shaking and sobbing he lay flat on his face on the boards. After a while the shelling eased off. He didn't hear any sounds of commotion outside; they couldn't have hit anything of importance. He began to get control of himself, to tell himself stories about when he'd been a kid, to recite scraps of verse. He turned over on his back; everything was quiet. He fell asleep.

He woke up with a start. Blue sky showed bright through the barred square of window. He was trying to tell himself the whole thing had been a nightmare, the questioning, the shelling, the thoughts, when the door opened and the same sentry came in with his steaming bucket and ladled him out what passed for coffee into his cup. The sentry was real enough.

Gradually from day to day his life lapsed into a routine of hunger and meals, and trips down the corridor to the latrine. All that varied was the sound of the guns. He started making marks on the plaster walls to keep track of the days. At the end of the seventh day he could hear machineguns distinctly. The next day there were men firing rifles from the roof above him. It couldn't be long now.

He started working on a mock heroic testament, writing with his finger on the soft blue wash that still covered parts of the walls. *I, Glenn Spotswood, being of sound mind and emprisoned body, do bequeath to the international workingclass my hope of a better world*, but he suddenly felt ashamed and rubbed it all out with the palm of his hand.

That evening the sentry didn't bring him any supper. The night was quiet and he slept well except for one bombing that set off a series of explosions that sounded like an ammunition dump, and brought down a lot of plaster from the ceiling.

When he woke up at daybreak he found that some pieces of tile roof had come hurtling through the bars of his window and had landed at the foot of his bed. He got up and yelled for the sentry and beat on the door of his cell, but nobody came. Finally he had to make water in the corner of his cell.

The racket started up again with a bang sometime during the morning. At the height of it the door opened and Morton stuck his head in. He needed a shave. He was wearing a helmet off which the khaki paint had scaled. "You still here?" He had to yell to be heard. "Well, I'm goin' to let you out. I'll probably catch hell for it, if I live long enough." He gave a dry snicker. "There's hell to pay, Spotswood." They stood there looking at each other and half laughing. Morton's eyes looked yellow in his face that was black with oil and dust. He was out of breath. "You said you wanted to go to the front?"

Glenn nodded.

"Well, there are some of our boys with two machineguns in a pillbox to the left of hill 14. They got to have water. You got to take it to 'em. They are the only thing that's keeping the wops out of this dump. Tell 'em to stick for another half hour, see, they got to cover us while we get some junk out of here." Glenn was following him down the tall corridor. Blue daylight shone through several jagged holes in the wall that had appeared in the night. At the end there was a cobbled court with a pump in the middle of it where a man with his scalp all clotted with blood was pumping water. The man was Peter.

Glenn, Peter, and Morton stood on the cobbles in the bright noon sunlight looking at each other. The sun beat down hot. Their shadows were small blobs underfoot on the bright cobbles.

Glenn took a deep breath of the dusty air. The artillery had stopped. Only occasional machineguns and rifles kept up a distant ratatat and a zing, plunk and a whining overhead. Above them in the very blue sky swallows circled squeaking.

"All right," Glenn said. "Where do I go?"

He lifted one of the buckets to his lips and took a deep swig of the clean cold water. Then he stuck his head under the pump and said to Peter: "Pump me a little, will you, I haven't washed for days." Peter seemed so astonished by the request he just stood there, but Morton stepped over and gave the pumphandle a couple of swings. Peter looked in Glenn's face with his narrowed, bloodshot eyes. "You vill go?" he asked.

Glenn looked straight at him. "What do you think I came here for?" he asked. Then he saw Peter's strained eyes move sidelong towards Morton. Morton's eyes dropped and he scruffed at the cobbles with the muddy toe of one boot. He kept from looking at Glenn. "Somebody's got to go. We can't," he said. Glenn understood.

His throat got stiff but he didn't let his mouth tremble. They had two new corrugated iron buckets. He picked one up in each hand. Morton motioned with his head and led the way to a door that opened under the arches of the cobbled court. He pulled it open and stepped back in a hurry.

Through the door they could see the crumbling walls of what had been a street of adobe houses. Under the brilliant sun every cobble of the street stood out clear. Beyond the houses a wagonroad curved up a bare yellow hill. At the top, in the ruins of a chapel, lighter shadows moved in the blackness behind some sandbags.

Morton pointed with a crooked forefinger that was black with powder and oil. He was careful to keep his eyes from meeting Glenn's. "That's where our boys are. You see way across the river; that's the enemy." Behind some walls in the distant purple shadow Glenn could see spots moving. Everything swam from the brightness of the sunlight after so many days of dark. "Now, when we get our gun in place we can shell this hill for a few minutes. Give you fellers a chance to run for it, see? No use trying to carry anything away. You'll have to be careful because they can enfilade that road."

Glenn had been telling himself the thing was just to put one foot in front of the other. He was busy keeping his knees from doubling up under him. When they hit him, they'd hit him. Maybe he wouldn't be killed.

Morton was still talking but Glenn couldn't hear his voice any more. He was walking, lifting first one foot then the other over the uneven cobbles between the yellow adobe walls. Sunlight danced in bright sharp rays in the water in the new buckets. Something that grew among the cobbles smelt like thyme when he stepped on it. He felt the deep regular breathing of his lungs, the one two, one two of his steps, the hot sweetness of the air.

As he stepped out from behind the last wall one of the buckets was suddenly empty. He must walk as carefully as he could so as not to spill the other. Something that must be bullets teased past him. On the slope ahead of him things were playfully kicking up little puffs of dust. The racket was beginning again. He was halfway up the hill before they brought him down. For a second he had no pain. He thought he'd stubbed his toe on a stone. Too bad the water was all spilled in so much blood. Must get out of this, he said to himself, and started to drag himself along the ground. Then suddenly something split and he went spinning into blackness. He was dead.

CPSIA information can be obtained
at www.ICGtesting.com
Printed in the USA
BVOW08s0850111116

467588BV00001B/80/P